FALL AND RISING

ROOT CODE, #2

SUNNY MORAINE

Riptide Publishing
PO Box 6652
Hillsborough, NJ 08844
www.riptidepublishing.com

Fall and Rising
Copyright © 2015 by Sunny Moraine

Cover art: Kanaxa, www.kanaxa.com
Editor: Carole-ann Galloway
Layout: L.C. Chase, http://lcchase.com/design.htm

ISBN: 978-1-62649-301-8

First edition
August, 2015

Also available in ebook:
ISBN: 978-1-62649-300-1

FALL AND RISING

ROOT CODE, #2

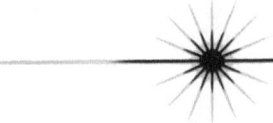

SUNNY MORAINE

For Megh.

TABLE OF CONTENTS

And Sarah saw the son of Hagar the Egyptian, which she had born unto Abraham, mocking. Wherefore she said unto Abraham, Cast out this bondwoman and her son: for the son of this bondwoman shall not be heir with my son, even with Isaac.

—Genesis 21:9–11

TIPPING POINT

(IN MEDIAS RES)

When Rachel saw they also had Becca and Dion, she began to scream.

It raked her throat, burned high in her chest. But the pain, the fear, the horror—they didn't quite touch her. Deep down she was numb. Even resigned. Hadn't there been whispers? About people who'd disappeared? People who hadn't seemed quite *right*, who hadn't seemed themselves. Sick? No, no one on Terra got sick. Long before birth, illness was rendered impossible, the potential for it engineered out of existence. That was where their great civilization had started: with sickness—with its erasure. It was the foundation of who her people were. The endless quest for physical perfection was a tree sprouted from this single seed: people who didn't get sick.

But her hands had been shaking for weeks now, and she was so often tired. Part of her had known something was wrong, even as the rest of her denied it. Denied there was any truth to the rumors. Of course she wouldn't vanish. They would never come for her.

She had been so wrong. And now they had her children.

She rose from her bench in the transport shuttle and tried to shove her way past the peacekeepers, ignoring their guns. Trampling everything to get to her children—following an instinct deeper and more profound than any genetic cultivation. Yet if she touched them, she would be sure they were here *with her*, and she had known the instant she saw them what that meant.

It meant that she and they might share this weakness. This sickness. Rachel might see them shake and fall, which would be worse than seeing her whole world do the same.

She was barely two feet from them when the peacekeepers knocked her to the floor with the butts of their guns. Their faces were covered by the white standard-issue helmets with their reflective blast shields, so she couldn't see if they felt any pity. If they might show any mercy. Her little boy and girl were crying, clinging and crying, her little boy and her little girl, and clinging to each other as another peacekeeper herded them forward—more gently, and she felt the tiniest sliver of icy relief. They might hurt her, but surely they wouldn't hurt children.

Rachel wanted to believe that.

She pushed herself up to her knees. "Not them. Please, not them. Look at them, they're fine, they're—"

One of the peacekeepers raised their gun as if they meant to strike her again. "Get back in there. Do it. Don't make this a problem and none of you have to get hurt."

None of you. It echoed in her mind, heavy and cold. So there was her answer.

They were willing to hurt children. *Children.* To maintain the carefully engineered, carefully perfected paradise that had birthed that next generation.

People didn't get sick on Terra. No.

"Where are we going?" Her sweet girl, oh, there were no words for how cruel this was. She would have traded never seeing them again to avoid this. "Mama?"

They hadn't even been allowed to pack anything, she realized. Somehow that was the worst part of this. They had their coats on but nothing else. None of their toys, no extra clothes, no pad for books or games. They had only each other, hand in hand. If they were going to be traveling, why wouldn't they have . . .?

She couldn't. She couldn't bear that.

The children moved forward, whimpering, and she opened her arms. It was all she could do. Everything was blurry, but she felt them come to her, pulled them both against her, felt their heaving breaths as they tried not to sob. Young but old enough to grasp the concept of stoicism. She was so proud of them. Now perhaps more than ever. Proud of them for simply being alive.

"All right, let's get in the air. They're not gonna hang around in orbit for that much longer."

Two of the peacekeepers slid onto the benches opposite each other. Their heads were bent together, and they were talking, tones low and casual, as if she and her children weren't there at all. The hatch hissed closed, and the engines rumbled as they fired, the shuttle jolting softly as it began to rise. She raised her head and blinked away her tears, holding on to those two small, trembling bodies—and thinking terrible things.

"You don't have to do this," she whispered—knowing it was pointless. "They're just kids, you don't have to . . . They're not even *sick*."

She was sure they weren't going to answer her, but one leaned forward, elbows on his knees.

"You know that doesn't matter. They're yours. They share your code, so they're as broken as you are. They should never have happened at all. Even if they don't seem sick now, they will. You're not an idiot, don't act like one." He sat back and turned his head, appearing to shoot his companion a glance before he directed his attention to her once more. "Maybe you're genetically degenerate, but you can at least have some dignity."

Small portholes were set into the shuttle's sides. As they ascended from the hangar, the light of a beautiful, crisp winter day flooded in, and sunlight gleamed off slender, graceful towers of crystal as they passed them. Left them behind. All those people, some aware of what was happening—and many more not. Many of them with no idea at all. No idea how many things were shaking—not just hands and not just bodies. Foundations.

They didn't conceive of the idea of an ultimate fall.

It'll tumble down. She lowered her head and squeezed her eyes closed as the blue sky began to darken. They were leaving all that beauty behind, that perfection, and now she understood—or was beginning to understand—that it was all a lie. A lie that, if there really were more like her, probably couldn't be sustained forever. *It'll tumble down and never rise again.*

And maybe, if this was what it did to children, to the foundation on which the future was built . . .

Maybe that was what had to be.

PART ONE

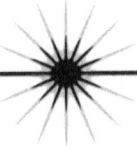

DESCENT

CHAPTER

ONE

The Plain of Heaven was a carpet of bodies.

Adam twitched where he lay in the dust, spasmed—not in pain but in shock, in an ecstasy of terror. He could see them stretched out in all directions, splayed and torn and bloody, staring eyes and faces twisted in agony. Protectorate and Bideshi. Young men and women and elders and little children. All dead.

All because of him.

He shuddered but couldn't turn away; they were everywhere he would turn.

There should have been screams, shots, metal on metal: the last echoes of the battle. And there should have been someone holding him—Lochlan's arms warm and strong around him. The pillars of the stone circle rose over his head—the circle where he had been led, the circle that had the power to cure the sickness in him at last. He knew this place so well by now. He knew what had happened here, what *must* happen.

But Lochlan was not with him.

He pushed himself up on shaking hands and scanned his surroundings, at once seeing and not seeing the desolation. He didn't want to see it, but he *had* to see it, because it was for him, all for him, a war which, if he hadn't caused it, he had coaxed to a fevered, lethal pitch. Blood that he had spilled, even if he hadn't taken up a weapon of his own in the end.

Lock.

He wanted to cry the name, but he didn't. He couldn't. It was lodged in his throat, choking him. He scrambled onto his hands and knees—and then he did see. What he had known he would see, and from which he had been trying to hide, because some truths were death to face.

Lochlan's body, lying broken and bloody at the edge of the circle, a gash in his throat nearly severing his head from his neck, his eyes wide and bulging and bloodshot. His dreadlocks were matted with congealed gore. He stared up at the sky, at nothing.

"Dead" was not a strong enough word. "Dead" didn't capture the finality, the violent end of everything. "Dead" didn't capture the agony, the void opening up inside him as he let the reality of Lochlan d'Bideshi's corpse crash over him in a poisonous wave.

His knees and elbows buckled under him, and he fell back into the dust, screaming and screaming. His mouth was full of the dust of the Plain of Heaven, the dust of Takamagahara, and it tasted like ashes.

"*Chusile.* Adam."

Hands shaking him, strong and firm and very familiar. Adam stirred, twisted—his legs were tangled in something, held down. He let out a moan and tried to free himself. His tongue tasted of dust, gritty between his teeth. He could still see . . .

Lochlan bending over him. A hand stroking through his hair. Adam dragged in a long breath and stilled.

"*Chere*, that was a dream and a half. Don't *scream* like that; you'll send me into an early grave."

"Don't say that." Adam shoved himself up and buried his head in his hands, the sheets pooling around his waist. It was too much. Part of him felt relief so deep it was almost painful. And part of him was still only terrified. "Just . . . don't."

Lochlan was quiet for a moment, hand on Adam's bare shoulder. Not caressing, not moving, but there, and Adam slowly pressed back against it, releasing himself into the touch. Behind his hands it was dark, and he could hear *Volya* humming around them, Lochlan's beloved, alive in her own way, and the life behind Lochlan's breathing. He was here. The Plain was far away now.

But it had been real. All that death.

"You were having that dream again, weren't you." It wasn't a question, and Adam didn't feel the need to confirm it. Lochlan wasn't oblivious, and in the weeks since they had left Ashwina, their knowledge of each other had deepened in ways Adam'd never expected. He knew the rhythm of Lochlan's heartbeat now, his breathing, the ways he moved as he slept, the ways he liked to be touched, what it took to make him smile.

And Adam was known in the same way. Sometimes it almost frightened him, because no one had ever known him like this. It had been too dangerous in his old world to share such intimacy with a man. That intimacy was dangerous even now in other ways. It gave him so much more to lose. Just the memory of Lochlan, broken and bloody in his dream . . . That wasn't how it had gone. Lochlan hadn't died in that battle. Lochlan was here. The sickness that had sent Adam to the Plain to be healed by power he couldn't hope to understand, power that had changed him in ways he was still discovering . . . It was gone. They were both well.

But the dreams persisted. Because how things had *ended* didn't erase how they had arrived there.

Lochlan sighed and leaned his cheek where his hand had been, pressing a kiss to the angle of Adam's shoulder blade. "I wish you'd tell me about it."

"I can't," Adam whispered. He had tried. But it had been like there was a block in his throat, like his body itself was keeping it all back, as if saying it aloud would invoke it in some way and make it true. The horror of the Plain, what had happened there . . . and the guilt that lay behind the dreams. Because if it weren't for him, none of those people would have died. Or if he didn't fully believe that—or didn't believe it could be so simple—he couldn't escape the idea. It lay on him, heavy.

"Dreams mean things. I don't mean to make it into more than it is, but you could . . . Maybe I could help. What happened to you back there—I don't completely understand it but that doesn't mean I know *nothing* about it." Adam felt Lochlan smile against his skin, though it seemed faint, and knew without looking that there would be a sardonic edge in it. "I know you Protectorate *raya* all think this star-reading and dream-seeing is obscene superstition and everything, but given that it did actually save your life . . ."

Adam shook his head, but he did find it in him to laugh. "Stop. I'm . . ." He took a breath. Even now, Lochlan teased—especially now, when he thought it might ease things. "It's just that so many people died," he murmured. "Your people. My people. Even Cosaire. 'Missy,' I think Aarons called her. Melissa, you know? I don't know why that one sticks with me at all, but—"

"You didn't put the bullet in her head," Lochlan said quietly. "He did. And it was a mercy killing. She was sick. You know that too. And in case you've forgotten, she hunted you halfway across the galaxy and back. She would have *killed* you if she could."

"Yeah. I do know it." He swallowed. *And she killed those people to get to me. Because I was everything she hated. Everything she feared.*

"You survived. We survived. That's what matters."

Lochlan kissed him once more, moving up along the ridge of his shoulder, and Adam let his head drop back and exhaled. Lochlan's hands could, at times, be a wonderful distraction, and his mouth doubly so. "You should try to sleep again, *chusile.*" Adam felt him smile again. "Maybe I can help you."

He didn't give Adam time to respond, and Adam wouldn't have needed to anyway. Lochlan's hand was already sliding down between Adam's thighs, his other hand pulling him back onto the bed, and Adam's sigh turned into a low moan as he gave over. This was real too. He could lose himself in this warm sweetness. He had permission. When Lochlan's hot mouth closed around him, he clutched at the dreadlocks spread over his belly and hips and held on as he shuddered in slow waves of pleasure.

This much remained easy.

Lochlan was dozing once more, but Adam still couldn't sleep. He lay on his back and stared up at the dimness of *Volya's* ceiling, lips moving slightly as he ran through recent events. Like counting sheep, maybe it would tire him out.

Or maybe it would just keep him awake.

At last he carefully disentangled himself from Lochlan, rose to his feet, and crept to the small alcove that served as the cockpit. There, he sank into the pilot's seat and activated the messaging system in the comm; he hadn't heard the ping of anything incoming, anyone responding to the feelers they had put out on some of the primary message bands. They had been forced to keep their queries vague— better to not attract more attention than necessary—but Adam had been hopeful.

Nothing. He sighed and scrubbed his hands down his face.

He was tired, tired in the kind of aimless way that came from prolonged periods of inactivity. Since leaving Ashwina in hopes of curing the rest of Adam's people, they had spent weeks skirting the edges of Protectorate space, looking for an unobtrusive way in. Making it into that space had been the objective from the start; Lochlan, usually the impulsive one, had counseled both care and at least some degree of planning—to the extent that planning was possible. There was so much they didn't know, couldn't anticipate.

And there were things they *did* know. As far as they could tell from trading rumors on outlying stations, little in the Terran Protectorate itself had changed: Its authority on its tributary planets was seemingly solid and its monopoly on trade and governance appeared stable.

If anything, it had circled its wagons, bulking up border patrols, sending reinforcements to its colonized worlds. The sickness that had nearly killed Adam remained invisible.

There was no real news about that sickness, nothing beyond vague rumors. Nothing about any of the Protectorate Peacekeepers who had been present on Takamagahara for the Battle of the Plain. Nothing about Commander Marcus Kerry, Kyle Waverly, or Eva Reyes—once an enemy, a best friend, and a low-ranking Protectorate officer, a total unknown. Nothing about Detective Bristol Aarons, though as an investigator for the Protectorate Military Police, he would be used to keeping his head down. They all seemed to have simply disappeared. Maybe dead, maybe imprisoned, maybe in hiding or on the run. If they had decided to return openly, Adam didn't imagine it would have been taken well, given their questionable loyalties, but he had hoped. He still hoped, if he and Lochlan could get across the border, they might learn more. Might be able to make contact with one of them— with more than one. And there were other potential contacts, if the contacts could be made safely; Adam knew others, people from his old life, though how many of them he could trust . . .

He didn't know.

They had to get into the center so they could find out what was really happening. What plagued Adam more than dark dreams was that he couldn't escape the intuition, deep and profound, that something was horribly wrong. He had set out to do this on an instinct and continuing to follow such an instinct was questionable at best—but something was leading him. His orbit was swinging wide, away from where he had come, and he had to follow it. He had to wait.

But he and Lochlan were being hunted.

He pulled up a few of the general public-band newsfeeds. Not much there either. A fleet of garbage scows outbound from Inarihad had been seized and searched and an enormous shipment of the powerful narcotic snake had been discovered. Thanks to additional terrorist attacks on Koticki, their shipments of minerals and heavy metals were down.

And there, in the list of criminals wanted by the Protectorate, right under a pair of fugitives named Theseus and Taur, were his and Lochlan's images. His drawn from his official dossier, Lochlan's blurrier—a man in motion. It must have been taken from the surveillance cameras the day Adam had been caught stealing credits and Lochlan had scooped him out of Protectorate hands. Saved his life.

Started everything.

There was a high reward offered for delivery of them both alive. But more for Adam. Lochlan was clearly a bonus.

He sat back and exhaled heavily. Not news. But seeing it still made his skin crawl. The Protectorate's pursuit of him hadn't ended with the death of Melissa Cosaire. She hadn't been the only one who felt he knew too much. That what he knew could break open their efforts to hide what had almost killed him. It could crack foundations. Pull everything down.

Strange, to have people regard him as so powerful. Powerful enough to break apart the system of faith that underpinned an entire empire.

Adam glanced down at his hands. Once they had shaken with the disease eating up his nervous system, but now they were steady. Strong. Yet he didn't feel strong, didn't feel as though there was any particular power in them. They were the hands of one man. In this moment, the idea that he could break anything so massive and ancient apart seemed ridiculous.

But there was something he *could* do. He and Lochlan could turn away from this whole horrible mess, head out to the farthest reaches of human-explored space, and make a life together that didn't involve the Protectorate at all. Or they could rejoin Ashwina, and the rest of Lochlan's Bideshi convoy, Suzaku and Jakana. Go back to a place that was, somehow and strangely, a home to him. Back to the friends he'd left behind—friends he had never expected. Kae, Lochlan's best friend, first to welcome Adam to Ashwina and the first there to be kind to him. Leila, his wife, brave and generous. Ying the healer, gentle and wise. They had all cared for him. He thought about them now and his heart clenched.

Running would be easy. But every time he thought of it, he saw Ixchel's face in his mind. Ashwina's Aalim, her wise woman, who had left her blood on the Plain and her spirit among the wandering stars and the ancient trees of Ashwina's Arched Halls.

She didn't look pleased with him.

After everything? After so many people died? For this? For you? For what you might become, for what you might make possible? You'd turn your back on their sacrifice? Child, I expected so much more from you.

It was as though she were right there with him now, her voice so clear, her blind eyes staring into and through him in the way she had always been able to. The mind that lay behind them, sharp as a jambia's blade. She had never let him get away with anything, had pushed him to the limits of what he thought he could do, and had given him massive, fierce shoves past the bounds of his comfort zones. Like her ancient trees, she had cultivated him, helped him to grow.

And in the end she had been among the dead. His dead.

Adam sighed, closed his eyes, and turned his attention out into the night. He had no idea which were his stars anymore, the ones that Ixchel had shown to him—had no idea if they were even visible. But he liked the sensation of them pulling at him, rooting him into the fabric of the universe.

He hadn't reached for that connection in a while. Maybe now it would help.

He focused on the stars, his hands loose in his lap, and let himself begin to drift.

The stars *were* pulling at him, was the thing. Not only his birth stars but all of them, knowing him like a son and beckoning him out of *Volya's* patchwork metal skin. The spaces between them, which more ignorant people—which he, once—assumed were made up of *empty space*. There were things dancing in those spaces, strings and lines that extended into him and everything else, their vibrations weaving the tapestry of reality. They made up the roots of the universe, and as he reached out unseen hands and combed his fingers through them, his own roots sung in harmony with them. A sine wave, rising and falling and rising again.

He wasn't alone. He would never be.

Ixchel was waiting in that crowded darkness. Unreal, but more real than he knew how to put into words. A dream, and yet not a dream at all.

Child, she said, taking his hand, and her face was at once as old as he remembered it and young, shockingly beautiful. *You're waiting for it to come to you because you're afraid to go to it. But this is not what I taught you. For anything worth having, you have to be brave enough to chase it, and ready to give up everything. Ask your sweetheart sleeping behind you there. He'll tell you what he was willing to give for you, in the end.*

"I don't know if I can do it," he whispered, unsure if he was speaking aloud or merely thinking the words. "I don't know if I can save these people. I'm just one man."

No. You're two men. And you may be more than that. You may be only the beginning of something else which will grow far beyond you. The universe is vast and very, very strange. Things have been set in motion the ends of which you can't possibly hope to see. We all of us are building something that we will never see to completion. Our children and our children's children must take up the work for us, and even they will never see it done. When we took the first trees from Terra and brought them into our homeships, do you think any of us thought we would see what they would become? Even the Arched Halls began as sprouts and saplings.

He frowned. "I don't understand."

Have you ever? She laughed, soft and musical, and it seemed as though the stars themselves laughed with her. *You don't need to understand, my love. Simply be ready. There is power in your blood. Power to take the hands of two warring brothers, two halves of the same human family, and unite them in the end. It was a gift to you. Many died for it. Don't waste it.*

The vision faded, as though he was being pushed out of the trance rather than coming out of it on his own. He sat, blinking, and looked at the time readout on the console, only faintly surprised to see that over an hour had passed.

And what had he gotten from it? What had he learned?

He was so tired.

He rose, stretching stiff muscles, and made his way back to bed. Lochlan was on his belly now, his tattooed arms under his head and the dim light making his brown skin appear darker and warmer than usual. Adam lowered himself down beside him and slung an arm around his waist, tangling their legs once more. He kissed the edge of Lochlan's jaw and smiled at the soft, sleepy rumble he got in response.

He didn't need to understand. Not right now. For the moment he was warm and safe. He closed his eyes again, and at last sleep took him.

CHAPTER

TWO

Isaac Sinder was trying hard to not be resentful. But he wasn't even meant to be here. He stood on the bright, polished bridge of the *Excelsior*, the lead patrol ship in this particular extension of the Protectorate's will, looked over the heads of the bridge crew and out at the star-speckled black, and brooded.

He had been third in command of operations on the planet Melann, an export center for refined plastics and as such it wasn't especially out of the way, but it wasn't by any means central either. He had done well there, but he'd been itching to leave, so when he had been offered a government liaison role on one of the larger warships, he'd jumped at it.

A week later, and he was starting to second-guess himself. They hadn't told him the work would be routine patrols in relatively empty space, with little to oversee—no direct, planned searches but merely regular, monotonous sweeps.

At least what they were searching for was interesting. Little was generally known about what had happened out there in that tiny nebula within which the Bideshi believed hung a central locus of ancient power—the rogue planet Takamagahara, the Plain of Heaven. Little was known about what Melissa Cosaire had done after she lost her mind. But people with access to privileged information knew that the name of Adam Yuga was mixed up in all of it. Even though he never should have been there at all, stricken by a disease that should have killed him—one of the core aspects of the man was apparently a stubborn refusal to die.

Adam wasn't just a fallen star, once rising—formerly a promising young engineer with a head for big-picture problems and a probable future in the halls of power. He was someone who sought to undermine the very foundation of the society that had been so kind to him.

He would make the career of anyone who was fortunate enough—or dedicated enough—to find him.

"Captain," Sinder said, clasping his hands behind his back and keeping his stance high and erect. No one at the command consoles turned to look at him, but that didn't matter—one had to maintain appearances. "Nothing on the scanners?"

Captain Amanda Alkor grunted and shifted in her chair. "Not since the last time you asked. Sir," she added—a little grudgingly, Sinder thought, narrowing his eyes. He knew well how peacekeeper officers tended to resent civilian overseers intruding into their commands, and he had come prepared for it, was ready to tolerate it even, but he was monitoring the situation closely in case it veered into something unacceptable. "Pretty sure we've covered this sector well enough. About time to move on, do you think?"

Sinder shook his head. "One more pass. By the book, Captain. We need to be systematic about these things. Do them right. Otherwise we might as well not do them at all."

Alkor grunted again, clearly annoyed, and finally turned, her neat gray eyebrows lowered, appearing even more severe for the tight bun that held her equally gray hair fast at the back of her head. "One might argue," she said, "that we're wasting time here."

Sinder regarded her placidly. "One might. That doesn't mean it would be a good argument."

Alkor rose and gestured to the door that led into the offices off the bridge. "Sinder, I'd like a word, if I may."

For a moment, Sinder considered refusing her. He knew how it would appear to the others on the bridge: a disrespectful child called into a private lecture session by a stern adult. That wasn't an attractive idea, not when backed by days of cold warfare, each of them trying to erode the other's authority. He was tired of it. It was counterproductive.

But refusing would look worse: petulant, weak. He nodded, gracious in the face of someone who probably didn't rate it.

"Of course, Captain."

The offices were small, more cubicles than anything else, and were arrayed around a central conference room where briefings and the other daily administrative business of the ship was conducted. Now it was empty, though brightly lit with the screens set into the glossy tabletop, as if a meeting was imminent. Alkor ushered Sinder inside and closed the door quietly after them. Sinder faced her, loose and relaxed.

Carefully so.

Let her make the first mistake.

"Let's get one thing straight, Sinder," she growled, all veneer of politeness gone now. "This is my command. I've put up with you for days, sauntering in here with your *orders* and your *credentials* and making a nuisance of yourself. If HQ says you have to be here, then I guess you have to be here. But if you want this to run smoothly, you back off and let me make the decisions on my own fucking ship. Is that understood?"

Sinder arched an eyebrow. Silence descended between them, and he let it play out until it felt uncomfortable. Then he cleared his throat softly.

"I understand, Captain." Sinder paused again, his head cocked. He might not yet have risen to any significant heights in the Protectorate's hierarchy, but he wouldn't have gotten this far without the ability to deal with things like this. "Now you should understand something. Try, at least." He leaned forward, bringing them about nose to nose.

"You have authority over your people, and I won't interfere with that. I don't especially *want* authority over you. I want you to do your job. If you do that, I don't have to report back that you're unfit to be doing anything but captaining a long-haul freighter on the outer edges. I don't want to do that. I want to complete this mission, and then I want to go *home*." He extended a hand and laid it against Alkor's upper arm, and it might have been a friendly gesture but for the ice in the room. "Let's work together, Captain. Not butt heads like a couple of stupid rutting goatworms."

Alkor looked at him for a long moment, and he noted how cold-blue her eyes were, like eyes that had stared at a star so long that all the color had been bleached out of them. At last she released a breath and stepped past Sinder to a cabinet against one wall, opening it and pulling out a crystal decanter and two glasses.

With pleasure, Sinder identified it—by the reddish tint to the gold of the liquid—as aged Albaran brandy. Fine stuff. A peace offering? Probably not, but he wouldn't reject it.

"I never wanted this mission," Alkor said as she filled the glasses, her back to Sinder and her head down. "I was supposed to retire a week from now. I had a little place all picked out on the west coast of the southern continent on Yefan." She turned back to Sinder, glasses in hand, and held one of them out, which he accepted with a nod of thanks. "You ever been to Yefan, Sinder?"

Sinder shook his head. He knew of the place, of course. A moon circling a small gas giant in one of the more out-of-the-way systems, it was nevertheless significant in how it teemed with an incredible variety of life forms. Half of it was given to nature preserves, and the rest of it was private land, owned by people who tended to value simplicity and quiet and therefore confined themselves to modest houses and cottages set on vast amounts of acreage. Some hunted, some did a little agriculture, and some did nothing much at all.

So now he knew more about what kind of woman she was. Interesting.

"The beaches there are beautiful," Alkor went on, lifting her glass to her lips and taking a slow sip, savoring the richness of the liquor. "Almost untouched. Just these long strands of dark sand with the forests behind them. There are plains too, and in the north there are the deserts, but that part of the coast is mostly trees. I already have a house there, right off the beach. There's a deck where I can watch the sunsets. I'm supposed to be there now." She took another swallow. "Instead I'm here. With you. Sinder, I want to go home as bad as you do. But you need to know, if you think getting me a shit assignment somewhere else is supposed to be a threat to me, you better think again."

Sinder considered this briefly, then nodded. It was probably a courtesy, Alkor telling him that so straightly. Whatever else might irritate him about her, she didn't seem the duplicitous type.

"Why didn't you turn down the mission?"

Alkor shrugged, turning toward the wide windows that lined one wall and gazing at the stars. "I've been a company woman my entire life. The Protectorate has been good to me. They're how I could afford that land. Seemed cheap to cut and run when they were asking me to serve one more time." She glanced back at Sinder, her mouth tight. "I wonder how much you'd know about that."

"I'm here too," Sinder said smoothly, moving to stand beside her. "I might only be a bright young thing, Captain, but I know what loyalty means." He sipped his drink and stared out the window for a few seconds. Then, "The Protectorate is the greatest civilization in the history of the galaxy. We bring order, wealth, and culture to the rest of the races. We benefit everyone and everything we bring under our authority. And we are the only ones to ever make the dream of perfection an achievable reality—in body, in genetic code, which might as well be in *soul*, if such a thing could be said to exist. We may not know what that ultimate pinnacle of our efforts will be, but we know that we'll eventually be complete masters of ourselves, of our bodies, able to control everything to the tiniest detail. Able to create ourselves almost from nothing. There are no gods, Alkor—only us. And one day gods are exactly what we'll be.

"The masters of ancient Terran philosophy used to debate about whether the perfect society was even possible. They called it 'Utopia.' Do you know what 'utopia' means, Alkor?"

Alkor shook her head. To her credit, she actually appeared vaguely interested.

"It means 'a good place.' That became the popular meaning, and then the only meaning. But it also means 'no place.' The assumption of its impossibility is inherent in its name." His hands curved delicately around his glass. He loved this story, and to the degree that any true member of the Protectorate could have holy scripture, he had made it part of his own. "Captain, we have made Utopia a place. Adam Yuga—and everything he represents through contamination, lack of control—threatens our work. That's why I'm here. So if you doubt I know the meaning of loyalty . . . Rest assured, I know it very well. It's quite literally in my blood." He allowed himself a faint smile. "As it is in yours."

Slowly, Alkor nodded, and something that looked like realization was spreading across her face. "You aren't just here to put in your time, are you? That's why you wanted us to do another sweep."

"Correct. If Yuga is out there to be found, I want to find him. If we fail to find him, I don't want it to be because we didn't try." He fixed Alkor with a keen eye; this might be someone with whom he could work. The trick was always in the approach. "I respect that you're at the end of your career, Captain. I respect your experience, as I do your dedication. To that end, let me come at this from a different angle. I'm young, at the beginning of my own career, and I'm asking for your assistance."

He took a minute step forward—this was the way to do what needed to be done, he was now sure. "Help me find Adam Yuga. At the very least, help me exhaust all the possibilities. At worst, you retire with honor, having completed your last mission to the best of your ability. And you'll have me in your debt. I don't think I need to explain to you how valuable favors can be."

Alkor appeared to think about this. But Sinder could feel the decision in the woman's bearing, the way she had immediately—though grudgingly—grasped the sense in it.

He would have no more trouble with her.

"All right," Alkor said at last, draining the remaining brandy and turning to set her glass down on the conference table. "I suppose I can—"

"Captain. Ma'am."

They both glanced up, startled. The door to the conference room was open and a young ensign was standing there, her face flushed and excited. "I'm sorry to interrupt, ma'am, but we've—"

Sinder opened his mouth to issue a rebuke, but Alkor was already ahead of him. "Ensign Diev."

The young woman drew herself up, her flush deepening and darkening. "Ma'am. I apologize."

"You should have paged me over the comm. Not barged in here like a wet-eared cadet."

"Yes, ma'am." She shifted, her hands behind her back and her gaze locked straight ahead. "It won't happen again, ma'am."

Alkor grunted and seemed ready to dismiss the matter. Sinder watched her, eyes narrowed—Alkor could look the part of the gruff disciplinarian, but from everything Sinder had seen so far, she was actually inclined to give her people a fair amount of rein. Sinder knew other peacekeeper commanders who would handle that breach of protocol with confinement. If not outright physical punishment.

It might be a good thing. Or it might be a liability.

"Well, then, Ensign, tell us what's so important that it caused you to forget how the comm system works."

"We found a ship, ma'am. Approximately six hundred kilometers from here."

A ship. Not that exciting, in itself. So there must be— Sinder stepped forward, eager. "Have you made an ID?"

"Yes, sir. It's not conclusive—we know a beacon signature can be forged—but we believe it's the last ship that Commander Marcus Kerry was seen piloting. Before he disappeared on Raltir, according to the last reports we have of him."

Kerry. Less high-value than Yuga, but still valuable. Potentially very much so. He would probably know things, and he might be willing to tell some of them. Or might be made to. "Is he aware of us yet?"

"Not as far as we can tell. He's flying a single-seater shuttle with low-range scanners. But as soon as we close within three hundred kilometers, he should know we're there. He could go to slipstream before we can do anything. What should our next steps be, ma'am?"

But Captain Alkor was already pushing past her, headed back to the bridge. Barely able to suppress a smile, Sinder followed.

The atmosphere on the bridge hummed with the same excitement that had gripped Ensign Diev. Alkor took her place in her chair, Sinder standing beside her. For now, Sinder was content to be silent and let her work.

They had reached an understanding.

"Bring him up on the main viewer." One of the other officers nodded and tapped their console. On the screen, a small pale ship snapped into focus, stubby and round, like a big toe.

"What's his speed?"

"Moderate. Not sure why he's not traveling in slipstream."

"He wouldn't," Sinder murmured, "if he had a specific reason to be here." Something was tickling at the edges of his awareness, at the edges of what he *knew*. At times things came to him this way—a knowing that went beyond mere knowing. He didn't entirely understand its nature, but he had learned not to question it. Discovering the ship like this was significant. He would find out how.

He shot Alkor a significant look, which she returned.

"Present distance?"

"Holding at six hundred thirty kilometers. We're prepared to close in on your mark, ma'am."

Alkor frowned. "Don't take us any closer for now, and don't hail. Tell the other ships to do the same and to move in. How spread out are they now?"

"Over several thousand kilometers, ma'am. It varies."

"Get them in as soon as you can." Alkor paused, one finger stroking the edge of her eyebrow. "Lieutenant Kwan, what's the absolute greatest distance at which a disabling shot would be effective?"

The lieutenant glanced over his shoulder. "Approximately four hundred fifty kilometers, ma'am."

"Good. Then bring us into range and as soon as you can, get a shot off. When he's dead in the water, close in and take him."

Sinder felt the momentary trepidation. There was always the chance that it wasn't Kerry after all. But Alkor wasn't ordering a kill shot, and apologies and compensation could go a long way.

The ship got bigger in the viewer. Marcus Kerry, the rogue commander. Along with Bristol Aarons, Kyle Waverly, and Eva Reyes, he was wanted for gross insubordination, conspiracy, treason, and the murder of a senior executive. If it was him, the man would face a firing squad.

But not before he made himself useful.

"We're in range, ma'am." The lieutenant at the firing control turned. "Do I have the order?"

Alkor nodded. "Fire at will."

"Wait. Ma'am." Ensign Diev sounded alarmed. "He's cycling up to go to slipstream. He must have detected us somehow."

"Then what the hell are you waiting for?" Alkor snapped, leaning forward, gripping the arms of her chair. "Fire!"

The screen flashed as the ship released a short volley. A single point on the surface of the small ship exploded in flames that quickly died, and then nothing more happened. No slipstream, no burn of engines. The ship merely sat there.

"He's immobile. Not even sub-slipstream propulsion. Shall we move in now, ma'am?"

Alkor sat back. She shot Sinder a glance that was faintly, grimly pleased. "You wanted a successful mission? Looks like we might be one step closer."

He smiled.

The ship didn't respond when hailed. But the channel was open, and Alkor delivered her instructions. Stay put—not that whoever was on board had much choice—and the flagship would dispatch fighters to tow it into docking. There was nothing to indicate that the pilot had survived, but the fighters towed it in and the docking bay door closed behind them. The entire thing took less than twenty minutes.

Sinder maintained his composure, but inside, he was practically vibrating with eagerness. This could end up being some hapless traveler, confused and angry. But he doubted it.

They would have responded to the hails, if that were true.

Once the ship was safely aboard, and an armed guard dispatched to watch it, Sinder followed Alkor down to the docking bays. They were silent as they walked, but in Sinder's chest his heart was anything but still. It was nearly pounding.

Things were happening. Finally.

The bay in which the ship had been installed was one of the smaller ones. The ship sat there, silent and surrounded by peacekeepers in full armor, the fighters parked on either side. Alkor came to a stop in front of the leader of the team, who saluted.

"No movement inside, ma'am. Shall we bust open the hatch?"

"No need."

As one, they turned. The hatch was open, and stepping through it, appearing tired and resigned and much, much older than the official photo in his dossier, was Commander Marcus Kerry.

The guards raised their rifles, and Kerry raised his hands, but except for that, he didn't seem to be aware of them. He fixed his gaze on Alkor, straight and unflinching, and nodded.

"You've come a long way," Alkor said, her voice low and perhaps even a little sad. "A long way in the wrong direction, Kerry."

Kerry barked a laugh. "So you think. I don't suppose I could convince you otherwise."

"Not likely. Are you going to come quietly?"

"Would there be any point in resisting?"

Alkor inclined her head. "You never were an idiot, Kerry." She motioned to the guards, who stepped toward him, weapons still raised. "Come down, then, and let's get you squared away. Then we can talk."

Kerry descended the short ramp to the deck. One of the peacekeepers grasped him by the arm and spun him around, shoving him forward. Kerry didn't resist, but he winced and stumbled, and Alkor put up a hand, shaking her head.

"What's the point in treating him roughly? He's dead anyway. And once he was loyal. We can still respect that past loyalty."

The peacekeeper finished restraining Kerry, and glanced back toward Alkor.

"The brig," Alkor said, nodding toward the door. "I'll be down to interrogate him directly. I have to confer with our *liaison* here."

The peacekeepers saluted once more and filed out, Kerry held in the middle of them. Alkor watched them go, then turned to Sinder, her expression unreadable. "What's our next move?"

"It seems you've already anticipated it," Sinder said, pleased to be asked so directly. "We put some questions to the man. He knows *something*. Something about what happened on that planet. Something about Yuga. He wouldn't have run, otherwise."

"And if he doesn't talk?" Alkor's composed expression flickered. "He's a strong man. Tough-minded. I knew him in the academy. If he does know something, he won't give it up without a fight."

"Well, then." He felt a smile pulling at his lips. There was something pleasant about it. "We give him a fight." He started toward the door, but then paused and glanced back.

He had been trained in this. But he had never had the opportunity to put that training to use.

"Do you have a neuro-stim unit on board?"

Alkor blanched. "Torture? Sinder, are you sure that's—?"

"Necessary? No, I'm not sure. But if he proves to be as resistant as you say he can be . . ." Sinder shrugged. "Needs must, Captain. Come on. Let's see just how *tough-minded* he is."

CHAPTER

THREE

Nio Station was humming. Humming was good, Adam thought as he and Lochlan wove their way through the crowd. A large long-awaited freighter had just come in, and people were here from all over the sector to pick through the goods it carried, to buy and to sell.

Humming meant they were less likely to be noticed.

It was a routine stop, to the extent that they made routine stops anymore. Fuel, food, some very basic repairs, and they were also gathering news, if there was news to be had. A busy station was always alive with gossip.

It would do.

But as Lochlan took Adam's hand in his and they walked a little faster, something in Adam stirred, a prickle of bone-deep intuition. There was more here than supplies and information. That much was clear, even if he couldn't perceive exactly what it was.

He scanned the faces as they passed, though he had no real idea what he was looking for.

"Adam. Hey, *Adam.*" Fingers snapped inches from his nose. Adam jumped and glared at Lochlan, a shiver of adrenaline moving through him.

"The hell was that for?"

"You were miles away. You need to stay with me. What's your deal?" Lochlan's voice was as light as usual, but his face belied that, and he grasped Adam's shoulder and herded him into an alcove apart from the stream of people. "You've been weird for days. The dreams, the way you've been fading out on me like some shala-addled youngster . . . Is there something you aren't telling me?"

There's so much I'm not telling you. But Adam shook his head. There wasn't any point, not yet. He was no Aalim, no star-reader. He had no gifts to help him untangle what was in front of him.

Except for what happened on the Plain.

"I'm fine." Adam glanced away, out at the people again. All those faces, and something in one of them that he needed to see. "I was just thinking."

"About what?" Lochlan persisted, and Adam closed his eyes. Lochlan wasn't going to give up. He was going to worry at it until he wore Adam down, though he wouldn't intend to cause pain.

"About orbits," he said, meeting Lochlan's gaze. It was easier than he had thought it would be. "About getting locked in."

"You're not locked into anything."

"But it still feels like we're moving in circles."

"Because we *are, chusile.* But we'll break out of them." Lochlan half shrugged. "Anyway, it's more than that. I can tell. Come on, I know there's shit you can't tell me, but there has to be shit you can."

Adam huffed a quiet laugh, glancing over his shoulder. "Here? Is this the place?"

"Is there a good one?"

"Fine. It's the Plain. You know where I got locked in? It didn't start there, but . . . All those people. Because of me."

Lochlan stared at him, clearly incredulous. "You're serious? Because of *you*? Not the fucking *raya* Protectorate? Adam, you didn't call them down on us. That wasn't your fault."

"They came because you took me in," Adam replied, and misery seeped into his voice. "To save me. Or you tried. You didn't, not completely. You couldn't have. I am what I am. But when you healed me . . ."

He raised a bare forearm to display the mottled, once perfectly even skin tone, and he knew that when Lochlan gazed into his eyes, he saw mismatched blue and green. Adam's very body rearranged, at the level of his code. An abomination in the life he had abandoned. That had abandoned him. "You changed me and that locked me into something new. Maybe not a circle, but . . . My orbit shifted. Nothing's the same now. Nothing deep in me . . . Nothing on the surface. Even small things. Maybe there's a reason behind it, what happened on the Plain, to everyone, to me . . . but it started with me, and it all adds up to something."

Lochlan laid a hand on his mottled forearm, his thumb stroking over one of the patches of browner melanin. "The small things? Let go of those. You know I think they're beautiful. *You're* beautiful."

Adam smiled faintly, sadly. "You think everything different is beautiful."

"Are you holding that against me?"

"You know I'm not. I'm just . . . Whatever happens next, what I started led to the deaths of all those people. And sometimes that's too heavy. Sometimes it's hard to breathe."

Lochlan nodded, slowly. His comprehension was like a rapid sunrise behind his eyes, and he reached up, hands framing Adam's shoulders. "Place like this, the less *legal* businesspeople will be marking the patrols. Someone here will have what we need. Let's go." But he hesitated, then cupped Adam's face with one hand, leaned forward, and kissed him.

It didn't come as a surprise, but Adam still stiffened for a split second before he relaxed. It was warm and sweet, and for the briefest, most wonderful of moments everything else faded into the background and there was only Lochlan, solid against him.

Solid and alive.

For how much longer?

"There's got to be a bar," Lochlan murmured as he pulled back slightly, one hand threading into Adam's hair. "There's always a bar."

Adam nodded, but with the loss of the kiss, he was freshly aware of where they were, of all the people, and though they were tucked out of the way, unease snaked through him. Being affectionate in front of the Bideshi was one thing—with them, at least as far as being with Lochlan went, he now felt a kind of comfort that he couldn't remember ever feeling within breeding-focused Protectorate society. There, the act of pairing and reproduction had taken on an almost religious significance. But these weren't Bideshi, and though no one seemed to notice them, it felt as though there were countless unseen eyes watching.

He pressed his hands against Lochlan's chest, feeling the beat of that well-loved heart under his palms. He was going to take what he had here. He was going to stop being afraid. "Okay. Let's find that bar."

The bar was an unnamed establishment on the lowest level of the station, and while it was clearly a large space, it managed—thanks to a thick crowd and low lighting—to feel claustrophobic. Adam and Lochlan made their way from the door to a long circular bar at the center of the room—slow and careful because all they needed now was to offend someone and end up in a brawl. The area around the bar was even more jammed with people than the rest of the place, but Lochlan had proven himself well versed in making use of spaces that Adam would have assumed were too small to squeeze through, maneuvering his way closer. Bemused, Adam followed.

Lochlan raised a hand as Adam pressed in alongside him and one of the barkeeps—a Koticki with its antennae waving—made its way over to them and clicked its mandibles in preamble to its greeting. "Gents. What can I get you?"

"Two house ales," Lochlan said immediately. "Chaser of whatever your cheapest whiskey happens to be."

The Koticki clicked an affirmative and turned to fill the order. Adam leaned close to Lochlan, glancing at the people who surrounded them—some human and others from a bewildering variety of other species, even for someone who used to live in the relatively cosmopolitan Kolyma City. They looked tough, weathered, and generally unapproachable. But they could clearly talk to each other, and they could all come to some form of communion. Not for the first time it occurred to Adam that it was sadly comic how such different species could often communicate with such ease—even learning each other's languages when necessary, and frequently without much difficulty, while two groups of humans had been at odds for centuries. And now that conflict had exploded into violence.

He turned his attention back to the task at hand: the careful, casual extraction of information. But not in a bar like this, and not from people so formidable.

Lochlan seemed to catch his trepidation, for he nudged Adam with his elbow and shot him a quick, cocky grin. "Relax. We got this." He leaned back slightly as the Koticki set their drinks down in front of them, and cleared his throat.

"*Khara*, you're right, those patrols are *such* a pain in the ass. But what can you do? We'll have to take the shipment back, I suppose." He nudged Adam again, raising his eyebrows as he picked up his ale, and Adam got it. *Play along.*

"But all that wasted cred," he groused. "Are you sure there's no way around them?"

Lochlan shook his head sadly. "Not sure, but I don't think it's worth the risk. But at this point I'd consider paying for the information. It'd be cheaper than getting boarded and seized, wouldn't it?"

Payment. Adam arched a brow. That kind of implicit promise might not be a good one to float. They had credits, of course, and some goods to trade, but they weren't exactly flush. Still, Lochlan could talk smooth when he had to. And even when he didn't. It was practically a sport for him.

They waited a few minutes, but no one came up to them. No one seemed to have noticed what Lochlan had said. The chaos continued around them much the same as it had before, and at last Adam leaned in again, sighing disappointment. He wasn't sure if he had really expected it to work, but he had hoped.

"I guess we'll have to try something else."

Lochlan shook his head. "No, just wait. You have to give the word a chance to circulate. And you have to give people a chance to do some considering." He squeezed Adam's shoulder and pushed away from the bar, drinks in hand. "Be patient, *chusile*. I must be a bad influence on you, eh?"

Bemused but willing to go along for the moment, Adam picked up his own glasses and followed Lochlan back through the crowd to a small table set against the rear of the room. It was dim and the low light made it feel secluded even as it was surrounded by people, and once more Adam felt a sliver of doubt as he slid into a seat beside Lochlan.

"You think anyone will be able to find us back here?"

Lochlan regarded him with a faintly amused smile. "*Mitr*, you haven't spent a lot of time in places like this, have you?"

Adam's mouth twisted. "I haven't spent *any* time in places like this. Until recently, anyway."

"Not even when you were on the run?"

"Not even then." Adam shrugged. "I was mostly trying to stay away from people. I picked up food in a few holes-in-the-wall, but I never went anywhere crowded. It seemed like asking for trouble."

"Well, trouble is exactly what we want right now." Lochlan looked up and grinned. "And right on cue, here she comes."

Adam followed his gaze and saw a woman approaching them, pushing her way past the people in front of her with a cool authority that matched her expression. She was both tall and softly round, but with a hardness under that roundness that suggested muscle, and Adam was struck by the deep-purple scar that cut down the right side of her face.

She stopped by their table and bent down, bracing on it with both powerful arms. "I hear you're trying to get past some patrols."

Lochlan inclined his head. "You heard right, lady."

The woman's face stretched into a quick smirk, there and then gone again, and her attention seemed caught and held by Adam, and he could guess why. Few people marked the unevenness in his skin tone or his eyes until they got close to him, but once they did it tended to hold their attention.

Try as he might, he was still noticeable.

"Might be able to help you." She dragged up a stool and sat without waiting to be invited, then leaned across to them. "I made the run past them twice last week. It's not easy, but there are ways."

Adam nodded. So it was possible. But it was unlikely that she'd proffer this information for free. "Are you the only one who knows about it?"

"You asking if I have any competition? Fat chance. Not saying I'm the only one who knows, but I'm the only one around here you're gonna find."

"We can pay."

"I know you can. You better." She tapped her fingers on the table. "Up front. Ten thousand credits."

Adam stared at her. This, he hadn't been expecting. He glanced at Lochlan, who gave him a minute shake of the head. *Let me handle this.*

"We don't have that much on us. Once we make the drop and get our payment, we can cut you in."

The woman barked a laugh. "What do you think I am, some dirt-fresh baby bird? I'm not telling you shit unless I have cred in hand."

"We can pay you after—" Lochlan started to say again, but Adam cut in. It was desperate, maybe stupid, but he was tired of waiting, and they didn't have the luxury of caution now.

"We'll give you what we have, and the rest later if you come along. That way we know you aren't trying to screw us. Is that acceptable?"

The woman's eyes narrowed. "How much are we talking?"

"Five thousand now, five thousand when we make the drop. For the full ten."

The woman was silent. Under the table, Lochlan gripped Adam's knee, and Adam was unable to tell what feelings were behind the grasp. Lochlan's face was unreadable.

She seemed to be considering, and when a tall, slender, green-skinned man moved past carrying a tray of glasses, she took one. She took a long swallow. "What's your story, anyway?"

Lochlan arched a brow. "Excuse me?"

"You. You're Bideshi, or you were. Don't bother trying to tell me you're not; I knew it the second I saw you. The tats? Please." She laughed again and took another swig of whatever was in the glass. Adam shot Lochlan a look, and the one he got back was both bemused and a bit tense.

Keep your mouth shut.

"So what if I am?" Lochlan's shrug was carefully casual.

"So, nothing. Except it does kind of have me wondering. There were some rumors a while back about a dustup on a planet closer to the galactic center. Protectorate. Bideshi. Lot of people killed. On both sides." She glanced from Adam to Lochlan, brow furrowed meditatively. "Just wondering if either of you know anything about it."

"Nosy, aren't you?" Lochlan's mouth tightened. "Is that wise?"

"I want to make sure you're not gonna screw me. What I know could get me in a lot of trouble. With the wrong people." She smiled faintly. "But you . . . Protectorate don't hire Bideshi. Even when they're desperate. Even if they could find any Bideshi willing to be hired. They wouldn't *lower themselves*."

"So you're satisfied?" Lochlan's tone had an acid edge. But he didn't, Adam thought, seem like he was about to drag them both away.

"I still don't know if you know anything about that little *incident*. I mean, you know that's why the patrols are as intense as they are right now. Looking for someone, people say."

Lochlan said nothing. There was tension gathering, and Adam worried that it was an indicator to pull out of this as quickly as possible, perhaps even get off the station, and he was lifting his foot to nudge Lochlan's under the table when the woman sat back, shaking her head.

"Look, man. You don't have to tell me anything you don't want to. I'll only say I have no love for the Protectorate. At all. Bideshi, no Bideshi . . ." She cocked her head at Adam and flashed him a brief but brilliant grin. "Whatever your deal is, Blotchy. I'm in, sure. You pay me, obviously, but I don't like the way they've been hassling people. Especially the Bideshi. And whatever happened on that planet . . . I don't like the sound of that either. You want to skim through under their noses, I like the sound of that just fine."

She drained the rest of the glass. "If you can forgive the questions, it's a deal. When are you ready to go?"

Lochlan's brows drew together. "We're refueling, picking up a few other things. Six hours?"

"Got it." She gave them another quick smile. "What names are we working with?"

"Yuri," Lochlan said immediately, then nodded at Adam. "And Sasha. You?"

"Skyler. All right, *Yuri* and *Sasha*." Her smile widened, her scar stretching. "I'll see you in six hours. I'm on a Finch J79 on the top ring, name of *Sybilline*. Disembark and hail me and we'll go from there." She stood up, gave them a slight bow, and left, vanishing through the maze of people.

Adam leaned close to Lochlan, one corner of his mouth twitching upward. "*Sasha*?"

"It's not always a girl's name." Lochlan downed his whiskey and rose from his chair. His lanky body was suddenly tense, almost twitchy, his eyes distracted. "And I liked the look on your face. Let's get outta here."

Adam emptied his own glass and rose, trailing Lochlan toward the door, feeling disquiet gnawing at him. Had something happened, beyond the obvious? Or was Lochlan doubting what they were doing entirely? Back in the main atrium, Adam caught Lochlan's arm and tugged him into a side passage, stopping them in a patch of shadow. "What's wrong?"

Lochlan's brows drew together, and his mouth pulled into a thin and unhappy line. "You just gave her the last of our cred, that's what's wrong. And those questions got *uncomfortable*."

"I . . ." Adam shook his head. "She wasn't going to budge. And we needed her. As for the questions . . . How were those my fault?"

"We would've found another way. Or I could've bargained her down."

"Is the money actually the issue, Lock? If it's about the questions, remember that you could have walked away when she started with them. I could tell you were thinking about it. But you didn't."

Lochlan's eyes widened, and Adam caught at least a little of what was really going on. Lochlan was scared. Scared and back into a corner.

"Regardless. That was stupid, Adam. You should've let me handle it."

Adam reeled back, stung. This was a taste of the old Lochlan, arrogant and bullheaded, snappish and impatient when it came to Adam and what Lochlan perceived as his sheltered Protectorate shortcomings.

Except it wasn't like the old Lochlan. Before, he hadn't seemed so tired. So worried.

"Okay," he said slowly. "So . . . Look, maybe you're right. Fuck, you probably are. I'm sorry. But we can get more, we can . . . This isn't necessarily a problem."

"'Not necessarily a problem'?" Lochlan sounded incredulous. "*Khara*, if you're going to go off all half-cocked every time you get impatient about something, then we're going to—"

"*You're* telling *me* to not go off half-cocked? Are you out of your mind?"

"*You can't do this*, Adam." Lochlan was close now, inches away from his face, voice an angry hiss. Someone pushed past them, and Lochlan glanced at their receding back, silent for a moment before focusing on Adam again. "You don't *know* this world. I know you've done . . . I know you've come a long way, but we're out in the shit now, and I worry about you, you don't know—"

Adam stopped him with a hand pressed quickly to his lips. The world was disintegrating around him. Lochlan had seemed so confident, so unconcerned, from the moment they had disembarked from Ashwina until only a few hours ago, but now it was as though a mask had slipped, revealing something raw and painful underneath. All at once Adam remembered the thick forests of the Klashorg homeworld when he and the Bideshi convoy had sheltered there from the pursuing Protectorate forces. He remembered sitting beneath the glowing bell of a massive flower, listening to Lochlan tell the story of what had happened on Caldor Station, the Protectorate massacre of so many Bideshi, of the small, terrified boy he had once been as he left the corpses of his family and went crawling through the passages and ducts of the station, blood and the screams of the dying outside.

Lochlan had two faces. Adam was still learning how to tell which was which.

"We're all right," he whispered, and Lochlan shook his head, pressing in, pushing Adam's back against the wall.

"*Chusile* . . . I almost lost you on the Plain." He leaned their foreheads together. "I came so close. The last few weeks . . . I can't stop thinking about losing you again. *Chere*, this could be so dangerous. I know you have to do it, and I have to be with you while you do. You just . . . I want to help you. Let me help you."

Adam let out a long breath, curled one hand around the coils of Lochlan's dreadlocks, and nodded their mouths together in something that was too light and careful to really be a kiss. "I want you to help me. But you have to trust me." He nuzzled Lochlan's jaw. He didn't care who saw them now. He didn't want fear to have any place here.

Yet it seemed it always would.

"You don't trust *me*," Lochlan said, and he sounded so sad that for a moment Adam couldn't speak anymore.

"I'll tell you," he murmured finally. "I promise, I will. I just . . . I can't. Not yet."

Lochlan nodded, but his face was still twisting, unhappy, and as Adam kissed him again the kiss was hard and a little desperate. When Lochlan pressed forward again, his hand slipped up under the hem of Adam's shirt, and Adam uncoiled under rough hands and a familiar body, as though there was nothing between their skins.

"I love you," he whispered, and Lochlan sighed in response and only kissed him harder, pushing his lips apart, demanding.

Yes, Adam didn't care about being seen now. But he was grateful for the shadows, all the same. This was theirs. This was for them. He wasn't going to let anyone take it away.

But the twisting in his gut didn't leave him. And even the warmth of the kisses, of Lochlan's touch felt somehow distant. What would happen if he moved further away? What would happen if, somehow, that space grew? What would happen if he had to make a choice?

CHAPTER

FOUR

Kerry didn't struggle in the bonds that held him fast to the chair. He didn't move at all, his face blank.

Sinder knew enough to recognize that as a form of resistance.

He, Kerry, and Alkor were in one of the brig cells. A med-tech sat on the bunk, and on her lap was the small box of the neuro-stim. Two wires extended from it, which branched into four and ended in adhesive pads; these were attached to Kerry's wrists and temples.

Normally it was a therapeutic device, to assist in the rebuilding of damaged nerves. Normally. It had other, less savory uses.

Kerry glanced from the pads up to Sinder, his eyes cool and oddly colorless. Alkor, for her part, was leaning in the corner, her mouth twisting with clear discomfort. This wasn't surprising. Sinder had gotten the feeling that she might not have the stomach for this kind of tactic.

She didn't have to. As long as she stayed out of the way.

"Well, now, Commander," Sinder said, his tone light and eminently reasonable. "I think we should talk."

Kerry shrugged. "Whatever. Sinder, is that your name? I don't see much of a reason why I'd tell you anything, but you can talk if you want to."

Sinder arched an eyebrow and gestured to the med-tech and her unit. "There is *that*, if you're looking for a reason."

"Torture?" Kerry snorted. "That's a little ham-handed, don't you think? Then again, the way your bosses have been going—"

"They were your bosses too, Marcus," Alkor cut in. More than anything, she sounded tired. "What the hell happened to you? You were one of ours. A true believer. How could you toss it all away like you did? *Why*?"

Sinder watched Kerry silently. These questions were rather beside the point, but he was prepared to let Alkor ask them.

Kerry was also silent for a moment. Then he shook his head, an awful smile stretching his mouth. "I know that's the line they fed you, but you weren't there. You can't imagine. You don't see something like that, all those people dying for *nothing*, and keep going the way you have. It's not possible, Alkor." He leaned forward slightly, his arms straining against the bonds. "Open your *eyes*. What's coming for you—for all of us—is so much worse than some kid who didn't die when he should have."

"Kid," Sinder echoed thoughtfully. Now they were getting somewhere. "You mean Yuga. So he's still alive."

Kerry pursed his lips. And said nothing.

"We were almost certain," Sinder went on breezily. "But it's nice to have anything in the way of independent confirmation. By rights he shouldn't still have been alive during the altercation on that planet, but given the fact, it makes sense that he would be now. Somehow he overcame what was happening to him, which is part of why we're interested in him." His voice dropped, grew more serious. "But we have to find him, Kerry. Him, the Bideshi, what they did to Melissa Cosaire and all those peacekeepers . . . We couldn't have predicted it. But now we know Yuga's a wild variable. He's destructive. If you ever valued the world that bore you, tell us what you know about him. Help us, Commander."

"'He's destructive,'" Kerry repeated, shaking his head. "You . . . You don't know, do you? They didn't fucking tell you." He laughed, sharp and bitter. "I guess I shouldn't be surprised. Cosaire knew, but she had every reason to. She was *dying* from it."

"What the fuck are you talking about?" Alkor stepped forward, shooting Sinder a worried look. "She died because Bristol Aarons put a bullet in her head. Because you helped him lead a mutiny. What's this bullshit we're supposed to know?"

Kerry smiled, that same awful smile. "Every one of us is dying from it. The alterations to our code, the first enhancements. Nasty little imperfections, hiding in the very thing that was supposed to make us perfect. They're in us, and they're twisting in on themselves. You know how fucking ironic that is? Given why they're there? Centuries of work leading up to the eradication of every cancer, of what the world feared then? Those initial enhancements. Then more and more, all built on top of each other, interweaving, combining. Now they're acting like a goddamn virus. That's what they aren't telling you. In some of us it'll go faster, in some of us slower . . . I haven't shown any symptoms yet, but I will— if you don't kill me before that. Adam . . . He wasn't alone. He wasn't even the first. He sure as hell won't be the last, and he knows it. What he represents—the truth, that *we* did this to him, that we're doing it to everyone, even now— it'll bring the whole thing tumbling down. Everything we've done . . . Every species we ever subjugated in the name of that. Every one of us who worked for it. Believes in it. You know what happens when faith gets snatched out from under you? 'Cause I do. It all falls down once people find out the truth. Our leaders, our people . . . They just deny and deny and deny, to themselves more than anyone else. He would destroy all that. He would destroy everything. Don't you get it, you stupid fucks? Why he's so dangerous."

It made no sense. And yet it did, like fragments of a sunken ruin protruding above the water—Kerry must be raving, but it was reasonable, perhaps, to wonder what he was raving *about*. How the mad idea had worked its way into him. How it might connect to other things. Isaac Sinder had been born with powerful instincts, and he had learned over long years to trust them.

He had to understand this.

It was another reason to find Adam before anyone else could.

"Then tell me where he is," he said, stepping closer, his voice low and even. "I'm here because I believe in protecting what we have. If what you're saying is true . . . Tell me where he is, and I'll see what I can do to help him. I'll at least hear him out. I know we have a mission, but if there's another threat to the Protectorate . . . Commander, I'm as loyal as you were, once. You're right. I don't get it. Help me."

Kerry stared at him. Sinder could sense the wheels turning frantically behind his eyes, the internal struggle that he had started. The man wanted to believe him. How long had Kerry been alone, facing his own impotence? Perhaps he hadn't been; perhaps he had been with Yuga and whatever other malcontents he had managed to scrape together . . . But he had a look of gaunt desperation that suggested that wasn't true.

This was a man hanging on by his fingernails.

"Anything you can tell us," Alkor said quietly. "C'mon, man. You can still turn this thing around. All those people who died on that planet . . . Don't make their deaths meaningless."

He was going to give in. Sinder was sure of it. He could see the facade cracking, a flood threatening to burst through.

And then it pulled together again.

"Fuck off," Kerry growled. "You think I don't know how to read you? I knew Cosaire. I knew that look in her eyes, like she'd do anything, say anything to get what she wanted. You have the same look. You're a snake, Sinder. You're a fucking snake, and I wouldn't trust you worth a shed scale."

Sinder stepped back, ice trickling down his spine. Not fear, but everything in him hardening, turning to cold steel. Not this way, then.

There were other ways.

"You know where he is," he said. "Or you know *something*. I don't care what you think of me, Kerry—I have a job to do. If you won't help me voluntarily . . ." He gave the med-tech a nod. She returned it and lowered her hands to the screen, which flicked on under her touch. It glowed and then glowed brighter, numbers scrolling across one side, a sine wave at the top. The line shortened, the troughs and crests lowering and raising, like a sea growing more turbulent. The tech touched the screen again.

Kerry screamed.

It wasn't a long scream, but it was tight with agony, strangled and then bursting from him as he failed to hold it back. Of course he couldn't. The neuro-stim seized the entire nervous system and sent waves of stimulation into it, wrenching muscles, jerking limbs, and simulating sensory input—including pain. Kerry was likely feeling as though the skin was being flayed off every part of his body at once, torn from him in a cruel yank.

Then the unit cut off and he collapsed back into the chair, breathing hard.

"I don't want to have to ask you too many more times." Sinder's tone was placid. He could feel Alkor glaring icily at him. "This won't kill you, but it *can* cause permanent nerve damage, and believe it or not, I have no desire to hurt you in that way. It would look better if I handed you over to the tribunal whole and well rather than in constant pain."

Kerry only stared at him in silence. Sinder sighed and leaned forward. He had hoped for a little more cooperation than this, but he had enough sense to know that was unlikely now. "You can go to your execution with all the dignity appropriate to your pedigree, or you can be carried there a drooling, paralyzed shell. It's entirely up to you."

"I don't know where he is." Kerry's expression radiated scorn. "And even if I did, I wouldn't tell you, you psychopathic prick."

Sinder nodded at the tech, who flicked on the stim once more. This time the scream went on for about half a minute, and when the unit finally cut off again and he went limp, there was a faint twitching in his extremities.

"You know something," Sinder repeated softly. "Give us anything we can use, and this stops right now."

Kerry shook his head, gasping, and then went rigid with a howl as fire leaped into his nerves.

"Sinder." Alkor stepped forward, holding out a hand. The tech, mouth tense—betraying the first emotion she had yet shown—cut the stim off, and Sinder gave Alkor a frown. This was something he would have preferred to avoid, though he hadn't imagined for a moment that the captain would have been willing to absent herself. "This has gone on long enough. Whatever he did, this is one of our own, we can't just—"

"We can. We will. We *have* to, Alkor; I thought we had this clear between us." He moved closer, his head down and his voice low and smooth, as if he were trying to soothe an animal. "He's not one of our own, not anymore. He's a destructive force. If he can't be made use of, then his value is entirely depleted."

He glanced at Kerry, hit by a wave of sudden and intense disgust. No, they didn't owe this man anything. Kerry had exhausted Sinder's store of mercy. "The man you respected—that we *both* could respect— died on that worthless planet. He can't be saved. He's already dead."

Alkor simply looked at him, her brow furrowed. For a few seconds, he expected her to protest further. But at last she stepped back, flicking her gaze away, her shoulders hunched. Sinder was satisfied.

She'd put on a show of strength, but there was profound weakness in her core. That was good.

"I don't know," Kerry moaned. *Speaking of weakness.* Sinder turned to him.

"I'm losing my patience, Commander. I told you, we don't have the luxury of taking our time here. Give us *something.* That's all I'm asking for. That's not so much."

Nothing. The stim's next thrust of pain went on for over a minute, and Kerry's screams took on a rough, breaking quality, as though the unit was raking his throat raw. He was crying now, eyes squeezed shut and teeth clenched, but when it stopped he simply shook his head and said nothing else.

So it went from there.

It was, Sinder thought as he watched the man's body arch and spasm, a little like the more delicate parts of mining, like wearing down solid rock until the ore could be extracted. You could blast your way through to some of it, but the rest took consistent, grinding pressure until at last it came away. That took determination. Faith.

He knew there was ore. It was just a matter of getting to it.

Fifteen minutes later, Alkor left, muttering something that Sinder couldn't make out, her face colorless.

Fifteen minutes more and Kerry broke.

"He's here," he whispered, barely audible. His voice was almost gone, his head lolling to the side and a thread of drool trickling from the corner of his mouth. Sinder had to crouch close to him in order to hear. A flush of excitement spread through him.

Finally. And better than he had hoped.

"Where? Where, Commander? You can tell me. This is almost over."

"In . . . this sector. I don't know exactly where. I was . . . I was going to make contact. Arrange . . . a meeting. Help him get past . . . patrols."

"How? How were you going to make contact?"

"They'd have to . . . put in for supplies. One of the stations. I could . . . I could get word through others. People there . . ."

His mouth stretched into an awful, sick smile. "They don't ask questions."

"All right," Sinder said gently. "Good. Thank you, Commander." He straightened up and turned toward the door, his hands opening and closing in reflexive fists.

Outside the cell, he nodded to one of the peacekeepers. "Get in there and see to him. Call another medic to assist. Have him cleaned up, see that he's resting comfortably. We might need him again."

In fact, there was no *might* about it. Commander Marcus Kerry had one last mission to carry out.

Whether he wanted to or not.

CHAPTER

FIVE

Lochlan shifted beside Adam, turned over, and slung a leg across his thighs. For once, Adam was sleeping soundly, and he didn't want to disturb him, but in the last week or so, touching him had been nearly impossible to resist.

Those touches had been desperate. He didn't like to admit it, even to himself, but it was still true.

After the Battle of the Plain, there had been a kind of peace that he now recognized as mixed exhaustion and relief. That peace had made the decision to leave Ashwina easier. Lochlan wasn't used to staying in one place for long anyway and Adam's determination to go had made the choice for him. Though what the man felt he still owed those who had tried every weapon in their arsenal to kill him, Lochlan wasn't sure, but he knew Adam would hold to it, this need to save them if he could. That he was driven in significant part by the fact that a lot of people had died because of the conviction that two civilizations who were truly siblings couldn't be at war forever, hot or cold, and someone had to make the first move. That someone might as well be him, whatever the risks.

It was what Ixchel would have wanted. What she believed, until the moment of her death.

Lochlan wasn't used to fear. It was there, but from long necessity he had gotten good at beating it back. Now the emotion was getting harder to ignore—fear coupled with frustration coupled with a heavy, sick boredom. Yet if they gave in to that boredom, if they moved too soon and too fast, they would likely be caught, even in slipstream. The Protectorate had demonstrated the ability to pursue them there before.

Everything had changed. Everything was wrong. He had been ready for it to be right at last, to be with Adam and to discover what it meant to love someone like this, which was so new, and here as well there was an element of fear. What it meant to need someone in this way, the danger that followed from it. Of vulnerability. Of loss.

What he had refused to do for so long.

Now they were facing death again.

They were stationed a few hundred kilometers from the patrol lines, Skyler's ship pulled up alongside. Hours before, when they had exited slipstream, she had hailed them and explained what they would be doing. It hadn't been a long conversation, and it all had seemed reasonable enough, but that hadn't meant Lochlan had liked it.

Not that they had much more in the way of options.

"I'm sure you've noticed that it seems like they have no pattern," she'd said. "To throw you off. It took me a week of watching them, but I have it all charted. We wait here a few hours, and then there'll be about half an hour where none of the patrol teams will be in sensor range of this one twelve-kilometer area. It's a blind spot, and far as I can tell they don't know about it. If we move fast, we can sneak through."

Adam had frowned. "No slipstream?"

"They've got some hot new sensor system that can detect ships in slipstream, even when *they're* out of it. It's actually got greater range than their sensors for normal space. Something about displacement or whatever; I don't totally understand the physics. Either way, we should use the sub-slipstream engines. They're slower, but safer."

So now they were parked, waiting. Trusting that in the meantime, they wouldn't be spotted. Trusting Skyler, which Lochlan wasn't sure he did, but that didn't mean they couldn't make use of what she knew.

Skyler did complicate things, because assuming they got through, she would want the rest of her pay. But they would figure that out. Lochlan was good at figuring things out. He was also good at wriggling his way out of tight spaces. From an early age, it had always struck him as blackly funny how he had acquired that skill. Expertise through misery and grief and terror. Crawling through the conduits of Caldor Station, wedging himself into places too small for anyone but a child. Staying alive.

Suddenly, he missed Ying so much it almost hurt. From the day she had taken him in after the murder of his parents, the Bideshi healer had been one of the few people able to comfort him, and now she was back on Ashwina, what felt like an impossible distance away, and it had occurred to him more than once that he might never see her again. And she might never know what had happened to him.

He could hope.

He lifted his head, leaned it on one hand. Adam was on his stomach, and the dim light fell across him in delicate patches of light and dark, which were a little like the soft mottling that had covered his skin since his healing on the Plain. Lochlan knew it now, the pattern of it, though—like the Protectorate's patrols—it appeared random. Perhaps he had merely created one in his own mind, like constellations seen from a planet's surface. A parallax view of someone's body.

He settled his hand on Adam's back and traced the marks with his fingertips, light and careful. *Perfect*, he thought, and smiled as warmth flooded through him.

But Adam's skin and eyes weren't the only things about him that had changed since he was healed on the Plain of Heaven. His build had always been slight, but even when Lochlan had found him, weak and starved and so sick, there had been remnants of the strength he had once possessed, and on Ashwina, much of that strength had returned, and he had filled out again. But now he was getting skinny once more, as if his body were melting away with each day without progress. His sleep choked with nightmares he refused to share.

There was distance between them now. It was small, but it was growing.

I could lose him.

There was more than one way to lose someone.

Lochlan lowered his head and pressed his lips to Adam's shoulder. Adam stirred, muttered, subsided back into deeper sleep. Like this, at least, there was a little of that peace they had had so briefly, a little of what they had begun to build together.

Maybe someday this would all be over. Then they could start to build it again.

There was a soft chime from the console. A hail. Lochlan sighed and pushed himself up, clambering over Adam's body. From behind him, he heard Adam stir again.

"Whassit?"

"Comm." He turned, bent, and combed his hand through Adam's hair, kissing his temple. "It's probably Skyler. I'll get it. Take your time."

But it seemed too soon. By his estimate, they should still have another hour or so. He crossed to the comm, stepping over piles of clutter, and punched the receiver without checking the sender ID.

"*Bienentad*, Skyler. What's the good word?"

"This is an automated message. The word is Takamagahara. Repeat, Takamagahara. That is the entire word. Seek location. Sender is plain orbiting body." There was a pause, a crackle of static, then, "Message repeat. This is an automated message. The word is—"

"What the hell is that?" Adam, behind him, sounding sleepy but awake enough to be confused.

Completely bewildered, Lochlan stared at the console as if it could tell him something, and called up the sender ID. Blank. "*Khara*, sender's blocked. Whoever they are, they don't want anyone identifying them."

"So what's the message mean?" Adam moved to stand next to him, glancing down at the ID, one hand at the small of Lochlan's back. "I . . . It sounds like some kind of code. *Takamagahara*." He glanced at Lochlan, his eyes wide. "You think it's . . . for us? Lock, who even knows we're *out* here?"

"No one. No one should." Except how sure was he of that? How sure did he have *cause* to be? They had been careful, but their faces had been seen, and if anyone had had reason to recognize them . . .

But this didn't feel like Protectorate. It was too . . . Well, it was too nonsensical, for one. Though Lochlan was certain, the more he considered it, that there *was* sense behind it, however elusive.

"'Sender is plain orbiting body,'" Adam echoed, settling himself into the pilot's seat and peering at the transcript of the message. "What could that . . . Takamagahara." He was quiet for a few moments, then lifted his head. "What was orbiting the planet?"

"When?"

"When the battle happened. There were Bideshi homeships . . . And there were also Protectorate ships." He looked back at Lochlan, eyes wide and his gaze sharpening. "Bideshi wouldn't send a message like this. What reason would they have to be so cloak-and-dagger?

Lock . . . What if this is coming from someone inside the Protectorate?"

Lochlan frowned. He had disregarded the idea as a bit improbable, but it made a kind of sense, as much sense as anything else made at the moment. "You think it's a trap?"

"I don't know." Adam closed his eyes. "If that part is referring to the Protectorate, it could also mean someone who was on one of those ships. I don't know why they wouldn't have contacted us before, but who knows what's happened to them since."

His mismatched eyes snapped open, bright and excited. "So . . . It could be Kyle. My friend, you remember? Or Eva Reyes, the woman who was with him. Even Bristol Aarons, though I don't think that's likely. Or . . ."

"That commander," Lochlan finished, as the memory came to him. "Kerry or something, wasn't it?" He had seen the man only briefly and had found his gruffness off-putting rather than possessed of the ornery charm it might have had in a Bideshi. But Kerry had seemed genuine in his desire for peace, and had kept the truce until the Protectorate fleet departed. He had even assisted in sorting through the dead and wounded of both sides, making sure that people—and bodies—were returned to their proper ships.

"Yes. Kerry." Adam frowned. "Okay, so leaving aside identity for a minute . . . What's the rest of the message? What's its actual purpose?"

"'The word is Takamagahara,'" Lochlan mused. He leaned over the pilot's seat, his attention momentarily caught by a scatter of light from the prisms that dangled over the console. The rainbow specks were almost like stars across the darkness of the console's face, moving slightly as the prisms swung in *Volya*'s gentle vibrations.

Stars.

"Takamagahara is a place." He set his hand under the lights, watching them slide across its brown back. "Is it telling us to go somewhere?"

"To Takamagahara?" Adam appeared to consider, then shook his head. "It can't be. If the rest of the message is that obscure, why would the location be so blatant? If it seems to be giving us specific directions it has to be referring to something else." He paused, then slapped a hand on the console's face so abruptly that Lochlan jumped.

"*Khara*, Adam, what're you—"

"What if we converted the letters of the name into numbers? In Standard, in terms of position in the alphabet." He was already doing it, fingers darting over the touch screen. "It's actually *really* basic, it could be wrong . . . But it's still worth a . . ." He shifted his gaze to the set of numbers softly glowing on the screen. "Are those coordinates? They are, aren't they?"

"I'll be damned three times over." Lochlan grinned, sudden and wide. For all the trouble he had slung Adam's way at first, for all the hard time he had given him, he had always known the man was sharp. "You're quite something, *chusile*."

Adam breathed a quiet laugh. "You're with me, aren't you? Seriously, though, it's not *that* complicated. Like I said, it's not even that secure. Anyone could probably figure it out if they had any context for it, though I guess it would be a lot harder to identify the sender if you didn't know about the battle." He tapped his fingers on the arm of the chair, brow furrowed, and Lochlan realized that it was the first time in a long time that Adam really seemed like himself again. Keen, alert, ready to move on something.

On impulse he swung the chair around, hooked a hand behind Adam's neck, and pulled him up and in, sealing their mouths together. Adam tensed, but then relaxed under him with a low groan, lifting a hand to grasp at Lochlan's dreadlocks.

"What was that for?" he murmured, when Lochlan pulled away enough to let them catch their breath. Lochlan smiled.

"Don't ask questions, you stupid *raya*. I like seeing you like this, is all."

Adam gave him a quizzical look, but he was still smiling, warm and happy. "So . . . I guess we go to the coordinates, then."

"You trust them?"

"Not really. Not sure I'd trust anything right now." He glanced back at them, lips moving silently as he mouthed the numbers. "Shit, there's Skyler, though. What's she going to do if we cut out on her? *Do* we want to cut out on her? We could still make the run through the patrol route."

Lochlan shook his head. "You think you can just ignore this? Act like we never got it at all?"

"No. All right. We should contact Skyler. Unless you think we should go to slipstream."

"Not very polite. I liked her. Anyway, she has our money for doing basically nothing. How mad could she be?"

Adam shot Lochlan a wry smile. "I don't suppose she'd give us a refund—I guess I should let you do the talking this time?"

"Oh, stop; I said I was sorry." Some of the words were teasing. Some of them weren't. He *was* sorry. It wasn't as though the outburst was unlike him, but he could tell when it was fairly justified and when it wasn't. "But yeah. I should." He leaned over farther—and then almost as if it were an accident, he slid backward into Adam's lap.

Adam let out a breath and a laugh that was dangerously close to a giggle. "What the fuck— You're *heavy*."

"You can take it." He rocked his hips back as he engaged the comm. It wasn't the time, not when something this huge and potentially dangerous had been dumped in front of them, but it was always dangerous now, and he could finally feel the better edges of the risks again. He had always been able to enjoy those edges before: the joy of daring, of being foolish, of running high both in slipstream and in life, and slipping away just as the jaws of danger began to close on you.

He understood that a great deal of that had been childish. But childishness had its place. It was worth holding on to.

"Whatever." Adam wrapped his arms around Lochlan's middle, shifting beneath him and resting his cheek on the center of Lochlan's back. "Make the call and get us out of here."

Skyler had clearly been asleep before she answered their hail; her hair was tousled and she swiped a hand down her face. "What the hell? We're not going anywhere for almost another hour. Told you to leave me alone until then."

"Yes, well." Lochlan leaned forward, giving the screen one of his most charming smiles. He wondered if Adam was visible from behind him, and mused on what an odd picture that would make. "There's been a bit of a change in plans. We won't be heading through the patrol route after all. We're needed elsewhere."

Skyler raised an eyebrow. She appeared less groggy now. "What about your *shipment*?"

"That's why the plans have changed," Lochlan said smoothly. "New drop point. More convenient, really. Regardless, we appreciate how willing you were to lend us your expertise."

"Whatever, you fucking paid me." Skyler eyes narrowed. "I hope you're not planning to ask me for the five thousand back. I still spent all this time out here. Regardless of whatever else is going on, that deserves compensation."

"Wouldn't dream of it. It's yours." Lochlan batted at Adam's hand—which had begun to drift below his waist—but without any real determination. "Thanks again. Maybe we'll cross paths another time."

"Yeah, maybe." Skyler allowed him a faint smile. "You're interesting. Clear skies to you, and don't get yourselves killed."

"We'll try our best." Lochlan tipped her a salute. "Safe flying."

The screen went dark, and Lochlan relaxed back against Adam's chest, sighing as Adam reached between his legs and curled his fingers around what he had been searching for. "Line and orbit, you . . . No blushing flower anymore, are you?"

"I'm alive," Adam murmured against his spine, his hand caressing. "Counts for a lot."

Lochlan laughed and spread his legs wider, trying to keep his own hands steady as he plotted the ship's new course. He managed to focus long enough to get them into slipstream, and then turned around and settled himself back into Adam's lap with his hands on Adam's chest and moving downward, parting Adam's lips with his own. No, this was definitely not the time. But this was something they had to seize whenever they could, now.

He had an awful suspicion that soon, these times might be fewer and further between.

CHAPTER

SIX

"How will we know they've taken the bait?" Alkor shot Sinder a skeptical glance. "If they're even really out there."

"They're out there." Sinder didn't return the look. His attention was fixed on the main screen, which was displaying a sensor sweep in all directions, as far as the ship's array could reach. The other, smaller ships in the fleet were arranged at distance. All together, they would see anything in the vicinity. "We wait. The message is cycling. If they receive it, they'll come."

Alkor still looked unconvinced. She shifted from foot to foot where she stood beside Sinder, restless. The bridge crew went about their work, calm and orderly, but Sinder could sense their anticipation as well. The details of the immediate plan had been largely kept from the rest of the crew, and the other ships knew even less, but they were all aware that *something* was happening. That they were waiting for someone.

Let Alkor wallow in her unease. In the end, she'd have to kiss Sinder's ring.

"How is our guest?"

Alkor grimaced. "Alive. You did a number on him, but the medic doesn't seem to think there will be any permanent damage. He can't walk, though. He hardly has any control over his limbs at all. If you want him to play his part, you're either going to have to have him carried up here or you'll have to go to him."

"You're speaking as if that weren't easily done." Sinder didn't spare her his scorn. He caught the eye of one of the bridge crew, a sandy-haired young man with a cold air about him. "Contact the sick bay. Have them send a grav-lift to the brig for Commander Kerry and bring him up here ASAP." He allowed himself a smile. "Tell them to be careful with him; we need him in top shape. He has an important job to do."

The man nodded and turned back to his console, leaning in and speaking into the comm. Sinder focused his attention back on the sensor display. If the target of their message was anywhere in the sector, they would be here soon.

And everything would be ready.

They came out of slipstream into a snake pit.

"*Khara*." Lochlan gaped. For a moment it was all he appeared able to do. Then he twisted *Volya* hard to the side, and Adam was beside him in an instant, staring out the window.

All his blood drained into his feet.

Ships. Protectorate. Five of them, spread out across his entire field of vision—and probably behind. They were likely surrounded. Adam lifted a hand to his mouth, silent, numb. Perhaps part of him had been expecting this for some time.

"He fucked us," he said, his tone even and calm. "Whoever sent that message, the bastard completely fucked us. Didn't he?"

"Looks that way." Lochlan sounded terse, too focused and too tense to really be angry. The anger would surely come later, if they lived that long. They were flying in a complex evasive pattern, swinging back and forth and doing wide loops in the center space between the ships. Only there wasn't, as yet, anything to evade. "It'll take me another minute to cycle the drive back up. Why aren't they shooting at us? Why don't they just blow us out of the fucking sky?"

"I don't know. I don't think I—"

The comm chimed softly, and they both froze. They were being hailed. That was something.

Every second they stalled was a chance to escape.

Lochlan hit *receive*. "So I couldn't help noticing we're not in a lot of very small pieces."

"No. You're not." No visual. Only audio. The voice was unfamiliar, but clearly Protectorate. It wasn't just its source; it was the tone itself, a tone so often heard from Protectorate authorities: quiet arrogance, implicit conviction that the speaker was better and more worthy of life than whoever was being spoken to. Melissa Cosaire had had that tone until she had begun to fall apart at the end. Adam wondered if there had ever been a time when he had sounded like that.

Lochlan was smiling grimly. "That's a start. You want to explain why?"

"You must be Lochlan d'Bideshi. The file on Yuga indicated that you might be together. Excellent." There was a short pause, then the voice went on. "My name is Isaac Sinder. I'm an executive with the United Terran Commerce Authority and a liaison to this peacekeeper reconnaissance fleet. I'm authorized to bring you into custody by whatever means are necessary, but believe me, gentlemen, I'm not interested in firing on you. Killing you, even by accident, isn't an attractive prospect. Give yourselves up peacefully, and you have my word that neither of you will be harmed."

Lochlan barked a bitter laugh. "You must be joking. You expect us to believe that? When has the Protectorate ever *not* harmed someone when they had the chance? You assholes live by harm. It's what you *do*."

"Nevertheless." Sinder's tone was unshaken, politely relentless. The politeness jabbed at Adam, and he almost hissed aloud. That had been one more vicious part of the Protectorate's poison—of *Cosaire's* poison—and it made his skin want to crawl off his bones. "I don't want to harm you at this time. I'm offering you a chance to end this without bloodshed."

"No way." He couldn't be seen, but Adam shook his head anyway. "You can try to shoot us down, if you want to see some of the best flying in the galaxy, and you know the Bideshi, you know that's not a bluff."

"Yes. I do. Perhaps this, then. There's someone who would like to speak to you."

For a moment, there was nothing on the comm channel. Then, very faintly, a broken voice slurred, "Yuga?"

"Holy shit," Adam whispered. "That's Commander Kerry."

He wasn't all that familiar with the man, not enough to be certain about the voice—especially not like *this*, raw and hoarse and cracking. But he knew, all the same. It was Kerry.

And he didn't think Kerry would sound like that if he had wanted to betray them.

Lochlan looked sharply at him. "Are you sure?"

"Yeah. That's him. Kerry? Kerry, what happened?"

A cough, rasping and harsh. Then, "I'm sorry, Yuga. They got me. Broke me down. I tried. I swear, I tried."

"They tortured him." Adam closed his eyes as new ice flooded his veins. *They tortured him because of me.* "Lock . . ."

When he opened his eyes, Lochlan was shaking his head, reaching out for him. "Adam, no, don't—"

"Yuga?" Sinder again, and Adam clenched his teeth as the ice turned to rage. The kind of rage that came when the last edges of resistance were wearing away. He was aware, now, that he was going to give in, even though Lochlan might hate him for it. Because he knew what Sinder was going to say.

"He's hurt, Yuga, as I'm guessing you can tell. He's a brave man, but even brave men have their breaking point. If you don't surrender in the next five minutes, I'll make him hurt as much as I can. And you'll listen to it happen. And if you outfly us, you'll still know what I did, and that you might have stopped it. You'll live with that. However much longer you have." He paused again, and when he spoke next, Adam could hear the thin smile in his voice. "Yes, you could turn off the comm. But I think we both know you won't. A lot of other people died because of you, didn't they? From what I know of your nature, that's not sitting easy with you. You may be a traitor, you may be a pervert and a degenerate and an enormous genetic mistake, and you may be dangerous to everything that we've built. But I don't think your heart is that cold."

The world blurred in front of Adam. He could feel Lochlan's hands on his shoulders, but he could no longer see him. How did Sinder know? How did he know what hearing that would do?

How did he know that was true?

"Don't listen to him," Lochlan was saying. "Adam, he's fucking with you, don't—"

"You couldn't save all those people on that planet, Yuga. You can't save anyone. Except this one man. That's the gift I'm giving you." He cleared his throat, becoming businesslike again. "You have four minutes to think it over. I'll be in touch."

The channel clicked off. There was silence.

"You can't do it." Lochlan's voice was small, hard, caught between icy and blazing with anger. Adam wasn't sure he had ever heard that tone from him before. "Adam . . . He's lying. He'll kill him anyway, and then he'll kill us. You remember Cosaire, you remember what she was like . . . How many people died on the Plain because she couldn't let you go?"

"She was insane," Adam murmured. How much had Sinder sounded like her? How much of her potential for madness lay in him? It was impossible to be sure. Impossible to know what they were dealing with. "Lock, I can't do this. Not again. Not someone else dead because of me. *Tortured* because of me. I'm haunted enough. I know he's just one man, but . . ."

"*Khara*." Lochlan slapped both his hands down on the console, shoved himself away from it, and stalked across the cockpit. Adam watched him, and what he felt—what superseded the horror and the helplessness that twisted at every part of him—was a profound sense of distance. He couldn't let himself feel too much. It would destroy him.

Lochlan whirled. "This again. This *again*, Adam. You stupid fucking . . ." He kicked a transparent container that had held some kind of food at some point in the past and it sailed into the far wall. "You wanted to run into their goddamn arms before. You remember that? You remember when Kae got put in the fucking clinic? You remember all those people, dead? You want to make what they sacrificed worth nothing now?"

"I remember." Adam swallowed. His throat was tight and getting tighter. Even breathing was becoming an effort, and for all the worlds this fear reminded him of being sick. Of his own body spinning wildly out of control, turning against him.

He had never been in control of anything.

"Adam. *Chusile*." All at once Lochlan's face softened, his jaw unclenched, lips parted. He crossed back to Adam and sank into a crouch in front of him, hands on his knees, staring up into Adam's face with large dark eyes. "Please don't do this. He's just . . . Like you said, he's *one man*."

"Lock." It was so hard to remember. "So was I."

"That's not the same. I don't believe it." But the look in Lochlan's eyes told a different story, and by now Adam could read him. "We can still run."

"If we try to run, they'll kill us anyway."

"No. No, I could outmaneuver them."

Adam lifted his hands and framed Lochlan's face. He felt an awful smile stretching his mouth, sad in a way that stabbed his heart. "No, you couldn't. I know you're good, Lock, but you're not that good. Neither am I. Not anymore." He leaned forward, tipped their foreheads together. "Maybe he'll kill us. But I don't think he will. If he was going to do that . . . at least now . . . he would have done it already. As long as we're alive, there's a chance. We might even be able to do some good over there. And I don't . . . Please don't make me watch anyone else die. Not because of me."

Lochlan shook his head, despair twisting his features, and Adam knew what he had to say next would make it all even worse. He didn't expect it to do much. But it had to be said.

"We should try to get them to let you go. They want me. I don't know what use they'd have for you. We should at least *try*."

Lochlan stared at him, mouth open, and Adam wished—violently—that he hadn't said it. As he'd thought, it was useless. Worse than useless. Because what he saw beneath the shock—faint but unquestionably there—was anger.

"Fuck off with that," Lochlan breathed. "You . . . Fuck *off* with it. I don't even know why you'd—"

"I know." Adam ducked his head. "I know. I'm sorry. I had to say it. I had to."

Lochlan let out a breath, clearly dangerously close to a sob. Here it was again, the edge they had been treading for what felt like years. "I can run anyway. I'm bigger than you, you can't stop me."

In spite of himself, Adam laughed. There was something childish about it, so heartfelt, so fundamentally *Lochlan*. "Yeah, you could do that. But you won't. You know what I'm saying is true." He pulled Lochlan closer and brushed their lips together. "We're surrendering. But we're not giving up. I promise."

Once more, the silence stretched out. They held on to each other, and the dimness of the cabin slipped away. When Adam closed his eyes, it felt as though they were spinning together in the black, nothing between them and vacuum. Just each other. All they had, now.

Even that was so delicate. So fragile.

"All right," Lochlan breathed at last, and then the comm chimed. Adam hit Receive.

"Well?"

Adam didn't hesitate. "We agree. We surrender."

"Excellent." His tone was deeply pleased, and Adam clenched his teeth. *Prick*. No. No, he wasn't going to let this man win. "Bring your engines offline and stay where you are. We'll be sending a couple of ships to tug you in."

Lochlan cut the comm. "So." He sounded as numb as Adam was. He was still crouched in front of him, leaning against him, but Adam could feel him pulling away all the same. Growing distant. "Should we have some kind of plan or something?"

"I don't know." Adam dropped his face into his hands and just let himself breathe. "I don't even know what to plan for. Let's . . . Let's let them take us in, see what we're dealing with."

"What we're dealing with." Lochlan's laugh barely counted as one, rough and harsh and utterly miserable. He pushed himself up and turned away, his shoulders hunched. "I'm glad Ixchel can't see this."

Adam sucked in a breath. It was involuntary, pained; it *hurt* to hear that, as bad as a slap to the face, and he couldn't hide it. But Lochlan didn't look back at him, offered no apology, and Adam turned to the console, staring down at it and at his hands, which sat motionless on its surface.

He had said they weren't giving up. He wanted to believe that.

But he wasn't sure he could.

CHAPTER

SEVEN

Sinder stood in the docking bay, watching as the Bideshi ship was brought in. Looking at it, it was hard to keep back one of those waves of disgust that came whenever he considered anything that originated with them. It was an ugly thing, patched together, a chaotic amalgamation of parts and designs that had clearly been added piecemeal as they were needed. It was a smaller version of their massive homeships, the same kind of structure that scorned order and planning. This was what the Protectorate could become if Yuga was allowed to remain free. He would bring this disorder, him and the Bideshi. A final, lethal treachery.

The two escort fighters set down on the bay's deck, and the Bideshi ship lowered itself between them with a hiss and a *clunk*. There was a pause. Five peacekeepers stepped forward, guns raised and aimed at the ship's hatch.

Sinder smoothed his already immaculate suit and cast a glance in Alkor's direction, satisfied. In truth, he was inviting the woman to be satisfied along with him. It was her triumph as much as his.

Well. Perhaps not quite as much.

"Come out, Yuga," he called. "You and your *friend*. Come out with your hands in the air and we'll have this over and done."

For another moment, nothing. Then, with a jerk and a creak, the hatch opened and a short stepladder extended. In the hatchway there appeared a slender man of strong build, pale blond, dressed in the rumpled and patched clothes of a Bideshi, but with features possessing the carefully crafted perfection that marked a child of the Protectorate.

There was his skin, however—mottled, uneven, imperfect. And even at a distance, Sinder could see his telltale eyes, that mismatched blue and green.

Yuga raised his hands.

"Come down. Now."

He did. Following him, hands also raised, was a taller man dressed in the same kind of disheveled clothing, his skin a rich brown and his head topped by a mass of gaudily beaded dreadlocks. Sinder's gaze moved over him, noting the complex black ink that wound over his arms, and his lip curled. Marring himself that way—not that his skin was much to boast of . . .

This. This *person* was who Adam had found refuge with. One among others, anyway.

Shameful.

"Lochlan d'Bideshi," Sinder said, allowing him a nod of the smallest degree. The man responded only with an icy glare. "I wasn't expecting the opportunity to take you into custody, but I have to say, it's a nice bonus. Captain." He nodded to Alkor. "Will you do the honors?"

Alkor stepped forward, her shoulders back and head high, now the picture of Protectorate regality. "Adam Yuga," she said, "by order of the Protectorate High Command, I'm—"

"That's not his name," the Bideshi growled. "He's Bideshi now. If you're going to do it, at least get it right, you stupid fucking *raya*."

Sinder's eyes narrowed, and he saw Alkor stiffen slightly, but otherwise neither of them responded. Yuga, however, shot the other man a warning look. The Bideshi returned it mutinously, but fell silent again. Alkor cleared her throat and continued.

"By order of the Protectorate High Command, I am placing you under arrest. You'll be transported to a detention facility until such time as a tribunal can be assembled, at which point you will be tried and sentenced."

Sinder smiled. He enjoyed the formality of this speech, and he would enjoy the greater pomp and circumstance of the trial, especially given that the outcome was a foregone conclusion. Yuga would be found guilty and executed, and likely his Bideshi lover along with him. Then this long, awkward mess would be at an end, and they could get back to the real work at hand: maintaining this exquisitely perfect garden of a civilization. Of an empire.

To his credit, Yuga didn't appear frightened, even when a peacekeeper ran a weapon scanning wand over him and the Bideshi, and Sinder felt grudging admiration. Whatever else Yuga might be, he hadn't lost all of the spirit that made the Protectorate great. Despite everything he had done, everything he had become, perhaps it was more fitting if he didn't go to his death shrinking and fainting.

Alkor gestured to the two peacekeepers who flanked her. "Take them to the brig. Put them in separate cells. It wouldn't do to have them doing anything . . ." Distaste flashed across her face. "Anything *unsavory*."

Once again the Bideshi seemed about to protest, but thankfully another look from Yuga shut his mouth. Interesting as this had all initially been, Sinder wanted to be done with it. He had reports to file. Later there could be questions, and that would no doubt be interesting as well.

"It's a pleasure to have you on board, Yuga," he said as the men were led past him, joined by two more peacekeepers. He turned to watch them as they moved toward the bay doors—Yuga's erect bearing, and the Bideshi's overtly casual slouch, maintained even when all hope was extinguished.

Whatever appearances they were keeping up, it would make no possible difference. Yuga, on his way to justice. And one less Bideshi loose in the universe. He gave the captain a smile. "I'd say this is a win all around. Wouldn't you?"

Alkor returned the smile, though hers was a good bit thinner than Sinder's. "Not quite all around." She pushed past him, not looking back. "I'll see you on the bridge, Sinder. You can speak to them whenever you want to, I suppose."

"Thank you, Captain." It might not be necessary at this point: it wasn't as though he needed additional evidence, or a confession of any kind. But there were some things he wanted to know. Things it seemed important to understand.

One had to know one's enemy. And Yuga was not the only enemy. There was an entire race of them.

They too would be dealt with, in their time.

As they were escorted down a corridor that led deeper into the ship, Lochlan tried to covertly scan their surroundings, checking for any escape routes. But he saw nothing.

They were flanked on all sides by peacekeepers, their blast shields down over their faces, making them look even less human than usual. And as their group passed other peacekeepers, each one was armed, and where their faces were exposed each one glared, eyes narrowed. Some verged on hateful. The whole crew must know who they were. If they did manage to break free, the entire ship would descend on them.

They would have to do this quietly. If at all.

Separate cells. He didn't like the idea of that, though he wasn't surprised by it. It wasn't just that it would make escape harder. The white pristineness of the ship was making it even more difficult, being in a space not only alien but hostile to him and everything he loved. He remembered the same hostile aesthetic from the flagship that he and Adam had boarded in secret, to clear the debt of the credits Adam had stolen before Lochlan found him—and to discover the truth about his illness. Then, Lochlan had been too focused on the task at hand to really notice his surroundings. But now he felt it and saw it, and hated it.

These people were *raya*. He knew that Adam still wasn't completely comfortable with the word, though with him it was always now affectionate, teasing. But he couldn't think of another that fit Adam's former people so well. Planet-bound, even though they flew. A slave to their own conventions.

That might be an advantage. If they weren't flexible enough . . . And the Bideshi were nothing if not flexible.

"Are you taking us to where you're holding Kerry?" Adam's tone was casual, though the effort in keeping it so was obvious. "I'd like to see him."

One of the peacekeepers on their left snorted. "You'll see him. You'll probably dine on bullets together. Won't that be nice?"

"Good," Adam said, as if he hadn't heard the last two remarks. "I hope you haven't hurt him too badly. He's an honorable man, whatever you think of him."

"I think he's a fucking traitor. Like you." The peacekeeper slapped Adam's shoulder and shoved him forward. "Keep walking, degenerate."

Lochlan knew he shouldn't. He knew it was stupid, bordering on suicidal. Whereas Adam was important, and he doubted that Sinder would let him die before he had a chance to deliver him to the Protectorate, Lochlan was likely expendable. He was a *bonus*. Any excuse he gave them to kill him might be enough.

But as long as Lochlan possessed any strength, no one was going to touch Adam. *No one*. As he lunged for the man, he heard Ying in his head, tired and reproachful.

Oh, Tommy. Tommy, Tommy, you never had the sense that God gave a glowbug.

Of course, he never reached the peacekeeper. The butt of a gun flew up and caught him in the mouth, exploding white pain across his vision, and the arm of another peacekeeper hooked around him, turned him, and slammed him face-first against the bulkhead. Blood was sharp on his tongue.

"Fucking asshole," one of the peacekeepers hissed from behind him.

"You do that again and I will *fucking kill you*, do you understand? I'll kill you in front of your *sweetheart*, and I'll do it slow. Make him watch. You get me?"

Lochlan didn't answer and was bucking back against the body pinning him, awash with rage, but then Adam cried out and the pain in his voice froze Lochlan. Not the high twist that came with physical pain. This was longer and closer to a moan. Pleading. Fear.

"Lochlan, *don't*. It's okay. We'll be okay."

Lochlan squeezed his eyes shut. *Okay*. Groping for any source of calm he could find, he imagined arms around him, warm and solid, and forced himself to ease. He wouldn't be any good to anyone if he died before they had a chance to formulate a plan.

Please don't make me watch anyone else die.

There was hot breath on his neck. The man behind him was still leaning in close, lips almost brushing Lochlan's ear, and in spite of himself, Lochlan shuddered.

What the fuck *was* this?

"Don't fight," the man whispered. "Not yet. Trust me, you'll have your chance. I'm a friend. Be ready."

Before Lochlan had a chance to respond, he was yanked away from the wall and pushed toward Adam. Adam reached for him, and Lochlan was once more intensely grateful to whatever power watched over them that their hands hadn't been restrained.

As if reading his mind, the peacekeeper who had insulted him sent Lochlan stumbling with a blow to the stomach. He bent over as pain racked him; coughing, he put a hand up to his mouth, and it came away smeared with blood.

His lower lip felt about three times its normal size. He focused on its throb. It drew attention from the thick, hot coal in the pit of his stomach.

"If you're done," one of the other peacekeepers growled, "let's get going. No more of that bullshit or we'll break your arm."

"That was stupid," Adam whispered, as Lochlan fell into unsteady step beside him, still half-hunched over with one arm wrapped around his middle. Nothing seemed seriously damaged, but the next few hours were going to be reasonably horrible. "That was so fucking stupid, Lock; I don't know why you—"

Lochlan touched his arm, shook his head. When Adam fell silent, Lochlan nodded at the peacekeeper who had spoken in his ear. The man was striding along ahead of them like the others, but Lochlan couldn't keep from studying him for details, any confirmation that he wasn't like the others.

Adam mouthed, *What?*

Lochlan jerked his head down. He didn't dare speak aloud, not now, and he was glad that Adam seemed to have adopted the same policy. They would have to find connections other than speech. Their hands were close, almost brushing, but his own were still stained with blood, and that closeness was its own kind of pain.

He knew what would happen if they touched again.

He's with us, Lochlan mouthed back. *He says.*

Adam stared at him, eyes wide. Lochlan returned the look, willing him to understand, and gave him a nod. Whether or not Lochlan believed it, he had no idea what reason the man would have to lie.

The Protectorate were cruel, cold, arrogant, inflexible, selfish, and conceited. But from what he knew, it didn't seem that they would fuck with someone for the sole purpose of fucking with them.

"You, there. No talking, or whatever the fuck you're doing." One of the peacekeepers behind them rammed the butt of his gun against Adam's side, hard enough to send Adam stumbling, wincing. Lochlan bit his swollen lip to keep himself from catching Adam, from curling his arms around the man and holding on.

It would only make it worse for both of them.

They went on in silence, down another series of corridors, a short ride up in a lift, then another corridor that ended in a heavy locked door. This hissed open to reveal a block of six cells, garishly lit and walled in clear dividers that looked delicate and thin but that would probably be almost impossible to penetrate. A peacekeeper out of armor sat behind a desk by the door, and she stood up as they entered, returning the salute that one of their escorts offered.

Lochlan barely noticed them. He was following Adam's gaze toward a cell at the back of the room. Like the rest, it was furnished with a bunk, a toilet enclosed only by a frosted screen, and was otherwise unremarkable but for the older, gray-haired man who lay curled on the bunk, his knees drawn close to his chest.

Kerry.

"This them? I'll open the cells." The peacekeeper bent to the console set into her desk and a section on the clear front of two cells hissed open.

Cells at opposite ends of the room. His heart sank yet again, though it was no surprise. Maybe the Protectorate weren't the type to play cruel games, but they still *were* cruel, and he understood what this was: a punishment, for the simple crime of being who they were and being together.

At least one of the cells was next to Kerry's. That might be useful.

Adam was shoved toward that one, while Lochlan was directed into the closer cell—by the same man who had pinned Lochlan to the wall. Lochlan managed to search what little of the man's face he could see under his blast shield, but the man gave him no attention except a final push inside. He stepped back without a word, and the cells closed.

The peacekeepers left, a couple of them chuckling. "Sweet dreams, lovebirds."

The woman behind the desk settled back down to whatever she had been doing when they had entered, her head bent over the console. He glanced across at Adam, who was standing with his hands pressed against the transparent wall, mouth drooping and eyes hollow.

"I'm sorry," he said, his voice muffled by the wall but still clear enough. Lochlan shook his head and laid his own bloody hand where the door had been. Its seams had vanished, and he couldn't be sure he was touching the right place.

"It'll be okay."

"Hey." The woman lifted her head, shooting them both a glare. "Shut up. Or you can wait a day for rations."

Even this was being denied them.

Adam gave him a final look, features twisted with obvious pain. It was almost enough to make him speak, regardless of the consequences but Adam turned away from him and moved over to the bunk, sinking down onto it and lowering his head into his hands.

Lochlan watched him for a while. It was all he could do, the last contact he could give. He couldn't touch Adam, couldn't hold him, so he imagined doing those things, giving him whatever comfort he could, taking whatever was given, and he prayed that those thoughts might be able to cross the yards that separated them and settle into Adam's own mind. Hands and warm arms and a chest to lean on. At last he went to his own bunk. When he lay down on it, he found himself curling up in the way that Kerry was, though the room wasn't cold. Perhaps it was merely this place. Perhaps it was cold in other ways. No, no *perhaps* about it. He could feel it.

Now all he could do was wait.

Trust me, you'll have your chance. Be ready.

CHAPTER

EIGHT

"Have we set a course for Terra?" Sinder strode into Captain Alkor's quarters as soon as the door opened for him, his stance wide and solid and his shoulders squared. His pride wouldn't be physically contained, and it was as if something unseen was buoying him up, almost setting him floating. His task wasn't finished, and he shouldn't relax until Yuga was safely in the hands of the proper authorities, but it was difficult to keep from feeling that the business was truly all but over.

Alkor turned in her seat at a desk in the room's office alcove. The room and the alcove were both simple, unadorned and functional, but for a drinks cabinet against the wall that was a good bit more ornate than the one in the conference room. Not even medals or other honors were on display, and Sinder knew from reading Alkor's dossier that she had been given her share.

"We'll be entering slipstream within the next ten minutes, in fact. ETA is five days. So relax. Enjoy your triumph." He could detect no sarcasm, but her lack of enthusiasm made Sinder narrow his eyes as he stepped closer to her.

"Our triumph, Captain."

"Of course." She thumbed off the small pad she had been studying and rose, stretching. "Sinder, to be honest, I'm looking forward to this being done with. I'm happy for you, really I am. It'll be a fantastic boost to your career. But my career is over. I have my house on the beach. That's what I want now."

Sinder inclined his head. Fair enough. He didn't entirely understand it, but there was no reason to argue against her decision. Perhaps when he reached her age, he would feel the same desire for peace and quiet.

He doubted it. But there was always the possibility.

"How about a drink, Sinder?"

Sinder smiled. "If you have any of that whiskey left, I'll take some."

Alkor nodded and went to the cabinet. It was one of the few signs of luxury in the room, carved from a rich, honey-colored wood and inlaid with intricate shapes that suggested vines and flowers. It appeared to be Klashorg. She bent to open it and produced a decanter and two glasses.

"Are you going to question them?" She glanced back at him as she poured. "I mean, what can they tell you that you don't already know? And Yuga is facing a firing squad. Nothing can change that. I'd guess that the Bideshi will face the same."

Sinder remained silent as he took his glass and raised it in a salute, which Alkor returned.

"It's not enough to simply hand him over," he said at last. "I need to understand why he did what he did."

"Understand?" Alkor raised an eyebrow. "What's to understand? He's a degenerate, like you've been saying. Mutated code. He's a walking, talking genetic *error*. Who knows why he's done what he's done? What matters is that he won't be doing it anymore."

Sinder shook his head. "That's not true. At least not for me. He *was* one of our best, Captain. Excellent at his work. Set to become a high-level executive. I know he took ill, and that was one of the first signs that he was an aberration. But joining the *Bideshi*? And then what happened on that planet. No, I need to have it straight from him, how he understands the meaning of his crimes. He's not a stupid man. That much is obvious. We're also sure that he's not the only one of his kind."

He walked to one of the wide windows, gazing out at the stars. Soon they would expand into the blinding white of slipstream and the journey home. He would have five days with Yuga. That would have to be enough. "This may not be the last time that we'll face the threat he presents. While barbarians are always beating on the gates of civilization, yearning to tear down what they can't comprehend, he's *not* a barbarian, though he's made alliances with them, and threats from within are the most insidious."

From behind him, Alkor grunted, and it sounded like agreement. "All right. But I'd be surprised if he tells you anything."

"I think he will." Sinder took another swallow of whiskey, closing his eyes briefly as he let the smooth taste and texture fill his mouth. "Men like him want to be understood. I think he has principles, however perverse." He returned to the cabinet and set the glass down on its polished surface. It was truly excellent whiskey, but he wanted to keep his wits about him. "I'll let him stew another hour or so, and then I'll see him. Do you want to be there?"

Alkor shook her head. "What I want to do is sleep. I haven't been doing enough of that. Just let me know if you get anything useful out of him. Or interesting." She lifted her glass again. "Good work, Sinder. From all of us."

Sinder gave her a bow and left.

In truth, he was tired as well—not even certain of when he had last slept more than an hour or two, except that it had been a while, and now, if at no other time, he could let himself indulge. But instead he went two levels up to the main security station. As he stepped through the door, he felt the gentle lurch and the instant of disorientation that accompanied entry into slipstream, and smiled.

They were on their way.

The three peacekeepers manning the surveillance streams nodded to him as he entered, but otherwise they didn't acknowledge his presence—which didn't offend him. They had their jobs to do, and kowtowing to a government liaison wasn't one of them. He looked over their shoulders at the streams, keeping his own silence. One of the views was of the brig, and he bent, peering at it.

Yuga, Kerry, and the Bideshi were all lying on their bunks. Kerry and the Bideshi appeared to be asleep, but as he watched, Yuga stirred, turned from his side onto his back, and swept his hands down his face. Even at the distance of the camera, Sinder could see the tension in his limbs.

A man in torment. Good. His distress would wear him down, make him more pliable.

Then Sinder turned his focus to the Bideshi, to his lanky form, his dreadlocks, the tattoos that covered his arms. The man who Adam Yuga had taken up with. Slept with. *Fucked.*

It was an ugly thought, but there was no way around it. And the truth was that this was the most fascinating puzzle of all. Perhaps no one else would find it so, but Sinder couldn't contain his interest. Men and women with Yuga's *tendencies* were not openly mistreated, or their rights curtailed. But they were never fully accepted, never allowed to rise very far. They were unnatural: such people were genetic dead ends, and in their hearts they had rejected everything that rested at the core of the Protectorate's greatness and perfection—the continuation of the species, its long evolutionary journey. As such they were of limited long-term utility. Had Yuga's desire for other men been generally known, he would naturally have been quietly prevented from rising any further through the ranks of the UTCA. It was true that his abnormality wouldn't have been considered an abomination like this coupling with a Bideshi. But the fact that he had done so was intriguing.

Because there was something *about* the Bideshi. For Sinder there always had been. Not spoken of, not because he was afraid but because he sensed that no one else would understand. They seemed to be aware of some secret aspect of reality, seemed to be able to use it. Some power into which they had tapped, which had allowed them to survive—against all reason.

Adam had been drawn to them. Accepted by them. He had been immersed in that awareness more than anyone else in the Protectorate. He might possess some of that same awareness now.

It might be abhorrent, but Sinder wanted to understand it.

When he left the security station, he didn't hurry on his way to the brig. There was no need for haste; Yuga wasn't going anywhere, and it was worth taking his time with every part of this examination. He believed Adam would talk. But the man would have to be coaxed, gently. No doubt he still held out hope that things might swing back in his favor, and that hope could be leveraged.

Yuga would see. If it took until the bullet crashed into his skull and tore his sick brain to shreds, he would see.

Adam wasn't sleeping. But he was dreaming all the same.

It was like when he had taken the shala, when he had gone into the Arched Halls to seek his name. When he had touched the roots of the universe and had felt the darkness that was choking his own. There was a sensation of being down in something deep, a heaviness over his head that made rising impossible.

But the air around him was thin, arid. He was kneeling on the Plain of Heaven with Lochlan bleeding to death in his arms.

I'm sorry, Lochlan rasped, the words forced out between bloody lips. *It's not your fault.*

But it was. He stroked a hand over Lochlan's face, his hair, fingers against his lips as he willed him not to speak, to save every last ounce of his strength and stay with Adam a little while longer. Once Lochlan left him, he would be alone with the dead.

I love you, he whispered, bending his head close. When he kissed Lochlan's mouth, he tasted blood. It hurt, to love someone like this. He had never believed, before Lochlan, that he ever would. He had wanted men—had lusted after them, if he was honest—but this *love*, this awful burning thing that was eating his heart . . .

And in the world above, Lochlan was far away from him. Across a room that might as well have been a galaxy wide.

I'm so sorry.

"Not yet. You will be."

Adam's eyes snapped open, and he lifted his head. By now, he knew that voice, and it sent rage surging over the cold grief that had settled behind his breastbone, and that was welcome.

Sinder.

"What the fuck do you want?"

"Merely to talk." Sinder had a slender folding chair with him, and he set it down just outside the transparency, settling comfortably into it as if they were having a relaxed chat over coffee. Adam pushed himself up, glaring, which felt about as impotent as anything else he could do.

"What about?"

"You." Sinder jerked a thumb in the direction of Lochlan's cell. He was blocking Adam's view, but when he shifted to one side, Adam could see Lochlan was standing at the transparent wall. Gaze sharp. Listening. "Him. Everything."

Adam barked a laugh. "That's not very specific."

"I like to keep things open. Flexible." Sinder folded his hands over his knee. "I think you're interesting, Yuga. Adam. What you did . . . Taking these . . . *people* as allies, using them to attack us the way you did . . . I might not agree with it—no, I might find it absolutely abhorrent—but I'll admit, it took some balls."

Adam shrugged. It wasn't praise. He wasn't stupid enough to think it so.

"I want to understand how everything happened," Sinder went on. "You were so high and you fell so far. Then you went to the *Bideshi*, of all people. Can you tell me? I promise, no judgment here." He smiled. "I've already passed all the judgment I care to."

Adam stared at him, incredulous. "How it *happened*? Are you serious? How it happened is your *Protectorate* completely fucking *screwed* me. You made me sick and you threw me under a liner. That's how it happened, you arrogant piece of *shit*."

Sinder blinked. There was no other indication that he was fazed by the burst of rage, but Adam saw the blink and took icy satisfaction in it. Cosaire had died before he'd been able to face her in person. Now he had a chance to face someone in her place.

"It was your Protectorate too, Yuga. Once." Sinder cocked his head. "What do you mean, *we* made you sick?"

Again, Adam stared, and this time his words were blocked by sheer surprise. Cosaire had known the truth of his illness, that it was hidden within everyone, and the knowledge had driven her mad in the end. He had assumed that people of any significant rank in the Protectorate government would know too.

But maybe Sinder didn't rank as highly as she had. Maybe he *didn't* know.

Was that prospect less terrifying, or far more? "It's in our code," he said slowly, stepping forward and placing one hand against the wall. "Don't you know that? What was wrong with me, really wrong . . . It's in *all* of the code. Ours. Bred in, ready to turn on us anytime. Anywhere. Everything you've built things on, everything you believe in—it's a snake in the grass and it's waiting to strike. You call me a degenerate, but that's what we all are now. We're falling apart from the inside. Do you honestly not know? Is that even possible?"

Sinder simply gazed at him, silent, his expression unreadable, and against his better judgment Adam went on, filling the silence.

"Maybe you've noticed that some people are dropping things. Their coordination worse than it should be. Maybe they have unexplained muscle pain. Dizziness. General suggestions that their nervous systems aren't working like they should be? Maybe they're hiding it really well, but you could have seen it anyway and not known what you were seeing. Maybe . . . Maybe you've even felt it. Maybe it's happening to you." He pressed forward, licking his lips. If Sinder truly didn't know . . . There could be a chance. To convince him. To change his mind.

"You're all sick, even if you're not showing the symptoms. The people in charge don't want anyone to know, because it would bring down everything they've built. Maybe we have structures, maybe we have institutions and rules of law, but foundations are always built on what people trust. What they *believe.* The foundations are rotten. It's going to come down anyway. Sinder, I was sick, but I'm *not* anymore. I can help us. I can help you, if you help me first."

Sinder was still quiet. Adam realized that he was breathing hard, his stomach clenching, desperate. If he could only make the man *see* . . .

Behind Sinder, he could now see Lochlan standing in his cell, his own hands pressed against the transparent wall. Watching.

Finally Sinder shook his head, a minute movement. But the sense behind the gesture was hard as steel.

"You're lying."

Adam closed his eyes in an ecstasy of despair. "I'm not."

"You are. You'd say anything now to twist this around, make me doubt what I'm doing. That's what you *do.* That's why you have to be stopped." Sinder pointed at Kerry, who was still curled up with his back to the world. "You see him? I tortured him to get what I needed from him. It wasn't something I wanted to do, but it had to be done. And it wasn't my fault, Yuga. It was *yours.*" He leaned forward, every word spat out of him like something poisonous. His impassivity had dissolved, and what had replaced it wasn't exactly anger, but rather ...

Sinder believed what he was saying. This man might be a fanatic. Adam saw it in his eyes, the spark of something that might be fanned into consuming fire. Cosaire had been cold. Inside Sinder was heat. Complete belief in everything he did. A man like that might do anything.

"You put him in that position. You twisted his mind, made him believe your sick, treasonous bullshit. Now he's going to die with you, and that's your fault too." Sinder sat back, his face a mask of disgust. "You have to be killed, just so you don't kill anyone else."

Adam simply looked at him. There was nothing to be done here. If there was hope, it wasn't with Isaac Sinder. "You'll find out," he said dully, and turned away. "I have nothing more to say to you."

"Why the Bideshi, Yuga?"

Adam clenched his teeth. No, he wasn't going to do this. He had played the man's game for a few minutes, on a wild chance. He wasn't going to give any more ground.

"I've been wondering that. If you had crawled off and died ... Well, that was clearly what the people who decided to expel you had in mind. If you had taken up arms yourself, fought back on your own, even that I could understand. But the Bideshi? And you're *fucking* one of them? I can't understand that at all."

Adam ducked his head. *Stop it.* "They saved me."

"Did you know they could save you before you fell in with them?"

"*He* saved me." Adam turned again, pointed at Lochlan—and fixed his gaze there, letting the man be his guide-star. Lochlan lifted a hand, as if to reach for him, and Adam remembered how Lochlan had found him on the Plain in the midst of the battle, fought to reach him though the death and chaos, and had held Adam as he waged his own war with the sickness inside him, as he drew power from the ground beneath them both until a silence that hadn't quite been victory settled over them all. "He did more for me than any of you ever did."

"Well, well," Sinder murmured. A slow smile spread over his face. "You actually love him. Don't you? It's not just about fucking. It's *romance*." He twisted the word into mockery, and Adam bared his teeth. "Does he feel the same way? Is he even capable of that?"

"I don't think you'd understand."

"No, probably not. For which I thank my code."

"Yeah, well." Adam gave a thin smile. "Like I said. You will."

"You love him," Sinder echoed. "You *are* degenerate."

"Whatever you say." For a moment Adam considered finally taking his own advice and ending the conversation there. But he didn't, and when he spoke next he heard pity in his voice. Pity for Sinder, for Cosaire, for the entire society of proud fools that he had once been part of. "I was trying to help you," he said. "I really was. And yes, if that meant destroying something that's killing us all, I would do that. If I could. But it doesn't seem like that's going to happen, does it?"

He stepped away from the wall focusing on Lochlan again. Lochlan was *all* he was looking at. All he would. "I'm done with you," he said flatly. "Leave me alone."

Sinder didn't move: maybe he would try to wring more conversation out of the stone that Adam was making himself into. But then he shook his head and gave Adam another smile, getting to his feet and folding up the chair.

"I'll be back," he said. "We'll have to have more of these chats. I'm enjoying them." He bowed. "Sleep well, Adam Yuga *d'Bideshi*."

It wasn't until he was gone that Adam could finally and truly breathe again. He sank back onto his bunk and pressed the heels of his palms against his eyes. He could feel Lochlan's gaze still on him, but suddenly he couldn't bear to meet it.

He had gotten them into this. All of them. Sinder was right about that much.

And he had no idea how he was going to get them out of it.

CHAPTER

NINE

Lochlan awoke to a scream, one that cut off so abruptly it left him lying on his bunk with his eyes wide, wondering if he had dreamt it.

He sat up. He hadn't.

In the cell opposite, Adam was also awake and on his feet, pressed against the transparency staring across the room to where the peacekeeper had been sitting at her desk. *Had been.* She was now slumped over it, a thin line of blood trickling from her temple. Lochlan gaped. He hadn't even heard the shot. When his gaze flicked to the peacekeeper standing over her, he saw why: the pistol he held was equipped with a silencer.

The peacekeeper glanced up, and though Lochlan couldn't see his face, he recognized him immediately.

I'm a friend.

"I didn't want to," the man said, his voice low and gruff. "But she wasn't going to be cooperative, and I didn't have time to handle it any other way. Even with the surveillance feeds outta commission." He bent over the console, his fingers moving rapidly, and a few seconds later the cell doors all hissed open. Lochlan crossed the room in what felt like a single stride, though his stomach continued to throb in time with his split lip and should have made moving that quickly difficult. Adam stepped forward to meet him, reached up to frame his face.

"Are you okay?"

"I'm fine." He turned to the peacekeeper, hands remaining on Adam's shoulders. He still didn't trust the man, but he was outside of the cell, and he wasn't going to argue with that. "What now?"

"Now we get the fuck outta here." The peacekeeper nodded to Kerry's cell, and Lochlan glanced back at him; the man was trying to push himself up, looking over at them with a dazed expression. "Can one of you help him? I'm not leaving him here unless we absolutely have to."

"I can." Adam went to Kerry, bending down and offering his arm, which the man took, though it was an effort to get him on his feet. Lochlan frowned. The idea of taking on someone who would probably only slow them down wasn't an attractive one, but again, arguing seemed ill-advised. Especially when he gathered that Adam would be the main one insisting they not leave Kerry behind.

So, sighing, he stepped forward to help, and as Adam staggered out of the cell, Kerry leaning against him, Lochlan slipped an arm around him from the other side, bearing him up.

The peacekeeper nodded shortly. "All right. There's a shuttle waiting in one of the lower bays. Out of the way. Let's get going."

"Who are you?" Adam asked as they left the brig and began to edge along the bright corridor. Lochlan had caught Adam glancing back at the woman slumped over the console, a pained expression twisting at his features. "You said you were a friend?"

"Didn't I do a friendly thing just now?" The man waved a hand at them. "Quiet. If you look like anything but prisoners we'll get stopped for sure."

Lochlan shot Adam a quick glance. "You don't think the lack of cuffs will be kind of a tip-off? I know we weren't cuffed when we got in here, but it'll look suspicious now. You can't seriously expect people here to be *that* dense."

"Nothing to be done about it. I need you to help Kerry. That might be enough of a reason for anyone who doesn't think about it for more than a few seconds."

Kerry, for his part, seemed to be getting stronger as they walked, supporting a little more of his own weight. "Yuga?" He focused on Adam, his brows furrowed. "Shit, they did get you. I'm sorry."

"It doesn't matter. It wasn't your fault." Adam's expression softened, then he swung his attention straight ahead of them again. "I know how persuasive they can be."

On the second level they descended to, they ran into their first officer, but she only gave the peacekeeper a nod and kept on walking. Another one passed without paying them any attention at all, and

Lochlan's confidence rose—this might actually work, especially if their luck continued. But when the third officer waved them to a halt, his spirits sank again.

Maybe it would be helpful if he appeared as dejected as possible.

"Where are you taking the prisoners?"

"Sinder asked to see them. Privately, in his quarters." The peacekeeper shrugged. "Look, I don't ask questions."

"All the same. Do you have an order for it?"

The man's tone radiated irritation. "Not *on* me. He didn't bother to give me one. He only told me to get them, so I got them. Why, do you want to explain to him why you delayed them?"

The officer frowned, reaching for her comm. "I think he'd be glad that all the proper precautions were taken. I'll page him, it'll only take a moment. Sit tight."

"Oh, wait." The peacekeeper lowered a hand to his side. "I think maybe I do have one after all."

Lochlan knew what was coming a second before it happened: the peacekeeper drew his sidearm, fast as blinking, and put a bullet in the officer's chest with a soft, high-pitched *thunk*. She went down immediately, an expression of surprise on her face. There was as little blood as there had been with the peacekeeper in the brig.

Again, Adam's features tensed. Kerry turned his head away.

"Had to," the peacekeeper growled. "C'mon, we really have to shake a leg now. Soon as they find her, they'll be raising every alarm in the place."

They moved on, Lochlan and Adam helping Kerry along as fast as they could. The rest of the way down to the docking bay—via another lift and series of corridors—they encountered no one, but as soon as the bay doors opened, two armored peacekeepers looked up from their station by the door . . .

And reached for their sidearms.

The peacekeeper with them squeezed off three shots before Lochlan had time to shout a warning, and the two other peacekeepers dove for cover. Lochlan turned back to the bay, adrenaline pumping through his veins; five shuttles were lined up side by side. "Which one?"

"Doesn't matter! Closest one! Run for it, I'll cover you." The peacekeeper went down on one knee, firing again, and a bullet whizzed past inches from Lochlan's ear. He didn't have to be told twice. He tightened his grip on Kerry and hurried forward.

"Adam, let's move!"

Adam was already moving, keeping pace with him as they made for the nearest shuttle, Kerry trying to run but managing no more than a brisk trot. More bullets missed them by almost nothing at all, and from behind them someone let out a harsh cry of pain.

If they had to leave the man behind, well, he wasn't sure he actually disliked the idea, whatever he had risked for them.

The shuttle, by some miracle, wasn't locked, and Adam pressed the hatch release, extending the small gangway and pushing them up it. "Come on!" He whirled halfway back, though Lochlan hissed a curse and tried to drag them all onward. "Run! It's open!"

Lochlan stole a glance behind; the peacekeeper pushed to his feet and ran. Blood was running down one arm from a wound in his shoulder, and the arm swung as if paralyzed, but the man managed to fire over his shoulder twice more before he reached them. "Go! Now!"

"I can fly." Lochlan handed Kerry off to Adam and pushed past them as the peacekeeper punched the panel to close the hatch. The cockpit was only feet away, and he dropped into the pilot's seat, rapidly scanning the console. It looked almost nothing like the patchwork of *Volya*, but it was standard enough. He could use it.

Volya. Fresh pain lanced through him. They were leaving her behind. He would probably never see her again.

Later, he would have time to mourn her. He engaged the engines and the thrust release, swiveling them in place to face the main bay doors. As the view out the front window spun slowly, he had time to see the far doors opening to spew about twenty peacekeepers in full armor, weapons drawn. Gunfire continued to rattle against the hull's shielding, and Lochlan gritted his teeth as he sent up prayers to anyone or anything who might be listening.

The peacekeeper fell into the copilot's seat, gloved hands flying across his end of the console—one of them streaked with blood. "The docking is automated. I have the departure code. Just a second." He cursed under his breath. "Unless they've locked us out. If we're in time . . ."

The bay doors rumbled and began to open. Beyond was the white maelstrom of slipstream. Lochlan let out a hysterical breath, almost twisting it into a moan, and then the ship rocked. Disembarking in slipstream was dangerous. But he had done it before. Many times.

"*Shit*," the man hissed. "Get us outta here. *Now.*"

Lochlan fired the engines, and the ship leaped forward, slicing through the force field and into the white.

And stuttered. Shook. Lochlan pulled up a quick diagnostic, and groaned. "We took a hit to the slipstream drive. We're coming out. I can't stop it."

"Well, whatever." The peacekeeper winced, a hand against the bullet wound. "If we're alive . . ."

All at once, the white snapped into black, dizzying him for a split second before the universe regained its normal shape. Lochlan called up star charts, scanning them furiously—a small star system, nondescript sun and only a few planets of no particular note. Exiting slipstream took a matter of seconds, and whoever was in pursuit had to have the coordinates they'd escaped at. They would be close behind. "If we can only run on sub-slipstream engines . . . *Khara*, we have to put down somewhere and hide. We won't be able to get away from them like this."

"Where are we?" The peacekeeper leaned over to study the chart and pointed to a planet that appeared to be only a couple hundred thousand kilometers distant. "That would work. Habitable. Dry, but it's still—"

"How are we doing?" Adam said from behind them. "I got Kerry into a seat; he's okay for now. What are we—"

"We're landing. We have to." Lochlan glanced back. "Slipstream drive is out of commission. I might be able to repair it, but—"

"Here they come." The peacekeeper cursed again, flicking on the rear screens. A collection of pale ships was blinking into existence behind them, and a large group of skirmish fighters was leading the pack. "Burn. Hard as you can."

Lochlan laid in a course for the planet and in another second the engines were in hard burn, thrusting them toward it at speed. But it wasn't as fast as the fighters would be able to go. Smaller and more nimble, they would be gaining, and he didn't need to consult the proximity sensors to know it. The planet swelled in the window, the part they could see rocky and barren, run through here and there with long, wide rivers. There had to be a hiding place. Somewhere.

The shuttle shivered, and warning lights flicked on. Lochlan assessed the damage in a few seconds, and gave the peacekeeper a grim look.

There was nothing to be done except to work with what they had. There was something perversely comforting about that.

"Landing is going to be rough. They took out half our atmo stabilizers."

"Can you get us down?"

"He can," Adam said quietly. "If anyone can."

"Thanks for the vote of confidence, *chusile*," Lochlan muttered, diverting what power he could spare to the stabilizers that remained. "No pressure or anything, right?"

The shuttle began to shake and rattle as they plunged down into the planet's upper atmosphere, as if it was being continually fired upon now—which perhaps it was. Lochlan gritted his teeth, staring at the ground hurtling toward them.

The sun was beginning to rise over the curve of the horizon. Lochlan was aware, in a distant way, that it was strangely beautiful.

The shuttle dipped, spiraled, then they were in free fall for a few seconds that made his stomach lurch before he managed to pull them out of it again. "Hold on," he cried. Almost every warning light that could be lit was flashing in panic. Close below them was a range of low mountains flanked by one of the smaller rivers, and they were approaching it at an alarming speed, a few thousand feet, a few hundred, less. "I think I can—"

Impact, so hard he felt himself fly out of the seat and tumble backward into something yielding that could only be Adam's body. He flailed and the world spun around him, and there was a yell of pain. They were bouncing, skidding, and something was burning. He reached for Adam, hands grasping desperately—

And then his head exploded with white agony.

PART TWO

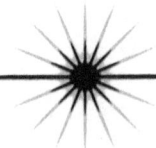

PLATEAU

CHAPTER

TEN

Nkiruka pressed her hands together and the glowbugs came to her.

They always came. They always had, from the time she had been a child exploring the roots and massive trunks of the Arched Halls, the trees brought from Terra when the first Bideshi had chosen their own exile centuries before to keep the roots of a long-lost home. Whether they were drawn to her extraordinary capacity to stay still for long periods—despite the abandon of her dancing—or whether they sensed kinship with her, no one knew, and least of all Nkiruka herself. What mattered was that they came, and they spoke to her in voices that no one else could hear.

Of the past. The present. Future things. They were like little stars, and like the stars they knew much.

Now they landed on her hands and forearms, on the coils of her hair, casting a warm and shifting light across her deep-brown skin. People said she was so still sometimes that she became one of the trees themselves, and that was part of why she was so at home in the Halls. In truth, she was more at home here than any other place on Ashwina.

"Little brothers, little sisters," she whispered, like the gentlest breeze moving through the branches. "Slow down. Slow down and let me listen."

They were chattering.

Something was happening.

It had been happening for a long time, she knew. Since the homeship and the convoy left Takamagahara, pushing out into a black more uncertain than it had been in many years. Nkiruka was comfortable with uncertainty in a way that few others were, but it wasn't as though it didn't trouble her at all, and now that uncertainty was rising in intensity. She frowned.

"Nkiru. Wingsister. They said you might be here."

She turned, startled, then smiled at the tall figure moving toward her through the shadows. Kae, walking with barely a trace of the limp that the Battle of the Plain had left him, bearing a tray of votives in his arms. Candles and prayers for the spirits of the dead that dwelt in the trees. Who was to say that the spirits weren't the glowbugs themselves?

It was good to see Kae. Before the battle, she hadn't known him well, but after ... After, everyone was a little bit closer in new ways, and she and Kae were no exception. Her, an untested pilot who had barely come through the fight alive. Him, the man who had trained her, who comforted her and her wingsisters and brothers in the aftermath when the air was still thick with fear and blood.

"It helps to listen." She shifted, and the bugs took humming wing, hovering around her as if reluctant to leave. She frowned. "It's more guidance than we get from the council these days."

"With no one to read the lines or the charts or the gut? I know." Kae set down the tray, dropping into a crouch beside her and catching one of the glowbugs in the curve of his palm. It crawled across his life line, flexed its wings, and took off again. "You'd think they would have settled on someone to take her place by now."

"She will be impossible to replace." Nkiruka hadn't known Ixchel especially well. Old Mother to the entire ship, beloved of all, Ixchel had nevertheless been inscrutable to almost everyone.

"Even so." Kae sighed. "We need an Aalim. We're the lead ship, it makes no sense for us to lack one. And given that Jakana and Suzaku picked theirs weeks ago ..."

"All things in their own time." Nkiruka fiddled with a beaded cuff on her wrist. "That's what she would have said."

Kae shot her a faintly sardonic smile. "Maybe it should be you."

"Me? No." But she couldn't pretend to be entirely surprised at his suggestion. Others had said it. Some careful to be discreet, but others increasingly less so. "I can't be an Old Mother. I can't be an Old anything. Only ten years ago I was Named, you know that." She injected gentle teasing into her tone, but there was an edge of something heavier under it.

"So you'll decline? If they pick you?" Kae sounded more solemn now. It was a serious question. In the past a candidate had declined their nomination, but it was rare and hadn't happened in the living memory of the convoy, though it had happened more recently in one or two others, and news of it had traveled even across vast distances. It was always a turning point in the candidate's life, and a difficult one. The point where they had marked their own desires more important than the needs of their homeship and their people.

After, nothing could ever be the same. It wasn't unheard of for a declining candidate to simply cast themselves into exile.

"I don't know," she said at last. She hadn't wanted to consider this, the real possibility of selection and what it would mean. Around her, as if sensing her unrest, the glowbugs were humming slowly away into the trees. "I don't want it to come to that."

Kae nodded but said nothing else. After a short period of silence he pushed himself to his feet and picked up his tray. But he hesitated, still looking down at her. Nkiruka waited, letting him come to the words in his own time.

"If I find you later," he said, "will you do a reading for me?"

Nkiruka hesitated. "I'm not very good. You know that, right? I'm not a replacement for Ixchel, no matter what the others think." Kae was searching for something. They were all searching for something, sensing the hole in themselves. More and more, people were coming to her. Pushing her in a direction she didn't want to take, but thus far hadn't been able to entirely resist.

How was she supposed to resist helping people who seemed to need her?

Oh, it's going to get so much harder than this.

"I know. I don't care. Do what you can." Kae's face briefly twisted, and confusion and unhappiness flashed across its handsome lines. "Please."

"I will," she said softly. "After the sunlamps dim. After Satya and I share a meal. Come to me then."

He nodded and moved off into the shadows without another word. The Halls swallowed him up.

Nkiruka sat for a long time after he was gone, absent the glowbugs or any of the other creatures that whispered and flew and crawled through the sacred spaces of the Arched Halls. She was thinking, but it was a directionless, scattered kind of thought, packed with so many things that it almost made her dizzy. She was already aware of what Kae wanted to ask. It was a question held in common among many of the Bideshi, at least the ones in this convoy, and especially the ones on Ashwina.

And she had no answer. No matter how much she wished she did. But perhaps tonight the stars would be kind to her, and give up secrets even to someone who didn't dance in the darkness in which they spun.

At length she rose, shaking out her skirts, and made her way toward some of the Halls' more traveled courses. Here were people praying, singing low hymns, meditating in the shadows. Inside her was still unrest, but as she moved among them, nodding and smiling to those who offered her greetings, she let their peace flow into her. Since Ixchel's death, the Arched Halls had been visited more frequently, though every Bideshi on the homeship went there occasionally, for the great Masses if for no other reason.

Need. It was everywhere.

The trees thinned out around her, the path widened, and then fell away entirely and she came out into the fields, the grass whispering in the breeze and carrying the sweet smell of heather and the bracken at the edge of the wood, mixed with the headier scent of honeysuckle. The light of the sunlamps was deepening into afternoon, and for a moment Nkiruka stood, breathing it in. She tilted her head back. Far above her, through the transparent ceiling, the stars shone in the night that went on forever.

She had not been born on Ashwina but on the residential homeship Suzaku, where the High Fields were drier and faded into patches of red desert, and the Arched Halls were—strangely—lusher and more humid, like the equatorial jungles of Terra, as people described them. She had grown up in those Fields and those Halls, had carried their dust and drifting pollen within her when she came to Ashwina in the year after her Naming, to learn how to fight, to dance the death dances, to pilot an escort fighter. It had been an adjustment. She would never love these lands the way she loved the lands that rested at the top of Suzaku's great bulk, but she had grown to love them all the same.

Anything growing. Miracles in the black.

She began walking again, following the path toward the great rock face and the stair that would lead her down into the winding corridors and vast chambers of Ashwina.

Like the quarters of most of the people on the homeship, Nkiruka's home was small, though larger than it had been when she first came to Ashwina to take up her apprenticeship. Not that she'd done anything particular to earn the size; quarters were assigned according to need rather than station. The reason for the relatively large size was waiting for her inside, and as she approached the door she smelled spices and cooking meat, turmeric and cinnamon, beef from Jakana. She smiled and the door opened at her touch.

Inside, the main room was in a pleasant state of disarray, cushions scattered on the floor in front of the wide couch, an easel and paints piled in a corner, a cup of forgotten tea on a low table, set perilously close to one of the paper books borrowed from Ashwina's great library. Nkiruka let out a fond sigh and moved to the table, shifting the tea away. She turned toward the kitchenette that took up one wall, around which bustled a curvaceous woman with black hair flowing loose all down her back. She was singing softly to herself, stirring something steaming in a pot on the stove. It was from this pot that the scent of spices came, seeming to grow stronger each time she stirred it.

Nkiruka slipped up behind her and curled her arms around Satya's waist, pressing a kiss to her shoulder. "Hello, *habibti*."

Satya laughed and reached up to comb her fingers through Nkiruka's hair, their tips stained yellow with turmeric. "Nkiru. I was starting to wonder if you'd be home for dinner at all."

"I wouldn't miss it. I just let slip the time." She pressed another kiss to the underside of Satya's jaw, Satya tilting her head to allow more access, humming happily. "Kae came to see me."

"Oh?" Satya arched a brow and reached for the jar of cinnamon that sat on the side counter, shaking a bit more of it into the pot. "And what did he want? Is he going to be a good neighbor and let Leila drag him here for dinner next week?"

"I didn't get a chance to ask him." Nkiruka stepped away, still tugging idly at a strand of Satya's hair. It was true enough. For those few minutes, talking to Kae, she had forgotten all about dinner, though not social niceties. And not Satya.

"No? Well, no matter. We'll see him again." Satya glanced over her shoulder and gestured to the meal table that sat against another wall, its one end melded into the wall's curved shape. It was piled with sewing. "Clear that off, would you? I meant to finish it all today, but they needed my help in the gardens earlier this afternoon."

Nkiruka began to gather up the sewing, quickly abandoning any hope of folding it into any kind of order and simply laying the pieces on one end of the couch. A length of bright red and orange brocade that might become a skirt or a form-fitting top, a bunch of gauzy black material that might be anything at all, and a bundle of pink silk that Satya had expressed the intention of making into a flowing dress. Nkiruka paused, this last in her arms, and again found herself thinking of fire and hot steel in the shadows of the Arched Halls. The ceremony that would make a merely gifted person into something much more.

No. Never.

"He's coming tonight," she said suddenly. "Kae is. He wants to see me." Where the abrupt honesty originated from, she wasn't entirely sure, but it came on strong and inarguable, an urge deep and instinctive in a way that she had long since learned not to fight.

Satya had turned, the pot in her hands. "Get some bowls . . ." she said, the last word trailing off just as Nkiruka finished speaking. She frowned. "Why?"

"He wants a reading."

Satya's expression darkened. For a moment longer she stood there with her hands tight on the handles of the pot. Her knuckles turned pale.

"You're going to do it, aren't you?" Satya's voice, when it came, was as tight as her hands.

"He asked me," Nkiruka said helplessly. No, she hadn't wanted to be this honest; it was peeling back what fantasy had covered and concealed since the death of Ixchel, since the rumors had begun. There had been a brief moment when the two of them had faced it all head-on, and then they had put it away. But it had still been there.

Now here it was in front of them again, something not only hungry but *needy*, wanting to pull at her, to devour her not from predatory malevolence but simply because it had no idea how to stop itself.

Like a child. A panicking child.

She always said she wanted children.

"You didn't have to say yes." Satya pushed past her, setting the pot down on a mat in the center of the table with a dull thud. "Please get those bowls for me. And some sticks, unless you want to eat this all with your fingers."

Nkiruka got the chopsticks and the bowls. She wasn't sure that there was even anything she could say. It was done; Satya was angry with her and it was too late to take any of it back.

Satya didn't say another word to her, not when Nkiruka stood close to her to set the bowls on the table, not when she was handed her chopsticks, not until she was preparing to ladle out spoonfuls of noodles and meat and sauce. Then she stopped with the spoon in the pot and turned to Nkiruka.

Her green eyes were shining with tears. Nkiruka stared at her, aghast. But not totally surprised.

"How can you do it?" Satya's usually melodic voice was thick and choked. "How can you *encourage* them like that? You know they want something, you know what that thing is, and you're *giving* it to them, and what happens when they actually start to expect it?" She released the spoon, her hands gesticulating with the force that filled her voice. "You're making these little choices now, and I know they don't seem like much, but what about when later they amount to *one big choice*, and it'll be too late for you to unmake it?"

She didn't have to say more.

But how was Nkiruka supposed to say no to anyone when the need was so clear and so great?

"They can't force me to do it, Satya." Nkiruka dropped her hand to her side again and faced Satya squarely, meeting and holding her tear-blurred gaze. "No Old Mother has ever been forced to take the vows. It has to be freely chosen. You know that."

"That was then," Satya murmured. Much of the anger seemed to be gone from her now. "As I said. All you have to do is make all those little choices. They'll lead you to the same place in the end. You won't feel like you can say no."

"I can say no to *that*." Nkiruka reached up and closed her hands around Satya's upper arms, pulling her closer, till their faces were barely inches apart. This was what it came down to. Becoming an Aalim— once that was done, love of the many must always take the place of the love of one. It was many decades ago, but everyone still remembered the only one who had broken that rule, who had been cast out forever. She had lost everything in the end. That was what was at stake, in that choice to cut love out by the roots. "I will *never* choose it over you, do you hear me? I will *never do that*."

Satya stayed silent for a few moments, her breath hitching, her eyes still glistening with the tears. The pot sat forgotten on the table. Everything else sat forgotten as well. The pain on Satya's face was raw and naked, and Nkiruka wondered how long it had been this bad, and whether Satya had simply hidden it that well or whether Nkiruka had simply been unwilling to see. "I want to believe you," Satya whispered at last. "I believe you believe it. Nkiru . . ."

None of this is fair. Nkiruka dragged Satya across the last distance between them and sealed their mouths together. There was an instant of resistance that dissolved almost immediately, and then Satya clutched at her, kissing her like it was the only thing that would keep Nkiruka there.

Five years. Not five years gone, not for this.

Nkiruka pressed Satya back against the table, then shoved her up onto it. Satya steadied herself with one arm braced behind her, and then she knocked everything onto the floor. The bowls shattered, the pot went with a crash, and noodles spilled in a slippery tangle across the floor. A cloud of spice scent enveloped them, and it was like Satya—it *was* Satya, the essence of the kiss. Satya spread her legs and hooked them around Nkiruka's slim hips, pulling at the cloth that wound around her torso and breasts.

It was hard and desperate and over too fast, the two of them gasping and still arching against each other in the aftershocks of their mingled orgasms, and when Satya touched Nkiruka's face, her turmeric-yellow fingers looked like the tips of flower stamens dusted with pollen.

"Never," Nkiruka whispered in Satya's ear, each syllable sending a shiver all through her. *Never, never, never.*

Nkiruka met Kae in a deserted corridor on one of Ashwina's upper floors, close to the outer hull.

She had left Satya sleeping, or at least lying in bed facing the wall, and Nkiruka hadn't found it in herself to risk disturbing her to make sure. She'd made herself ready, trying to calm her own mind, trying to remember how one had to listen in order to be able to turn the listening into a true reading. She had her own small deck of pads, but they were nothing to Ixchel's, nothing to her power, nothing to what any Old Mother would be capable of.

They were in the pocket of the shawl she'd wrapped around her shoulders. Because the truth was that Satya was right. Nkiruka couldn't say no.

She knew what this place was. Everyone knew the Old Mother enough to know where she kept her councils, where she wandered in pursuit of her own odd, esoteric ways. The light spots of dust—the remains of old footprints—made Nkiruka even more certain.

What had truly led her up here?

"Here," Kae murmured, turning in place. He gazed back at Nkiruka, and something passed between them. *She* was there. Maybe only her echo, lingering traces of her, like her footprints, in a place where she had woven her magic and listened to her stars. Or maybe more. But she was there. She was waiting.

The pads tucked in Nkiruka's pocket felt as if they were vibrating at the edge of what it was possible to feel.

"I think we can do it right here." Nkiruka nodded at a cluster of the spots with thinner layers of dust, perhaps some place where Ixchel had stopped for a time. "Sit?"

Kae nodded. They sat down opposite each other, silent, as if the dust was eating up all sound. On impulse, Nkiruka laid a hand against the floor and lifted it up again, examining the gray handprint that she had made.

You're not my ghost, a voice whispered in her ear, and with a shiver she recognized it as Adisa's. Once the man—leader of Ashwina in all but name—had stood here and said those words to a woman now gone to join the branches of the Arched Halls and the stars beyond. Nkiruka had no way of knowing that—but she did.

What she might become, where the potential rested . . . That woman would know it well.

"Nkiru?" A touch at her knee and she shook herself; Kae, peering at her with open concern.

"I'm fine." The smile she gave him didn't feel especially convincing. "It's just strange, being up here." She reached into her shawl and pulled out her deck, untwisting the scarf that wound around it. Undid the cord that bound them together, shuffled the thin pads through her hands, letting the rote movements calm her. Part of her already knew what was coming and the anticipation wasn't pleasant, but it had an inexorable quality, the feeling of something that couldn't be turned aside. Something that touched too many people, that exerted a tug on too many orbits.

She laid the deck down in front of Kae. "Cut."

Kae cut the deck in a single smooth movement, well practiced. She'd expected this. Kae, steady Kae; everyone familiar with him knew how he placed deep importance on personal readings, on consulting the dance of the stars—unusually so, even for a Bideshi. It was because of what he had learned, so early in his life, about himself. It was because of how early he had gone to be Named. And it was because of the reason that he was here now.

In some ways, he was more comfortable in this moment than she was.

She selected the first few cards and began to lay them out, facedown. "Ask." It wasn't usually done this way, with the question laid out beforehand. But sometimes it was appropriate to query directly, to do what one could to shape the direction of the answer before the wave function collapsed.

Kae took a slow breath. "Are Adam and Lochlan alive?"

Here it was. Finally. Nkiruka suppressed a shiver. She had never met Adam—many people on Ashwina hadn't, or had only seen him in passing—but as everyone did, she knew what part he had played in what had happened on Takamagahara. Was Adam alive? By extension, was his lover alive as well? They were questions that most of the people on Ashwina had certainly asked, were certainly asking, but here was Kae, the one with the courage to give it voice and send it out among the stars.

She turned the first pad, its sine waves twisting through the dark.

Kisin. The death star.

Nkiruka glanced up and saw that Kae was sitting rigid, his face frozen and unreadable.

"Wait," she murmured. There was a cold stone in the pit of her stomach, but out of the night, something was whispering to her to hold back her fear. It was only the first pad. There was no way to know what it really meant, not yet.

The second pad.

Sol.

"Not them," Nkiruka said softly. "Not Adam, not Lochlan. Not yet." She tapped the pad with her fingernail, its waves shifting gently and rhythmically. Kae was sharp enough to draw his own conclusions, but the words still wanted to be said. Needed to be said, to confirm themselves. "The Protectorate. The death that touched Adam now touches his homeworld. The source of protection."

"As we expected." Kae was nodding slowly, his hands clasped together. He stared down at the pad and then up at Nkiruka again. "I'd hoped . . . I'd hoped they might have stopped it before now. But I guess if they had, we would have heard something. Even this far out." His gaze was fixed on Nkiruka, but she got the distinct impression that he wasn't seeing her anymore, that he was searching through and past her toward the answers that he so badly wanted to come through her.

"But what about *them*?"

Nkiruka said nothing. The third pad.

Jana. The Lady of Secrets.

"In hiding," Kae said, before Nkiruka could issue her interpretation. "Good. That's . . . Yes. That's good."

The attitude of his body had subtly changed. Part of him seemed to be sagging, though some tension remained. *There is no one to guide us through the night.* Nkiruka fought back another shiver. *Our future is hidden from us.*

The final pad. That very future. As she slid her fingers under it to turn it, Nkiruka realized that she was holding her breath. And she kept holding it when she saw the image of the vibration, a dark dance full of violence, a close embrace of Kisin. Its distant sibling.

Ares.

War.

They stared at it for a long time. This too, she knew—she *felt*—was not unexpected. The current period of doubt and greater distance from more populated parts of space, as the convoy traveled on its far outward arc toward the galactic rim, had begun in battle and bloodshed, and that darkness had ghosted their path, subtly changing their dance. It was something else that everyone sensed but no one wanted to speak about, no one on Ashwina or on the other ships, and—she was sure—no one in any of the other convoys.

War. Not in the past. But war, coming. Coming like the paths of comets, the long orbits of stone and ice. Coming to strike them all.

At last Nkiruka began to gather up the pads, returning them to the deck. Kae continued to sit in silence, his head bowed, almost as if he was praying. She let him be. If she could have taken time for herself right now, she might have as well. Perhaps later she would, in her quarters with Satya sleeping a room away, her presence both comforting and nothing of the sort.

"What are you going to do?" Kae asked, once the deck was stowed in her shawl again, his hands still clasped in his lap. "What now, Nkiru?"

Nkiruka rolled a shoulder in half an uncomfortable shrug. It was easiest—to the extent that it was easy at all—to let it be something that was for Kae and Kae alone, his own question and his own answer. "What do you think I should do?"

"You can't ask me that." Kae hesitated, then laid his hand over hers. "No one can decide for you."

"I know." Nkiruka sighed. "So in some universe where I make certain choices, I go to Adisa, I tell him what I've seen, and things slide into motion that can never be stopped. Things that . . . We already suspected. But this is worse. And if it's in the reading, it's more imminent than any of us imagined."

"But it hasn't happened? We still have time before it does?"

Nkiruka made a vague gesture. He was right. Was this cowardice? How could she understand what she was feeling? "You know what I'm saying."

"I do."

Nkiruka pushed herself to her feet and gathered herself in a way that was as mental as it was physical. "I'm tired."

Kae rose and nodded. "Come on, then."

"No. You go." Nkiruka turned away, her gaze fixed on the stars. They were hinting at things that went beyond what the pads had shown. They were unclear and gentle but so persistent, like water wearing down stone. "I'll stay here for a while." This time for herself, here, high and close to the stars that whispered, Ixchel's ghost lingering around her and perhaps whispering loudest of all.

Kae left her. After a time she closed her eyes and laid her hand flat against the glass.

All the dark and all the dancing.

CHAPTER

ELEVEN

Pain. A world of it.

Adam groaned. Even that much hurt, the sound scraping against his raw throat. Slowly, he became aware of his limbs, and then the fact that he could feel them, could move them, though he didn't much want to. Then he focused on what was around him, and he saw something strange.

Two pilot's chairs, set into the ceiling above him. Who in their right mind would put chairs *there*?

Slowly he pushed himself up on his hands, pausing as his head spun and nausea swept through him. He looked blearily around. They weren't on the ceiling. The cockpit—the shuttle. They had gone down, *hard*.

And no. Wait. *He* was on the ceiling. The shuttle had come to rest upside down. He scrubbed his hands over his face, squeezing his eyes closed as his stomach wobbled again.

Well, this was an auspicious beginning.

Lochlan.

He scanned the debris around him, panic rising. Simply because— by some miracle—he didn't seem to be badly hurt didn't mean that no one else was. Part of him thought about blood, about torn flesh, so vividly that for a few seconds it was all he could do not to give in and vomit . . . And then a moan under a piece of fallen bulkhead got him moving, scrambling forward across debris.

The bulkhead wasn't as heavy as it appeared, and with a yank he pulled it away, revealing Lochlan crumpled beneath it, bleeding from a long scratch down the right side of his face and a sizable gash in his forehead but otherwise apparently unharmed. He sat up, his fingers going to his face, and he winced at the blood that stained them.

"*Khara*, how exactly are we not dead?"

"Unbelievable luck, I guess." Adam tore away a strip of his shirt—which was already torn—and pressed it against Lochlan's forehead. Relief was crashing through him, but he was trying to ignore it. If they were still being pursued . . . "Hold that on there. I need to find the others."

"I can help you. I'm not *that* hurt." Lochlan caught Adam's arm with his free hand, pulling him closer. "*Chusile*, are you all right?"

"I'm fine." He allowed himself to pause, covering Lochlan's hand with his own. They were alive, and still together. That had to count for something. That might count for almost everything. "Let's go, then."

The curvature of the cockpit's ceiling and the scattered debris made the going awkward and more difficult than it seemed. Several times Adam's balance lurched in a way that made him wonder if he might not be quite so fine after all. Then a pile of loose wiring shifted and a man pushed himself up through it, shaking his head.

The peacekeeper. His blast shield had been nearly sheered away—it must have taken the majority of the force from a blow to the face. Likely it had saved the man's life. Even so, his lip was split, blood crusting his chin. He let out a rough curse and reached up to remove his helmet.

As he pulled it off, the face that came fully into view was a horror. Twisted pink scars ran all down one side, the hairline burned, the eye gone. In its place was a bionic implant, its reddish pupilless center and eerie internal glow hard to look at.

The face was familiar. But not like the man from his memory, not quite. The other side appeared so much older than it should, the eye a different shape, the angle different as well.

The man gave them a thin, pained smile. "Hello, Yuga." He paused, flicking his gaze from Adam to Lochlan. "You don't recognize me? Wouldn't be surprised, I saw you for only a short time. And I've had some work done. Much as I could. Wouldn't do for them to be recognizing me."

Adam blinked. He had thought. For an instant, he had. But it *couldn't* be. It made no sense.

"*Aarons?*"

"Now he gets it. Always knew you were a sharp one, Yuga."

Adam shot Aarons a glare. He didn't like the man. He had never been given much of a reason to. That Aarons had engineered their escape didn't change that.

"It makes no sense." He stepped forward to help Aarons up, but moved back when he was batted away. "You, helping us? Why? And then there's also— Shit, Kerry."

The three of them shouldered their way out of the cockpit— Aarons still moving with obvious discomfort—and toward the back of the ship, where Kerry had been installed. It was even worse than the cockpit, the floor—which had been the ceiling—invisible in most places under twisted metal and wrecked seats, foam padding littered around like some kind of bizarre fungus. Scanning it, his heart sinking, Adam again wondered how they were alive. "Kerry?" Aarons groped his way forward, and Lochlan and Adam followed. "Kerry, man, you in here? Make some noise. Anything. Help us find you."

Silence. The three of them froze, listening; there was only the creak of the ship and a single metallic clang as something else fell elsewhere in the shuttle.

"Well, this isn't all that—" Lochlan started to say, but then a low moan and the shuffle of debris cut him off. Aarons hurried toward the source of the noise, shoving things aside as he went. A couple of yards away he stopped and lifted a fallen seat, and went still.

Adam approached, Lochlan muttering darkly at his back. But when they reached Aarons, even Lochlan fell silent.

Kerry lay where the seat had pinned him. His lower body was twisted at an angle that no body should be able to twist, and his torn face was a mass of blood. One arm seemed to have grown an extra joint, and pale bone protruded from the skin. But that wasn't the worst of it. A jagged shard of metal had speared him through, jutting up from his belly, scraps of cloth and what appeared horribly like flesh clinging to its razor-sharp edges.

Somehow he was still alive. He blinked up at them and raised his unbroken arm, his hand shaking.

Aarons dropped into a crouch beside him, clasping his hand. "*Shit.* I'm sorry, Marcus."

No pointless platitudes about him being *all right*. No useless hope. Adam didn't know Kerry well, but he knew that he wasn't a fool. He would know how badly off he was. He would know that he was dying.

Adam shouldn't have much reason to grieve for the man. Kerry had been in command when Bideshi men, women, children had been slaughtered, many of them without a chance to defend themselves. He had overseen the butchery of hundreds if not thousands of people. He had worked with Cosaire, and chased Adam across the galaxy and to the point of death.

But now he was dying because of the two of them. Standing there, staring down at Commander Marcus Kerry's ruined body and the agony twisting what remained of his face, Adam was sorry. He curled his fingers around Lochlan's.

Lochlan didn't seem sorry. Adam didn't blame him.

"You made it out." The words were slurred. Was the man's jaw broken? "Aarons . . . I didn't know it was you."

"I couldn't help you. Not until they got there. I couldn't risk it. I'm sorry," Aarons said again, and there was a tremble in his voice.

Kerry tried to smile. It was awful. "At least I'm not getting . . . that fucking firing squad. This is better." He coughed, his hand going to the metal that impaled him, his fingers dancing along its edge. Lochlan looked away, swallowing. Adam didn't. It seemed like his duty to witness this man's passing. "It hurts, Aarons. Hurts a lot. Better hurry it along."

Aarons nodded. He reached for his sidearm. "You did good," Aarons said. "Thank you. I'll take it from here."

He pressed the muzzle of the gun against Kerry's temple. Kerry closed his eyes.

Even with the silencer, the shot was quiet.

"So now what?" Lochlan asked.

They were seated in a circle in the cockpit. What few supplies they had managed to scavenge from the wreckage were scattered around them. A survey of the outside from the hole that had been torn in the side of the hull revealed no signs of pursuit, no sign of any Protectorate presence. The terrain was every bit as barren and dry as it had appeared from the air, except for the ribbon of the river that shone in the morning sun. But that seemed to be miles away. They had come down on a rise in the lower foothills of the mountain range, and ahead of them was nothing but dry, brownish desert.

He kept ending up in deserts. Kolyma, Takamagahara . . . and now this place. Wherever it was.

"Now, we get outta here." Aarons gestured around at the wreck. "Call me crazy, but I don't think this thing is flying again. If we stay here, we'll die of thirst or hunger or probably both. Not to mention, the crash site has to be visible from the air, and I promise you, they're still looking for us."

Lochlan grunted. It sounded like reluctant agreement. "I can't believe they didn't catch where we went down as it happened. We keep getting lucky, I guess."

Adam smiled thinly. "Yeah, well, I'm not into arguing with it." He scrubbed a hand over his face and glanced back at the weak light coming from the hole behind them, wincing as pulled muscles in his shoulders twinged. Everything still hurt—if anything, twice as much as it had—and it was obvious that Lochlan and Aarons were no better off. Aarons a good bit worse, the blood from his wound painting his uniform, though the bullet had gone straight through, and Aarons had torn a strip of cloth away and bandaged it as well as he could. Traveling across country—especially across a desert— would be difficult. Perhaps even suicidal. But Aarons was right. They couldn't stay.

Maybe their luck would hold.

"So let's get going." Aarons shoved himself to his feet, groaning, and pulled his makeshift pack—made from wiring and the cloth from ruined seats—over his shoulder. They each had one, Lochlan and Aarons with canteens of water that had probably been there a while, all three with dry rations found in a supply cupboard in the back of the shuttle. It was meager, but it would have to do. "While we still have daylight. I got no idea how long the days are on this rock but we shouldn't get confident."

"What about Kerry?" Adam asked softly. "What should we do with his body?"

Aarons frowned. "Don't know that there's much we *can* do. We can't bury him, we don't have the tools to dig, and I'm not wild about the idea of cremation. I guess we could use trithosite for accelerant, but smoke and flame would draw even more attention than we already have."

"Then let the ship be his tomb," Lochlan said, and there was something about his tone and cadence—almost formal, reminding Adam vaguely of Adisa—that made Adam study him, searching for any sign of mocking.

There was none. Adam touched Lochlan's knee and nodded, hoping that Lochlan could read his gratitude.

One didn't have to like the dead to honor them.

When they stepped onto the hard-packed dirt, Adam's stomach sank. The landscape was more barren than it had seemed before, the river distant and the ground between them and it hilly. Low clouds drifted across a small, pale sun, and as soon as they were a few yards away from the crash, Adam looked back and saw the mountain range, its peaks blunt and dusted with snow. Between them and it, dark clouds rolled, promising storms. The air itself was chilly, and he wished that they had come dressed in something other than their own light flying clothes.

Of everything that he had imagined happening to them, death by exposure hadn't been on the list.

Moving warmed him a bit, and he drew closer to Lochlan, though the heat he felt from the other man's body was probably in his head. In the meantime, he continued to scan the land around them, searching for a sign of anything they could use—plant life, an animal, other sources of water. People. Anything.

The desert resembled the Plain, but it felt completely different. The wind whipped across the flats and up into the hills they moved over, and there was none of that stillness that marked the Plain of Heaven: the held breath of its power. Takamagahara was a desert, but it wasn't a wasteland. This was.

Lochlan caught Adam's arm and pointed. "Over there."

A few yards away, there sat a cluster of small tufts of some grasslike plant. It didn't appear particularly edible, but Adam glanced back at Aarons, who had also halted. "You see it? We should check it out."

"Waste of time, if you ask me. That shit looks about as eating-worthy as hair." But he started toward it, hefting his pack again, grumbling under his breath.

Aaron's estimation turned out to be correct. The grass was devoid of moisture, fine and wispy, but it was alive: when Lochlan tore a blade of it, the inside was a light green. Things were growing. There might be more.

"We'll keep an eye out," Lochlan said, straightening up. "Wonderful, we can graze like cows."

"If we're lucky," Aarons said dryly. "Let's stop dawdling, gentlemen."

They reached flatter land and the river by midafternoon and stood on its banks, surveying it. It was wide but appeared shallow, and there was a faint orange tint to the water. It smelled, a metallic odor that burned slightly in the nose.

Adam's mouth tightened, and he shot Lochlan a grim look. "No way we're drinking that."

"No?" Lochlan chuckled thinly. "You sure? I know resorts where it'd be labeled 'rejuvenating mineral water' and sold for fifty credits a bottle."

"I don't feel especially in need of rejuvenation." Aarons sighed and scanned the bank. "Well, we have a choice now. Forward, left, or right."

"It might be good to follow it downstream." Adam squinted left, into the distance. Nothing but more of the same, but given that, they had little to lose by taking the chance. "If there are any settlements here at all . . ."

Lochlan shrugged. "Might as well. You could be right, and even if you're not, it's something to keep us from going in circles."

Aarons looked back the way they had come, and Adam followed his gaze. The crash was only the faintest speck nestled in the gray hills. It was now too late to turn back. "Fine," Aarons said. "It's true, might as well."

The bank of the river was mostly dry, hard, and cracked, as if there were periods when the river swelled and expanded. Again Adam thought of the storms in the distance. Rain meant floods, and that could be another danger; floods in the desert usually came on hard and fast with little warning. He remembered on Kolyma when an unusually strong storm had caused a flash flood that had washed away the homes of many trithosite miners. Thirty people had died, their bodies never recovered. They were buried somewhere in layers of mud.

The land continued much as it had, flat and then rolling up into foothills, but as the sun sank toward the horizon, the mountain range fell away, and the ground began to descend into a series of rocky crags and low cliffs. These were newer, and looked as if they had been carved by flood and rain, some of the cliff edges leaning precariously forward.

"Getting dark." Aarons stopped and glanced up at the deepening purple sky. "We should—"

Screams from overhead. Engines, ships in the distance and speeding toward them. They were low, drifting back and forth in what Adam recognized—with cold fear—as a search pattern.

"*Khara*," Lochlan hissed, and lunged toward one of the cliffs. "C'mon!"

The cliff they were making toward had a shallow depression, a hollow that wasn't quite a cave, and when they reached it they pressed themselves into it, their bodies hunched. Adam pushed himself against Lochlan's side, a hand on his chest, feeling the racing beat of his heart. The three of them scanned the part of the sky they could see, and as far as Adam could tell, none of them were breathing at all.

"If they have infrared," Adam whispered, and winced when Aarons slammed a fist into his arm.

"Shut up, Yuga. Or I do it for you."

Adam obeyed. If the ships had infrared and scanned at the right angle, they would be spotted. But if their uncanny luck didn't leave them . . .

He had no idea how long it took. But at last the buzz of the engines faded. Then they could see them, flying in formation toward the setting sun. Together, the three let out a long breath.

"They might be back." Aarons crept to the edge of the hollow, peering out. "We need to stay here and hope for the best. In the morning we can move again."

The chill bled further into the air, and gradually sharpened. A fire was risky, but the oncoming cold was riskier. With the last of the daylight, Lochlan and Adam left the hollow and searched along the bank and near the cliffs for anything that might burn. There were a few more clumps of grasses, a couple of stunted plants with woody stems, but not much else was in evidence. Lochlan stopped and straightened up, looking toward the horizon and the rim of the sun that remained, golden orange and glaring.

"This is fucked," he said flatly.

Adam walked up beside him, his hands full of grass. "I know."

"I mean . . ." Lochlan turned to him, and though his face was cast in shadow, unhappy tension gripped every line and angle, augmented by the ugly cuts the crash had given him. "Aarons. You trust him? Seriously? He was trying to *kill* you."

"I don't think he's trying now." Adam sighed. He knew a fight over this was probably brewing, but he had been hoping with all his heart to avoid it. "They already had us imprisoned. What would be the point in pretending to let us go? And getting his own people killed in the process? Hell, killing them himself. Why would he do that, Lock?"

"I don't *know*." Lochlan gripped one of his own dreadlocks and pulled. "It's . . . You can't expect me to trust one of them. You just can't."

"I'm not. But I used to be one of them. Did you forget that? Maybe you've been trying to. When we first met, I thought you hated me." Adam's mouth twisted. "Maybe you did."

"Adam." Lochlan's shoulders slumped. "I never hated you. You know that."

"Yeah, well. Could've fooled me."

Lochlan stared at him incredulously. "Are you trying to pick a *fight* with me?"

"No, Lock, I'm not." Adam dropped the grasses in a heap and stalked toward the edge of the water. It was lapping the mud of the shore. He was angry now, but it was a dull anger, one without fire or force. It didn't even have much in the way of direction. He had long ago made his peace with Lochlan's initial dislike for him; it didn't matter now, because what was between them had outgrown any ill feeling that might have existed before.

But it wasn't even about that. It went deeper.

"I could tell you hated us," he said softly. "Maybe not me specifically, but . . . When you told me what happened to you, on Caldor Station . . . how your parents died, how the massacre happened . . . I got it. I understood. I don't expect that to vanish overnight. I don't even expect it to vanish ever. But they're still my people, Lock."

"Ixchel said they were our brothers and sisters." Lochlan's smile was utterly devoid of humor. "Mad old bat."

"But she was right about a lot."

"They're the reason you were dying, Adam."

"They're dying too." Adam folded his arms around his middle. The wind was picking up. "You came with me to help them."

Lochlan walked to him, settled hands on his shoulders. "*Chusile*, I came with you for you."

Adam gazed at him for a long moment. Again, he remembered those early days—Lochlan supporting the proposal to cast him out, insulting him, blaming him for what seemed like every small inconvenience in his life. And now this.

"You trust me," he whispered. "That has to be a place you can start from."

"Adam." Lochlan said his name in a heavy breath, curled his arms around Adam, and pulled him close. Adam went without resisting, let himself be held. From their earliest time together, Lochlan's body had been like an anchor, warm and solid, even when it was still frightening and new. Now it was familiar. It was home, to the extent that he had a home anymore. To the extent that he had ever had one at all. He pressed his face into Lochlan's neck, then lifted his head again.

"If you can't make yourself want to help the Protectorate, sooner or later you're going to leave me."

Lochlan pulled back, eyes wide, shaking his head. "What are you *talking* about?"

"This. All of it." Adam met his gaze without flinching. "It's going to get worse. It's going to get harder, and I think death might end up being the best we can hope for. I don't know if it can work. I have no idea what I'm even doing. And I . . . I don't know if love is enough, Lock. I just don't."

It was getting seriously dark, and as far as Adam could see, there were no stars in evidence—the clouds perhaps now too low and too thick. They would have to get back soon, though finding their way would probably not be too difficult, with the river to follow. But neither of them moved, and at last Lochlan spoke.

"I don't know what else I have." He shook his head slowly. "But I'm not leaving you, Adam. Don't you fucking talk like that; I'm *not*." After a few more seconds of silence he pulled away, and there was a jerkiness in his movements. "Let's . . . Let's get back. This'll have to do."

Together they scooped up the grass again. Lochlan led the way and Adam followed, silently.

But it was true.

Death might be the best we can hope for.

CHAPTER

TWELVE

Adam stirred but didn't wake, and Lochlan sent up a silent prayer of thanks. He needed to sleep. Really, they both did, but if one of them had to be awake, he preferred it be himself. Lochlan slid a hand into Adam's hair and tugged his head to rest against his chest, trying to wrap himself around Adam's sleeping form. Again, he couldn't help but feel how fragile he was getting.

Weak.

Adam, who even in the worst of his illness had been so strong.

I'm not leaving you. The words clenched in his throat, though he didn't say them. *Shut up, I'm not.*

Except he had before. Not Adam, but others. So many, fucked and enjoyed and left soon after, because connections were their own horrible weakness, and when you loved someone and lost them it *hurt.* If life had taught him nothing else, it had driven that cruel lesson home. So of course, of *course* he had let himself fall into the arms of someone who was dying.

Who was now charging toward lethal danger. Or trying to. And weren't they in lethal danger already? Before long their food would run out. Their water was already very low. A few more days without replenishment, and . . .

I'm not leaving you.

The bird lying in his open palm; Ixchel's knife; the tangle of guts on her kerchief. The story they told.

"The fuck're you thinking about so hard?"

Lochlan looked up sharply to see Aarons staring at him. The fire had long since gone out, but in the distance two small moons had risen and they cast enough light to see by. Aarons's face was unreadable, his eye keen as a blade, and his bionic one glowing brighter in the shadows.

A face maybe not even a mother could love.

"None of your business."

"Suit yourself." Aarons rolled a shoulder. "Just seemed like it was troubling you, whatever it is."

"We're in the middle of a desert with no transport and no idea where we're going, and we'll be out of food and water in another day or so. Yeah, I'm troubled." Lochlan allowed himself a crooked, humorless smile. "Aren't you?"

Aarons returned his smile. On his scarred face it was even more crooked. "I'm not sleeping, am I? But what the fuck good is worrying about it gonna do? Won't make rations appear outta thin fucking air, will it?"

Lochlan inclined his head.

"We're alive," Aarons went on. "That counts for everything. As long as we're alive, there's a chance, and I'm not giving up on that chance until I am quite literally dead. If that happens, it happens."

It probably wasn't false bravado. Aarons sounded too matter-of-fact, with no element of boasting in it.

"You know why he's here. Adam. What he's . . . What he's trying to do."

"I saw it. Missy. Before she died. She wasn't only out of her mind, boy. She was sick. Bad. I think that's some of what drove her to it. She knew she was dead anyway." He chuckled. "Most elaborate fucking suicide plan I ever saw. I did her a favor when I killed her."

"Is that why you're helping us?"

Aarons gazed at him for a long moment, and Lochlan could see the thoughts turning and grinding behind his eye. "I saw something on that worthless little rock," he said finally. "I saw what might happen to us. What *is* happening. Look, boy, I never had much love for the Protectorate, even when I was military police for 'em. Even though I was born to 'em. Given all their benefits accordingly. You think that's crazy, right? Like I said, I worked for them. Not only that. I did *dirty* work for them, shit that no one else wanted to do. But I never liked 'em. I can see what they are. They've been striding along, confident as you please, so sure that what they do is always *right*. They can't even imagine any other way of doing things anymore." He fell silent again for a few seconds. Then, "So I got no love for them. But people are people. The people at the bottom—Hell, the ones in the middle—they're trying to live their lives. Most of 'em are good people, as far as *good* goes. They're doing their best and they're being lied to. Propping something up when it's just gonna fall on 'em. Probably *should* fall. Sooner than later, if we want to minimize the damage.

"Maybe I'm sick and tired of seeing people die for no good fucking reason. Maybe Adam's right. Maybe forcing everyone to see their worlds differently is exactly what we need to do to get this whole thing toppled in just the correct way for us to be able to build something better. Maybe *you're* right, all you mongrels."

Lochlan bristled at the word, but Aarons was smiling again, and there was something bizarrely affectionate about the smile. The word. *Mongrels*. And he thought of *raya*.

Maybe they weren't so different. Not in every way.

"You love him."

Lochlan blinked. "What?"

"Adam. You love him." Aarons gestured toward the man in his arms, smile lingering about his mouth. Nothing accusing, no sign of distaste. Strange. "It's pretty damn obvious."

"I—" Lochlan looked down at Adam, his face relaxed in sleep, mouth open, features that spoke of careful craftsmanship, and long, delicate lashes. He was perfect. Always perfect. There wasn't much point in denying something as visible as his feelings. And why would he? Just because someone thought he should be ashamed of it didn't mean he had to give a fuck about their opinion. Every reason not to. "I do." He lifted his gaze. "Do you think that's disgusting? Isn't that what you *raya* say about it?"

"No," Aarons said quietly, and there was a sudden softness in his expression that Lochlan couldn't interpret. "I don't say that."

Lochlan nodded and relaxed a bit. He still didn't trust Aarons, didn't like him, but he didn't think he was lying now.

"I didn't at first," he said after a few more minutes of silence. "He was . . . I saved him and I didn't even know why. He was annoying, he was a goddamn prude, and he was judging *everything*." Lochlan leaned his cheek against the top of Adam's head and closed his eyes.

"The man grows on you," he murmured, and smiled again. "Like a weed. Or a vine. He winds himself into you and you can't get him loose."

"A lot of people died for him. On that planet." Aarons sounded curious more than anything, almost eager, as if he was asking a question that he had held on to for a long time. "Was he worth it, do you think?"

Lochlan considered. At any other time, the question would have put him on the defensive, but now he was far too tired, and it was a fair question for an outsider to ask. It was one that he suspected Adam still asked.

"It wasn't really about him, then. It was about all of us. That was the line, anyway." Lochlan opened his eyes, met Aarons's half gaze. "I'm not sure what I think about that. All I know is . . ." He sighed. "They asked me if I would die for him. I said yes. I'd still say yes. That's all I know."

Slowly, Aarons nodded. "We do what we have to do," he said again, and closed his own eye. The bionic one, a little alarmingly, didn't close at all but continued to stare unblinking into the darkness. "Try to get some sleep, Bideshi. I'm not sure, but we might not have a lot of night left. And I got a feeling we'll have a long day tomorrow."

Lochlan responded with a nod of his own. Aarons said nothing more, and within several minutes he was snoring gently. But Lochlan stayed awake for a while, holding Adam tightly, thinking too much and too hard.

We do what we have to do.

CHAPTER

THIRTEEN

Isaac Sinder wasn't sleeping.

It was deep in third shift, and the ship was quiet, but Sinder paced through his quarters, fists clenched, now and then slamming one into his open palm, part of him itching to slam it into something else that could scream and cry. He wasn't sure he remembered being this kind of angry before, because he couldn't remember experiencing this kind of failure. Failure itself, yes, sure; one had to go through some of that, or one forgot how to deal with it. But to fail when success was all but assured . . .

Apparently he couldn't trust anyone. Those who were not actually duplicitous were probably incompetent. Had Cosaire gone through this, when time after time Adam Yuga slipped through her fingers? Kerry, gone. Yuga and his Bideshi lover, gone. And a fourth man, about whom he had suspicions that he dared not voice aloud even to himself. He had combed back through records, reports, dossiers. He had pulled together every single thing he could find that was even tangentially pertinent. None of it was conclusive, but together the picture they hinted at was nearly impossible. And awful. One man who was, for all intents and purposes, a Protectorate spymaster. A man who had been close to Cosaire, present for that final battle, who had turned against her. A man who had been regarded as loyal but not prone to doing things by the book, who weaved and dodged as the situation demanded and was a general irritant to the people who charged him with the work he did.

A traitor, charged and vanished and hunted, to no avail. Here under his nose all this time. Perhaps someone he had passed in the corridors. Had seen on the bridge. Had spoken to. He had no way of being sure. But it made sense; wasn't the man knowledgeable in infiltration techniques? Of everyone who had been present at the battle and who were suspected traitors, wasn't this man most capable of something like this? Sinder felt the shape of the thing, the outlines of the threads that bound it together, and between those threads he leaped and swung and grabbed for a name.

Bristol Aarons.

But skilled though he was, how had he slipped through all the checks?

Except there were ways. The truth was that anything could be forged, and out in the farthest reaches of human-occupied space, where law was only a word, it was possible to obtain the methods of such forgeries. Ways to slip through code checks and scans undetected, unidentified. Ways of altering one's appearance. It was difficult, but it could be done.

A man from the secret military police would know how to do it. He would have contacts.

Aarons, working with Yuga. Kerry, working with Yuga. It was worse than he thought. Who else? How highly placed?

He stopped in the center of the cabin and closed his eyes, forcing his breathing to slow. He had to be calm, cool. He had to think.

Their escapees were still on the planet, after all. The search fleet had been deployed in orbit at regular intervals around it. They would catch anything that took off. Yuga and the others were effectively trapped.

The only task was to find them.

His door chimed, and he started, turning. "Come."

Alkor stepped inside, the door shutting silently behind her. Dark circles had settled under her eyes, and her hair, though pulled back in its customary bun, still managed to appear disheveled, as if a few unseen strands were out of place. Her demeanor was slumped but tense and vibrating around the edges. Perhaps she had taken stimulants. It wasn't uncommon, though it wasn't admirable.

Sinder clasped his hands behind his back as he faced her. "Anything?"

"Nothing yet. We're employing a grid approach, but so far there's no sign of them except for the crash itself. Or there's no sign of the survivors."

Sinder raised an eyebrow. "Survivors?"

"Yes. High winds right around the site kept us from setting down at the crash site initially, but an hour ago we were finally able to land, and I just received the report. Kerry's body was found in the wreckage."

Kerry's body. Sinder turned away again. That simplified things a little, though it was frustrating. It would have been better to deliver Kerry alive. Still. "What about the others?"

"No sign. We can only assume they left the area on foot."

"Any tracks?"

"None. As I said, the high winds. They swept the ground clean. I'm sorry, Sinder." But there was no real apology in her voice. Only vague impatience. "We'll keep searching. We'll find them."

"I find it difficult to understand," Sinder murmured, "how you haven't found them already. *High winds* or no." He didn't look back at her, and didn't feel the need to. Probably his back was expressing itself well enough. "They were on foot. Likely injured. They can't have gotten that far away. How is it possible that you've found no sign of them at all?"

"I don't know," Alkor said flatly. "I can only speak to what we *have* found."

"Which is almost nothing." Sinder sighed and pinched the bridge of his nose. He didn't want to be angry. Everything had been going so well. It wasn't even that he didn't appreciate what Alkor was trying to do. But the facts were the facts. "Captain, we need to find them. I . . ." How much to tell her about what he suspected?

Only as much as necessary.

"I have reason to believe that the threat Yuga presents is greater than we imagined. I have no real proof as yet, but I suspect a conspiracy, perhaps a huge one. If I'm right, Yuga is the key to uncovering it, and he may be the only remaining key, now that we can't question Kerry any further." At last, he glanced back at her. She was listening in respectful silence, but more to the point, her eyes were alight with understanding, and if skepticism pulled at her mouth, there wasn't enough to pull very hard. "I need everything you can give me, Captain. Please. Even the most minor thing might make all the difference."

Alkor's mouth tightened. "We have only what one pass gave us, though we managed to capture some images from orbit. But that isn't much."

"What, Captain? Tell me."

"It's a settlement," Alkor said, moving forward to stand beside him. "Not large. Doesn't look like more than a few hundred people at most. And it's a long way from the crash site. Nearly a hundred and seventy kilometers. I don't see any way they could make it there, not on foot with limited supplies."

Sinder's eyes narrowed. "Tell me more. There *is* more, isn't there, Captain?"

"Like I said, we only got the briefest look, but it doesn't seem like *settlement* is really the right word. We saw what appear to be guardhouses. And fences." Again, she hesitated, but before Sinder could prompt her, she went on. "We can't be sure, not yet, but it could be a detention camp."

Sinder stared at her. Of all the things he might have expected . . . "A detention camp," he echoed, his focus drifting as his attention turned inward. "What would— Have you hailed them?"

"Not yet. The thing is . . . It's strange. They must have seen our teams; we were flying low. If they can scan orbit, they must know we're here. But we haven't heard a peep from them. It might be simply that they don't have the capability, but . . . we also saw what appeared to be ship hangars. Repair bays. They have garages for heavy vehicles. Whoever they are, they're set up pretty well there."

Sinder nodded. This wasn't about Yuga, had no obvious connection to Yuga at all . . . But every instinct in him was screaming that this was worth his attention. All of it, maybe, instead of search grids that were turning up nothing.

"Captain." He laid his hands on her upper arms, peering into her face. "I need everything you've gathered on it. I need new images. Intelligence. And then I need to talk to them."

They saw it in the distance, shimmering and hazy, and for a moment Adam was sure it was only his imagination, until he saw that Lochlan and Aarons had both halted as well, staring in its direction.

Aarons lifted a hand to shield his eyes, squinting. Adam did the same, but whatever it was seemed to have gone. Then it was there again: a long, low shape, speeding across the horizon.

Getting bigger. Moving toward them.

"Another search ship?" Lochlan asked under his breath. Aarons shook his head.

"Not that kind of ship. That's a groundcar: a big one. The fleet has groundcars for landing parties, but nothing like that." He dropped his hand and turned to them, brows drawn together. "Gentlemen, I think we're not alone."

Adam frowned, and shot Lochlan a worried look. "We can't assume they're friendly. We can't even assume they're not Protectorate."

"No, Yuga, we can't. But I don't see anywhere to hide around here, do you?" They'd reached the flat, dry remains of what had once been a wide delta, the river nothing more than a small trickle in its center. "Our water's almost gone. This passes us by, and we're as good as dead unless we get lucky again."

Lochlan's mouth twisted, as tense and worried as Adam felt. But he nodded. "I don't like it either, *chusile*. But I think he has a point. We need to risk it."

"Anyway, it's—" Aarons was squinting at it, and Adam swore that he could almost hear the man's bionic eye whirring as it focused. "No, it's not Protectorate. Not any Protectorate car I've ever seen, anyway. They have that model, but the markings are all wrong." He lifted a hand and waved. "C'mon, even if they might've seen us, we need to make sure we have their attention."

Reluctantly, Adam joined the others in waving, standing as tall as he could. If Aarons said it wasn't Protectorate, he was inclined to trust his judgment, though that didn't quiet the unease that was tugging at him. His every instinct was clanging a warning bell.

But there was nothing for it.

The car got larger and larger, and at last Adam saw what Aarons had meant about the markings. They appeared vaguely martial, but they didn't correspond to anything he'd seen on any peacekeeper vehicle. Now they could also see the driver, hunched down in the open-roofed interior, and that he wasn't alone: a woman was seated above him, her blond ponytail whipping in the breeze. She was manning a large mounted gun. The gun was pointed at them.

"*Khara*," Lochlan muttered, lowering his arms.

Splashing across what was left of the river, the car rumbled to a halt in front of him. The woman leaned forward on her gun and pushed her goggles up onto her forehead.

"The fuck're you doing here? How did you get out?"

They all glanced at each other. Aarons turned to her, making no attempt to hide his confusion. "Out?"

"Of the quarantine, wiseass." Her eyes widened. "What the fuck, man, you're in a peacekeeper uniform. How did you get that through processing? Or did you pick it up inside?" She kicked at the back of the driver's seat. "Harlow, I keep telling you, they need to be better about checking for contraband."

Harlow grunted.

"I *am* a peacekeeper," Aarons said gruffly, and shoved Adam forward. "We crashed, a few miles from here. These two are my prisoners. If you can take us into—"

"Yeah, we've heard it all by now. Don't even try it." The woman's tone was flat, slightly drawling—bored. "Look, I don't really give a fuck where you came from. We have our orders, either way. Harlow." Another kick. "Cuff 'em and get 'em in the vehicle. I've got you covered."

"No, wait." Lochlan lifted his hands, his expression pleading, and Adam wasn't sure how much of it was an act. He gritted his teeth, silently willing Lochlan to be quiet, but of course Lochlan wasn't. "He's telling the truth, he's—"

"Shut the fuck up." Aarons slammed a fist into his shoulder and turned his scowling gaze back on the woman. "Who are you with? Protectorate? I'm a lieutenant commander, and I can have you demoted for this. Thrown in the brig to cool your heels for a few days. Take me and my prisoners to—"

The gun roared. Adam flinched hard and almost dropped onto his belly, except for Lochlan's hand at his shoulder. But Aarons remained where he was, staring at the cloud of dust that rose from the bullet impacts at his feet.

"I told you," the woman said placidly, "shut up. One more word and I'll take your legs off. Don't think I won't. Harlow, now."

The man, still silent, slid open a door and clambered out, reaching down to his belt and unhooking a handful of wrist bindings. Adam stood still, hands at his sides, as an awful resignation sunk its blunt claws into him. She meant it.

They were out of options. Again.

Harlow put the wrist binders on them, and for once Lochlan had the sense not to resist. Aarons accepted his in stony silence, glaring at the woman. Cuffed, they were shoved forward toward the car.

"Between me and him," said the woman. "C'mon, we need to get back before nightfall."

The seat was cramped; not really a seat at all so much as a depression probably meant for light cargo. Adam sank into it, his knees nearly at his chest, pressed against Lochlan's side—which wasn't much of a comfort. As Harlow climbed back into the driver's seat and the engine revved, Lochlan leaned close.

"We got out of it before," he breathed. "We will again."

We don't even know what this is. But Adam said nothing, only gave him a tiny nod.

They kept quiet as the car tore across the desert at high speed, its heavy treads chewing up the ground and billowing dust up around them. The desert itself continued on in flat monotony, without even hills or a river to break it up. In spite of everything, Adam felt himself drifting toward a doze, and it seemed as though there wasn't much point in fighting it. Escape, just now, was impossible, boxed in the way they were. Lochlan slumped against him, but he was awake, and when Adam managed briefly to focus on him, Lochlan's dark eyes were alive and keen. Watching.

At last the car began to slow, and Adam jerked himself back to full consciousness, scanning the landscape ahead of them. There was nothing, but then he looked to the left and any words he might have said died in his throat.

Fences. Long and high, topped with cruel loops of razor wire, and what appeared to be guard towers cutting through at intervals. Behind the fences, a mass of rough shelters were crammed, constructed of scrap metal and plastic. Through the gaps between, he caught glimpses of people dressed in rags, their shoulders hunched. Some of them were stumbling. One, a child who couldn't be older than ten, turned to watch them with hollow eyes.

"Home sweet fuckin' home," the woman muttered as the car made an arcing left toward the fences. Adam looked at Lochlan and the eyes that met his were wide and shocked and horrified.

He had no idea what he had expected. But this . . .

They stopped at a reinforced gate flanked by bigger guardhouses. There was a pause, then a loud rattle as the thing opened and closed behind them, followed by another gate in front. Then they were inside, rolling along a wide, muddy track flanked on the left by another fence. To the right was a series of long, low buildings that could be anything from garages to barracks. Here and there were more people dressed in the same plain clothes as the woman and Harlow, though more than a few of these also wore light body armor.

All of them carried rifles.

The car stopped. The woman leaned in, placed her boot in the center of Aarons's back and shoved. "Gate on the left. They're expecting you. If you're lucky, you'll get rations tonight along with the rest."

Numbly, Adam followed Lochlan and Aarons out of the car, staggering a bit on stiff legs. Harlow held his own rifle trained on their backs.

At the fence, another guard cut their bindings loose without a word. He nodded up to someone unseen in one of the towers, and the gate rattled open.

"Go on. We'd just as soon shoot your asses, but that means body disposal and that's a pain."

Aarons walked silently forward. Adam trailed Lochlan, staring at the horror ahead of them. The sun was going down, casting that same weird, orange light over everything, and glinting dully off the metal roofs of the shacks. It made the faces of the people who glanced at them appear sallow and dead. Then again, Adam suspected they might look like that anyway.

The gate closed behind them with a clash. It sounded like finality. They were prisoners once more.

CHAPTER

FOURTEEN

In the soft morning glow of Ashwina's sunlamps, Nkiruka made her way through the winding corridors to Ashwina's great central hall and let its busy sights and sounds and scents settle over her, familiar and comforting. Peaceful, too, in their way, though they also served to stir her to alertness, to help her see the world more clearly.

She spent almost as much time here as she did in the Arched Halls above. The two were, in a way, cousins, and both drew people together. They provided places of connection, communion, and centers for life. The air in the hall was sweet, and Nkiruka had found it soothing since she had first made her home on Ashwina and turned her thoughts to the more distant future.

She had come to Ashwina to learn to fight, to do violence to those who would harm her people, but almost everything she had found here had been focused on anything *but* violence: life, growing things, family, creation, the nourishment of the spirit. All on a ship of war.

Not that it was entirely unexpected. It was common among Bideshi convoys for the defensive ship to be the most in tune with the dance of the stars, for their Old Mother to be the most powerful of the three. Fighters had to be ready to move the quickest, had to be able to see the blow before it came. And anyone who killed had to be able to keep a place inside them that was still compassionate, calm, full of life.

It was about survival. The balance between life and death was part of the routine business of staying alive, every day. Every night.

And the last couple of nights had been difficult in smaller ways. Satya had been calmer, maintaining her own cheerfulness, though Nkiruka could tell it was stretched thin, almost pained. At least there hadn't been coldness between them. If anything there had been a hotter fire, their lovemaking edged with desperation that had been there before—since Ixchel's death and the whispers about replacing her—but had never been so sharp.

Things were coming to a head. They both knew it. And for Nkiruka, the reading had confirmed it.

War. Not just conflict. Not just clashes. Open war. And soon.

She hadn't told anyone but Kae. Not even Satya. But sleep had been elusive since, and she had taken to wandering Ashwina's corridors, losing herself in their harmonious chaos. Always, always, she ended up in the same place. The dusty corridor with the stars outside, where a ghost lingered.

Ixchel.

Now she had some time before the scheduled practice run in the fighters, and though she wasn't hungry, she knew she should eat. She was going sleepless; it didn't mean she also had to starve herself.

And there was something about Ashwina's hall, the sounds of talk and laughter and the transactions in the small marketplace that woke her up. There were smells of spices and cooking food, sweet oils and perfumes, herbs both for cooking and for medicine, as well as for their pleasing scent. Children ran underfoot. People smiled at her and lifted their hands in greeting, and if they wanted something from her, if they expected things that she didn't want to give, their warmth made it easier to forget. For the time being.

Thankfully, none of them tried to drag her into lengthy conversation.

She found herself a bowl of seasoned rice and moved into one of the small gardens to eat it, hoping that her solitude would maintain itself. As she ate, she used that solitude as space to examine the problems before her, and felt herself instinctively shrink from them. For the first time she noticed that the thoughts most hateful were the ones that involved her. Primarily her. Not war on her people, but the prospect of losing the things she wanted. Satya. A future she had been sure was hers.

She shook herself, staring down at the food she had suddenly lost any appetite for. *Chere. Am I really that selfish?*

Surely such a selfish person could never make a good Aalim anyway?

"Nkiruka."

The voice was low, rich, and familiar. Her stomach dropped even farther. She looked up, steeling herself.

"Hello, Adisa."

The old man nodded, the barest hint of a bow. His brown face was deeply lined now, more than it had been before Ixchel's death on the Plain, and though he appeared as hale and hardy as ever, it was no secret how it had aged him. It had left its mark on all of them, but as the leader of the ship's council—unofficially but something didn't have to be official to matter—he had borne the loss harder than most others, and the loss had been heavier. The loss of so many.

The loss of her.

But he still did what was necessary. What was demanded of him.

So naturally he was here now.

"May I sit?"

Nkiruka slid a little farther down the bench, gesturing at the free space. "Please, Elder."

He did so, gathering his robes as he sank down with a sigh. "Thank you. My bones aren't what they used to be. Kindness to your elders now will serve you well when you join our ranks, young lady." He shot her a smile, and some of her tension slipped away. These days he was often so serious, but now and then there were glimpses of his old humor.

Nkiruka hazarded her own smile. "You're not that ancient, surely."

"Aren't I? I feel it in me, despite your courtesy. But I'm not here to discuss my age. We must talk, Nkiru." Her familiar name. Less formal. It did nothing whatsoever to put her at ease. "I think it would be best if we didn't do so here. Will you walk with me?"

Nkiruka swallowed. "I thought you wanted to sit." She cringed inwardly. Part of her had meant it as gentle teasing, since he seemed amenable to it today, but instead it came out like the protest of a child.

But Adisa ignored it. Slowly he rose and held out a hand, beckoning. "I do. But my position requires that I not put my own desires first. Please, come."

That was pointed. Sharply so. He led her out of the main hall and into the winding corridors again, the ship closing in around her in a way that was comfortable rather than claustrophobic. It was more comfortable than the hall had been, and depending on their eventual destination, it might be a good move after all to avoid conducting whatever business he had with her in that great open space.

Except that, after a few minutes of walking, it became apparent that they were heading upward. Up toward the High Fields and the Arched Halls.

She sighed.

"You know that this could go in a particular direction," Adisa said as they climbed the winding stair that would take them to the wide stretch of rolling meadow. "Or at least I could get there by particular means. I could sidle my way around to it through pleasantries and conversation that made you no challenge and no threat, and then when you were lulled I could let my real object stand, and force you to deal with it by surprise."

He fell silent again, and Nkiruka let the silence linger, not because she didn't want to break it but because she honestly had no idea how to do so. She had always found Adisa somewhat intimidating, though he had never been anything but kind to her in the few times they had interacted beyond a glance and a passing nod.

"I could do those things," Adisa said. They were passing through the meadow now, the wood rising up ahead of them with its treetops kissing the curved, transparent ceiling and the sunlamps set into the spiderweb of its frame. "But I think there would be no real surprise in it for you. More, I think it would be an insult to you. You're not a stupid woman, Nkiruka. I know it. You know it. Everyone else is well aware." He halted and abruptly faced her. "Why else would they come to you the way they do?"

Nkiruka shifted from foot to foot. There wasn't really any point in denying it. "You know of that, then."

Adisa smiled faintly. "Of course I do. It's a difficult thing to *not* be aware of, and in my position I have to make it my business to know things. So," he continued, starting to walk again. "I won't take that approach. Instead I'll be direct."

But he said nothing else until they were under the spread, interlaced branches of the Arched Halls, the dimness settling around them like a blanket, along with the quiet creaks and whispers of the trees and the distant singing of those observing old rites.

As every time, the glowbugs came to her. Nkiruka lifted her hands as the two of them walked and the little specks of light circled her fingers as if she herself was bringing them into being.

She could feel Adisa watching her.

"The council has decided that we must choose a new Aalim within two weeks' time," he said. "You are the foremost candidate at this point. I need to know whether, if called, you'll serve your people."

He didn't stop, didn't turn to her, but she gazed at him, her mouth working. It didn't matter how he came to it. There it was in the end. Here, in this moment, she was being asked to choose.

She closed her hands and the glowbugs flew off and were gone.

"I don't know," she whispered. The corners of her eyes prickled and stung.

Adisa stopped. This time he halted her with two hands on her shoulders, and when she scrubbed the tears from her eyes and looked up at him, she saw that his face was grave.

"You must know."

"I *don't*." Didn't he realize what he was asking? Didn't he know what it *meant*? She was opening her mouth to let those words go when it hit her like a slap to the face: of course he knew. "I have a woman," she said, still barely above a whisper. "Satya. I mean to marry her."

"I know it." Adisa gave her shoulders a gentle squeeze and let his hands drop. "So you know that I would prefer not to ask this of you."

"So don't ask it." Nkiruka turned from him and started to make her way toward the deeper halls, half-blind, almost blundering. "There must be others."

"There are." Adisa was following her easily, his voice low and calm behind her. "None of them half as promising as you. And Nkiruka— Nkiru." He stopped her with a hand on her arm and she faced him, flushed, so much angrier than she wanted to be. This time when he spoke his voice wasn't much more than a murmur. "You know the consequences for refusal. Nothing will ever be the same for you. I'm here to tell you now that you *will* be asked, because I'm only one member of the council, one in a group of many, and I won't be able to dissuade them from you. They wouldn't consider romantic attachments a sufficient reason. They never have before."

"'Romantic attachments,'" Nkiruka echoed scornfully, and barely stopped herself from spitting into the dirt. The once-welcoming Arched Halls now seemed to threaten her, branches becoming hands reaching down for her, intending to clutch and squeeze. "That's all they are? I'm *not suited*, Adisa. Do you think I would be fighting it like this if I were? Do the suited ones say no?"

Adisa was silent for a few moments, and Nkiruka gazed at his unreadable face, trembling. She had overstepped. She had overstepped so far. But she was no longer certain where the line was. Maybe it was moving.

"Many times."

Nkiruka closed her eyes, tears escaping down her cheeks.

"I saw her dancing," Adisa said softly. "The death-dance. Her knives in her hands, burning with life. I had never seen anything so beautiful. I never have since. I would have made her my wife. Lived out my life with her. Not a day goes by, Nkiru, when I don't wonder what might have been. Not *one day*."

Nkiruka took a long, shuddering breath. She knew it. Most people on Ashwina knew. But he had never spoken of it, nor had Ixchel. The subject had never been so blunt, so soaked in pain. "Maybe you never should have had to choose."

"Maybe. Nevertheless. We did. And you remember Lakshmi. I know you do. We all do. She chose—and then in the end she chose poorly. She chose one over many, after she had sworn to do the latter, and now she no longer walks these halls. Regardless, she had to choose. So will you." He glanced away from her, up into the branches through which the stars shone. Somewhere among the tangled roots of the place, Ixchel had been laid to rest, but there was no record of where, and those who had interred her had done so under the influence of shala, their memories blurred and muddied.

She might be anywhere. So she was everywhere.

"Will I?"

Adisa looked down at her again, and what she saw on his face was kindness and hardness and a sadness so deep and so vast it was like gazing into the night itself.

"Yes, you will. Sooner or later, my dear, we all must."

CHAPTER

FIFTEEN

"Well, this might actually be a step up."

Together, Adam and Lochlan stared at Aarons. Lochlan coughed a laugh—he had grown to respect Aarons in the past day, if not exactly to *like* him—but this seemed like the babbling of a crazy man. "*What?*"

Aarons lifted his bowl of sour mush. "We have food, such as it is. They gave us water. And we're alive. Tell me that's not at least sort of better than we were doing before."

"Yeah, *mitr*, I think you might be working from a different definition of 'better' than I am," Lochlan said dryly.

They were seated on a set of dirty crates set against a wall of one of the shacks—helping to hold it up, as far as Lochlan could tell. Since they had stepped inside, they had been left alone, and the people even appeared to be taking pains to avoid them. But they were being watched, and from all sides. Not only by the guard towers but by the ragged people of the camp, peering at them from doorways and makeshift alleys and from under lowered brows as they passed. When a harsh horn blast had announced supper, they had experienced their first real close contact with any of the camp's other inhabitants, but even crushed together in a line to receive a plastic tube of water and a bowl of watery gruel, no one had spoken to them, and no one had met their eye.

No one was looking at them now either. People were heading inside their shacks. Threads of smoke were drifting up here and there as the chill of the night descended, prisoners taking what snatches of warmth they could make with whatever they could find. Everyone seemed exhausted, stooped, some nearly staggering. More than a few trembled, holding their hands close to their chests.

They must be suffering from lack of wholesome food as much as anything else.

Lochlan glanced down at his bowl and, twisting his mouth in distaste, tipped it back and drank the last of it before tossing it to the ground.

"Tastes like hydrated nutrient powder." He made another face. "You know, like chalk."

"Might *be* hydrated nutrient powder," Adam said, draining his own bowl and discarding it beside Lochlan's. "Or chalk. Both're cheap, and I don't get the sense that they care all that much about keeping these people alive. Or healthy."

Aarons grunted. Lochlan nodded. A woman and two children stopped in passing, the children—a girl and a boy—staring at them with huge eyes. The woman appeared to be in her early thirties, her black hair cut short, her skin a deep brown—almost as deep as Kyle's had been, though not quite. Hesitantly, Adam waved, and after a moment of apparent internal warfare, the girl darted forward and scooped their bowls out of the mud, backing away just as swiftly with her gaze locked on them, as if she expected them to lunge at her.

"No, hey," Lochlan said, lifting a hand. "It's okay, you can—"

Muttering something, the woman ushered the boy and girl onward, and they were lost in the maze of shacks.

"You see her?" Adam murmured. He was looking after the small family with a strange expression. Almost, Lochlan thought with a ripple of unease, haunted.

"Yeah, she seemed fucking terrified of us." Aarons scowled—if possible—even more than he already was. "How's that make her any different from anyone else here? Seriously, I know I'm intimidating, but come—"

"No, I don't mean that." Adam was rubbing his hands together, almost dry-washing them. Lochlan put out his hand, closed it over Adam's, and Adam met his eyes, his own as wide as the children's had been.

"The woman. Her hands. Did you see her hands? Lock, they were shaking." He drew in a sharp breath. "What did she call this place? The woman who picked us up? 'Quarantine.' Shit, I can't . . . I don't know why I didn't think of it until now."

"Adam—" Lochlan could feel the direction this was going in. He could feel the shape of it as if it were emerging from the darkness, weaving itself into sense second by second. A quarantine. Yet, clearly exhausted, malnourished, and generally hopeless as these people were, none of them had any obvious signs of contagious disease. No explosive coughing, no sneezing, no lesions, no rashes or flushes of fever. Of course, not all serious illnesses would have visible signs, but even so . . .

"Look." Adam spread his hands out in front of him. "In a place with conditions this bad, wouldn't you *expect* to see some sick people? Sick in really obvious ways, I mean. Imagine if they were Bideshi."

Aarons hunched forward, narrowing his eyes at him. "You're saying . . . Holy shit, Yuga."

"They're all Protectorate," Lochlan said. He knew it, now. They had only taken a close look at the one woman and her children, but now that he thought back, there had been more. People in the line had stumbled, nearly fallen—he had chalked it up to weariness and hunger, but now he wasn't sure. And there was their appearance, their eerily perfect features, even worn and haggard and filthy. Like Adam's, more than one way.

"They're all Protectorate," Adam echoed. "And they're all sick with what I had. This is what they've been doing with the people who can't be ignored anymore, Aarons. When there were too many of us to exile, they had to find another way." He pressed his palm against his mouth, then let it fall. "I never thought . . . I should have."

Lochlan lowered his head. He hadn't thought either, mostly because it was unthinkable. He'd supported sending Adam away, but the truth was that exiling someone dying and in need of help and comfort would be one of the most shameful possible acts for a Bideshi. People were exiled for other reasons. Transgressions. Crimes.

This . . . Never. Never for any reason.

"Fucking hell." Aarons didn't sound horrified. He fell silent, and the three of them were quiet for a few moments. Lochlan reached once more for Adam's hand and held it, and to him it felt as it always did: like an anchor.

He could only hope his was the same for Adam.

"So why haven't they simply killed them?" Aarons asked, glancing around at the camp again. It was now almost deserted, but for sickly lights showing from inside the shacks and the few thin lines of smoke. "That would be a lot easier. If they can disappear these people, you'd think dumping them in a pit somewhere would be nothing to them."

Adam shook his head, eyes wide and face slightly pale. "I don't know. Maybe we can find out." Abruptly he got to his feet, twisting his hand free from Lochlan's. "We have to talk to them, find out more. We can't just sit here, I need to—"

"What you need to do is *rest*." Lochlan stood up beside him, touching his arm. He had seen this in Adam before, this determination to do whatever he thought was right, whatever the consequences for himself, and each time he had dragged Adam back from the brink, but each time it was tiring. "They'll all be bedding down, anyway. You waltz into their houses and wake up their kids— I don't think that's going to make you many friends, *chusile*."

"I can't *wait*." Adam turned on Lochlan, his eyes wilder than they had been. "Lock, this is . . . This is what I came out here for. This is what I was trying to find. I didn't know it then, but I came back to help people. These people *need help*."

"And how exactly are you going to do that?"

"I don't *know*." Adam spit the final word out and stalked a few feet away, raking his hands into his hair and tugging at the strands. When Lochlan glanced back at Aarons, the man shot him a warning look. *Get a handle on him*. "I'll figure it out. I can't do that by . . . I'm not going to drag an answer out of the air, Lock, you *know* that."

"I know a lot of things," Lochlan said softly. Soothingly. Once this had been the kind of thing Kae had done for him, kept his manner smooth when Lochlan had been passion and jagged edges. Settling calm over him with his even, controlled temper. Lochlan had never been good at doing that for himself. "I know these people are scared, Adam. I know they have every fucking reason to be. And I know that if you charge up to them all 'Hi, my name is Adam Yuga d'Bideshi and I'm here to save you but I don't know how yet,' you'll only freak them out, badly. They'll think you're insane. You need to be careful about how you do this. And you can't do it when you really *are* pretty much out of your mind."

He moved forward, curled his arms around Adam's waist from behind and pressed his lips to the nape of Adam's neck. "Rest, *chusile*. Rest with me. We'll plan in the morning."

Adam tensed—and then let out a long breath, relaxing back against Lochlan's chest. For a moment the rest of the world fell away—the horror of the camp and the fear of the future, and it was only them, orbiting each other in that dance they knew so well by now.

We fit. We fit better than anything.

"Rest where?" Aarons said from behind them—his tone less gruff and the words less pointed. "I got no idea how we'd find a vacant shelter, and I'm guessing we wouldn't be in for the most pleasant night bedded down in the mud."

"You can stay with me."

As one, they turned. Standing behind them all, her hands folded in front of her, was the woman they had seen before, the one who had led her children away. They weren't with her now, and in the garish light that came from the guard towers, she appeared older than she had before.

Adam pulled himself free from Lochlan's arms and took a step toward her—slow, hesitant, raising his hands. "Are you sure? That would be—"

"That would be very kind," Lochlan finished. In happier surroundings he would be turning on the charm full blast, but that felt wrong here, so instead he worked to keep his outward self calm, undemanding. *Be like Kae,* he thought. *Kae would be perfect here.* And suddenly, in a wave of dull pain, he missed his old friend so much. "We're new here, and I—"

"I know." She gave them a thin, wry smile. "That much is obvious. No one gets much out of being neighborly here, at least not right away, but usually it doesn't cost much, either, so we tend to hang together if no one makes trouble. It's all we have here." She pointed at Aarons, who looked back at her with his unscarred brow raised. "Why is he dressed like a peacekeeper?"

"Because he was one," Aarons said gruffly. "Not anymore."

The woman nodded. "You're not the first one I've seen. There are peacekeepers in here. They got fucked like the rest of us." She sighed and glanced over her shoulder. "I need to get back. Are you coming?"

"Yeah. Yeah, we're coming." Adam nodded at Lochlan. *Come on.*

Together they walked down a row of shacks and then another, turning to the right and heading toward the fence. There was no rhyme or reason in the way the shacks were constructed, no indication at all that they'd been constructed by whoever had established the camp. The prisoners appeared to have been given a pile of scrap material and instructed to fend for themselves.

The woman stopped and gestured to a shack on the end of the row, nearly pressed up against the fence itself. It wasn't large, but it looked strong and tidy, and there was even a window beside the plastic-covered doorway, shaded in the same material.

"The fence is electrified," the woman said. "So it's more dangerous out here. But the air is better. And the kids know not to go near it. I guess everything's a trade." She pulled the sheeting aside and nodded into the shack's dim interior. Adam moved forward without hesitation, Lochlan following, and Aarons bringing up the silent rear.

The ceiling was so low that Lochlan had to bend his head slightly. What light there was came from an ancient plasma lantern. Bowls were stacked in the corner, a few clearly in the process of being broken apart; the material might have some use, though what wasn't clear. There was a low sleeping mat made of scrap cloth, and the boy and girl were seated on it, huddled together, watching them with those same huge eyes.

"Hey," Lochlan said, dropping into a crouch in front of them and putting on his friendliest smile. He liked children, had always done so, but these were nothing like the open, usually gregarious children of Ashwina. "Nice to see you again."

"They don't like strangers." Lochlan glanced back to see the woman lowering the sheeting across the door again and securing it in place with a metal hook set against one side of the doorframe. "They don't like anyone, really. I'm not sure they even like me anymore." She stared at Lochlan, hard and unflinching. "You're Bideshi."

Lochlan straightened up. There was no point in denying it. Though her tone left him unsure as to whether this was an accusation or merely an observation. "I am."

"What the hell are you doing here, then?" She studied him. "You wouldn't be sick, would you? Seems like this only hits Protectorate.

Not that they tell us anything," she added bitterly. "But we pool what we know."

Adam looked from Lochlan to Aarons, and after a fraction of a second, Lochlan knew what he was searching for. He nodded. Aarons said nothing; his eye narrowed. Adam turned back to the woman again.

"We're not from the camp. Our vessel crashed outside the fence. They found us and just assumed. Or they didn't care."

"That sounds like them." The woman crossed the room, pushing past Lochlan, and sank down next to her children, tugging the girl into her lap and beginning to comb her fingers through her hair, working out some of the worse tangles. "They don't give a damn about any of us. Far as we can tell they're here to pull their time and get off-world as soon as possible. You know why we're here." She didn't look up, and as Lochlan studied her hands, he saw the same shaking that Adam had seen. It was faint, barely a tremble, but it was there and it was constant. And very familiar.

"Yes." Adam took a seat on the boards opposite her. After a second or two, Lochlan sat down beside him. Aarons remained standing against the wall, watching them all in silence. He seemed to have withdrawn into himself, and it was making Lochlan uneasy. More than he already was. "We've seen it before. But we didn't— We didn't know they were doing *this*."

In the woman's lap, the girl's eyelids were drooping. The boy was leaning into her side, his eyes already closed.

"I know you don't know much." Lochlan glanced up and back at Aarons, startled. Aarons ignored him. "But it would be helpful if you could tell us everything you do know."

The woman appeared to consider, her hands continuing to move. Then she nodded, her mouth tightening. Outside, the wind let out a sudden howl, but she gave no indication that she had heard it at all.

"I'm one of the better-off ones here," she said. "It started showing in me a couple of weeks ago, and it's progressing more slowly. I went to a doctor and he didn't say much, just gave me a referral to a specialist. Who turned out to be a group of peacekeepers with guns. I should have known—a *specialist*? Come on. Those are never good news anyway. But I guess I was afraid." She dipped her head, her hands going still—or mostly still but for their slight palsy. "They rounded up my kids. Seems like it's what they do as a matter of course. There are a lot of kids here, and most of them are manifesting. Maybe it's worse in the next generation."

"What about their father?" Adam asked.

"We're . . . estranged. I'm not sure he even knows we disappeared. Or cares. I don't know how, but they're good at keeping this quiet."

"They're *excellent* at keeping things quiet." Adam's voice was low, but it was full of such bitterness that it burned in Lochlan's ears. "You might even call them specialists in it."

"Yeah, well." The woman rolled a shoulder. "Like I said, I'm better off than most. I haven't seen it yet in them," she nodded at the children, "but I get the feeling it's just a matter of time. And then . . . I have no idea. People here are dying. One or two a day. And they keep bringing more in.

"We know that this isn't the only quarantine. A few people are transfers from another one. What we also know is that they *are* trying to find some kind of cure, here. We think that's one reason why they don't kill us all outright. This isn't only a place to dump inconvenient people until they have the courtesy to die."

Adam started. "What do you mean, a 'cure'? How do you know?"

"People disappear," she said simply. "Some of them come back, much worse. They have scars, needle marks on their arms. Someone's been performing medical procedures on them. None of them talk about what happened. Most can't talk at all, and they die within a few days. Once or twice people have claimed to see where they go. There's a building on the far end of the compound. Separate from the rest. No windows. We obviously don't know for sure what's going on, but . . . If they're doing experiments on people, I can't think of why else they would be."

"*Khara*," Adam whispered, and Lochlan echoed the word in his mind. He had been ready to assume the worst of the Protectorate since long ago, but now "worst" was revising its meaning every few hours.

They called themselves civilized. But he couldn't imagine anything more barbaric than this. Even if he hadn't seen the massacre on Caldor.

"So we try to survive," the woman went on, either ignoring the Bideshi obscenity or not understanding it. "Day by day. I'm not even sure why, a lot of the time. Either we die out there or we die in here. They give us enough food and water to make it slow, and sometimes that feels like torture. But the starving and the thirst are most of what we have to worry about, at least from them. We're immune to everything else, of course, and something keeps us all going. Keeps me going." She turned to the boy as he lay down on the rags, wordlessly tugging his sister with him. They curled close together, their eyes still shut tight. "I think maybe it's them. That's instinct, isn't it? See the next generation through. It's what we're supposed to do."

"You love them," Aarons said, as if commenting on the weather. "That's enough."

"You think so? I wonder." The woman swiped her hands over her face, her shoulders hunched. "Go to sleep. The nights here aren't very long, and tomorrow I need you to move on. You can't stay here again." She nodded to the boards. "That's all I have. But I guess it's better than the mud."

"It'll be fine." Adam slid back, trying to arrange himself. "Thank you."

The woman shrugged and lay beside her children. "Shut off the lamp before you bed down."

The three of them settled in silence, Lochlan and Adam close together and Aarons a little way away. As Lochlan closed his eyes, the light on the other side of his lids dimmed and darkened. Then there was only the wind and breathing, and the soft creak of the fence as it flexed.

Adam's warm body was against Lochlan's arm, close to his side. Half on instinct, he pressed closer to it, reaching for Adam's hip, but Adam stopped him with a hand on his arm.

"Maybe we shouldn't," he whispered.

"*Chusile.*" A dry smile pulled at the corners of his mouth. "I'm not exactly going to fuck you in a single-room shack with children less than a foot away."

"No, I know that, I just . . ."

Lochlan frowned. Adam actually sounded flustered, a tone he couldn't recall hearing in weeks. "If she sees . . . I want to stay on her good side. Okay? She's already noticed you're Bideshi, she—"

"I thought you were Bideshi now." Something in Lochlan grew cold, and he withdrew his hand. This shit again. Except no, this was different shit. This was shit that he honestly hadn't expected, and it stung. "Anyway, she didn't seem like she cared. Not sure why *touching* would bother her."

"Lock . . . That's not what I meant, I—" Adam's whisper was pleading, but Lochlan shifted away. Maybe it was petty. But it still *hurt*.

Don't sulk, Kae's distant voice came reproachfully. *He's still new to this. Don't throw a tantrum.*

"It's fine." Lochlan turned onto his back, slinging one arm under his head. "You're probably right. Whatever. Get some sleep."

But he could tell that Adam wasn't sleeping. And he didn't either, not for what seemed like a long time.

Aarons, meanwhile, snored away on the other side of the room, and the last thing Lochlan remembered thinking that night was, *Bastard.*

CHAPTER

SIXTEEN

Morning started with a horn blast.

Adam sat bolt upright, every muscle in his body tensed, pumping with adrenaline. For an awful moment he had no idea where he was—walls of scrap metal and canvas? Foul air. Then he remembered, and the core of him sank into a deep pit somewhere in the vicinity of his stomach.

That didn't explain the horn. But early morning light was coming in through gaps in the doorway, and the woman was already getting up from her mat, her children stirring and blinking. "Morning rations," she said by way of explanation, and nudged Lochlan with her foot. "Get up. I'm not going to miss a meal on your account, and if you know what's good for you, you won't miss one either."

Getting up hurt. Whether it was the night on the board or the bruising from the crash or both, Adam wasn't sure, but an ache had settled deep into every muscle, and it was obvious that Lochlan and Aarons were feeling the same. Lochlan sat up and shook his head, trying to blink the sleep out of his eyes. The woman stepped past them, her children in tow, and stopped in the act of lifting aside the sheeting over the door, shooting them an unreadable glance.

"You have about five minutes before there won't be any point in getting in line at all. I'd hurry."

And then she was gone.

"C'mon," Lochlan muttered, getting to his feet and reaching down to give Adam a hand. "Lines, I reek."

"We all do." Aarons stretched his limbs gingerly—wincing as he flexed his wounded shoulder—and heading for the door. "My guess is you get used to it. Nothing to do about it now, anyway. She's right, we can't afford to miss a meal, not with what they're feeding us. Let's go."

The entire camp was moving, a slow mass of people seething to where the food had been given out the night before—the same gate they'd been pushed through—vats on wheels and a stack of bowls, flanked by armored guards. Were they actually peacekeepers? Were they drawn from some other source? It was impossible to say for sure.

The lines were already long by the time they reached them, and they slipped into what seemed like the shortest line, though it likely made no real difference. He searched the crowd for the woman, but she was nowhere to be seen.

They had to find her again. This was an opening, a chance to connect. He couldn't let it slip away.

There was no conversation to speak of, though there were voices—grunts, groans of pain. The woman had been right about how many were seriously ill, and now in full daylight it was even easier to see: many of the gathered people appeared to be walking with difficulty, some leaning on others. The majority of them had shaking hands, some quite badly. The middle stages of the disease. Those in the later stages probably couldn't stand or walk at all.

So what happened to them? Were they fed? Or was each person in line only allowed their share and nothing else?

He guessed the latter. He didn't remember seeing anyone from the night before receiving more than their own helping.

The line edged forward. Lochlan moved a little too quickly and bumped into Adam's back, catching himself with a hand on Adam's hip, lingering—and then flinching away. Adam was puzzled—Lochlan was always watching for excuses to touch him. This wasn't like him.

But then he remembered.

Shit.

He had royally fucked that up, hadn't he? His simple precaution, drawn from a memory of what his people were like and what they expected to see and not to see. Aarons didn't care, so far as he could tell, but Aarons was Aarons, and Adam recalled enough of his life before—all his anxieties and fears—to know that Sinder's attitude was far more representative.

He was with a man. He was with a *Bideshi*. So why shouldn't he keep that particular piece of information under wraps until he had a better sense of where he stood?

I thought you were Bideshi now.

He knew why. He knew perfectly well.

All through the line, Lochlan didn't speak to him. Adam was handed his water and gruel and he lingered on the edges of the crowd, waiting for Lochlan and Aarons to catch up. People were dispersing. Latecomers were arriving and being turned away. A few of them raised their voices angrily and were shoved back with the butts of rifles, but most simply left with their heads down. What afflicted them was worse than merely sickness, Adam thought, watching them with his food going cold in his hands. There was no fight in most of these people. They had accepted their fate.

They had been told all their lives that sickness was a sign of unworthiness. Perhaps they believed it.

Lochlan and Aarons joined him. Lochlan kept his distance, not meeting Adam's gaze, but Aarons drew up alongside him as they walked farther from the gate, appearing not to notice the coolness between them.

"Today we need to scout the fences, see if we can find any weak points, any blind spots." His already twisted mouth twisted further. "I don't expect to find any, of course, but we may as well know what we're dealing with."

Adam glanced back at Lochlan. "So you're thinking escape."

"I'm not thinking anything yet." Aarons leaned closer, his voice dropping. "But we can't stay here. We might actually be hidden pretty well in this place, maybe better than we would be anywhere else. Even so, it's only a matter of time before Sinder and his people track us down. And then they'll have us backed into a corner. Again."

"It's not enough to merely get out," Lochlan said quietly from behind them. "We'd need a ship. Some way of getting off-world."

"Yeah, that sort of occurred to me," Aarons muttered. "I'm working on it. You work on it too."

They settled where they had the night before, and while people passed them, the three of them still only garnered looks and no words. They ate in silence. Adam barely tasted his food; not that there was much to taste. Unbidden, the memory of his first meal on Ashwina came to him: Kae leading him into the great central hall and to the stall in the market, getting him the savory meat and the cooked greens.

How good they had been. How beautiful the place was, how it had caught his attention and didn't let it go. How it had been so far beyond what he had ever imagined, in a lifetime of stories about savagery and darkness. How much would he give to be back there now?

When they were done, Aarons stacked their bowls against one of the crates, since there was no refuse deposit point in evidence, and the children had seemed to have an interest in collecting them. Aarons got to his feet and Adam and Lochlan followed, Adam groaning as the pain rushed back into his muscles.

"Not much point in waiting." Aarons gestured to the fences. "Let's split up, go in opposite directions and meet in the middle. I guess you two want to go together?"

Lochlan glanced at Adam. Adam stared at Aarons, jaw working, and finally said, "Yeah. We do."

He didn't catch Lochlan's expression then. He wasn't sure he wanted to.

Aarons looked from one of them to the other, brow raised, and nodded. "All right. You go left along the perimeter. Adam, a word?"

Lochlan moved on ahead, down the row of shacks toward the fence. Adam watched him go, and then Aarons touched his arm. It was a surprisingly light touch from a man so rough around the edges. Adam turned to him with new unease in the pit of his stomach.

"Is something going on between you two? Anything I should know? Or is this your average lover's quarrel?"

"Everything's fine."

"Yeah. Sure it is." Aarons's lips twitched in what might have been thin amusement. "Look, whatever. It's none of my business, and I frankly don't give a fuck. Just don't let it get in the way of getting out of here. We need to *go*, and *soon*. If you think I won't bury my foot up both your asses, think again. Now get."

Adam lingered for a few seconds, searching his face. Aarons's scars made it difficult to read him, but he could detect no disgust on the man's face, only impatience. He didn't care. He really didn't. At last Adam followed Lochlan's receding back.

The next half hour or so was spent in silence as they walked. Nearer the fence, the mud wasn't quite so thick, and the air was, as the woman had said, a bit better. They walked slowly, casually, and if any guards saw them, they might well conclude that he and Lochlan were simply wandering with the same kind of aimlessness most of the prisoners seemed to feel, and leave them be. One thing that he gathered might work in their favor—whatever plan they came up with—was the general disinterest that the guards seemed to have in their prisoners. The three of them had undergone no processing on entering, though the woman who had brought them in had mentioned the possibility. He had seen no counting of people, no care taken to regulate what went on behind the inner fence. Provided people stayed within its bounds, they appeared to be left mostly to their own devices.

But a healthy part of his focus was elsewhere. It was on Lochlan's back, his profile, the tense line of his mouth. Searching for a way in.

Finally he put out a hand and stopped the other man, his determination steeling itself. "Lock, hold up."

Lochlan turned to him, eyes narrowed. "What?"

"We need to talk. About last night."

Lochlan huffed out a laugh. "You honestly think we've got time for that right now?"

"I think we can make time. What the hell are we doing here, anyway? Aarons said, there's probably no weaknesses."

"There might be." That familiar, petulant tone was creeping into Lochlan's voice, the mode of speech that always made Adam want to punch him. "You don't know either way."

"*Lock.*" Adam rolled his eyes. "Could you be an adult for five minutes? Please?"

"Oh, fuck *you*, you fucking *raya*." Lochlan spun away from him, throwing up his hands. "You know, I don't get you. Not even a little. You reject them, you say you want to be with me, and I think maybe you've shed all that fucking bullshit they stuffed your mind with back when you were one of them. Then you pull this. She wouldn't have *cared*."

"You don't know that."

"I'm pretty fucking *sure*." Lochlan faced him again, arms folded across his chest and his dark eyes even darker than usual. "I would— Do you have any idea what I'd give for you? At all? You didn't know me before; what I was like. What it took to let go of that. Do you have *any* idea what you mean to me?" The anger was still there, but now it was being overridden by something else, something that sounded more like hurt than anything else, and Adam's throat clenched.

"I have some idea," he said softly. "Lock . . ." He pushed past Lochlan, closer to the fence. "You keep saying I'm one of you."

"Well? Aren't you?"

"Yes. And no." Adam sighed again and closed his eyes. "Lock, I'm never going to be completely one of you. I can't be. I'm not from your world, I haven't gone through what you have. I'll never know your whole history, everything that makes your people who you are. I want to, I wish I could—you were so kind to me . . . But I can't. I'll always be a little bit of an outsider. I'll always be a tourist. No matter how much you love me, you can't change that."

He paused, chewing on his lower lip. Lochlan didn't speak at all.

"All that 'bullshit' they stuffed my mind with? That might never go away. Not totally. I don't see the world through your eyes, and you *can't* see it through mine. You don't know what it does to you, living your life in fear of who you are. That fear doesn't simply leave you because you want it to."

His voice died. When he felt Lochlan's hand at the small of his back, he stiffened, but Lochlan didn't remove his hand. "*Chusile* . . . Look, I'm sorry."

"I didn't think I could ever have this." He pressed back, his shoulders against Lochlan's chest. They were in full view of anyone, and he wanted, so much, to not care. "I thought I was always going to be alone."

"Would you believe I did too?"

Adam turned, staring. "You were . . . You were never alone. You had friends, you had . . ." He didn't entirely succeed in stifling a chuckle. "You had a *parade* of people marching into your bed. Some of them marched right over me."

"And believe me, I had a *lot* of fun. But that wasn't the same." Lochlan laid a hand against Adam's cheek. "It was . . . I don't know.

Maybe I was making up for something. Trying to, anyway. But you have to know . . . I've never felt like this before. About anyone. Not even . . ." A strange expression passed over his face. "Never mind."

"No, what?"

"This is the weirdest fucking place to be having this conversation."

"It was always going to be weird." Adam gave him a crooked smile, and it all felt better. A little. "Weird is what we do."

"I guess. Okay. If you must know . . ." He tipped his head back, exhaling. "I was in love with Kae. Once. I thought I was. Sort of."

Adam barked his own surprised laugh. "*Kae*?"

Lochlan scowled. "If you're going to laugh at me, I'm sorry I told you."

"No, no, it's just . . . *Kae*."

"Yeah, and he's *beautiful*. You've seen him; you're really that shocked? We were best friends growing up. We understood each other. I knew him better than anyone. I was one of the first people he told when he decided that he had to . . . remake himself. Strip away everything that wasn't him. I *do* love him. You know him. You know it would be easy . . . to feel that way."

"I do know him," Adam said softly. "Yeah. I do see how it would be, with how he is. He was . . . You remember how kind to me he was, when I came to Ashwina." He gave Lochlan a faint smile. "Much kinder than you. Maybe I should have fallen for him."

"If you're not going to take this seriously . . ." Lochlan rolled his eyes, but his exasperation clearly wasn't meant. "You know, then. He might be easy to fall in love with, but when he knew who he was . . . He told me I couldn't be with him like that. Shut me down gently. But yeah, I carried a torch for a while. Lovelorn and sighing, that was me." Lochlan's mouth twisted, and there was a hint of fondness in it. "I needed to know someone that deeply in order to be with them that way. Or I thought I did."

"You couldn't have known me." Adam shook his head. "I was so different from you. I still am."

"Maybe not that different. I know it doesn't make sense; why does that matter? *Chusile*, all I really *want* is to be with you. That's why I'm here. Don't question it. Don't make *me* question it."

"I'll try," Adam whispered. His throat was closing up again, his eyes prickling, but it wasn't unpleasant. They were standing in the midst of shit and sickness and people with guns, but somehow he felt lighter than he had in days. "I can't promise I'll always get it right . . . But I promise I'll try."

Lochlan gazed at him for a long moment. For once, his face was difficult to read, and Adam felt something tug at his gut. Lochlan was *always* easy to read. The man couldn't hide anything, didn't ever try. And that didn't seem like what he was doing now—his tone was all raw honesty, but his expression was shifting, difficult to pin down. It seemed more like . . .

It seemed more like *he* wasn't sure of what he was feeling.

"That's all I want," Lochlan said at last. "That's . . . Adam, that's all."

And there didn't seem to be much more to say.

There were, as Aarons had predicted, no obvious weaknesses, and no blind spots that they could see. The fence was solid, in good repair, and the guard posts were placed at perfectly regular intervals, all of them occupied.

But there was something else.

They'd just finished their inspection, and Aarons had come into view down the fence, and Lochlan waved at him. Adam did the same, then turned his attention back to the fence again, past its links and coils of wire—and to the distant buildings on the other side.

Hangars. Ships parked beyond. The hangars weren't especially large and neither were the transports, but potentially large enough. Enough to hold . . .

He halted, grabbed at Lochlan's arm. "Look."

Lochlan drew in a breath. "*Chere*, why didn't we see them when we came in before?"

"I think that line of buildings was in the way. Or maybe we were just distracted. Whatever. Lock, those are big enough to . . ."

Lochlan stared at him for a moment. Then he shook his head vehemently. "Adam, you *can't*. Stop it. Get that out of your head right fucking now."

"No, it could work." Adam's heart was racing as he glanced back at the ships again. "We just have to figure out how to do it."

"Do what?" Aarons stopped beside Lochlan, following his gaze. "Oh . . . Fucking hell, of course. They have ships, they have to. They need ways of getting up and down."

"He doesn't mean only us," Lochlan said tersely. "Lost his fucking mind, if you ask me."

Aarons arched a brow "So what does he—" Then his misshapen mouth dropped open. "No. *Absolutely* fucking not."

"I'm not leaving these people." Now that the idea had come to him, he felt abruptly calmer. Determined, but coolly so. Suddenly everything was making sense. He had no idea how he would get to it, but he could see the endpoint. What he had been seeking for weeks. "You can't ask me to do that."

"I'm not *asking* anything. You're leaving them."

"I'm not."

"Adam," Lochlan said desperately, "They're all *sick*. Did you see them, before? Some of them can't even fucking *walk*. You're going to break out, steal a ship, load them onto it, and run?"

"I don't think one would do it. We'll need at least two."

"*Adam.*"

"I know they can't walk. They will." Adam smiled, and the smile felt a little hysterical in a quiet kind of way. Crazed. This *idea* was crazy, Lochlan was right.

But his entire life had been crazy for quite a while.

You must, Ixchel whispered into his ear. He sensed her, tossing a glance over his shoulder at the hangars with eyes that were whole and bright and saw everything. He was remembering the Arched Halls on the night he was Named, sinking into the roots of the universe, spinning madly through a chaos of possibility. Being on the Plain of Heaven, the agony and the death all around him, but along with it the sense that he had reached something, touched something, let part of it enter him. Only it had always been there, waiting for him to find it.

"On this ground, my beloved child, you may be an Aalim."

When she had said that, he hadn't understood. He had barely even marked it as significant. But what he had done . . . The Plain had allowed him to find power in his core, power for which he hadn't been trained, hadn't been *bred*. Power, according to the precepts of the Protectorate, that he shouldn't have had.

Except perhaps that was what she had truly been showing him. He had it. He always had.

The gifts he had uncovered in himself weren't confined to such a select few. They couldn't be. Not if he had somehow used them.

"I'm going to get these people out. But first, I'm going to heal them."

CHAPTER

SEVENTEEN

"I'm not *demanding* anything," Sinder said patiently. "I'm *asking*, and I'm trying to ask nicely. I told you, we're seeking Adam Yuga, and I'm guessing you're aware of how high-priority a fugitive he is, so if you assist us, I can't see how it wouldn't be—"

"And I keep telling you," said the woman on the comm screen, her perfectly coifed hair and her neutral expression nearly disguising her calculating eyes. She had been speaking placidly since she had answered the hail, and it was beginning to be infuriating. The fact that she resembled images he had seen of Melissa Cosaire wasn't helping at all. It was, in fact, freaking him out a bit. "You're not even authorized to be down here. I don't care who you're looking for. I could have your entire fleet commandeered merely for having seen what you've seen. I still might, if you push me."

"If you would explain what it is we're supposed to have seen—"

The woman laughed. "Are you serious? Then we really *would* have to take some extreme measures. This is all classified, Mr. Sinder. The facility, the planet, all of it. Highest code clearance only. If you don't have that, you're entitled to nothing from me. So take my advice, turn around right now and go. Somewhere. Else."

Sinder sat back and closed his eyes briefly, watching the patterns dance on the inside of his lids. He was seated in his quarters, without even Alkor present, and he was bullshitting his way through this as best he could, but he was rapidly realizing that he was in over his head. They wouldn't let his people land. They wouldn't even let them into the airspace anymore. They were clearly Protectorate, but not any branch of the government or of the quasi-private UTCA security corps that he had ever encountered before. It wouldn't be wise to assume he outranked them. Secrets like this were usually kept for powerful reasons.

And what were they guarding? What could be in that camp that they didn't want him to *see*? They had claimed to be able to detect images being captured from orbit, and while Sinder had his doubts about the existence of such technology, he didn't want to risk it. Not so long as he wasn't sure what he was dealing with. His rank, if this went well, stood to improve a great deal. It would be wise to exercise a little caution.

"What if," he said slowly, leaning forward. "What if I were to apply for clearance? Would you be able to cooperate with me then?"

The woman looked skeptical. "*Able* is one thing. You can't merely give me your proof of clearance and expect to be able to waltz down here and do whatever you please. I have orders. I'd need orders that supersede those."

"I can get those, too." He carefully maintained his confidence; he had gotten where he was by assuming that he could get what he wanted and then finding a way to make it happen. He would. He had cause.

The woman shrugged. "You want to try; I guess I can't stop you. But you'll need to withdraw from orbit while you take care of that. I can't have you hanging around here for the rest of whatever. If you come back here without that clearance, your entire fleet is mine for breakfast. And you're in a brig. You get me?"

"Perfectly." Sinder smiled, showing his teeth. *Bitch.* "I'll return as soon as I can. Thank you *very* much for all your kind assistance."

The woman gave him a sharp nod, and the screen went dark.

Sinder sat back, his head tipped up toward the ceiling, and stared at nothing at all. He should report in to his superiors anyway, but he hadn't done so since Yuga and the others had escaped. His superiors didn't need to know about that, because it was only a matter of hours before he had them all in hand again, except now there was the woman and the fucking camp and some kind of required clearance that he hadn't known existed.

So he would have to tell them. But he knew Yuga had to be down there. He knew that he *was*. He knew it with everything in him, every fragment of instinct, with the part of him that could sense the weaving and pattern of the universe. That part was irrational. It was a step or two away from superstition. But it was also right, consistently.

It had developed early. He remembered playing with his friends, pretending to be the heroic explorers and bringers of civilization that made up Protectorate legend. Those more perfect than perfect, set up as a new standard for a new generation to meet. He had loved those heroes and the idea of striking out for a new world and carrying a new way of life with him to the benefit of all.

But there'd been something else. A secret fascination.

The Bideshi.

He hadn't shared this with his friends. But by himself, he read what he could when his parents weren't watching, about Bideshi superstitions, rituals, dark magic, and spells. The witches that they called their "Aalim" and obeyed as if they were gods. The way they could read the future in blood and gut, in murder and evil impulse.

Reprehensible. Dishonorable. Filthy.

But in all the stories, powerful.

What could he do with that power? Of course, he'd understood that the stories lied—young Isaac had been a good student and had absorbed every lesson at school with perfect comprehension. But in the midst of all that learning, the idea had come to him: what if the stories of that power *weren't* completely lies? What if there was truth in it, however small, however mutilated? So it was that Isaac would sit on the balcony of his childhood home in the ancient city of Berlin, looking up at the stars and trying to read the future in their movements. Trying to know what the next day would bring. Killing rats, the occasional stray dog, cutting them open in the narrow alley behind the residential tower and sliding his fingers into their guts. Grasping at things he'd only half sensed, or perhaps had only wanted so badly to believe he could.

But he *could* sense them. There were things he predicted before they happened, positions that he could put himself in, to be noticed, to be at the right place at the right time, to catch the right person's attention. Flashes of intuition that were uncanny in their intensity and accuracy.

It wasn't Bideshi magic. There was no future written in strings of gut, and the stars told him nothing. But he could still know.

Yuga.

He touched the comm, and called the bridge. "Captain." He paused a moment, eyes open, his tongue pressing itself between the ridges of his teeth as he considered. "Let's withdraw to the outer edges of the inner system. But stay ready. Make sure you have people who can fill landing parties on short notice. I need to make some calls."

"How are you going to heal them?" Lochlan was puffing to keep up—it wasn't weariness so much as his muscles protesting, but he could also tell that he was getting weaker, and that troubled him. Though at the moment, Adam troubled him far more. "You can't do simple laying-on-of-hands. You're not Ying. And remember, that was only ever a temporary thing. She couldn't heal you in a way that would stick."

"I'm not going to heal them the way she did."

"*How*, then?" Lochlan slipped in the mud, almost fell, swore sharply and stumbled after Adam again. Aarons had peeled off a while ago, muttering something about waiting until certain people came to their senses. So now Lochlan was cursing himself, cursing his own damn stubbornness, his refusal to give up when giving up was clearly the smarter option.

He never could give up with Adam.

"*Chusile* . . . I'm not doubting you, I swear I'm not, but—"

Adam laughed but didn't turn. "Yes, you are. That's exactly what you're doing."

"I told you last night: you need a *plan*." Lochlan grabbed Adam's arm and finally succeeded in tugging him to a halt, and though Adam twisted free, he didn't immediately start off again. Lochlan fixed him with a pleading look and sent up a silent and very general prayer for strength and guidance. To Ixchel, maybe. It would be like her to eavesdrop. "I know you; you're plunging yourself into this because you always do that. And don't you *dare* start with me about how impulsive I am; this is *not* the same thing."

"Lock," Adam said patiently. "Yeah, I always do this. I've always done it. Listen." He held out his hand, palm up, as if he were holding an invisible pad. "In school, when the other kids would go at their problems all conventionally, step-by-step, the way they'd been told . . . and I would dive in and feel my way out. I'd use the steps, sure, because that *was* usually the best way, but when I was in the middle of it, I wouldn't even be thinking about it. I'd just be . . . feeling through the problem. The shape of it, the way it could be rearranged to give me the answer I wanted. Equations, proofs, spatial calculations, physics . . . It all worked the same. I didn't need to think. Thinking actually got in the *way*."

Lochlan simply shook his head. He couldn't remember when he'd last felt this helpless. The previous few days—if not weeks—had made him feel more and more like there was little he could do but hold on for the ride.

"I'm going to do this," Adam said, softer now. He stepped closer and laid a hand against the side of Lochlan's neck. "I need you. I don't need you to buy into it, not totally, but I need you with me. Can you do that?"

"Of course I can."

Adam nodded. "Good." And resumed walking.

They were outside their ex-host's shack when Lochlan yanked him to a stop again. He wasn't surprised to see that they were here, had in fact had a growing sense of dread. He had to make one last attempt to stop it. Before it went too far to take back.

"Adam." He took a breath. "*Chusile.* If you try . . . however you think you can . . . and you fail, they're going to hate you. They're all going to hate you. They might try to kill you."

Adam frowned. "What? Why?"

"Because," Lochlan said, choosing his words with care. "The worst thing you can do for people like this is sell them hope and then destroy it in front of them."

Adam looked at him for a long moment, his face unreadable. "I'm not going to fail," he murmured. He turned and pushed the sheeting aside, stepping into the dimness of the shack. Fighting a wrench of despair, Lochlan followed.

The woman was seated on the mat again, her eyes closed in a doze. The children were once more lying curled together, but their eyes were open, and they'd locked onto Adam and Lochlan as they entered.

Lochlan tried not to let his trepidation show, but he didn't think he was all that successful.

Adam, meanwhile, radiated confidence. It was bizarre. Lochlan wasn't sure he had ever seen Adam like this before.

"Hey." Adam dropped into a crouch beside the mat and touched the woman's shoulder. She jerked, her eyes snapping open.

"What the fuck?" She shoved his hand away. "I thought I told you not to come back here."

"I know. I'm sorry." Adam shifted even closer. "The thing is . . . I think I might be able to help you."

The woman's eyes narrowed. "Help me? How?"

He has no idea—he's out of his mind. But Lochlan bit his tongue to keep it still. Even if he couldn't believe what Adam intended to do, even if his doubts were overwhelming, he couldn't stop it now.

"I used to be sick too. I'm not anymore. I was healed."

The woman let out a harsh laugh. "Bullshit. That's not possible. Why would you be, if they can't do it here already?"

"I went elsewhere." Adam glanced back at Lochlan and the woman's gaze followed his. *God, no*, Lochlan thought desperately. *Leave me the fuck out of this.* "I was dying when he found me. I was sure nothing could help me. But he did. His people did. I think I can do the same thing."

The woman stared at him. "You mean to tell me," she said slowly, "you were cured by . . . by Bideshi *magic*, and now you're going to cast the same spell on me, and that's going to cure me. Just like that."

Adam gave her a vaguely wry smile. "I don't think it'll happen 'just like that,' no. And I don't think it's magic. It's something else. It's definitely not a spell, either . . . but that's basically the idea, yeah."

For a long moment, the woman was silent. Lochlan searched her face for some indication of what she was thinking, but could glean nothing. She looked into Adam's eyes and he looked back, his expression open, a little pleading. Lochlan had the sensation of a nightmare, everything moving sluggishly forward with no way to sidestep or stop any of it.

At last she shrugged and gave another quick, dry laugh. "Okay. Sure. What the fuck."

Adam blinked. "Really?"

"Yeah." The woman smiled crookedly. "It's bullshit and it won't work, and *you're* crazy, but what exactly do I have to lose? I'm already dead. Can't hurt."

"Thank you." Adam glanced down at his hands as if he expected to find something changed in them.

"So what do I do?"

"Just sit there. I think." At that, the girl sat up and tugged at the sleeve of her mother's shirt, shaking her head.

"No," she whispered. "Mama. No."

"Oh, baby." The woman pulled the girl into her lap, cradling her head against her breast and rocking her gently. "It's okay. This nice man wants to try something. I'll be fine."

Adam sat back on his heels, waiting. After a few minutes, the women pressed the girl back onto the mat. The girl was still sniffling, but had otherwise fallen quiet. Lochlan fixed his gaze on them. Children the age he had been when he'd stepped onto Caldor Station and his life had exploded. What would seeing all of this do to them? Assuming they even survived?

Adam no longer seemed to be aware of them. He was taking the woman's hands in his, hunching forward. "Just close your eyes," he said, then added, "I'm not sure how this is going to go. I've never done it before."

"Oh." The woman smiled thinly at him. "That's very comforting." But she closed her eyes, and then for a moment there was nothing at all. Only her and Adam, sitting hand in hand across from each other, in an attitude of what might have been prayer.

Then the woman arched with a ragged breath. Her eyes snapped wide open, rolled back in her head so that they seemed pale and sightless.

Like an Aalim.

Lochlan almost lunged forward, but something held him back, staring. The children were sitting up and shifting backward, their faces twisted with fear. Adam's body was as rigid as the woman's, the muscles standing out in his arms and his fingers clamped so tight around hers that his knuckles were white. He threw his head back, his mouth stretched into a grimace.

They were both clearly in pain. A lot of it.

"Adam, *no*." But Adam didn't let her go. Perhaps he couldn't. The woman's body bucked and her mouth opened in a silent scream.

This was worse. It was so much worse than he had feared, than he had even imagined. Because there *was* power here. It hummed through the air, raising the hair on his arms. He'd thought that nothing would happen. Now the woman was writhing, shaking her head, her breath harsh and shallow. Now her teeth were closing on her tongue, and blood trickled from the corner of Adam's mouth. The children were screaming, scrambling away from her, and Adam wouldn't let her go.

Lochlan reached for the children, and perhaps they were too scared of what Adam was doing to their mother to be afraid of anything else, because they rushed into his arms.

And then it was over.

Adam fell back with a rough cry, releasing the woman's hands. She crumpled as if boneless, her body sprawled, her eyes closed, and her face gone lax.

"Is she—" Lochlan couldn't say it. Saying it might make it real. The children were still crying against him, their fists clenched in the dirty fabric of his shirt. Adam pushed himself slowly up, shaking— it seemed as though that simple movement was taking all of his strength.

He fell forward onto his hands and knees, reached for the woman, and laid a hand on her chest. His head dipped—and every muscle in his body stiffened at once.

No. Oh, no.

"Lock." Adam swallowed hard, and turned stricken eyes on him, blood still showing at the corners of his mouth. "Lock, she's . . . she's not breathing."

"Try to revive her."

Lochlan sounded numb, the words mechanical. Adam stared at the woman, her limbs askew, her lips slightly parted and stained with blood. Chest compressions. Of course. He knew how. But it wouldn't do any good. He was as sure of that as anything, even as he somehow got himself up to his knees, placed his hands on her chest, and pushed.

Where she had gone, he couldn't reach her. She would return riding her own strength, or she would not.

The next few minutes were hazy. He was aware of fragments—the soft weeping of the children, the hot pain in his own body, the overwhelming desire to fall down and sleep. Death in the body under his hands. The nothingness that seemed to surround the shack, pressing in from all sides. A starless void.

Then the body beneath him convulsed.

He fell back, shock blasting through him. The woman shook, and the shaking became a cough that wracked her from the deepest part of her chest, her breaths making their way in between gaps in her coughing, rattling and sharp. Her hands twitched weakly.

The world blurred as tears filled his eyes. It was too much. All of it.

And then it sucked him down again.

The sensation of falling wasn't as deep as before. If anything it felt like an aftershock. Except . . . *He* hadn't done anything except open a door and lead her to it. She had gone through. And like him, she had known what to do once she was there, struggling amidst the grinding tangle of her own roots, battling the sickness that lay at their heart. It was the Plain all over again, and yet it wasn't—the power that had gripped him there was fainter here. But it was still *here*. He had been right. It had gone so deep into him that it had left pieces of itself behind.

Or maybe it had been there all along.

Maybe it was in everyone.

Now he stumbled through the dark of himself, groping for anything that would help him find his way back. He was aware of Lochlan's hands on him, the children still sobbing with fear, the woman coughing as she reclaimed her breath. But all of that was distant. His own weakness was devouring him, the living things in him withering, their dances erratic and stuttering. It wasn't like before. It wasn't death eating at him. But so much of him had been drained in only a few seconds, and now it was all he could do to keep his head above the surface.

He remembered lying on the Plain in Lochlan's arms, smelling blood and terror. But there he had felt safe, as if Lochlan really could protect him. As if he could bring Adam out of the dark with the simple force of his love.

Like now.

He twisted weakly and finally managed to shake himself free, light flooding back into his vision. Lochlan was cradling him, his face bent close, his eyes wide and frightened.

"I'm all right," Adam whispered. "I'm—" Then a kinder darkness closed over his head, and he welcomed its coming

"What the *fuck* was that?"

The woman was holding her children again, though they were still whimpering, pressing themselves into her as if they could crawl beneath her skin and hide themselves. Lochlan looked up, dazed, Adam's body gone limp in his arms—but he sensed that it wasn't unconsciousness but the kind of sleep that would heal if it was given time. He met the woman's gaze, and it was keener and brighter than it had been before. Her brown skin had less of a gray tint and appeared healthier. But the tone was also a little uneven, a hint of mottling. Like Adam. Though her eyes were both still the same color. Perhaps whatever had happened to her—if she had been healed, permanently—was similar to what had happened to Adam.

How he carried the Plain in his blood.

He wasn't sure how else to explain what he had seen. How else it could be possible.

"He healed you," Lochlan said dully, and ducked his head. *And he almost killed you. Along with himself.*

"How did he do that?" She didn't sound doubtful. She almost sounded angry, in fact, though there was a quaver in her voice that suggested fear.

"He did it once before." Lochlan stroked Adam's damp hair away from his head, holding him closer. "When he said he used to be sick, he wasn't lying. It nearly killed him. It *was* our magic that saved him, if you want to call it that." He shot her a sardonic smile. "He left my people to try to save *your* people. I suppose you're the first."

The woman nodded but said nothing else for a moment. She was gazing at Adam with a strange expression, many emotions passing through it in waves. Shock. Wonder. Admiration. Suspicion.

"Will he be all right?"

"I don't know." Lochlan shook his head. If he had known it would do this, potentially damage Adam in this way . . . Would he have tried harder to stop it? Would he have argued that it wasn't worth the risk? He had no idea. "Like I said, he's never done this with anyone else before. I don't know what's going to happen now."

The woman hesitated, then gently shooed her children off the mat, getting up and motioning to the vacated space. "Put him here."

"You don't need to rest?"

"I feel fine." The woman gave him a small smile. "Better than fine. My mouth hurts; I think I bit myself, but . . . It's okay. Least I can do, maybe."

Lochlan nodded. The question had been out of uncharacteristic politeness and little else. Adam was the most important thing in the world. Awkwardly, he lifted Adam's deadweight onto the mat and arranged him into as comfortable a position as he could. Then he sat back, his hands in his lap, and closed his eyes, though he probably wouldn't sleep. Aarons needed to be told. Because this changed everything.

"I just realized," the woman said quietly from behind him, "I don't know your names. Any of you."

"Right." Lochlan sighed. "I'm Lochlan. Lock. There's other names in there, but I guess . . . I guess they don't really matter right now. There's a lot of them." He gestured toward Adam. "He's Adam. The handsome fellow with us earlier is Aarons."

"All right." The woman seemed to mull that over, then added, "I'm Rachel. The kids are Becca and Dion."

"It's good to know you, Rachel." And he realized then that he meant it. Their circumstances were horrible, everything at the moment was horrible, but it was also good. Because for the first time in a long time, it was as if light was pushing through the black, like stars emerging through a dust cloud.

Maybe there was a chance. Maybe.

"I want to help you." Rachel touched his arm, careful and hesitant. "I have no fucking idea how this works, and I don't even know if I trust you, any of you ... But if he's here to help people ... Then I want to help you. Tell me what I need to do."

Lochlan glanced back at her, nonplussed. Of all the things he might have expected her to say, that wasn't one he had considered in the wildest corners of his imagination.

But it felt right. And that sense of possibility, of *hope*, was hitting him relentlessly, beating its way inside.

"Okay." He took a breath. "He has an idea. A crazy goddamn idea. It's probably a terrible one, and it's probably suicide. But if you want to help ..."

He told her. She listened in silence. At some point, around the time he got to the part about the ships, she started to laugh.

CHAPTER

EIGHTEEN

I n her dreams Nkiruka ran the corridors and halls and secret places of Ashwina.

She'd had these dreams before. She suspected everyone on a Bideshi homeship had them sooner or later. The ships folded into themselves, claimed and marked their own. One wandered through them in sleep as well as waking. But in those other dreams—the ones Nkiruka had always had—the ship had been full of life, voices and footsteps and the smell of growing things.

Now it was dead and her feet left tracks in the dust that coated its floors.

She wanted to call out. She wanted to find someone else alive on the ship, even one person, because to be alone in something this vast was to draw dangerously close to the night that went on forever. That night cradled them and kept them free and unbound, but it was also so cold, so cruel, and it could be like a devouring mouth. Now it was open to swallow her, the darkness battering against the glass that capped the great halls and the high corridors.

At length she found herself on the ground of the High Fields. But the grass was dead and dry, the trees in the distance like skeletal hands, the nearby lake nothing but cracked mud. She was standing in one place but it was as though her awareness lifted and flew, everywhere at once. Everywhere she saw the same infertility, the same death. The same deep loss.

When she focused on the Arched Halls, she opened her mouth to scream—which choked itself in her throat.

Like everywhere else, they were dry and dead, but the death was of a different kind, because the life there had been of a different kind also. She searched along its paths, touching each trunk, but she sensed nothing. No glowbugs came to greet her. No singing echoed through the branches. The candles had all gone out.

There were no stars.

But there was light.

She watched it draw nearer, red and orange and gold—familiar. It was like a tiny flame. For a few seconds she allowed herself to hope that it was the life returning to the ship, that it had perhaps fled into the night but was now coming back, because Ashwina would draw life back to herself.

But then she knew the light and she knew it wasn't so.

She whirled and ran.

She could hear its roar now, feel the heat at her back, blistering her skin. Suddenly it was all around her, screaming for her life, more ravenous than any cold night could be. She hurled herself through the Arched Halls and the branches reached out to claw at her, to yank her hair and clutch at her clothes. She beat at them, but she only succeeded in scratching her palms open, and the dead trees sucked greedily at her blood.

Finally, in an ecstasy of terror and dull rage, she faced the fire. It reared up in front of her like a horse, and she saw faces moving inside it, their features twisted with agony and their mouths wide to make up the massive howl of the flames. Some of the faces, she knew. Many others she didn't. But she knew they were all Bideshi—not only the ones from Ashwina but *all* the Bideshi, and she was the last one both free and living.

And the rest had come for her. Because she hadn't been able to save them. Because they had died, consumed by what was coming, and she had turned away from them. Now they were enraged, drowned in the fire. That rage would destroy her.

Please, she gasped, all the strength draining out of her, as if through her feet into the roots of the place. *Please, don't.*

The fire crashed down on her like a breaking wave, and at last she could scream.

She knew it was a dream, of course. She knew it before she burst into waking, shoving herself up with the covers tangled around her sweaty legs. She knew it before she saw Satya's bare back, the lines and curves of it warmed by the dim light given off by the walls. She had known it was a dream the moment it came to her.

It made no difference. She knew a true dream when she felt it.

Letting out a huge, shuddering breath, she pulled her legs free, turned, and sat on the edge of the bed with her head in her hands. Her skin was hot, almost feverish, but her sweat was drying and slightly cooling her.

Sleep wasn't going to come back to her. She had lost it completely. Slowly she rose and reached for her silk robe.

Perhaps because of what the dream had forced her to do, or perhaps because she wanted to assure herself that nothing was as she had seen it, she walked. She went barefoot, padding softly over the decks, the fingertips of one hand trailing over the bulkheads.

It was in the midst of what was, for Ashwina's internal clock, the small hours. The sunlamps that lit the larger spaces and the smaller lights that illuminated the corridors were both dimmed, and while a few people moved here and there, attending to work or merely wandering sleepless the way Nkiruka was, there weren't many of them. However, the place wasn't empty and dead. She could see that for herself.

But of the sleepless, she saw more than she once had. She could always tell them apart from the others, and not just because she was one of them. It was their gait, either shuffling or a little too quick, and their expression, distant and preoccupied and often faintly worried. Some of them were pallid and hollow-eyed, suggesting more than one night with not enough rest.

We are the ghosts which sleep has left behind. Nkiruka fought back a shiver.

She was unsurprised to find her feet carrying her up toward the top of the ship, to the High Fields. This, too, she needed to see, to confirm to herself without a shadow of a doubt that it was still whole and living. And it was, the fields thrown into darkness broken only by starlight that glittered across the grass and trees and water and almost as bright as any moon. A soft breeze whispered. She stood there, wrapped in silk, and goose bumps prickled her bare skin.

In the distance, a shape sat under a tree. She made for it, the grass cool underfoot, already somehow sure who she would find.

Kae glanced up at her as she approached, his knees drawn up against his chest. Someone sat up beside him—Leila, her long hair pulled back into a simple ponytail. The two of them lifted their hands in greeting.

"You're awake too," Nkiruka said as she reached them, sinking down cross-legged. They were near one of the lakes, and the starlight glittering on its still face was a distraction in the corner of her vision.

"Often these nights." Leila smiled a bit wanly. "It's better to have company at these times. I take it Satya isn't suffering the same as you?"

"Not as far as I can tell." Nkiruka pulled at a loose cuticle. "When I do sleep, the dreams are bad. I don't . . ." She sighed and raked a hand back through her thick cascade of braids. "Everything feels wrong right now. Worse than before."

Her eyes met Kae's as she spoke, and the expression that met her was grimly knowing. She wondered if he had told Leila about the results of the reading.

"War," Leila murmured. Well, that answered that. "It's not just in the pads, Nkiru. Not just in the lines and the orbits. Kae was privy to a council meeting yesterday. They wanted his input as wingleader. It wasn't only our three ships—they had messages from other convoys as well."

Something under Nkiruka's skin ran cold. She already knew what this would mean. What it was about. In what direction the pressure would fall. Like everything, she had felt it coming, whispers from the stars. "And?"

"There's a sense among some," Kae said, leaning forward with his voice low, "that we should all withdraw from this part of space. Head toward less-traveled parts of the galaxy and remain there, out of the way. Find new species and new worlds to trade with and steer clear of the Protectorate entirely. And then there are others who seem like they're spoiling for a fight. They actually want to go on the offensive. They want revenge."

"*Chere*, that's . . . It's not what Adam wanted. He tried so hard to avoid it." Nkiruka shook her head. Revenge. Slow dread twisted at her; it hadn't been there in any intensity immediately after the Plain, but she had sensed a general inclination toward vengeance gathering, like low rumbles of distant thunder. "It's not what *Ixchel* wanted. She wanted the *healing* of this rift, not the widening of it. Adam was supposed to be that connection. That was what we were hoping for. What he was hoping for. Now they might use him as an excuse for more conflict? That's . . ."

"I know. Believe me, I know. So does Adisa. So does at least half of Ashwina's council. But the rest of the convoys didn't know Adam the way we do. All they know is that they lost hundreds on the Plain, and all for a Protectorate outcast they didn't even meet. For a people who have been nothing short of enemies to us. Now the word is that the Protectorate isn't planning to ease up. If anything they're harassing us more. Everyone is *scared*, Nkiru. Either way, we're not equipped to do any fighting."

"But the Aalims were there. They accepted him, didn't they? They—"

"Half of them are dead. The newly appointed ones never knew him either. They're under a lot of pressure." Kae sighed. "And *khara*, we have no Aalim at all. The whole convoy is out of balance. If we're one of the few dissenting voices . . ." He shrugged. "We don't have a lot of pull."

"So. We go sleepless," Leila said. She sounded beyond tired, more so than Nkiruka had ever heard her, even after the Battle of the Plain. "We know Adam is alive. We're sure of that much."

"If Adam is, so is Lochlan," Kae added firmly. "I'm just as sure of that. I have no talent for star-reading, but I *feel* it."

For a few moments there was silence except for the whisper of the grass and the leaves. It was an uncomfortable silence. At last Nkiruka shook herself. "Couldn't we refuse to go? Even if the rest of them do?"

"We could." Leila tilted her head back, the starlight glittering in her eyes. "It would put us in a bad position, though. Cut off from the rest. If we got into trouble, we'd be completely alone. And it would weaken our standing with pretty much everyone else."

"We can't abandon Adam and Lochlan," Kae said. Now his tone was positively steely. "We can't. We stood for him when no one else did. He's still a brother. And Lochlan is . . . No."

"It may not be up to us." Nkiruka dug her toes into the grass, down into the soil beneath. "Things are moving. Big things." Again she thought of fire and death, and couldn't keep back her shudder.

"And," Leila said quietly, "if the faction counseling a fight wins out, what then? Do we stand idle and let our brothers and sisters commit suicide?"

Kae laughed suddenly, arms curled around his knees. There was something awful about his laugh: dark amusement and sadness and anger all expressing themselves at once. "Sometimes I envy Lochlan. How he got so totally away from all of this. I understand why he used to spend so long out there in the black. We can be so . . . *Khara*. All of us, stubborn and sluggish as goatworms."

"And selfish." Nkiruka wanted to laugh too, but it wouldn't come. "Whatever Ixchel said about exiles. Line and orbit, she would be so *angry* right now."

Kae laughed again, this time joined by Leila, and it sounded less strained. "That would be a thing to see, wouldn't it? No one ever dared cross that old witch, not to her face. She'd see them snapped into line soon enough."

Nkiruka nodded, but she said nothing. Her own words were haunting her. *Selfish.*

The universe itself wouldn't leave her alone when it came to this.

"Was it hard?" she asked presently, not looking at either of them. "To watch Lochlan go?"

Kae let out a surprised breath. "Why, it was . . . Yes, it was hard. It was hard to see the backs of both of them. Adam was my friend in the end, Nkiru, almost as much as Lochlan was. My brother. I miss them both every day."

"It's strange," Leila added, "how attached one can get to someone so quickly. But we went through hells together, all of us. I saw him when he was fresh and new, and so afraid. He was like a child. Something in me wanted to keep him safe." She shifted, sliding around to Kae's front and settling back between his legs, his fingers toying with a few loose strands of her hair. "You remember. Even if you didn't yet know us that well."

"We all remember." Nkiruka dug her fingers harder into the dirt, as if she might be able to push her way down to the roots of the Arched Halls themselves. It was said that those roots grew far beyond the land occupied by the forest itself, spreading out beneath the fields and meadows. That the entire top of the ship lay cradled in a great, tangled, wooden hand. "So . . . You don't think that what he did was selfish? Or Lochlan? Leaving the way they did?"

"Do I— No, I don't think anything of the kind." Confusion mingled with the surprise in Kae's tone. "If anything . . . They almost certainly went into greater danger than they would ever have faced here. Who knows, maybe doing what they did gave us a bit more space to breathe while the Protectorate focused its efforts on them alone. Anyway, they're cut off from us. Their family. Lochlan might have spent every minute he could spare away from us, but this was always his home. More than anywhere else in the universe."

Leila cocked her head to one side, and though Nkiruka couldn't see her face clearly in the dimness, she could feel the woman's penetrating gaze. Maybe no one would have crossed Ixchel to her face, but Leila too, was also formidable in ways that belied her years. "Why are you asking us these things, little glowbug?"

It was the pet name that threw Nkiruka off, and in the end probably what knocked the truth out of her. Or it was that in part. But that name . . . No one had called her by it in years, not since she had shed the last physical traces of her childhood.

Leila seemed to remember.

Maybe it should be you instead of me, Nkiruka thought, and was immediately ashamed.

"They're going to make me choose," she said slowly, miserably. "Adisa told me. They're going to . . . lay it out in front of me like a poisoned meal and call me traitor if I don't eat."

Leila and Kae were silent. Nkiruka sat there with her head down and her hands loose in her lap. Once again the tears were a hot pressure behind her eyes. She hated even saying it like that. She hated saying it at all. She was so *tired* of feeling young and foolish and not good enough, when it came to this. Like there was no good choice to be made. Like every turn she took would take something away from her.

There was a touch on her hand and she lifted her head to see Leila kneeling in front of her, her face gentle and open. "Nkiru," she murmured, and Nkiruka let herself fall forward into Leila's arms, shaking as everything tight in her released.

She was vaguely ashamed that it was Leila, and not Satya. *It should be. It should.*

Finally Nkiruka lifted her face from Leila's shoulder, wiping her eyes and letting out an embarrassed laugh when she saw the damp spot on Leila's shirt. "I'm sorry."

"Don't be." Leila took her hand, glancing back at Kae, who gave her a nod. "Walk with me, Nkiru. There's something I want to tell you."

Puzzled, Nkiruka nevertheless allowed Leila to pull her gently to her feet and lead her across the grass toward the small lake. The water caught the starlight, amplifying it somehow, and the entire thing seemed to glow faintly in the night, casting rippling illumination over Leila's face and dark hair as they walked together along its edge. Nkiruka didn't try to break the stillness. Leila would speak when the time was right.

Presently she did.

"You know the story of Adisa and Ixchel?" She went on before Nkiruka could answer. "Many of us don't. It's not considered polite to be too free with it. It was in another life, and it's a story that holds much pain for him. Once for her as well, though she would never have let it show."

"I . . . think so. A little of it." Nkiruka frowned. There was really only one thing this could be referring to: What Adisa had told her when he had spoken to her last. Watching Ixchel dance. Thinking about the future. "He loved her, didn't he?"

"He did. With a passion that few on Ashwina had ever seen. The moment they first saw each other—it was said—all they wanted was to be together. When they were, they lit the world around them. Some people whispered that they would destroy whatever came between them. But of course that wasn't true."

Now it was clear. Why Adisa had told her in the first place. What he was trying to make her see.

"They chose . . . *She* chose to go to the fire. Didn't she? She chose to become the Aalim."

Leila squeezed her hand and nodded, facing Nkiruka. She took Nkiruka's other hand in hers. "It was agony for her. She never spoke of it, but everyone could tell. It must have been a choice that tore her in two. And Adisa . . ." She shook her head. "I think he would have stopped her if he could have. But of course no one could ever change Ixchel's mind when she made it up."

She paused a moment, then stepped closer, reaching up to briefly lay a hand against Nkiruka's cheek. Her palm was cool and smooth. "You must understand: She didn't make the choice out of fear. Her people needed her. She answered them."

Nkiruka nodded. When she closed her eyes, she was distantly irritated to feel more tears spilling over, trickling down her cheeks. But naturally Leila wouldn't care.

"I'm not telling you this to sway you one way or the other, little glowbug. It was all a long time ago, before you or Kae or I were born, and we only know the story from others. I can't tell you what to do, and I can't tell you what's right. You have to decide that for yourself, and live with the decision. I'm telling you simply so you know that you're not alone—that if you're suffering, others have suffered as you have. I think . . . I think there's always suffering in this choice. I think, to be an Aalim and to guide our people, one has to have suffered terribly. To know loss as great as any her children might suffer."

"I'd never have children," Nkiruka whispered.

"No." When Nkiruka opened her eyes Leila was smiling at her, sweet and sad, tears shining in her own eyes. "No, you wouldn't."

Nkiruka simply let that hang in the air. Somehow that was all of it, that future absence. That blocking-off of a pathway by virtue of a single decision, a choice that precluded so many other choices and implied so many more things placed forever out of reach.

She hadn't even been sure she *wanted* children.

But all the ship would be your children, she could almost imagine the council saying.

Her heart instantly replied, *That's not even close to the same thing.*

Leila was no longer looking at her. She was gazing off toward another one of the lakes, shining like a small pocket of liquid light. "One of the early days Adam was here," she said quietly, "we took him swimming." She laughed softly. "God, he was so afraid. Of everything.

But that night, when he pushed himself through the awkwardness, the fear, stripped naked and jumped into the water, I saw a little of the other side of him. That part that would act despite the fear. The part that could even use it as an excuse to push ahead."

She looked back at Nkiruka again. "You have that same stubbornness, I think. Kae has it as well. It may make you doubt yourself, intensify your fear . . . but you should be grateful for it. If you trust it, what it pushes you toward and pulls you away from, it won't lead you wrong." She reached out then and cupped Nkiruka's face in both hands, leaning in and pressing a kiss to her forehead. "You're strong, Nkiru. You're stronger than you know."

Nkiruka wanted to answer her. The words seemed to demand an answer. But once again no answer came. So instead she merely nodded, closed her eyes against the darkness and the starlight, and felt herself slowly calming.

It's going to be all right.

Even if she sensed, so deeply, that it was a lie. Maybe some lies were necessary, at least for a while. Maybe they held you up when nothing else would.

Unless they let you fall when they disappear.

"Come on back." Leila stepped away, taking Nkiruka's hand once again. "Sit with us awhile longer, until you feel sleepy. You shouldn't be alone at a time like this." She smiled. "We don't have to talk if you don't want to."

Nkiruka nodded. Part of her still wanted to be alone, completely so—wanted it very much. But she thought of the empty ship, all that death, and she knew that Leila was right. It wouldn't do. Not now.

She let Leila lead her back to the tree, sat down, and listened to Kae and Leila's sleepy chatter until at last, quite without meaning to and without really noticing that it was happening, she drifted off to sleep in the shadows, and did not dream.

CHAPTER

NINETEEN

"You're certain?"

Sinder nodded. "Quite certain. There's nowhere else he could have gone. We've found tracks that lead away from the crash site." A lie, but not entirely. There had been no tracks around the crash site itself, but miles distant they had found the tracks of a groundcar, one that had come from the east, stopped, then turned around and headed back again. That in itself wasn't conclusive, obviously—but he knew what it meant. He simply *knew* it.

"And you know that you can apprehend him?"

"If he's there, he's trapped. They've done that much for us. All we need is the clearance to go in and get him."

The woman on the comm screen frowned, her elegant lips pursed. She was one of the top people he had access to, stationed in the halls of power on Terra. Not as high up as the ancient things in their climate-controlled towers on Terra, living on a diet of hormones and concentrated nutrients, stumbling through the hollow shell of their rule while the real rulers did the work beneath them. In truth, he wouldn't want to talk to them anyway. There would be no point.

"This is a sensitive matter, Mr. Sinder." The woman regarded him with narrowed eyes, passing a hand down the perfect angles of her face. "You understand that. This isn't merely a matter of getting the formalities taken care of. This isn't just about stamping and turning in the proper paperwork. If you're allowed to do this, you and your people will have to be granted the highest clearance available. In terms of access to information, you would be the equivalent of both a top executive and a top administrator. I can't hand that kind of thing out like candy."

"I understand." Sinder took a breath, trying to keep his impatience from showing. None of this was anything he didn't already know. "If you could expedite the process at all, if I can give you anything that would make the whole machinery run a little faster—"

"Send me whatever intelligence you've compiled. I'll need to take this up the chain."

So the ancient ones *would* need to be brought into it. The Founders. Old gods, fog-minded and weak-willed, thinking they were strong enough to resist death itself, when in fact they were simply too afraid of it to face it. Sinder felt increasing scorn for their apparent belief that their desperate, hollow half-life was perfection, instead of the effortless, intrinsic thing he imagined perfection must truly be: an existence in which pristine, perfect life was so deeply written into the code that weakness and death would never touch it. To even hint at disrespect for the Founders was one step from blasphemy, though Sinder was almost certain that more than a few people held his opinion. The Founders were the fathers and mothers of everyone. They had set down the foundations on which the Protectorate was built. Their word was law.

Their word was bullshit.

"Whatever you have to do." Sinder inclined his head; a tiny version of a bow. "I appreciate you taking the time to consider my request."

The comm screen flicked off, and Sinder sat back, letting out a sigh before he went about the business of compiling and sending the pertinent files.

Of course no part of this could be easy.

Suddenly restless, he got up and left his quarters, heading out into the corridors in the direction of the bridge. But halfway there he turned and started on the route that would take him down to the gym. He wasn't dressed for a workout, but his traveling clothes would do, light and loose as they were. Even if he only lifted some weights, it might take the tension out of his muscles. Maybe he could even sleep after.

It was second shift, the ship alive in its own version of midday, but the gym wasn't especially crowded. It was a relatively small facility, with weights, a few treadmills, and a ring for practicing hand-to-hand combat. Adjacent to it was a firing range. The idea of using that was briefly attractive—but no. No, he needed to work his body. His body was the thing getting in the way.

It was strange. He hardly ever felt like this. Then again, he tended to get a good deal more in the way of sleep.

He was only mildly surprised to see Alkor on one of the benches, the muscles in her arms straining as she hefted a hand weight, her silver hair pulled back in an even more severe knot than usual. He had been able to perceive under the crisp lines of her uniform that she kept herself toned and strong, but now he could see how true that was. He took a seat beside her and smiled. For her part, she glanced at him, nodded, and turned her attention back to her reps.

"Sinder."

"Captain." He paused, watching her, then went on. "I wanted to say, I appreciate your flexibility."

She flicked her gaze up at him again, arching a brow. "I'm not even stretching."

He laughed lightly. "You know what I mean. I realize you wanted to be done with this mission a good many days ago. I won't forget your dedication. And I'll make sure important people are aware of it."

"I'm not doing this for pats on the back." She shifted the weight to her other hand and began another set of reps. "I told you, I care about a job done right. I'll see this through to the end."

"Regardless. I appreciate it."

"Did you hear back yet?"

Sinder shrugged, got to his feet and headed over to the sets of weights, selecting fifteen pounds to start and returning to the bench. "I spoke to someone. She said she had to run it up the chain. I don't know exactly what that means, but I'm confident." He flexed the weight upward, enjoying the pleasant strain. "We have him. All we have to do is get him."

"And you're really that sure?"

"I am." He let out a hard breath. "I know I have no proof. But I feel it. He's there."

She paused, wiping sweat away from her forehead, peering at him. "You're a strange man, Isaac Sinder."

He laughed once more. "It's not the first time I've been told that." He fell silent, thinking, then glanced up at her, suddenly oddly shy.

Shyness wasn't common to him, but it came along with the memories that were washing over him, so he didn't resist it. "When I was a child, I think everyone was a little put off by me."

Alkor set the weight down and retrieved a bottle of water from under the bench. "You didn't have many friends?"

"No, I had a few. Not good ones." He shrugged again, a little awkwardly, an echo of much older, much worse awkwardness. "I was . . . focused inward. I thought a lot. Spent a lot of time alone. It served me pretty well, in the end."

"I guess I can see how it might." She was still studying him, and as he continued to lift, he found himself enjoying the scrutiny. "What was your major? In university?"

"Would you believe philosophy? With a focus in ethics?"

"Actually, yes." She favored him with another of those small smiles. "You've shown repeatedly that you're a man of convictions. Pragmatic, but . . ." She rolled a shoulder. "I think I can respect you. Even if I don't always agree with your . . . methods."

Sinder barked a sardonic laugh, shifting to his other arm. "That's a relief." And it was. He wasn't sure when he had started to care what Alkor thought of him, or why—though he did. It was important, of course, that they have a good working relationship, but although the captain could be exasperating, difficult, and altogether prickly . . . he liked her.

Which he didn't often do with anyone.

Alkor inclined her head in mock graciousness. "I do believe you'll get Yuga, for what it's worth." She hesitated, then went on. "Do you really think he's that great of a threat?"

He stopped and stared at her. How could she still question something so self-evident?

But then again, she might not see as clearly as he did. She was a soldier, first and foremost. Her mind was made for specifics, for the completion of clear tasks, and larger scale thinking was perhaps beyond her. As it should be. So he nodded, trying to appear as patient as he could.

"He might be the greatest threat we've encountered in generations. Not because he's one man, but because he *isn't* only one man. Alone, he might be barely more than a nuisance, whatever ability to destabilize he might possess, however much he might try to sow seeds of doubt and disloyalty. But there was Kerry. Now there's Aarons. We have to assume that he has other friends in high places. It might be a conspiracy the scope of which we can only guess. And the Bideshi..."

His voice darkened. Very little of the whole business made him afraid ... except this. "They've showed that they're willing to attack us now. After generations of relative peace, they might well be massing for direct conflict. Not only with us but with everything we are. Adam is part of the reasons for that. I know it. He must be. More than connected—he's the *center*. Dead, he's once again merely one man, and we lose our one chance to comprehend what's actually going on here. How far it goes, how far it might go. We lose our one chance to truly understand what's already happened."

Alkor nodded. "So what's the camp?"

Sinder blinked. "What?"

"The camp he's supposedly hidden in. It's one of ours, we know that. But I know the locations of all Protectorate detention centers, even the black sites, and I've never heard of this one. What is it?"

Sinder's eyes narrowed. "She didn't say. But . . ." *Might as well tell her.* She would know soon enough. "Its purpose seems to be the barrier here. We don't have clearance to know what it is. Whatever it's for . . ." He shook his head. If it was secret, it was for a reason, and it wasn't his place to question it. He started lifting again, sighing.

"I don't like it," Alkor said quietly. "I don't even know why. I just . . . There's something about it that doesn't feel right. If we—"

All at once, Sinder's muscles seemed to *disintegrate*. There was a wobble, a tremble, and all the tension in them disappeared, the weight dropping to the floor with a reverberating *thud*. Around the gym, people paused and stared in his direction. Sinder stared back, wide-eyed, then down at the weight.

What had *that* been?

"I ... must be tired." He picked up the weight—the movement was normal. One by one, everyone turned away again. But the adrenaline in him had taken on a sharper edge, and when he caught Alkor's eye, she was frowning at him.

"Maybe you've noticed that some people are dropping things. Maybe you've even felt it."

"Maybe it's happening to you."

"You should maybe get some rest, instead of tiring yourself out even more down here."

Sinder nodded. No doubt he was only overworked. Wasn't this exactly what Yuga had been intending? Confuse, worry, sow the seeds of doubt and second-guessing. Letting him succeed would be to grant him one tiny victory, and Sinder wasn't going to allow him that. He got up and set the weight back on the rack, lifting his arms behind his head and stretching his shoulders.

Really, he was much better now.

"I'll speak to you soon," he said, turning to go. "Please make sure that any messages for me are put through directly to my quarters. I'll take them whenever they arrive."

"Will do, Sinder." He didn't glance back, but it seemed to him that Alkor's voice still held a hint of the keen scrutiny that he had seen on her face before. "Sleep well."

He did, in the end. After a drink and some sedatives. But his dreams were troubling, and when he woke a few hours later, there was still no word.

Yuga, he thought. He lay on his back and imagined knocking the man to the ground, standing on his throat until he stopped struggling. Not death but total domination. The elimination of all resistance.

Yuga.

CHAPTER

TWENTY

Aarons listened in silence. At the end of it he shook his head slowly, scanning Adam up and down, and Adam's stomach dropped a bit. Dusk had fallen across the camp, and in Rachel's shack the lamp was flickering, its power cells clearly running low. Adam guessed that she would have no easy way of getting new ones once they ran out. Light probably wasn't a luxury afforded to many of the inmates by their caretakers, though the camp did seem to contain a black market of some kind.

Rachel was out on an errand—she hadn't been clear about what exactly. In the corner, Lochlan was playing a game with the children that involved a series of sticks of splintered scrap wood and a little ball of clay. Adam couldn't quite make out the rules, though his attention kept being strangely drawn to them.

He had never seen Lochlan with children before.

"Hey." Aarons snapped his fingers under Adam's nose, and Adam jumped a bit, turning his attention back to him. "Focus. We need to go over this."

"Right." Adam sighed. "I know it sounds crazy. Lochlan and I have—"

"You're fucking right: it sounds crazy. It *is* crazy."

"If we can get these people well, we can get the ships. I've gotten a good look at the guards by now: they're all convinced that no one here is sufficiently strong enough to pose any significant threat. If they're suddenly overrun by a bunch of *healthy* people—"

"Even if you *can* heal everyone here, a significant number of them aren't what I'd call *healthy*." Aarons scowled. "They're malnourished. They're exhausted. They're dehydrated. They'd be weak no matter what you did. And maybe you missed the part where they don't have *guns*?"

"We can get them guns." Stubbornness rose in Adam, not least because part of him was whispering that Aarons was right. About all of it. "I've been watching, and I'm pretty sure the building to the right of the main gate is the armory. If we can get enough people in there—"

"How exactly would you get past the inner gate? Huh? Have you thought that far ahead?"

"I have." Adam's jaw tightened. Though maybe it was good that he was getting this kind of resistance. Having to reconsider. Convince. Which he would have to do over and over, if this was going to work. "We obviously can't go over. I considered rushing the guards when they come to give us breakfast, but with the ones in the watchtowers, they'd mow us down. It'd be a massacre."

Aarons smiled grimly. "So you *can* see sense."

Lochlan glanced over his shoulder and snorted. "Oh, just wait."

Adam shot him a glare—but Lochlan was smiling at him, and the smile wasn't cold. So he did believe. Or he was open to it. He had scoffed when Adam had first told him the idea, but otherwise he had been quiet, had listened, though he hadn't said what he thought.

"We can go under," Adam said, turning back to Aarons. "We can dig."

Aarons stared at him for a moment, then coughed a laugh. "*Dig?*"

"Yeah. They might've installed the fences so they go down a ways, but we won't know until we check."

"They'll see us."

"They actually won't," Lochlan said. "Not if we're careful about where we do it. I went out an hour or so ago, and took a gander at how the shadows lie. About halfway down the left side of the inner fence, there's a spot where the shacks obscure about five feet of space from either of the guard posts, and there's no direct line of sight from the other buildings. Not that I could see. There's patrols, but they're predictable. It's absolutely goatshit, but I think it could work. If we get *fabulously* lucky."

Aarons looked from one of them to the other, his twisted face even more twisted than usual. Adam watched him carefully, but— also even more than usual—it was almost impossible to say which way he was leaning.

After a few minutes, he coughed and passed a hand over his tousled hair. "Okay. Leaving aside how completely ridiculous that is *for one minute*, how are you going to heal so many people? What's your time frame? 'Cause near as I can see, healing this one person almost fucking killed you. There's hundreds here. Let's say you can *maybe* do two or three a day. Maybe. At most. It would take you months. Months that we don't *have*."

Adam was silent for a moment. This was what he kept coming back to. He didn't need to ask what Lochlan thought. Lochlan probably wouldn't see any point in trying to dissuade him.

"I don't know," Adam said at last. "I . . . I haven't figured that out yet. Maybe I'll get better at it the more I do it."

"Or maybe you won't."

"Yeah, maybe I *won't*." It came in a sudden snap and his fists clenched. "Are you telling me I can't try? Are you telling me I just waltz out of here and leave all these people behind? Leave those *kids* behind? Leave what I came here to do?"

"I don't think anyone's going to be doing any waltzing," Aarons said dryly. "But yeah. Yeah, if it was up to me, that's exactly what you'd be doing."

"Well, it's *not* up to you." Adam crossed his arms over his chest. Necessary or no, talking like this made him so tired, and if he was honest, the weariness from before hadn't left him. For better or for worse, Aarons was right. This drained him. It drained him dangerously. "You can leave if you want. I'm staying until everyone here is free."

"Or dead."

"It's not up to you, either, *chusile*."

Adam looked back at Lochlan, who was gazing at him with grave eyes. There was love there, though there was still anger. And sadness, deeper than he had seen in the man in a long time. Lochlan seemed older now, he realized. His face still held the youth it had had when they'd first met, and fragments of the cocky rogue he had been, but now there was a seriousness there that Adam wasn't sure he liked.

It reminded him of Kae, and he loved Kae. But Kae was Kae. Lochlan should be Lochlan.

You knew you couldn't come out of this unchanged, child, Ixchel whispered. *None of you. That brat of a boy is finally growing up. You did that. Love him for who he is. God knows he needs it.*

"You can't just save these people unless they want to be saved. It's up to them. You're not some hero riding in with shining armor, waving your sword and slaying all the dragons. If you were thinking that, you stop it now." A hard edge came into his voice, and again Adam thought of Kae. Kae's words coming out of Lochlan's mouth. And true. "They know what they want, what they need. If they want to put their lives on the line to get out of here, that's one thing. But if they choose not to, you have to listen to them and leave them be. I know you care. I know you only want to help. But you have to *listen*."

Adam looked at him for a long moment. He wasn't sure what he was feeling, as he considered the concept. *Hero*. He hadn't thought of himself that way. He didn't think.

Had he?

"What if only some of them want to go?"

"Then we help those people the best we can," Lochlan said simply. "But we let them work it out among themselves."

This, it was true, hadn't occurred to him. Why wouldn't people want to fight back? Why wouldn't they want to be well, to be free? But there had been a time when he hadn't wanted to fight, either. Stealing, scraping by, waiting to die—that had been the easier path in some ways, though he hadn't thought so at the time. Easier to accept. Far more difficult to resist.

Who was he to say which choice was the right one for everyone?

"All right," he said heavily. "All right. Whatever they want. We'll get Rachel to help us find out. We'll—"

The plastic door-cover was torn aside and Rachel stumbled in. Held under the arms, clearly barely able to walk on her own, was an older woman, pale, probably middle-aged but ravaged by the disease that gripped her. Her head nodded forward, bobbing with the palsy in her neck, her face partially obscured by greasy, gray-streaked hair that hung in front of her eyes. She didn't appear fully conscious.

Rachel moved toward the mat. At once Aarons was on his feet, sliding an arm around the woman from the other side to help her. Adam stood as well, apprehension prickling down his spine. "Who's this?"

"Her name is Naomi." Rachel grunted with effort as she and Aarons laid the woman down. "She's one of the more respected people in here. Or she was, before the sickness hit her hard. People still care for her, save rations so she doesn't starve. She's among those who've been here the longest, helped a lot of people adjust. Stood up for them when the guards got abusive." She straightened up, panting. "She's dying, Adam. I don't think she'll last the night. You have to help her. You help her; the rest of us will be with you."

"I don't . . ." Adam dropped to his knees beside Naomi, reaching out to push her hair back from her face. Trembling, she tried to pull away from him, her eyes half-closed and rolling. She was so far gone. Much further than Rachel was. Much further than even he had been.

I don't know if I can. But he couldn't say it.

"Adam, *please*." Rachel knelt, grasping his hand. He could feel Lochlan and Aarons gathering close behind him. "She's cared for the entire camp. She was there for me when I came in with the children, when we had nothing. We can't lose her. Please try."

After all his insistence that this was what he had come to do, to let fear stop him now . . . He stared into Rachel's desperate eyes, and nodded, reaching for the woman trembling before them.

He heard Lochlan and Aarons suck in a breath as he laid his hands on her. Then he was down, *falling*, dropping into the deep, dark void that the core of her cells had become. Blackness devouring itself. It hurt, wrenching at him, airless like the vacuum of space. He cried out as he groped for her, gasping in pain and gasping her name both at once. He had to find her. If he could find her, he could show her the way . . .

But he was too deep, and it was too dark. Evil tendrils were winding their way out from her diseased roots, curling around him and dragging him farther down. Squeezing his chest. Taking away the last of his air and eating his heartbeat. He couldn't help her. He wasn't strong enough now. She would die with him.

Lock. Help me.

Light exploded. Something—some*one*—closed a hand around him and pulled, yanking him free and drawing him rapidly upward. *Lock* . . . But it wasn't Lochlan. There was a difference in the dance. It was someone he had felt in this way before. Someone he had been this close to.

Rachel.

She shoved him aside, putting herself in his place, and he hovered in the void and watched as she sent her light crashing against the dark, pushing it back until a woman was revealed, coiled in on herself, rigid with terror. Rachel closed the light over her, wrapping her in it like a blanket and lifting her up. Awe flooded Adam's core as they melded together in a paroxysm of surprised joy, spinning as one being and beating back the last of the nothingness. Revealing the full shape of the roots and cutting like a bright blade through the tendrils that choked them.

Now, Rachel cried. And they all exploded up and out, surging like ocean-creatures toward the surface, breaking hard into the air.

Once again, Adam fell into Lochlan's waiting arms. He was aware of gasps, surprised shouts, someone saying his name and the fitful blurs of bodies in front of his vision. Cringing away from them, he turned, pressing his face against the warm skin of Lochlan's throat. Hands stroked his hair, and there were whispered words that he couldn't make out. For a time he lost himself in it, and let everything else go.

"You're not some hero riding in with shining armor, waving your sword and slaying all the dragons. If you were thinking that, you stop it now."

Gradually—he wasn't sure how long it took—he reemerged to find Naomi lying on the mat, her eyes closed, peaceful. So relaxed, in fact, that he had a horrible moment of dread before Rachel turned to him. Her face was drawn, exhausted, and she looked as if she might be about to collapse herself, but though her dark eyes shined with tears, a gentle smile curved her lips.

"She's sleeping," she murmured. "She's all right now. Adam, we—"

"No." He shook his head, leaning forward, Lochlan reluctantly releasing him. He felt beyond weak, more so than he had when he had healed Rachel. Aarons was right. There was no way he could heal everyone. Even one a day would kill him within a week.

But he wouldn't need to.

Rachel arched a brow. With an effort, he reached out and laid his hand over hers, and felt something electric pass between them. "It wasn't us," he said quietly. "It wasn't me. I failed. It was you. It was all you."

He let out a long breath and settled back against Lochlan once more, his eyes falling closed. "You were right," he added, his voice dropping even lower. He needed to sleep. He would sleep, and in the morning everything would change. "I'm no hero. I'm not going to save these people."

"No?" Lochlan tilted Adam's chin up.

"No." Adam smiled. It was relief. It was beyond relief. It was finding his place in what was happening, at last understanding— or finding that he had understood—what his purpose was. He could almost see Ixchel smiling back at him, her eyes full of good-humored mischief. "They're going to save themselves."

CHAPTER

TWENTY-ONE

Sinder was emerging from a particularly unpleasant dream—a deep pit that he was crossing on a thin wire, his balance wavering and wobbling, and the pit like a mouth open to swallow him—when the call came. He sat up with a rush of gratitude at being awake, and then excitement and anticipation drowned it.

He hit the comm receiver by his bed and rolled upright as the small screen in the nightstand slanted upward and flicked on. Of course, it was the woman from the surface again, and there was something about her that seemed. . . chastened.

"I've heard back," she said. "Mr. Sinder— I'm sorry, did I wake you?"

"No. I mean, yes. It doesn't matter. What's the word?" Not his normal manner when speaking to a superior, but he didn't care, and sensed that it didn't matter. She had what he wanted. It was coming toward him with an inexorability of the most pleasant kind.

"The word is that you're to have whatever access you require, immediately." She said it all in a rush, as if in a hurry to have the words out. She had enjoyed flexing her muscle over him at the time. Now her muscle had been removed, and she didn't appear to be enjoying *that* much at all. "And I must also apologize for delaying you as much as I did. You understand the need to adhere to strict procedure regarding—"

"Yes, yes." He waved a hand impatiently. "It's all right. So I can return to the planet? You'll accept a landing party?"

"Yes. However, before you do . . ." She coughed. "I'm sending you an information packet on our facility. It's very detailed. You should make sure you look at it closely before you send anyone into the facility itself."

"Is there any danger to my people?"

"Not directly. But the purpose of our facility should be known before you have any contact with its occupants. Those are my orders. By extension, they're yours." She gave him a tight smile. "You may proceed, Mr. Sinder. Retrieve your prisoners and vacate the facility as soon as possible."

"Certainly." Sinder gave her a polite nod. There was no reason to not be gracious, now that he had what he needed from her. "I appreciate your expedition. I'll be in touch as soon as I can."

The screen flicked off without another word from the woman. Sinder picked up the pad that lay beside it, which was already flashing with a message notification. Attached to a textless communique was a single large file, which he opened.

He read it for over an hour, sitting in bed with the blankets pooled around his waist. When he was done, he lowered the pad into his lap and stared at nothing.

Yuga.

Not lying. Not lying at all.

After a few more minutes, Sinder lifted his right hand in front of his face and looked closely at it. Was that a tremor he detected in his fingertips? Was that a shaking deep in his muscles?

He was superior stock. He had always believed that would protect him. That it was a shield against harm, ironclad, unbreakable except by his own error.

But Adam Yuga had been from superior stock, too. And where was he now? Melissa Cosaire had gone mad. What had driven her to that? Had it simply been some inherent weakness in herself, something that he couldn't possibly share with her? Or had it been something else? Something she had known, some horrible secret that had eaten her away from the inside until she simply collapsed into panic and rage?

No. He let his hand fall, steel bracing itself inside him. Yes, she must have known. And yes, that might well have driven her into the madness that had helped to destroy her, or delivered her into the hands of the mutinous conspiracy that had resulted in her death. But he wasn't her. Regardless of what was or was not happening to him, he was going to remain focused. Calm. He had a job to do. He had a higher purpose to serve—one that went beyond superiors or orders and into the heart of what the Protectorate was. What it meant. Its ideal. Its legacy. He would serve that purpose for as long as he was able, and in the end, if he could be of no further use to it, he would take his leave with grace and dignity.

Later, he could fret about himself. Yuga was still the greater danger. Him, the people with whom he had surrounded himself, the tendrils he might have already extended into the Protectorate's structures of power—these were the barbarians pounding at the gates. Whatever solution they seemed to offer would taint the Protectorate's core, its beating heart. The Protectorate would not poison itself with "solutions" from the very things they'd purged from themselves. There would be another way. But before searching for that, the barbarians would be dealt with. Everything else was secondary.

He punched the comm on again, calling up the bridge and Alkor's personal channel. Her voice came through immediately, sharp and alert. She must have known about the previous call. She must have been ready.

"Yes?"

"We have our clearance," Sinder said, and allowed himself a faint, hard smile. "Take us back to the planet. Prepare your landing party. We're going in."

Adam stood some way from the shack, staring out past the double fences. In the distance, the sun was rising, thin and pale. He had been up for something like an hour already, had extracted himself from the heavy, tangled sprawl of Lochlan's limbs, and was taking what fresh air he could, every breath seeming to pump a bit more strength back into him.

He would need it for what was coming next.

A hand touched his back. He started but didn't turn.

"Can't sleep?" Rachel asked, her voice almost at a whisper. She moved to stand beside him. She appeared tired, though not worryingly so. There was a new energy about her, a strength that hadn't been there before. Not only hope.

Life. Life, and a grip on the same.

He shrugged. "I was. Then I woke up and it didn't seem like there was much point in sleeping. We'll have to move fast once the rest of the camp is up."

Rachel nodded. "Naomi is awake too. We've been talking. She understands. She wants to speak to you before we start, but she's with us." Her mouth twisted. "Apparently she was talking escape when the first people came here. Then she stopped when it became clear that she'd only end up getting people killed. But if she broaches the subject again, people will listen. A lot of them, anyway."

"You don't think all?"

"I don't know. They're afraid. Some more than others. You might be a problem, honestly. You and your . . . friend."

Adam met her gaze levelly, though there was a sinking sensation in his gut. "How so?"

"Oh, c'mon. I'm not oblivious, you know." She paused, teeth worrying at her bottom lip. "You're together. Aren't you? You know. *With* him."

He laughed. He couldn't help it. "Yeah." As usual, there was no point in denying it. He didn't want to, anyway. Not anymore. He owed Lochlan that much. "We are. That's a problem?"

"He's a Bideshi." She was quiet again. "I mean . . . No, it's not a problem for me. It would've been, but that was before. Now . . . I don't think it matters. You do whatever you have to; I don't honestly give a fuck." She sighed. "But the others—I'm not sure they'll be so open-minded. Naomi knows and she's mostly okay with it, and that's a start, but . . . Yeah, I don't know."

"Well, I can't exactly change it." Adam raked a hand through his hair. It felt lank and greasy. When had he even last bathed? At least he had long since stopped smelling the stench of the camp. "You think we just . . . hang back? Keep a low profile?"

"I don't know." Rachel still looked uncomfortable. "Why *him*?"

It always seemed to come back to this. "He and his people are a huge part of the reason why I'm still alive. Him more than others." He paused as memories welled in his mind. The feeling in those memories stretched into the present: weariness and the sensation of being pulled forward, exhorted to continue. "But that's not all of why. He's . . .

He's not like anyone else I've ever met. I thought he hated me at first, but he was there for me when I needed him most. He never asked for anything in return. He helped me . . . accept who I am."

He flashed a wicked smile as a very Lochlan-like impulse gave him a push. "And he's *fantastic* in bed."

Rachel made a choking sound, but when he glanced at her she was smiling.

"He *hates* the Protectorate, Rachel. He has every reason to be content to see us all dead. But he came with me anyway. I don't even think he hates our people, anymore. I think he hates the idea the Protectorate is built on. What it stands for." He tilted his head back, watching the lightening sky. "I think I'm with him there."

Rachel stood silently for a few moments. Then she let out a breath. "I think I am too. If it does this to people. Why should I feel any fucking loyalty to something that doesn't care if my children die?"

"Yeah." Adam turned to her. A shiver swept through him as he realized what this moment meant. It wasn't the first step toward what was coming next, but it was another one of them along the way. If he could talk about the Protectorate this way with her, about what it had done, then he could talk about it with others. And he would need to. "Let's get back to the shelter. I need to talk to Naomi. And then we need to move."

Naomi sat on the mat and listened as Adam talked, and then Adam listened as she talked, until the sun was high in the sky. They talked through the breakfast summons, barely noticing the siren, ignoring their gnawing bellies. Lochlan sat beside him, making his presence felt though not interjecting. Once or twice Naomi glanced at him, but otherwise seemed to ignore him.

They couldn't have been much more than an hour into their discussion before Adam was sure that Rachel was right: this woman was the key to everything. Maybe not everyone would listen to her, but most would.

And she agreed. She could convince them to do that much.

"I don't know how this *healing* is possible," she said. "But I don't think I need to understand it. What matters is that it works." She ruminated. "Rachel and I will head out into the camp and do what we can. *Show* people what's possible. I doubt we can get through everyone today, but if we move fast, probably by the end of tomorrow. It'll spread like a virus." She smiled, steady and cool and determined. "We have to keep it quiet, though. Make sure everyone pretends to still be sick. The last thing we need is the guards wondering what's going on."

"You trust everyone here?" Aarons spoke from the corner. He had appeared to be dozing upright, but now both his eyes were open. "People have a way of turning traitor when they're hungry enough. Will anyone blab to the guards? Maybe for extra rations?"

Naomi appeared to consider his words for a moment, then shook her head. "I've never known anyone to do that. It might be that we all feel the whole common enemy thing especially keenly. Or it could be that the guards have never really made it worth anyone's while. Anyone who snitched would be persona non grata around here. We'd make their lives even more miserable and they know it, and they wouldn't get help from any other quarters."

"And you don't think they might assume that there wouldn't be anyone left to make their lives miserable?"

"The guards wouldn't kill us all." Naomi shot him a grim smile. "That would be a lot of bodies for them to dispose of, and they don't have the best work ethic."

"Really?" Aarons appeared unconvinced. "I hope you're right. In any case, I guess there isn't much we can do. Either we risk it or we do nothing."

"Tonight the camp will meet." Naomi turned back to Adam. "There's a place in the center of the quarantine. It looks like more shelters, but under the roofs it's a bigger space than that. Sometimes it works sort of like a market, when people manage to scavenge or save anything worth bartering from the shit they chuck in here sometimes, but it's also big enough to hold most of us without drawing too much attention. They don't care what we do anyway, as long as we're not trying to escape."

"Good." Adam paused. Here was a question that he should have asked before. "Aarons over there was military police. Is there anyone else here with peacekeeper training?"

"A few," said Rachel. "Not that many."

"That's fine. If we're going to take a group under the fence to break into the armory, a small team is better than a crowd of untrained people."

Lochlan coughed. "You're along for the charge, eh, *chusile*? You, the ex–desk pilot?"

Adam gave him a look. "You really expected me not to?"

"I suppose not." Lochlan returned his gaze, level and hard. "So you know of course I'm coming with you. *Someone* has to keep your perfect ass alive."

Adam smiled faintly. "I wouldn't want it any other way."

The cure was passed on slowly. Outwardly, there was no sign that anything was changing. The horn blared for the midday meal, and people stumbled and shuffled toward the vats of watered-down porridge the same way they always did. This time there was a little dried meat and some bread—which Adam gathered was a fabulous luxury. At first it had struck him as odd that the inmates were so poorly fed—after all, it wasn't as though the Protectorate was suffering from food shortages, and there wasn't any obvious reason why it would serve anyone to keep them all at a low level of starvation. But now he understood that it was a symptom of the same phenomenon that might also serve them well in the end.

The Protectorate fundamentally didn't care. Food shipments from off-world were probably infrequent, and nothing particularly edible appeared to grow on the planet itself. He guessed that the porridge was watered to make it stretch.

That, and a camp full of sick, weakened people was a camp full of people who were unlikely to launch any concerted resistance.

They would never see it coming.

And it was coming. Standing in line among them, Adam could feel it. The staggering, the shaking—in many of them it was genuine.

However, in more than a few of them it was an act, and underneath, they were alive and keen and stronger. Their bodies were already healing, some of their ingrained, bred physical hardiness clearly remaining. Another day and they would be ready.

Adam curled his hand around Lochlan's, squeezing. After a second or two Lochlan squeezed back, firmly.

Despite everything that had happened, they were still together.

"So fast," Lochlan whispered, looking around. "*Chere*, I never thought it would happen this quick."

"That's the thing. The healing ... Doing it comes naturally. It felt like something I had always known how to do." Adam suppressed a smile. He couldn't possibly assume that everything would work from here on out, but the temptation to do so was strong, and persistent optimism had been nudging at him all day. "Naomi was right; it's like a virus. It'll be all over the camp by the end of tomorrow. Before then, I think we'll have enough people."

Lochlan shook his head. His face was unreadable, but his hand tightened even more.

"Lock. It'll be fine."

"You can't know that."

"No, I can't. But I can have faith. Can't you?" Adam did smile then, quick and soft. "I thought you were the irrational, superstitious one. Lost in whatever gibberish you get from the stars and animal guts."

Lochlan huffed a laugh. "Shut up, you goddamn *raya*."

Adam lifted Lochlan's hand to his lips and kissed his knuckles, and if anyone saw, he couldn't have cared less. Compared to the other risks they were taking, this was no risk at all.

So night fell. And they waited.

Inside the large central shelter, Rachel was playing with her children in a little alcove set between two roughly connecting walls and keeping half an eye on the entrance as people trickled in. The children were laughing and chattering to their mother. Adam wondered if it was simply relief at seeing their mother well again or better health in themselves, since he gathered she had healed them.

Or maybe, once shown how, one of them had healed the other.

The shelter was easily ten times the size of Rachel's, and the ceiling was draped canvas, the walls the same scrap material as the rest of the camp's shelters. The floor was a series of boards and pieces of sheet metal, all of it caked with mud. The light of a few hanging lanterns cast weird shadows around the place, making it seem both larger and smaller than it was.

Adam supposed that uprisings had been started in less grand places.

Lochlan stood behind him, one hand at Adam's back. Aarons, for his part, was leaning against one of the sturdier supporting walls with his arms crossed. It was, as usual, difficult to say for sure what he felt, but he had come, and that meant a great deal.

At one end of the shelter, the tarp over the door was lifted aside, and in stepped Naomi, posture even straighter and her color better than it had been a few hours ago. She nodded to Adam and approached him, while the others hung back, looking him up and down with no little skepticism.

"I've told them what's going on," she said when she reached them. "They're not sure about you. Or the Bideshi." Lochlan let out a dry breath of a laugh, which Naomi appeared not to notice. "They *are* sure that they've been healed, and all of them want to know more. They'll listen. But again, I have to ask you to let me do the talking."

After another half an hour or so, the place was filled to capacity. Adam tugged Lochlan toward the back of the crowd, taking a place near Aarons. As they settled themselves, Naomi raised her hands and at once the crowd went silent. All eyes were on her.

"You know why you've been called here. We have a matter of vital importance to discuss," Naomi announced. "All of you have been healed of the sickness that's been ravaging us. I can't tell you exactly how or why. You've felt it—you have to make sense of it for yourselves. What you do need to understand is that this gives us an opportunity. The guards don't know yet that we're healthy. They've gotten complacent. They won't be expecting resistance. If we move fast, and we stick together, we have the chance to win our freedom."

No one spoke, but many people glanced at each other, brows furrowed but without any hint of incredulity or scorn. Many looked thoughtful. A good sign, overall. After a few seconds, Naomi continued.

"We have a short period of time where we can hide what's happened. We've discovered a blind spot near the fence where the guards never get too close. I believe we can take advantage of it."

"The fence is lethal," someone toward the outer edges of the crowd called. "You touch it, you die. How are we supposed to get around that? Even if there *is* a blind spot."

Murmurs of agreement. Once more Naomi raised her hands for quiet.

"We can't go over or through it, no. But I believe that it's possible to go under."

Again there was silence, and this time the exchanged glances were accompanied by raised eyebrows, widened eyes. Before anyone could speak, Naomi went on.

"Digging a safe distance down will take some time. But if we begin tonight and keep going after dark tomorrow, I think we can be done before the following sunrise. Then a small team could go through and make their way to the armory, gear up with whatever they can find there, and release the rest of us. There are transport ships near the hangars. We can hijack a couple of them, load everyone up, and make our way off-world."

Still no one said a word. Adam took a breath and held it. This wasn't good. It didn't *feel* good. Maybe he had put too much faith in Naomi's clout.

Maybe Lochlan was right. Maybe he *did* have a little too much faith here in general.

But then Lochlan took his hand once more, thumb stroking behind his knuckles. "Just wait, *chusile*," he whispered, warm breath close to Adam's ear. "Give them a chance."

"Where will we go?" Another man's voice spoke up, skeptically, but Adam took note of the phrasing. *Will*. That couldn't mean nothing. "Even if we make it off-world without being massacred, without failing completely, no one in the Protectorate would take us.

Nowhere would be safe for us. Where could we go where we wouldn't be caught again? Or killed outright."

"There's more than the Protectorate," Rachel said, moving to stand beside Naomi. "There's the frontier. The Protectorate doesn't have a lot of control out there, and pretty much anyone has their price. Or we could go even farther."

"Regardless." Naomi folded her arms across her chest, her face set and stern. "It's better than just sitting around in our own shit waiting to die. Which is all there is for us here. Now. I need to know who's with me and who *is* content with that last option."

Nothing. Adam realized that he was holding his breath, every muscle tense. But then a young woman with brown hair cut close to her scalp stepped forward.

"I'm with you. We'll probably all fucking die anyway, but what the hell." She barked a laugh. "You're right. Almost anything would be better than this."

It happened in a wave. Other people nodded and raised their hands, first a few and then more and more until the entire space was a sea of upraised hands. Naomi watched them, a smile spreading across her face.

Lochlan squeezed his shoulder, murmuring, "I told you."

Aarons muttered something about *fucking suicide*, but when Adam glanced his way, a smile was playing about his distorted mouth.

"Good." Naomi waved for silence again. "We move now, then. Get anything you can shift dirt with. There can't be more than ten of you working at a time or we'll draw too much attention. And those of you with peacekeeper training, report to me. Anyone on the team going for the armory has to know how to use a weapon." Something cold and sharp passed across her face, though her smile remained. "There's only a hundred or so of you in here, and I know all of your names. If the guards find out about this, if we're betrayed . . . Maybe they'll kill us. But I'll find whoever's responsible, and I'll make sure that they go first. And slow."

There were nods. A few grim smiles that mirrored Naomi's. Even a laugh or two, though just as grim, and a little thin. They believed she would do it. They believed she could. And they were behind her if she had to.

"All right. Let's get going. Everyone who doesn't have a job right now . . ." Naomi let out a long breath and pointed toward the door, direct and steady and commanding. "Go out and heal people. As many as you can. Don't tell them exactly what's going on, but tell them to be ready. Tomorrow night, before dawn, we'll either be free . . . or dead."

CHAPTER

TWENTY-TWO

Lochlan's arms ached. His back ached. His knees ached: the result of keeping himself in a low crouch for what seemed like hours. He was exhausted to dropping point and felt as if he might simply fall into the trench they were digging and go to sleep. Still, he kept carving away at the ground, gouging it, scooping soil into makeshift buckets and passing it back to the people behind them to be hidden away, so no mound of dirt was left behind as a giant red flag to the guards.

They weren't digging a hole so much as boring a crawl space under the fences. It was currently tiny, and Lochlan could tell that when it was finished, it would be barely big enough for an adult to wriggle through. The ten people on the dig team weren't working all at once but rather were operating in shifts, one by one replacing those who were too tired to go on. Every half an hour a single guard passed a few hundred yards away, and everyone dropped onto their bellies, as still as stones.

Incredibly, it appeared to be working.

At last Lochlan rolled to the side and lay on his back, panting. Someone shuffled past him to take over, but he didn't move away. He gazed up at the stars, which were hazy through a thin layer of cloud, and let his muscles gripe at him for a bit.

Adam sat down next to him, tugging a stray dreadlock away from his face. "You okay?"

Lochlan coughed and smiled. "Brilliant. Fucking brilliant. This is a lovely honeymoon, darling; thank you *so* much for thinking of it."

"*Honeymoon?*"

"Well . . . *Yeah.*" Lochlan pushed himself up on his elbows, which complained, but he ignored them. "Don't you know how Bideshi weddings work?"

Adam now appeared distinctly worried. "No."

"Two people who are deeply in love must endure pain and the threat of death together and for each other," Lochlan said in a singsong voice that bespoke well-known tradition. "So. That's that, then. Pretty sure we've done it several times over."

Adam stared at him. It was delightful. "I— I didn't. You mean we—"

"The thing is . . . And I really think you should know this."

"What?" It was almost a squeak. Lochlan nodded solemnly.

"I'm completely fucking with you, you stupid *raya*."

Adam stared again, then sputtered and punched Lochlan's upper arm. Lochlan let out a barely hushed peal of laughter.

"Your *face, chusile*."

"You *asshole*. That's not even sort of funny."

"Yeah, pretty sure you're wrong there." Lochlan slung an arm behind his head, settling back. It had been funny, and more than that, it had felt *important*, as if he had grabbed for and briefly held a fragment of his life as it had been.

And yet. Adam's reaction kept tugging at him.

"Does it bother you that much?" he asked quietly. "The idea of being married?"

Adam turned his face away, his hands moving uncomfortably over and over each other. "I mean . . . I don't know. I . . . I never thought about it. Two . . . people like us. Getting married. Does that happen?"

Lochlan pushed himself up, shaking his head in wonder. "Of course it happens. Why the hell would you think it didn't?"

Adam shot him a sharp look. "You know why."

"Yes, I suppose I do." He sighed. He hadn't been ready to be disappointed. If he was honest, he hadn't thought about marriage either—not at all. It simply hadn't been on the scanner. Yet now he realized that he was. A little. "Never mind, then."

Adam was silent for a few minutes, his attention fixed in the middle distance. Lochlan was starting to slip into a light doze when Adam spoke again.

"I think I . . . I would want to know it when it was happening. That's all."

Lochlan turned to Adam. The spotlights around the perimeter fence were on and bright, but Adam's face was thrown into shadow, with only its barest outlines showing. Like that, he appeared both incredibly young and profoundly old, a man who had already seen and done more than enough for one lifetime and would do more still. Lochlan hoped.

He hoped so much.

"So does that mean you want—"

"Patrol!" one of the diggers hissed, and Adam dropped flat beside Lochlan, his face to the ground.

And when the patrol had passed, Adam took one of the diggers' places, and for the rest of the night they hardly spoke to each other at all.

The morning dawned exactly as the others had. Lochlan and Adam returned as the sky was beginning to lighten, curled up together on Rachel's floor and fell into a precious few hours of exhausted sleep. When Lochlan opened his eyes, it was well past midmorning. They had missed breakfast, but he wasn't hungry. Perhaps it was nerves. Perhaps he had simply moved past hunger for the moment.

Leaving Adam sleeping, he got quietly up—groaning as his abused muscles let out fresh protests—and made his way out of the shelter. Beside the door there was a small barrel that appeared to have been set to catch whatever rain fell, and he dipped a hand into it—it was only about a quarter full—and scrubbed at his face. He wasn't sure it did any good, but he felt slightly more human.

"Morning."

Aarons was coming toward him, lifting a hand. Lochlan lifted one in return and dropped into a crouch, trying to stretch the worst of the stiffness out of his thighs.

"How's the dig coming?"

Lochlan shrugged. "Naomi was right; we'll finish tonight. Probably not even that long after dark. I'm not going, though. I'm in the lucky bunch that gets to storm the armory; I need to not be about to fall the fuck over." He huffed a laugh, rubbing his eyes again. They felt gritty and too big for his head, as if he had drunk too much lovina the night before. "Where've you been?"

"With the team you're on." Aarons grunted. "Looking 'em over since I guess I'm the one with the most actual combat experience. They're not much, but they *might* not all get killed."

Lochlan shot him a glare. "I can more than hold my own, old man."

"Old is right. Like I said, experience. I didn't say anything about your capabilities, boy, so watch your damn mouth." Aarons paused, then added, less tersely, "For what it's worth, I believe you. I've seen what the Bideshi can do. I'd trust you before any of them. It's good that you're with us."

Lochlan nodded, flicking his gaze away. "Yeah. Well. We have to work with what we've got."

"Don't we always?" Aarons dropped down beside him, letting out a breath as his knees cracked like breaking twigs. "Like I said, you're right. I *am* old. Older than I wanted to be." He lifted his head, as though to scent the air. "But something is happening. Can't you feel it? It's like the whole place is waking up."

It was. Lochlan could. Life, in a way that there had not been. It was nothing that he could see or hear, but the despair that had hung over the place like a noxious cloud had lifted, and the sky was clear.

Would the guards feel it too? Would they have any idea what it really was?

He glanced at Aarons. "Can I ask you something?"

"I guess."

"You people . . . You care about perfection more than anything else, isn't that right? Perfection of all kinds, but especially physical. No weakness. No sickness. No place in your pristine world for the likes of Adam fucking Yuga. Or any of these people. That's so?"

Aaron's brow inched higher, but he nodded. "Not sure it's *mine* anymore. Not after what happened to me. And honestly I never felt like it was the best fit. Never obsequious enough when it came to those *ideals*. But yeah. Essentially."

"So why did they let you stay after you got the scars? Looking like you do?"

For a long moment, Aarons didn't answer, and Lochlan wondered if he was offended by the question. He had half expected the man to be so, and had decided that he didn't much care—he still wanted to know. It had been eating at him for days: a thing that didn't make sense.

At last Aarons shook his head slowly. "Honestly? I have no fucking idea."

Lochlan laughed, surprised. "Honestly," he echoed, and believed that it was. He supposed that Aarons had no reason to not be honest. "How did it happen?"

"Bomb went off just a little too close to my face." Aarons smiled thinly. "I was good at what I did. Really good. Counterterrorism. Translated well into detective work after they couldn't let me keep my old job. Was never sure about the reason for that, either. I think maybe they were hiding me, but I dunno. It never mattered."

"You had a lot of trouble with *terrorism*, then?"

Aarons gave him a hard look. "You know what the Protectorate is. Funny how it's called that, given how and what they protect. The term is supposed to apply to space under the control of Terra, but I don't know how much Terra even matters anymore."

He turned his face away again, moody. "The *Terran* part is just a word. There's only the Protectorate now. The people who used to be in charge, who presided over some of its greatest days . . . They're barely even human anymore. They don't remember why they're alive, only that they want to stay that way more than anything. That's what the Protectorate is, Bideshi. It's a dying thing that won't lie down and die, and it's getting its own people killed instead. I'm not the first one to notice that, and I'm sure as *fuck* not the only one out there who's angry about it. So yeah, we have trouble with terrorism. Not that anyone likes to talk about it."

He smiled faintly. "That's why they're so scared of Yuga. Someone somewhere knows what he is, what he means. This whole thing is ready to come down. All it needs is a push in just the right place."

Lochlan nodded. This was all making sense. An entity as sprawlingly powerful as the Protectorate could only ever be a top-heavy, blundering, blind animal operating on pure instinct; it was one of the reasons why the Bideshi kept themselves scattered in small

SUNNY MORAINE

groups, nimble and quick and responsive to a changing environment.
He looked at the Protectorate as a small, agile creature regards a
lumbering beast and found the idea of toppling something so large
attractive, the part of him that reveled in chaos delighting in the
prospect of watching it fall apart.

But Adam.

"You want him to push. That's why you're here."

"Boy, I don't think he needs to do any more pushing than he's
already done." Aarons pointed at the camp, the stirring that filled it.
"If he died now, what he's started wouldn't stop. It might not go as
far, it might not have as much fire under its ass, but you give people a
taste of what they were missing and they'll run you over to get more."
He smiled again. "You don't have to lead a revolution in order to
start one."

"I don't want to see him hurt," Lochlan said softly. "I don't . . . Not
again. I don't know if I even care about anything else."

Aarons nodded, lowering a hand to trace lines in a dry, dusty
patch of ground. "Y'know, you and him could probably take off, once
we get free. Leave this all to the rest of us and find yourselves a quiet
spot somewhere. Settle down. Raise a family or whatever." He grinned
suddenly, and it was a grin with a sharp edge. "But you won't. He
won't. You can't let yourselves. You're both in it to the end, now."

"You guys talking about me?"

Lochlan glanced over his shoulder and saw Adam standing in the
doorway, yawning and scrubbing at his face. He was still pale, deep
pits under his eyes, but it would have to do. There was work to be
done.

"Talking about what's next," Lochlan said.

"Ah." Adam leaned over and pressed a kiss to Lochlan's bare
shoulder. "I feel good. I know I shouldn't, every fucking part of me
hurts, but . . . I do."

"Well, that's one of us." Aarons pushed himself to his feet with
a grunt and dusted off his hands. "Bideshi, when you're ready, come
meet the rest of us in the center of the camp. We need to go over the
plan of attack." He tipped an imaginary cap, gave them both a sardonic
smile, and walked away.

"I'm coming with you," Adam said, staring at Aarons's retreating back.

Lochlan had been thinking about this, thinking hard, and all at once he was decided. "You'll do no such thing."

"Lock, what— Come on, we talked about this. I'm not letting you go in there without me." Adam's mouth was drawn into a thin, stubborn line: familiar and well loathed. "You knew I wouldn't, Lock. I already said, don't fuck around."

"*Khara*, no. I don't care what you said. I've been thinking about this since then. You're not a fighter. You have no training at all. And your *perfections* got stripped away when you fixed yourself on the Plain. Maybe you were cured then, but all those perfect little cells of yours are in tatters, all jumbled up and messy. I don't know for sure, I can't know, but I'd be willing to bet the healing is worse for you because you're the source. You're the conduit. The *roots*. You'll get yourself killed." Lochlan took a breath—this felt cruel, a stab into a weak, raw spot, but it also felt *true*. "You'll get other people killed."

Adam fell silent, jaw set and eyes narrowed, looking mutinous. More than that, *stung*, and again a wave of guilt swept over Lochlan. But he couldn't pretend it wasn't so. Not even out of kindness. Sometimes kindness could be the worst decision.

"*Chusile*." Lochlan laid a hand against Adam's cheek; Adam stiffened but didn't move. "They need you here. You need to help organize the rush once we get the gate open. I'm not just saying that. You don't always have to be the one in front. Sometimes that's not where you do the most good. You see?"

After seconds that stretched out like minutes, Adam seemed to loosen, and he nodded, eyes lowering. "If something happens to you," he said quietly, "I can't stand the idea that I . . . could've been there. That I could've done something."

"*Mitr*, you can't save everyone. You know that."

"Yeah, I guess I do." Adam sighed, then reached up and covered Lochlan's hand with his. "All right. Shit, I . . . I don't want to fight about it. But you better come back in one piece. Or I'll pull the rest of the pieces off and hit you with them."

"How can I say no to a deal like that?"

Adam laughed, though it was a bit thin, and everything lightened, eased. If only a little. Lochlan leaned forward and nodded their mouths together, which was all he could think to do now, and around them the world spun on toward the dark and whatever came after.

CHAPTER

✳

TWENTY-THREE

When the fleet arrived, the part of the planet that housed the camp had already swung into night. Sinder stood on the bridge, freshly washed and pressed and perfect, staring out at the dusty ball, which appeared as a pale crescent, spinning in the dark. The crescent was expanding as they slid into orbit and away from the camp, and the fleet was dispersing around the planet, forming a sensor net. They would see everything.

They wouldn't lose what they had come for.

Sinder took a place beside Captain Alkor, who had been quiet ever since he'd briefed her on the nature of the camp. Sinder had omitted the details of the illness, saying that it was a disease that was manifesting in a tiny percentage of the population from one particular system, that it wasn't yet well understood, but it didn't seem to be contagious via air or bodily contact.

She had seemed to believe it. But she clearly hadn't liked it.

Well, she didn't have to. As long as she did her job.

"Give the order to launch the landers," Alkor said, consulting a readout on the screen in front of her chair. "ETA?"

"About three hours, ma'am." The crewmember she'd addressed glanced up. "We just got word that there's a hardware problem with the guidance syncing. Fleet-wide. We have multiple repair crews working on it, but we can't launch until it's fixed."

Alkor muttered a curse. "Fast as you can, then, Lieutenant."

"Yes, ma'am."

Sinder felt a prickle of alarm. They had been surprised by one traitor already. "A hardware problem, Captain? Is something like this—"

Alkor waved a hand. "I wish it was unusual. Been an issue with a number of classes of ships ever since they overhauled the designs. It's been a while since it happened; I thought maybe the last round of repairs dealt with it, but . . ." She let out a growl. "You'd think we could get something this small *right* on the first try."

"If you're sure," Sinder said evenly. His suspicions weren't completely done away with . . . But the explanation was enough. For the moment. "There's no reason to get so upset. Not if what you're telling me is true. They're penned in; all we have to do is go in and get them. Now, three hours from now, it makes no difference." He smiled. "We've waited this long. We can wait a bit longer."

In truth, inside—under his carefully maintained composure—he was jittery, a walking ball of nervous energy. Yuga, so close and yet still out of reach. But he wasn't going to appear more eager than he could help. It was unbecoming. It was also useless.

Alkor looked up from her display. "Hail the base down there."

There were a few seconds of static as the channel opened. Then an impatient, disembodied male voice said, "Yes?"

"This is Captain Amanda Alkor of the PSS *Excelsior*. I'm contacting you in regards to—"

"I know why you're contacting us." Still impatient, but now resigned as well. "We've already heard. We're to allow you unfettered access." A pause, the cause of which was unclear. Then, "Come on down, then. The sooner we get this over with, the sooner you're out of our hair."

"We'd love nothing more," Alkor said dryly. "Unfortunately, we've been delayed due to a technical problem. Our best estimates put us at about three hours from reaching you. However, perhaps in the meantime you could—"

"Captain," Sinder cut in. "A word."

Alkor shot him a scowl. "Please excuse us for one moment," she said, motioning to the comm officer to mute. "What is it?"

"I suspect you were about to suggest that they conduct a preliminary search for us. Is that correct?"

Alkor arched a brow. "Yes . . ."

"Let me request that you not do so."

"And why not?" Alkor's voice rose slightly, pitch higher.

"Because they might well alert him to our intentions before we're on the ground, and that's risky." Sinder meant what he said, but there was more. He wanted it. The satisfaction. The credit. It should be his alone.

And Alkor's, of course.

"I thought you said he was penned in, that all we had to do was collect him."

"Provided he doesn't see us coming. But you'll forgive me, Captain, if I'm reluctant to place my faith in anyone but you and your people." He smiled.

Alkor frowned, but she appeared to be giving the matter real consideration, and finally she nodded. "I suppose it doesn't matter. But before we go in, I want my people briefed by the facility guards. We can't hunt blind."

"Obviously." Sinder inclined his head in thanks. "I appreciate your commitment to doing this right, Captain."

Alkor turned back to the comms officer, nodding, and the channel was unmuted. "Belay that," she said. "We don't need anything from you at this time. We'll contact you when we have a more definite arrival time. In the meantime, we appreciate you standing by."

"Yes, Captain," the voice said—he had never given a name or a rank; clearly these were rough, unmannered people—and the channel clicked off.

Alkor sat back with a sigh. "I'll be honest: I can't wait for this to be over."

"Soon, Captain." Sinder folded his hands between his knees and took a breath. Hours. If nothing else, the wait would heighten the anticipation. "Very soon."

Ten people crouched in the shadows by the fence. They were armed, such as they could be: makeshift cudgels and clubs, wood and plastic and metal and various combinations of all three. Lochlan recognized how little of an edge the weapons gave, but it was better than nothing.

If everything went according to plan, they wouldn't need them for long. Might, in fact, not have to use them at all.

Beside him, Adam pressed close and squeezed his shoulder. "I want you to appreciate how hard this is for me," he said under his breath.

Lochlan pressed briefly back against the touch, then shrugged him off. "I'll meet you outside the gate."

"Right." He both heard and felt Adam moving away, felt his barely suppressed fear as if it were Lochlan's own. And he *was* afraid, however much he was trying not to be. Then again, maybe fear was good. Fear, Kae had said more than once—echoing the hard-edged old woman who had first trained them in fighting with the jambia—made you keen, alert, ready to fight to stay alive. Fear *kept* you alive. People who could no longer feel fear didn't feel much of anything for long.

Ahead of him, Aarons raised a hand—and then dropped it. As one they slid onto their bellies and began to crawl forward toward the trench under the fence.

It wasn't deep. It didn't need to be. Whether through a simple lack of imagination or because of a conclusion that it wasn't necessary, the electrified wire barely extended below ground level. One by one, they wriggled into it, heads down to avoid the fence. As he crawled in, Lochlan found himself taking little gasps instead of real breaths, fearful of touching the wire.

And then he was through.

The ones who had gone before him were already up and crouched, their weapons at the ready. They were still in that blessed patch of deep shadow, deepened further by cloud, and no patrols were in evidence. If the guards kept to their schedule, the team had fifteen minutes or so to get across the space between them and the cover of the closest building.

Aarons made a hard, horizontal slashing motion in front of his mouth. *Silent.* Then pointed and chopped his hand down. *Move.*

The stretch of ground between them and the building couldn't have been more than fifty yards, but it felt more like five hundred. He clutched his metal bar as he crept, fast and as silent as he could, hardly daring to breathe.

Then they were there, and just in time: a few hundred yards away, a guard was approaching, whistling something low and tuneless. "No movement," Aarons breathed, and no one did.

The guard passed, never glancing their way. Aarons nodded to them and started around the side of the structure, avoiding the periodic pools of light and heading for the next building over—before the armory, which they had gathered was a set of general offices. Lochlan was one of the last three to go, and as he did he checked the fence. A form crouched there, watching him, one hand raised, blond hair silver in what little of the spotlight's glare touched him.

Lochlan blinked and there was nothing. Pulling in a huge breath, he followed Aarons and the others.

It was surprising how few guards were about, though it had been established most would have bedded down in the barracks by now. When they reached the next building, they edged close to the outer fence, where the lights were dimmer and no one seemed to patrol regularly. They were still within sight of some of the guard towers, but they kept to the shadows and behind what little cover they could find—crates, a set of barrels, a small ATV.

The armory rose in front of them. It was small and low, and a guard leaned beside the main door, rifle in hand, but head down and shoulders relaxed, possibly in a doze. Aarons held the team back, scanning the space in front of them.

There was no rear door, not that they could spot. In that, their luck wasn't holding.

"We'll have to take 'em out," Aarons hissed. "And then move fast, because odds are we'll be spotted." He pointed to a young man and an equally young women crouched close to him. "Mell, Farrow. Like we talked about. Get whatever you can find in the way of long-range precision weapons and use them. Then remember: four of us to the front gate and four to the inner one. Everyone stay down and make your shots count."

They all nodded. Aarons swept a hand forward, and moving in close and swift, they went for the door.

The guard's head jerked up and he said, "What—" when the burly man to Lochlan's right broke the man's jaw with his club. The club was spiked, and the spikes stabbed deep into the man's throat; he went down with a pained gurgle, twitching and bleeding. Aarons dropped over him, going through his pockets. Smiling grimly, he produced an access card on a chain. "Fan-fucking-tastic."

There were already shouts of alarm as Aarons got the door open, and they pushed inside. Shots rang out, and a whine sliced through the air above him. There was a pained hiss behind him, and he reached back, grabbing someone by the arm and pulling them through the door after him. Someone else pushed it shut and—with the help of another—braced it closed with their backs.

"This isn't going to hold," one of them grunted. "Move fast."

The room Lochlan found himself in was as small as the building itself: gray and unadorned and harshly lit. There were other rooms beyond, but his team probably wouldn't need to do much exploring, because the far wall was taken up entirely by a rack of rifles, sidearms, body armor, helmets. Even—

"Holy shit," Mell said, raking a hand through her short hair. "Are those grenades?"

Aarons headed for the crate, bent and pulled out a shining sphere the size of an apple. His face twisted into a pleased smile. "Yeah. They are." He tossed it to Mell, who caught it automatically, and then turned to the others. "Gear up. Use the armor. It might confuse them, make 'em unsure about who's who on first glance."

On first glance, yes. Lochlan seized one of the armored vests and a helmet, then added a rifle to the ensemble. On second glance, not so much—dirty, skinny people with ragged clothing couldn't really pass for well-fed Protectorate peacekeepers. But it was dark, and the guards would be confused, and that could only help their chances.

Someone was pounding at the door, and the two braced against it strained to keep it closed. They were both tossed rifles and vests of their own and managed to catch them, glancing at the team and gritting their teeth.

"We'll pull back," Aarons said. "Everyone else, get ready to take down whatever comes through that door."

With a *crash* the door burst open, light flooded into the room, and a mass of peacekeepers followed, already firing. Lochlan shot without thinking, without aiming; he was trained but this was chaos, and even a skilled fighter would have trouble picking it apart.

Suddenly it was quiet. Lochlan blinked, scanning his surroundings, taking it in as his ears buzzed gently. Three peacekeepers lay sprawled and dead on the floor ahead of them. A fourth was moaning and clutching a bleeding wound on her thigh.

"Anyone hurt?" Aarons called, and his voice was muddy against Lochlan's abused eardrums. A few negatives—no doubt people were dazed from the sound—and one woman was crouched against a wall while a teammate wrapped up a shallow graze on her hip. A man, grimacing, braced himself on a chair while a neat hole in his upper arm was examined. Neither was bleeding heavily, though both were clearly in pain.

"Can you all keep going?" Affirmatives, though they sounded dazed and a little unsure. Still, it wasn't as if they were swimming in options. "Okay. Let's move. Mell, Farrow, you know what to do."

What happened next flowed forward with a feeling of inexorability, as if Lochlan was following the script that someone else had set for him. The ten of them burst out of the building, Mell and Farrow dropping behind a parked groundcar and lifting their long-range rifles. Aarons grabbed Lochlan's arm as more shots cut through the air, missing them by what seemed like inches. The meal siren began to blare.

"You take three and get back to the inner gate," Aarons bellowed over the din. "I'll take the others and head for the main gate. We all meet up at the hangar bay. *Go.*"

Lochlan ran. Three—he couldn't remember their names, wasn't entirely sure which ones they were—trailed him. He ran as fast as he could with his body hunched low to the ground, and when a guard rose out of nowhere in front of him, he put a bullet in the man's throat without thought.

He was thinking about only one thing. Not the people they were liberating, not the distance they still had to go, not the odds stacked against them.

Like on the Plain, in the worst of the violence and fear, the only thing that mattered was Adam.

Adam heard the shots, and everything in him froze. Everything was difficult to see clearly—there were shapes moving across the outer edge of the compound, lights shifting, but nothing clear. He had to stop himself from pressing against the wire, had to remind himself that it would kill instantly.

There were no guards nearby. They had all gone to hunt the other team. To hunt Lochlan.

"Everyone get ready," Naomi called. "If this works, we won't be waiting long."

Beside him, Rachel touched his arm. She kept a tight grip on the wooden club she had been armed with. Becca and Dion were pressed against her legs, their eyes huge—but somehow steely, determined like he had never seen Protectorate children be before.

They reminded him suddenly of the Bideshi children in the dojo, whirling with their knives.

There were other children, close to the center of the group. Some of them were too small to run and were in slings on people's backs. They would be targets.

They were all targets now.

"It's going to be okay," Adam said quietly, dropping down and fixing the two children with what he hoped was a calming gaze. "We're going to get out of here."

"You're goddamn right," Rachel murmured. "Look."

Adam snapped his head up and straightened as his breath stilled in his chest. Across the compound, Lochlan was running toward him, flanked by three other people. He was helmeted, clad in guard's armor, but Adam saw the beaded dreadlocks swaying, and his heart lurched.

"All right." Naomi's voice lifted above the siren. "Here they come. Everyone get ready to run for the main gate!" Adam scanned the crowd; he wasn't sure if they had managed to collect everyone, but it had to be close, and anyway it was too late to take a full count now.

One of Lochlan's team vanished to the side. A few seconds later there was a rattle and a creak as the gate swung open, and as one the crowd wedged itself through. He was swept on by the wave of humanity, Rachel lost in it beside him, and was past the gate before he realized it. He stopped and shoved his way back through the tide of people, glancing wildly around.

Someone dragged him in, sealing their mouth over his. It was hard, desperate, and there was a fierce joy in it as he returned the kiss with everything in him. The ferocity surging through his veins wasn't only because of the short time they'd been apart. He was letting go of something, maybe letting go of a great many things, and he didn't need to be a hero. He didn't need to save anyone. They were rushing on without him, not needing him anymore.

"All right, *chusile*," Lochlan breathed against his lips. "We'll have time for the grand romantic reunion later. Right now, let's just not get shot."

Adam laughed shakily. "Right." He took Lochlan's hand and pulled—now he heard the gunfire. People were, indeed, shooting at them. *Love makes you crazy.* "I'm bored with this place. Let's leave."

"Ma'am." The comms officer turned toward Alkor. His eyes were wide. Sinder didn't like that. Not at all. "We're getting a transmission from the planet, but . . . it's confusing. I'm not sure what—"

Alkor sat forward. "Patch it through."

There was a crackle of static over the main bridge speakers. Then a terse female voice snapped, "*Excelsior*, come the fuck in. We could really use some damned assistance here."

"This is Captain Alkor." She shot Sinder a bewildered glance. "What's going on down there?"

"We don't know. Seems like a group of the inmates got to the armory, got some weapons. Now they're— Fuck, there's a whole bunch— They're rushing the gate. Repeat, they're rushing the gate. No, get out there and fucking shoot them, I don't care what you have to—"

Nothing but more static and garbled voices. Then, "*Excelsior*, we are under attack. Please tell me you can get your asses down here."

Alkor looked around at the bridge crew. Two of them shook their heads. "At least twenty more minutes," one of them said. "We've isolated the problem, but we're still coordinating with the repair teams."

Alkor cursed under her breath. "I'm sorry. You'll have to hold them off as best you can. Is there any other assistance that we can—"

"Unless you have orbit-to-surface guns, no. Fucking hell. They're all over. They're *sick*, they're not supposed to be able to— They have snipers, what the fuck are they even—"

The channel cut out. Stunned silence settled over the bridge. Alkor looked at Sinder again, and he stared back without a word.

This was *not* supposed to be happening.

"It's Yuga," he whispered. "They have ships there?"

Alkor glanced at her screen. "Yes. Why?"

"Because he's running. He's going to try to make it off-world. Captain, if you want to lend those people some assistance, you can shoot down anything that tries to make it out of atmo."

Alkor's eyes narrowed. "I thought you wanted him alive."

"Disable if you can. But kill if you can't." *Fuck*. His gut clenched— whatever Adam knew about the poisonous seeds that might be taking root in the Protectorate itself, beyond even the sickness . . . He would no doubt be able to ferret it all out without Adam's help. But with Adam it would have been quicker, easier, and far more satisfying. Well. He had to be flexible. He dragged in a hard breath. He sure as hell wasn't going to make Melissa Cosaire's mistakes.

He wasn't going to end up like her.

"He is *not* getting away from us again."

CHAPTER

TWENTY-FOUR

A dam heard, rather than saw, the main gate crash open. That was followed by a roar that wasn't quite a cheer, and everyone flooded through it. Two people close to him fell, but he managed to pull them to their feet before they were trampled, before he was tugged away by Lochlan. As he ran with the rest of the human tide he could see the fence, the guard towers and the gun nests that flanked the main entrance, but no gunfire came from them. Aarons's designated snipers appeared to have done their jobs well.

Really, it was all a bit too easy.

"Nearly there," Lochlan panted, and laughed. "*Chere,* this is almost fun. Let's do it again sometime."

"Yeah, let's not. Not even for a honeymoon." Adam's side was aching, cramping—once it wouldn't have, but that was before he had been remade a little less perfect, a little less strong. He imagined that he could pull strength from Lochlan's hand, and that made things easier.

"So you do want to marry me."

Adam stumbled, dragged himself upright, and held on to a young girl beside him who had stumbled as well. "What?"

"Later." More shots—not from above them but directly behind. To their left there was a series of explosions, and Adam almost stopped, startled, before he was shoved onward.

One of the buildings was on fire. Above it, a spindly metal spire was slowly breaking into pieces and dropping onto the roof.

"Comm tower," Lochlan gasped, and laughed again. "Aarons said he was going to try for that, in case they call for backup. Probably a bit late, but *khara,* that gloriously crazy old bastard."

They all rushed on, curving to the left like a flock of birds. Adam saw the hangars rising ahead of them, and parked outside, as if waiting for them—

Transports. Two. Enough.

"Remember the plan," Lochlan cried in his ear. The siren was still blaring, and though its tone hadn't changed, to Adam it now sounded panicked. "We're in the nearer one with Aarons."

Adam nodded, not enough air in his lungs to speak agreement. It was a plan cobbled together with lots of chances for confusion, but it was the best they could do: half of the escapees in one ship, half in another. Everyone'd been assigned to a particular ship, but he had no idea how well frightened, exhilarated people would hold to them.

But the group split with surprising neatness as they sprinted toward the ships. The first people to reach them released the main hatches and the transport's cavernous mouths opened to receive their human cargo.

More shots, closer. Lochlan had kept his armor, but somewhere in the confusion he had abandoned his rifle. It probably didn't matter; the time for fighting was over. Lochlan dragged Adam toward the open hatch—

And fell to one knee with a sharp grunt.

"*Lock*!" Adam skidded, whirled, saw a line of guards advancing on them and firing. He groped for Lochlan's arm, panic turning to a cold focus as bullets flew around him. There was no more fear as he hauled Lochlan up and onward, bearing almost his entire weight. Lochlan was saying something, but what didn't matter; all that mattered was that he *was*. There was the hatch, and then the dimness swallowed them and the sea of people packing in beside them and behind.

It was horrible to think of them as a shield. But he did.

"Everyone, come on! We're closing up!" Aarons, standing by the hatch, was dragging stragglers on board. The engines were firing; someone must already be in the cockpit. Adam stumbled to one of the walls of the main bay, and Lochlan slumped against it, a hand pressed against his right side.

Adam dropped down in front of him, pushing his hand aside. "Lock, are you—"

No blood. Adam exhaled so hard that he was almost dizzy. He felt something flat and still hot and picked it out, letting it fall into his palm.

The bullet, flattened by the armor.

"I think my fucking ribs are broken," Lochlan hissed, and batted Adam away. "*Khara*, quit it, you mother fucking hen. I'm fine."

"You're *not*." Adam straightened up, ready to argue, but the ship gave a great lurch and began to rise. He braced himself against the bulkhead beside Lochlan, dazed as he scanned the bay. Again a cheer went up, people lifting hands and clubs and waving in triumph. Adam stared at them, and Lochlan took his hand.

These people will save themselves.

"C'mon." Lochlan pushed off the wall and gave him a tug, and started forward through the crowd, limping but moving well enough. "Let's find our scarred friend and reconnoiter. This isn't over yet."

The rest of the way up to the cockpit was chaos. The transport clearly hadn't been designed to accommodate this many people, and they seemed to be crammed into every available space, in the corridors and in the dormitories they passed, in the mess hall, leaning against walls and binding their wounds. A few glanced up as they passed but most ignored them, and again it struck Adam that some of them might have no idea who he was. That he had helped to start it all.

He was fine with that. More than fine.

Like the rest of the ship, the cockpit was crammed with people, everyone talking at once, Aarons especially loudly. Two older women were seated in the pilot and copilot's seat; their hands on the controls. Out the main window, Adam could see the fiery mess on the ground falling away and the low clouds closing over them. Just ahead and to the right, the other transport.

"Everyone *shut the fuck up*," Aarons bellowed, and amazingly, everyone obeyed, turning toward him. He raised a hand. "Hands up if you think this is actually over."

No one moved. Aarons barked a laugh. "You're fucking right it's not. We have no idea what kind of heavy artillery they've got on the

SUNNY MORAINE

ground. They might be able to shoot us outta the sky. We might need to do some evasive flying, and in a bucket like this, I think you can imagine—if you have *any* idea how piloting a ship works—that that might be a tricky prospect. So what you all need to do is stand back, shut the hell up, and let our pilots here *do their job*."

The atmosphere took on a sheepish air. A couple of people muttered and shuffled their feet, but otherwise said nothing. Close beside him, Lochlan laughed and then winced.

"*Chere*, I feel sick. Adam . . ."

Adam slid an arm around him and guided him a few feet to a side console he could lean on. Inwardly he was growling a stream of curses, but there was relief there too. No, it wasn't over, though now that they were airborne, the sky in front of them beginning to show stars, it was easy to feel as if they might be in the clear.

He slid his hands carefully over Lochlan's body, feeling for the straps of the vest. "Let's get this off you."

"Everything okay?"

Adam looked up as Aarons approached. "He took a bullet. He was wearing armor, so he's banged up but he's—"

"I said, I'm *fine*," Lochlan grumbled. "Stars, *mitr*, if you're going to lose your damn fool head over something like a couple of bruises—"

Adam pushed up Lochlan's filthy shirt—and drew in a sharp breath. "You idiot, this isn't a few bruises. Your whole side is purple."

"You might have some fractures. Those rifles have a lot of stopping power." Aarons tugged the worn fabric up higher, arching his unscarred brow. "There's probably a medic somewhere—"

An alarm sounded, harsh and penetrating. Adam and Aarons whirled, and Lochlan yelped as he stumbled.

"Proximity alert," called one of the women at the helm. "There's— *Shit*, there's at least three ships in close orbit around the planet. Large. Protectorate."

"It's Sinder," Adam whispered. He knew it instantly and with absolute certainty. He could feel it, the rhythm and the dance of events, as if he was touching part of those deep roots that he had gone among before. It wasn't merely the Protectorate. It was Sinder. He was here. Waiting for them.

As part of Adam had always known he would be.

Aarons pushed his way through to the pilot's seat, leaning over its back and staring at the console. "Are they hailing us? Making any attempt to get in touch at all?"

"Nothing. They're only . . . sitting there." The woman in the copilot's seat paused—then shook her head, her eyes widening. "No. No, they're not, they're—"

Another alarm. At the same moment, one of the ships swung into view. A small flash of light sparked on its underside, and then another. The light became a bright line, a trail of the thing plunging toward them.

"They're firing," said the woman. She sounded eerily calm. "Trying some evasive maneuvers."

"So I guess they've given up the idea of trying to take us alive." Lochlan's tone airy, smooth and even, but strained around the edges. "Makes some things simpler, don't you think?"

Adam shook his head. "I don't think it's just about us anymore."

"It never was," Lochlan said softly, and then they were almost sent sprawling to the floor as the ship was rocked by an impact. Lochlan let out a cry and clutched at Adam, who felt a stab in his own middle—but they were still alive to feel it.

"It didn't hit us," called one of the pilots. "Shock wave was too close, though. Gonna have to run past them and get to slipstream if we want a chance of staying alive. If the other one doesn't follow us close enough—"

"I'll get in touch with them," said the second pilot, her hands flying across her console. "They already—"

Another impact, and although everyone managed to remain standing, shouts of surprise and alarm rang through the large cockpit. "That's two of them firing now! Everyone hold on, I don't know how much longer we can—"

Her voice was lost as Adam was seized by the shoulder and spun to face Rachel, her eyes wide and frightened and her face bloody from a gash high on her cheek. "What's happening? Why are we—?"

"They're throwing us a going-away party, what do you think?" Lochlan was leaning against the bulkhead again, one arm around his middle as if he were holding himself together. "Nice of them, but it's getting a little rowdy. We should probably put the drink away."

Adam opened his mouth to say something else, but he would never be sure what. At that moment, out the window, the second transport surged into their field of vision, between them and the closest Protectorate ship. Simultaneously, the comm crackled as a channel opened.

"They're hailing," said one of the women, and then a voice sounded over the cockpit's speakers. Unfamiliar. Flat.

"Rogue ships, you have ten seconds to signal surrender. Our next shots will be kill shots."

"They weren't *already*?" Adam coughed a laugh. He was scanning the faces of the people in the cockpit, looking for what they were feeling. They had risked death to make it this far. But now they were being offered a way out, a chance. It was possible that some of them were considering it. Considering their own deaths.

More people potentially on the chopping block because of him.

Except this time, it had been their choice.

Every eye in the place turned to Aarons. He didn't move, his gaze locked on the ships in front of him. Then, slowly, he shook his head.

"They'll kill you. All of you." His mouth stretched into a thin, grim line that wasn't even close to a smile. "Don't make it easy for them."

Not hesitating, the woman who appeared to be in charge of the comm system opened another channel. "You guys hear me? You hear that? Don't do it. It's a trick. Run for the gap there, go for it *now*—"

Multiple explosions of light, multiple streaks. Adam watched it happen in eerie slow motion, unstoppable, horrible. There were an infinite number of ways things might have gone, but this was the path they were on, and there could be only one outcome.

The side of the other transport exploded in a ball of debris and flaming gas. It rocked, then arced downward, burning, pieces of it falling away and spinning off into the void. It was almost graceful, the way it fell back toward the planet, the rest of the shards glowing brilliant red and gold as it hit the thicker atmosphere.

Then it was gone.

"Naomi," Rachel whispered.

The cockpit was silent. In front of them, the gap between the ships was widening. There were more impacts, but Adam hardly felt them. His hand found Rachel's and held on and somehow he sank beneath her skin and joined her again down in the deeper reaches of her. Naomi was there too, tiny fragments of her left from the communion that she and Rachel had shared. Together, he and Rachel gathered them up and clung to them and felt their song going out, the rest of the universe small and distant and unimportant. And it wasn't just Naomi. It was all those people, all joined by the same communion. All bound together by so much more than blood and history.

He hadn't truly understood what this larger communion would mean. This was something deeper than grief, more visceral than pain. Loss like the loss of a limb. He tried to hold Rachel up, only to find she was also holding him. And through it, there was something more, something distant—something so close.

Eyes that saw nothing. And everything.

The white of slipstream closed over the ship, and they were gone.

CHAPTER

TWENTY-FIVE

At some point, Nkiruka and Satya's relationship had become defined by everything that *wasn't* being said. Nkiruka had no idea if it would ever go back to the way it had been before.

She sighed as she and Satya walked hand in hand down toward Ashwina's docks, and of course Satya didn't ask her what was wrong. It would have been a stupid question.

The more crucial question hadn't yet been officially posed. Nkiruka's back wasn't yet officially up against that official wall. But the sense of what faced her was already there—something a little like death. An ending. Everything between her and Satya had already changed, and it would change more once—yes, *once*—the selection was made fact. Perhaps that was what people meant when they said nothing could ever be the same after a candidate refused. No matter what happened, something would be ruined, even between the candidate and the one they had said no for. Because a person was always the reason why. A person or persons. Records of candidates who said no were spotty at best, but the ones that existed did include the given reason. No more than a line or two, sometimes only two or three words, but *something*.

It was always ties. Ties that were stronger than the ties an Aalim was supposed to feel for their people, ties that couldn't be broken. Except now Nkiruka thought she knew the nasty secret behind all that.

They were already broken. As soon as the notion was raised, they were severed as if with an Aalim's bone knife.

"You don't have to walk down with me," Nkiruka said after a moment. "It's only a routine training flight, it's not like I'm—"

"Don't be silly." Satya grasped at her hand, and Nkiruka held on, by instinct if nothing else. They had been holding each other's hands for years now. "It's not like I have anything better to do. Anyway, I like seeing you off. I told you."

"You did." Nkiruka smiled faintly, letting go of Satya and stepping to one side to let a laughing group of teenagers past. "Many times. And you know I like when you do it; I'm only saying you don't *have* to."

Satya spun, stopped Nkiruka with a hand on the center of her chest, and leaned in to press their lips together. Today she smelled like rosemary. Nkiruka bit gently at her lower lip, reaching up to tangle her fingers in Satya's thick black hair and making the little chimes braided into it here and there tinkle softly.

Sometimes she could almost believe that nothing was wrong at all.

"I don't have to," Satya repeated, pulling back. Her smile was warm and sweet, but there was darkness behind it. As there always was now. "I don't have to do anything. I make choices, Nkiru. I do what I want."

She turned again and started to walk, tugging Nkiruka along with her, and Nkiruka went willingly. That had been something more than it seemed, and they both knew it. A step up to the very edge of that not-saying and peering into the chasm beyond. *Like all of us*, Nkiruka thought. *All of us, on that hard edge and making believe that we aren't.*

She focused on their joined hands, her head briefly spinning. *You are my tether. You are my gravity well. Keep me falling around you and never let me go hurtling off into the dark.*

All the dark and all the dancing.

The docks weren't especially busy, the training flight only involving about a third of Ashwina's pilots. The ones going out were making their leisurely way to and fro, getting into their flight suits, talking amongst themselves, laughing and joking and a few of them even shoving. This, too, was a scene in which nothing seemed to be wrong.

It was like a clean bandage over something beginning to fester.

"All *right*, you *voel*. Get yourselves together. I've never *seen* such a sorry display." It was Kae, striding across the deck with his gunner—a petite woman with short red hair who didn't look a day over fifteen—in tow. Everyone glanced up at his call, but no one appeared apprehensive; Kae's tone was play-gruff at worst and everyone could tell when he was in a good mood.

So that was one thing.

"You heard him." Nkiruka nodded at Kae when he caught her eye, then turned back to Satya. "I should jump to it."

"Such a hard taskmaster." Satya leaned up and kissed the corner of Nkiruka's mouth. "Go, then. I'll be at the kilns until later this evening. I'll meet you there? We can go to that place two decks up that has those red bean buns you like so much."

Nkiruka nodded and let her fingers linger on Satya's collarbone as she pulled away. But she didn't speak. All of a sudden she had no idea what she could say.

Kae touched her shoulder as she headed to her gear locker. She turned, half-prepared with an apology, but as soon as she saw his face she knew she wouldn't need it.

"Is everything all right?" He jerked his chin toward Satya. "With her?"

It's not your business, Nkiruka almost snapped, and bit the insides of her cheeks in time to keep it back. Maybe it wasn't his business, not technically, but she never would have cared before. Kae was her teacher. Her mentor. In a few short months he had begun to feel almost like an older brother to her. There was little she had ever kept from him.

But now she was facing two futures, and in one of them, what she did was everyone's business.

Perhaps in the other one as well, if it came to that.

"It's fine," she said, not expecting for a minute that he would believe it. "I'm holding everyone grounded, I should get my gear on."

"There are at least a few others," Kae said, following her toward the lockers. "Everyone's slow these days. Think they're enjoying how much downtime we've been having."

Nkiruka grunted agreement, opening her locker and pulling out her suit. "It's strange that we're having any at all." And it was. Reports from all over of convoys being harassed, finding it difficult to dock at stations, and a few individuals who did manage to board finding themselves detained on petty offenses. And always, always, the questions, which grew more overt with each instance.

"An exiled Protectorate man was involved in the fight on the planet where you have your meetings. You know anything about him?"

Nkiruka had decided that if she ever met Adam Yuga, she was going to make a level effort to break his nose.

"Not going to question it too closely. Relaxed training now could save lives later." Kae lingered a moment more, as if there was something else he was trying to say, then gave her a half shrug and turned, heading off across the deck to where his own fighter was docked.

Climbing into her little single-seater used to be a nerve-racking experience. But now it was almost soothing. It was something about the ritual of it, feeling the way her body fit into the larger body of the fighter, listening to the chatter on her comm. What people were saying didn't even matter; what mattered was the sense that she was not and would never be alone. That, as with everything on a homeship, she was a single part of a much larger whole.

Or such an idea used to be a comforting one. Now she buried her attention in her preflight checks and tried to ignore the comm noise.

"All right," Kae said—she should probably listen now. "Once we get out there, everyone form up on me. We're going to try gamma and delta attack formations and roll back into beta defense. We're only focusing on the *motions* here, people, so it goes without saying that I don't want to see a *single* instance of fire, but here I am saying it anyway, so take me seriously. You all know who your leaders are. Stick with them, hold to the formations, and we'll all be back in time for the first round of lovina."

There were crackled affirmations, and Nkiruka issued one of her own, short and clipped. And a little absent. Good thing she wasn't a flock leader. She really *might* get someone killed.

She engaged the engines and the night wrapped her in its arms.

Immediately and automatically she checked her proximity sensors. She waited, poised to swoop into an attack on an imaginary enemy—and as she did so, the stars in front of her caught her gaze and held it.

They were moving.

Of course, stars were always moving; they danced and spun and made stately journeys across the universe. But not like this. Not like the ships themselves, shifting position and slipping into patterns.

Coming toward her.

She blinked, and they were back where they had been, apparently stationary. She pulled in a breath, shaking herself—and realized that she was out of formation. The others had begun their runs.

"Nkiru." Kae, sharp in her comm. "What's up? Get moving."

She didn't wait to acknowledge, pushing her fighter to rejoin the rest of them, the two groups splitting off and arcing outward. The idea was for the wing to divide in order to approach multiple targets but also to remain in sync, re-forming easily and turning to attack again.

There was nothing save space all around them except for Ashwina, and Jakana and Suzaku some distance away, but in her mind's eye she could see the targets: big, bulbous Protectorate ships hanging there, cold and perfectly lethal. Fighters were coming to meet those targets, rising like a swarm of angry insects from multiple hives, carrying stings that exploded into fire. As they had been when they had all been far too real.

She strafed through them. Turned with the wing. Strafed again, almost seeing the gunfire.

"Delta formation. Go."

Moving with the others, she spun off into the familiar pattern and found her place. The formation consisted of two flocks made up of two smaller groupings, intended to come from below and above, taking advantage of a ship's probable blind spots. Aiming for a larger target than the Protectorate fighters. Like the gamma formation, it was almost second nature to her now, and she nestled into it like a pebble into the palm of a hand, focusing her attention on the empty place where the target would be.

Which wasn't empty. She froze, gaping.

It was full of stars.

Not some stars. Not even many stars. *All* the stars, all of them at once, the rest of the universe gone dark and cold. They seemed to coalesce into a single star. Such a thing should collapse into a singularity.

But space itself was not the shape it had been. Nothing was as it had been.

Nothing ever will be, she thought, gazing into what should have blinded her in an instant, tears streaming down her face. *Everything is a center.*

The universe took a breath and held it.

The star's light blasted the darkness from the roots and Nkiruka cried out and breathed again, the universe breathing along with her.

Adam reached for her. A hundred thousand hands opened at once.

And the star went out.

"*Nkiru!*"

The voice was more than shouting at her. It was practically *screaming* at her, its upper registers disappearing into comm static. Nkiruka frowned, stared down at her hands and then at the fighter's console. None of it looked quite right. And lines, she had *such* a headache.

"What? I'm here." Her own voice sounded strange to her as well, distant and rough. "Did something happen?"

"Did something *happen*?" It was Kae, Kae both angry and frightened. "*Khara*, Nkiru, you're on a collision course with Ashwina! Pull up! Pull the fuck *up*!"

Nkiruka moved without thinking, and that was probably what saved her life. She turned the ship toward the direction her proximity sensors—unheard before now—were indicating and *jerked* the attitude control, pitching up so hard that she was slammed back into the seat, the breath shoved out of her as if from the blow of a fist. Ashwina's bulk rushed by beneath her, the chaos of its hull, the glow of its windows and portholes, no more than a hundred feet away. In a few of them she could have sworn she saw faces staring back at her, eyes wide.

She still wasn't afraid.

Star-speckled darkness rushed up at her again and then she was clear, arcing around to find the wing in front of her.

"Kae?"

"Nkiru." Kae cursed long and lavishly before he went on. "You scared the *fuck* out of us. What the hell *happened* to you?"

"I don't know," Nkiruka said vaguely. Everything was wrong. Alien. Everything was different somehow.

It's begun.

"Whatever. Get back to the docks. The rest of you, one more run and we're done for the day." Trying to shake off the last of the fog that had settled over her brain, she turned the fighter back toward Ashwina, angled down—maybe flying a little more cautiously than she usually did—toward the row of docks. What *had* happened? What had she—

Oh God.

She glided through the force field and into the ship, engaged the clamps and landed. Then she opened the hatch and pushed herself out of the seat, unsteady, her limbs jerking.

She was far too connected to everything.

As soon as her feet hit the deck, she stumbled and went down onto one knee, breathing hard. Distantly, she heard shouts and saw figures running toward her, but fragments of the world had faded out, other parts of it fading in and becoming as real as the edge of a jambia. She stared down at the deck and could almost *see* each atom, each electron, each quark, strange and charm, each vibrating string.

Yes, child. Now you see them.

Someone was standing in front of her. Slowly she raised her head and found herself staring into eyes that were not eyes at all, but were instead replicas of that star that was all stars that was every star, burning eternally.

Ixchel, old and strong and sad.

Now you see. Others might be able to take the role, fill the barest minimum of what an Aalim might do. But you have gifts beyond any of them, and you have always known it. You can turn away from this now, choose your own love and your own path, in isolation from your people. But that will be the end. It will be the end of everything.

Either way you will have blood on your hands. The only true choice given to you is how much, and why it is there.

And either way, once your choice is made there will be no going back.

"But I can't . . ." Nkiruka was weeping again. The figures rushing toward her were now moving so slowly that they seemed not to be moving at all. "I can't do it. I can't, I'm not strong enough." Not strong enough to make the choice. Not strong enough to say good-bye. Not strong enough to put every one of her people on her back and carry them through the night that went on forever.

You can. There are no mistakes, daughter. Ixchel smiled, a ghost of her own knowing and mischievous smile. *Anyway, it's already begun.*

Help them find the center.

"Nkiruka. Are you all right?" Hands were on her, lifting her; she tugged herself free and blinked at faces she should recognize but didn't. "Do you need us to get you to Ying? Here, hold on, we'll—"

I'm all right, she started to say. *I'm all right, she said I was strong enough. Let me be strong.* But the deck was lunging up to meet her, and after the dull thud of its impact against her head she knew nothing more.

CHAPTER

TWENTY-SIX

She was fighting her way out of darkness. Beating herself against it as though it were a wall, as though she were a thing of stone and wood that could break through to the light beyond. It was night but not a good one, not a kind one, and not one she'd chosen. A final night, without fire stitched into her bones and no greater sight to follow the darkness.

No, she wouldn't allow it to take her.

"Nkiruka." Hands on her. Soft, soft—she wanted to see whose they were. The voice, too. Was this all she would have now? Darkness and sound and touch? She wanted to cry, but her eyes were burned and white and useless, and she knew no tears would come.

"Nkiru, *please*."

All at once she burst through the wall, falling back into the world, jerking and gasping as those hands held her down. "Nkiru—*God*, it's okay, you're all right . . ." Satya was leaning over her with her smooth hands cupping the sides of Nkiruka's face. "You scared me so much. I could *hit* you." But she sounded as though she were close to laughing, tears shining in her dark eyes.

"I'm all right," Nkiruka echoed softly. It was there. It was all there inside her, behind the broken wall. Everything that she had brought back from the dark, pressing, insisting, demanding that she move. She pushed herself up and no dizziness came. Her head was level. Every part of her was level. She felt almost as if she hadn't been unconscious at all, scanning the curtained clinic space, clear-eyed. Seeing everything.

How long had she been out?

She had to hurry now.

"Whoa. Hold on." Satya placed a hand in the center of her chest, trying to push her down. "Ying said you shouldn't rush things. She doesn't even know what happened to you. Kae told us what he could, but even he didn't—"

"I have to talk to Adisa." Nkiruka turned, gaze moving over Satya's face, so well loved. Memorizing every line, every angle; the elegant slope of her nose, her full cheeks, her equally full mouth and her skin like sun-warmed olives. "Satya, I'm sorry. But I have to."

Satya stared at her. It was one apology for one thing, of course, but it was also for something else. It was the first of many good-byes.

Satya blinked, hard, and the tears rolled down her cheeks as she straightened and stepped away. "I'll get him," she said dully.

Nkiruka shook her head, already sliding her legs out from under the sheet that covered her. Beneath it she was dressed in a clean, white clinic shift—not the best garment, but it was decent enough. It would do.

"I need to go to him myself. There isn't time."

Satya paused, misery evident in every part of her face, her body, the way her hands hung at her sides. Suddenly Nkiruka remembered seeing her for the first time in a lower corridor, arms full of a stack of small pots, glazed and painted with delicate lines of winding flowers. She'd almost dropped them, and Nkiruka had noted the grace with which she moved, though she was stumbling. Somehow even her mistakes were beautiful.

This isn't fair.

Ixchel's touch on her mind, light as the tip of a finger. *Since when was life ever fair, child? Life is cruel. Life is a mad bitch who spits you into the world, bloody and screaming and drowning in air, and then never forgives you for it. Life is a ravening demon that eats you, cell by cell, and grinds your bones between its teeth. Life drinks your hot blood until your veins crack like dry riverbeds. The greatest lie you have been told is that life and death are different things.*

And life is also your dear mother, who loves you and wants to see you grow. Growth is painful. But we all must grow.

You are strong enough for this. You are stronger than you know.

"We never got enough time," Satya said. She stared down at her hands, where all her unhappiness seemed to be flowing like blood, and raised them. For a moment she looked as if she might simply turn and run. Or as if she might strike out at Nkiruka, rage overtaking her misery. But instead she reached out and took Nkiruka's hands in hers. "Come with me, *habibti*." Her voice was soft and sad. "Just promise me you'll tell me what happened to you."

Nkiruka squeezed her hands and it was like squeezing love into her core, waves of it, along with gratitude. "If I can. If you can stay when I speak to Adisa. I think I can only tell it once. It's that big, Satya. I thought maybe it was too big for me."

"And now?"

"I think it's big enough," Nkiruka said. "I think . . . I think I can carry it. Because I have to."

And every one of her children on her back, through the night that went on forever.

She met Adisa in the dusty hallway at the top of the ship, the windows opening out to their side and the stars looking in on them. She hadn't told him to meet her there. She had somehow known where to go, just as it seemed that he had; she was sure that she wasn't the only one the ghost of Ixchel was speaking to these days.

Satya had helped her along, though Nkiruka hadn't needed it. She hadn't attempted to resist. Satya had to help her, needed to feel needed herself, for a little while longer. In truth, it had been good to lean against her side, feel that familiar arm around her shoulders.

Will I be allowed even this much? When it's all over? Except that was a foolish question. It was never over. And an Aalim could lean on no one, for an Aalim was always the support for everyone else.

Adisa turned as she approached, his eyes hooded. He studied her and didn't smile.

"Nkiruka. We had heard you were ill. It's good to see you up."

"I wasn't ill." She gently pushed Satya away, standing on her own, and Satya went without a word, withdrawing into the shadow of one of the wide metal window frames. "I'm not ill. I was given a message. I have to give it to you now."

Adisa nodded slowly. She had known that he wouldn't doubt her. He had perhaps been waiting for this to happen, something that would push her irrevocably in a particular direction. She didn't resent him for it. She was too tired.

And her work was only beginning.

"Some time ago I read the pads. Consulted the stars. I wasn't looking for guidance for us all, but it came. I read war in the stars; war connected to the name of Adam Yuga." She paused, watching him carefully, but his face remained impassive. "I should have come to you then. I'm sorry I didn't. Some part of me knew what it would mean for me. And I was afraid."

Adisa didn't speak for a moment, his expression still unreadable.

"Sooner or later fear pushes us into doing things we later regret," he said quietly. "That you've come to me . . . I regard that as the most important thing."

"Thank you." Nkiruka bowed her head. "But my coming to speak with you isn't about regret. As I said, I've received a message in my fighter. I don't know why it came to me when it did, why there and not elsewhere, and I still don't fully understand what it means. It— It means many things at once.

"One of them is that war is indeed coming. We won't be able to escape it. No one will." She paused again, drawing in breath and trying to slow her heartbeat. Everything would come. All of it that she could tell, anyway.

"Another part is that Adam is at the center of what's happening, what *will* happen, and I felt the center shifting. He's begun to heal others. Or at least . . . No, that's not quite right." She frowned. "He healed one. What he did is sending out . . . ripples. Ripples that might grow into waves and sweep everything before them.

"There's one in particular. A Protectorate woman. She's the beginning of something bigger. Unless . . ."

She met Adisa's gaze, hard and direct and very sure. "Unless the danger I sense kills them all. Which it might."

She fell silent, suddenly weary. Adisa stayed silent as well, turning a little away from her and gazing out at the stars, seeming to slip into a meditation. She felt Satya close, almost at her back, and wanted nothing more than to lean against her again and close her eyes. But she couldn't. Not now.

Now she had to stand alone.

"I've feared something like this," Adisa said at last. "No visions as you have had. No readings. But hints in dreams. Premonitions. Nothing I could point to, nothing clear enough. Nothing that I could take to anyone else." He sighed. "So now I suppose I have my answer."

He lowered his head, almost as though he were praying. Perhaps he was.

"If Ixchel were here, no doubt she would tell us that something like this demands action on our part. That what we began on the Plain isn't done yet. That we must take the next step and go to Adam's aid." He lifted his head again, a faint smile playing about his mouth. "*Chere*, I can practically hear her now. She would be so *irritated* with us for delaying so long."

Nkiruka tried to smile too, but it felt more like a grimace and she abandoned it almost immediately. "I've been hearing her. I don't know if it's simply my imagination or if she really is speaking to me, but . . ." She shrugged. "I can't ignore her. Not anymore. Not after what I saw."

"You know that many of the others of us want to run." He faced her, his face as grave as his tone. "And some want to attack the Protectorate directly, before they can do the same to us. It seems like you might be ready to present us with a third way." He pursed his lips, his expression thoughtful. "What do you advise, Nkiruka?"

She hesitated. She knew that she shouldn't, that she already understood what had to be done, and these were just the last few steps, but oh, they were hard ones. Her first act of counsel. It might seem like a small thing, but . . .

Small things start ripples. And ripples grow.

"We need to go," she said. "Not *should*. *Need*. If we fail at this moment . . ." She shook her head, fighting back a shiver. "I don't know what will happen to us. I mean, I can't see it at all. It's darkness."

"What of Suzaku and Jakana?" Adisa's voice was soft, but merciless. He was pushing her gently toward the rest of it. The harder steps. "Our communications with them lately have been strained. I doubt they would agree to come." He let a significant pause fill the air between them. "And Ixchel counseled unity above all things."

"Unity can be weakness when it leads you away from what's right." The words came quickly, though not easily. Each one hurt, each one was heavy on her tongue. "If they refuse to come with us, we can't force them. They should join another convoy."

"Such a thing is almost unheard of. Except in the most terrible extremity." Adisa wasn't chiding. He wasn't objecting. He didn't even seem surprised by the idea. He was merely stating a fact, letting it face her. "There are always three. The three need each other. One cannot survive without the others."

"If we don't help Adam and Lochlan and the others—if we don't help the *Protectorate*—none of us will survive at all." Nkiruka glanced back at Satya, pleading with her eyes. *I'm so sorry. Forgive me.* "You have my counsel. This is what we must do. There's nothing more I can say."

Adisa was silent again, regarding her with a stare that seemed to see her completely, every broken piece and everything she was struggling to make strong. Everything she was still clinging to and everything that she would have to give up.

"I will take this to the council," he said simply, in the same tone he had used to lay the facts before her. "I will tell them just as you have told me. We'll have an answer in a matter of hours."

Only one answer is the right one. But Nkiruka only lowered her head once more, in thanks and in acknowledgment that he was shouldering a heavy burden of his own. For though Jakana and Suzaku would be nearly impossible to convince, she didn't expect the council of Ashwina to be any easier.

"I'll let you know as soon as our meeting has concluded." He stepped forward, preparing to head past her for the corridors that would take him down to the council chamber. "Thank you for coming to me, Nkiruka. Thank you for your counsel."

Nkiruka nodded again. And for a moment she stood there, her hands clenched at her sides, the stars ruthless and old.

"Wait."

Adisa turned. "What is it?"

She faced him. She didn't look at Satya. Maybe it was cowardly, but she simply couldn't. It hurt too much. All these good-byes, and each one would be more difficult than the last, until the darkness swallowed her.

She let out a long breath.

"Tell them to prepare the ceremony," she said softly. "Tell them to set the fire and heat the iron. Tell them that if they want me as their Aalim, I will be that for them."

Tears prickled at the corners of her eyes, but she wouldn't let them fall. In the shadows, she was certain that Satya was once more weeping silently. She could feel it, a wrenching beneath her breastbone, the crying of a limb that had yet to be cut off but knew its time was coming.

"Tell them I'll go into the dark."

PART THREE

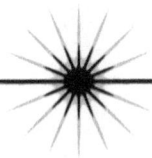

ASCENT

CHAPTER

TWENTY-SEVEN

"Report."

Alkor spat the word out like a curse, and every eye on the bridge swung in her direction. Watching her, ice settling into his veins, Sinder thought of a predator with eyesight based on movement, and a room full of prey animals keeping motionless.

It wasn't working.

"One of them went down, ma'am. The other one . . . got to slipstream." An older bridge officer, a man with a face that somehow managed to be both perfectly formed and unattractive, stood at attention, his apprehension barely concealed.

"I can see that, you idiot," she snapped. "*How*? We had five ships to their two."

"Good flying, ma'am. Luck. Otherwise, I— It would take time to produce a full analysis of it, we could—"

"I already have, and it's that you *failed*." Alkor made a disgusted noise and spun away from him. "At least we got one of them. Yuga might have been on it."

"Yes," Sinder said quietly. It was possible. There was a fifty-fifty chance, but he didn't like those odds. He liked none of this. "He might have. How can we be sure either way?"

"The ship broke up at an extremely high altitude," said a younger officer. "A great deal of it would have burned up in the atmosphere before it hit the ground, and after that whatever was left would be scattered in a debris field hundreds of kilometers long. I—I'm sorry, ma'am, sir, but I think it's unlikely that we'll recover much in the way of remains."

"So the only way to be sure is to find the other ship." Alkor tapped her fingers on her arm. "Can we track them?"

"If we chase them *now*, we might have a chance. But not a good one. They'll be too far away; their drive trail will have mostly dissipated."

"*Fuck*." Everyone on the bridge jumped. "All right. We're going, then. Contact the *Vanguard* and the *Superior* and tell them they're with us. The *Orion* and the *Advantage* will stay behind and comb through the debris. And tell them to get the hell down to the camp and debrief whoever's still alive there. We need to understand what happened and how."

"Ma'am." The officer nodded smartly and spun back to her console.

"Go to slipstream as soon as possible. *Find them*, people. No excuses. I'll be in my cabin. Contact me immediately if there's any news." Without waiting for a response, she turned toward the door that led off the bridge, motioning for Sinder to follow. Which he did, silently.

There was nothing to do for the moment. And strangely, where before he had been full of jittery energy, now he was calm. Coolly determined. If he was going to get through this, he would need his composure.

The trip to Alkor's cabin was full of quiet tension, and when they entered and the door hissed closed behind them, she stalked to the windows and slammed a fist against the transparency, letting out a sound somewhere between a sigh and a wince of pain. Sinder remained close to the door, his hands clasped behind his back, waiting.

It was good that she was angry. It meant that she was in it with him, to the end, whatever that should be.

"Why is everything going wrong?" She whirled on him as if he bore personal responsibility. "You said this would be simple. That it would be *easy*. I know he's *more than one man* and all that shit, but how the hell is it possible that a bunch of deathly ill people overpowered a facility full of armed peacekeepers and stole two ships? How does that *happen*?"

Sinder smiled coldly. "Welcome to a universe with Adam Yuga in it, I suppose."

Slowly, still calmly, he glided over to her desk and took a seat in front of it, crossing his legs and leaning back.

In a way, he felt a degree of sympathy for the man. Adam clearly believed that what he was doing was right. His convictions, though they were ghastly, appeared sincerely held. He was even right, at least a little, about his mysterious illness. But it didn't matter. His way, his method, how he proposed to *cure* people and what that cure might mean—revealing it all would destabilize everything. Create panic. Sow dissent. If things were as they were beginning to seem ... It wasn't even about a conspiracy. It wasn't just about a few traitors in their ranks. It was about everything on which the Protectorate was built. Purity, superiority, separation from everything irrational or unclean. Perfection almost to the point of invincibility.

If what Adam had said about his illness was at all true, the foundations of the whole thing might begin to wobble. They couldn't be undermined any further. And no one was going to crawl to the Bideshi for whatever they claimed to offer. No one was going to sink that low, to sacrifice the soul for the body. Solutions would be found elsewhere. It was only a matter of time.

Yuga couldn't be allowed to succeed.

"Have you read the full report we got on what happened on that little planet in the nebula? With the Bideshi?"

Alkor frowned. "I looked it over, yes."

"Then you saw how difficult he was. How elusive he proved. Yuga was no warrior, nor is he now if any of his breeding holds true, but he was a gifted problem-solver, and he could find his way through tight spaces. He could see things that others couldn't—he developed a certain viewpoint that few possess. A significant element of his ability was pure analytical thinking, but I believe he also possesses unusually powerful intuition." *He and I might have that in common.* "We shouldn't be surprised that he's still alive. And ... I believe that he is."

Alkor arched an eyebrow. "You do? Why?"

Sinder shrugged. "I feel it, and I've learned to trust those feelings. And it's reasonable, given his origin. He wouldn't simply burn in a senseless meteor of twisted metal. He would demand a better end than that, and he would probably be able to get it. He was, after all, a Protectorate man with the highest quality of code, however perverse and ruined. Our society produced him. If he's survived for this long, I don't think it can be through unusually good fortune."

Alkor looked doubtful, but she nodded, crossing her arms. "So he's alive. Maybe. We chase him, if we're *lucky* we find him—"

"We'll find him."

"You know that too?"

"I do." Sinder inclined his head. There was no way to explain the certainty he felt. It was as though he could see lines twisting through the surrounding space, through the larger universe; lines that bound pieces of it together and tugged them closer. Tethers that held people and places and things into orbits. Branching paths of probability and chance, seemingly chaotic but in fact possessed of a profound order.

He would find Adam Yuga because he must. There was no escaping that fate.

"Well, we'll see." Alkor sighed and sank down into the chair opposite him. "In the meantime I suppose we should get some rest. We'll need to be sharp. Whatever happens."

There was a soft lurch, and the stars outside the window swelled and filled the void with brilliant light as they went to slipstream. Sinder watched the transition for a minute, losing himself in it, then shook it free and got to his feet.

Rest. Yes.

"Sleep well, Captain." He gave her a small bow. "I hope you know, I don't regard this as any failure of yours."

Alkor seemed to hesitate, then gave him a smile, wry but genuine. "I appreciate that, Sinder. I sincerely do."

Sinder nodded, and left as silently as he had entered.

Back in his cabin, he hesitated between stripping off his clothes and sliding into bed. Naked, he approached his own window, laying his hands on its pristine surface as if he could touch the slipstream itself. All those stars, rushing past. Space-time warping, twisting in on itself. It *was* a kind of magic. He was in the midst of a maelstrom of the spaces between everything. Impossibly tiny, impossibly large. He had never really given it a thought before.

He lifted his hands away. Slightly, so slight it was hardly perceptible, they shook. He dropped them and took a long, deep breath.

There was freedom in surrendering. That was the wisdom he had been waiting for. He had his path to walk. He would walk it with grace. At the end of it he would look Adam Yuga in the eye.

And kill him.

When he had been very young, Adam's mother had told him stories. These were profoundly romantic stories, and they revealed parts of his mother he hardly ever saw. She was a cool woman, efficient and more than a little distant, but when he lay in bed at night and she lowered the light and spun her tales, her face would contort with emotion—fear and excitement—and it would make its way into him and he would feel it too. She'd tell old stories, of brave warriors and proud, graceful royalty, heroes and heroines who fought for love and justice. There was one story, a woman who had been cursed by a Bideshi witch to sleep for a thousand years, but a Protectorate peacekeeper who loved her fought his way to her side, took her in his arms—though he believed she must be dead—and gave her one final, sorrowful kiss that woke her from her charmed coma. It was a rare moment when the magic of the Bideshi made its way even into the lives of the Protectorate heroes as something powerful and real. It was thrilling, beautiful, and at the end he had felt a rush of joy as the two were reunited.

Like that woman, he had fallen into his own sleep, deep and dark and still, but somewhere in that darkness he felt a hand stroking through his hair, lips on his, and he opened his eyes.

Lochlan smiled. "Thought you might sleep the whole way to wherever-the-fuck-we're-going."

Adam groaned. The dark was receding, and he wished it would come back, because now he felt his own body. He was sore, still exhausted no matter how long he had slept, and when he moved every muscle rushed to tell him what a bad idea that was. As far as he could tell, he was lying on a bunk in one of the ship's dormitories, and the sounds—and smells—of other people were all around him: muttering, groaning, the shuffling of feet.

Ignoring his body, he pushed himself up on one elbow. Lochlan slid back to give him room. "How long was I...?"

"About five hours. I wanted to let you sleep." Lochlan took his hand and held on, and the tension in it pulled Adam back to a fuzzy memory. Something that had happened before he and Rachel had—

The ship.

"She's dead, isn't she?" he breathed. "Naomi?" But he already knew. He sensed it, how she wasn't there anymore.

Lochlan nodded, pain briefly etched across his features. "Her and a couple hundred others. I mean, I assume. No way anyone could've survived that crash." He sighed, glancing around the room. "No one is really talking about it. I don't think anyone knows what to say."

"They'll be in shock," Adam said softly. He sat up and swung his legs over the side of the bunk, taking a few seconds to let his body reorient itself. "At still being alive. I . . . I know how that feels."

Lochlan didn't say anything else, just held on to his hand. Adam was aware of people moving past, others lying in their bunks, a few sitting close together and talking. Some were stripping off filthy clothes and gathering spare bedding around their waists and chests in makeshift togas, presumably so they could wash what they had. Getting clean, that would make sense as an escape. It would be something to care for the body and occupy the attention.

It sounded amazing.

"Are there showers here?" He raised his head, grateful for the idea. "There have to be, this is a transport ship."

"There are. And a lot of *very* hot water. They were pretty crowded a couple of hours ago, but I think we could find a spot." Lochlan smiled faintly. "Not much privacy, but I'm guessing you won't mind that."

"I don't care." Gingerly, Adam stood, stretching the kinks out of his spine and shoulders. "Just come with me. Make sure I don't fall asleep in there."

The showers—there turned out to be two large chambers devoted to them—were indeed communal, and though the two rooms were probably once divided by sex, people were ignoring that now, throwing Protectorate propriety to the wind in favor of scrubbing weeks of dirt and oil. Men and women huddled together under the spray, using soap and cloths and their hands to clean themselves, whatever they could, some of them laughing with tired joy and some of them merely standing there, heads down. Adam couldn't tell if they were exhausted or grieving or both, and then, as Lochlan began to strip off his clothes, he didn't care.

It was strange, how he hadn't realized that it had been days since they had seen each other naked. Days since he had even thought about sex as something that they might do together. He was still far too tired and too generally overcome with everything that had happened to want to do anything of the kind, but as Lochlan's body came into view, he felt a low hunger that bled into relief, though there was a flash of anger and sympathetic pain at Lochlan's bruised and now tightly wrapped side.

He undressed, leaving his clothes in a pile beside Lochlan's— even though he didn't want them anymore—and followed him to a miraculously free spot under one of the showerheads. The water was scalding the first time it touched his skin, and he jumped and gasped, but Lochlan curled an arm around his shoulders and held him, and he remained where he was, loosening and uncurling as he became accustomed to the heat. He became freshly aware that everyone could see him, could see *them*, and that, if they remained close like this, anyone with sense would be able to tell what was going on.

But that seemed beyond unimportant. He leaned back against Lochlan's chest and let the water run over him, sluicing off everything that had accumulated over days that had seemed like weeks, freeing him of it. Lochlan had gotten soap from somewhere and his hands moved slowly over Adam's skin, half cleaning and half simply stroking, soothing. And as Lochlan's hands drifted lower, it became a little less soothing, and he turned in Lochlan's arms, leaning in close. In part he was trying to hide the fact that he was suddenly getting hard, but it was backfiring badly.

"You don't have to," Lochlan murmured, but Adam shook his head.

"Just stay here for a minute."

When he glanced up, he saw that no one was watching them. Adam had a sudden, insane fantasy of letting Lochlan push him up against the wall of the shower and take him right there in full view of everyone, and he shivered.

There was nothing left to be afraid of.

"My turn." Lochlan turned them again, slid in front of Adam, and began to work the soap over his own body—but without thinking, Adam took it from him, and began to lather up Lochlan's skin. It felt smooth, easy.

And then they simply stood, heads tilted back, skin pressed together and thrumming as the last of the soap ran down past their feet and away.

"Let's get out of here," Adam whispered, and when Lochlan kissed the edge of Adam's jaw, he felt the other man smiling.

They didn't stop to dry off. They didn't even stop to dress. The ship was still in chaos—no one would notice. There was a small alcove off one of the corridors, for storage or something, and they edged themselves into it, clumsy and laughing. Somewhere, a great many people were dead in senseless fire, but that knowledge only—perversely—made the pleasure sharper, sweeter. They were alive. They were together. Adam rolled his hips into Lochlan's hand and kept his moans locked behind gritted teeth, his own hands doing as best they could with almost no room to move in.

But there didn't need to be any skill involved. They tensed and shuddered against each other, Lochlan muffling a low cry in the hollow of Adam's throat. Then stillness, as they leaned together, breathing hard.

"We need another shower," Adam mumbled, and Lochlan barked a laugh.

"*Chusile*, we need to sleep again."

"Did you sleep at all?"

Lochlan pulled back enough to frame Adam's cheek with one hand, lifting the other to his mouth and idly sucking his fingers clean. Adam watched him, vaguely entranced. "No. I'm okay." He paused, licking his lips. "No, scratch that. I'm about to pass out on you right now. Let's go."

They finished cleaning themselves up as best they could, and were still naked as they made their way back to the dormitory, but as Adam had guessed, those passing barely glanced their way. It had been a kind of arrogance to assume that they would be so important that anyone could spare them a second thought after everything else that had happened. He didn't need to carry that with him any longer, and as he lay back down in his bunk, Lochlan curled close along his back, the weariness that stole back over him was almost welcome. For the moment, he had no responsibilities. Later, he could deal with the death, the uncertainty, the guilt that he knew was waiting in the wings.

He could deal with anything. He had everything he needed now.

Aarons scanned the people around him. "So where are we going?"

The cockpit was considerably less crowded than it had been, occupied only by the two de facto pilots—Tamara and Kara were their names—as well as Rachel, who seemed to have taken Naomi's place as the former prisoners' leader, Aarons, Adam, and Lochlan, who was leaning against a console toward the rear of the chamber.

Adam didn't need to ask him to know that he wasn't comfortable with this, playing a part in the decision making. Lochlan would probably be better pleased if the two of them removed themselves from the front line of things completely. But even now, Adam couldn't. He didn't have to be the center, he didn't have to be the one directing them, but he had to be present.

He was in too deep to pull back.

Aarons's question hung in the air for a moment. The white light of slipstream streaked over their faces. Kara looked around at each of them, her young face showing unease, while Tamara—the older of the two—kept her attention locked on Rachel, who met her gaze and sighed, raking a hand through her hair.

"I have no idea. Somewhere where we can hide for a while. We have a lot of exhausted people, and they all have more healing to do. Simply getting this far took almost everything they had. I know *I* don't have much left in me." She paused, her mouth twisting. "They've also lost a lot, some of them. Almost everyone had friends or family on that ship. And everyone loved Naomi. They're in mourning, and they need space for it."

Adam nodded. "That means somewhere on the edges of Protectorate space."

"Everything out that way is at least a few days from our current position in slipstream." Tamara frowned. "We've got some nonperishable foodstuffs—mostly protein bars—but not enough for everyone, not for long. We'll either need to find a place ASAP or make a stop somewhere to take on supplies."

"So let's pick a planet and head for it," Aarons said. "The more random the better, probably. Anywhere sparsely populated. There have to be a few of those closer in. We ditch the ship, find the most middle-of-nowhere place that still has water and food, and lay low as long as we can."

"We have another option."

Everyone turned toward Lochlan, and Adam could feel their faint surprise—as well as his own. Lochlan, for his part, shifted slightly, mouth tense, as if he felt deep dislike for what he himself was saying. But he pulled in a breath and pushed on. "My people. We didn't cast Adam out, even when it was in their best interest to send him packing. I don't think they'd turn a whole gaggle of refugees away, not after we explain what's going on. We make contact with a convoy, we see what they say."

Slowly, Adam shook his head. "I was one person, Lock. We have hundreds. No way they could accommodate that, regardless of whether they'd be willing."

Lochlan's mouth twisted. "You'd be surprised what we can do, *mitr raya*. There wouldn't be one homeship, remember. There'd be three. If they spread us out—"

"Wait." Kara held up a hand, frowning. "The *Bideshi*? I know we're desperate, but we— You—" She shot Lochlan a look of mingled apology and distrust. "I know you helped us and all, but you can't really expect us to—"

"You think we're in a position to be that picky?" Rachel's voice was sharp, edged with disgust. "Shit, Kara, get over yourself. I'm not sure I like it either, but I want to stay *alive*, and at this point I'll do whatever that takes. I have children. So do a lot of people here. Think about that for a second."

Silence. Adam let his gaze pass from one to the other, halting on Lochlan, who stared back at him, a hundred different emotions swirling behind his eyes.

And then something *shifted*.

At first Adam thought the deck was rocking, that an object had impacted with the ship itself. But no one in the cockpit seemed to have noticed anything, and when it hit him again, he realized that it was coming not from outside himself but *inside*. The world around him faded, drifted over him as if he were falling down a long tunnel that led into the core of a vast space. Tendrils of darkness wrapped around his limbs, around his neck, but they were gentle. They meant him no harm.

There was something they wanted to show him.

This was the center. This was the Plain—only not the Plain, but everywhere that the Plain might be, the part of it that he carried within himself now, that was also a door to everyplace and everything else. There were people here waiting for him, strange people, whose faces he had never seen and did not know. They were watching him approach, faces tilted up and arms lifted to greet him: two women, one very old and one young, dressed in the scarves and beaded chaos of an Aalim.

Their eyes were pale and sightless. But he knew they saw him better than anyone could. He drifted toward them, and as he did he heard Ixchel laughing.

Child, perfect, yes. Follow one, bring the other one to you. You are the link between them. You are what I couldn't be. You are the last piece needed to bind them together, the future and the ruined past.

He reached them, his feet touching a solid surface, and he saw that they weren't in darkness but in the center of a field, with the stars spinning over them. Wind in the grass whispered secrets to the sky. There was a little house some way away with low trees around it, and a garden. The old woman smiled; the young one's face crumpled with pain and loss. Then the faces were reversed, then reversed again.

The stars changed, moved, danced. They spun into new forms, wheeling in strange orbits, and after a few seconds—or minutes, or hours—Adam realized that he was gazing at an atlas in the sky, a map to where he now stood.

A way forward.

Go, Ixchel murmured into his ear. *Find her, my lost sister. She has been waiting for you for a very long time.*

Who? Why? But as he asked it, fire bloomed under his feet, spreading in an instant across the grass and eating its way up the trunks of the trees, wreathing the house in flame. There was a scream, or maybe only the wind howling, and he was rushing upward again, the vision spitting him out like sour and unwelcome food. Part of him didn't belong. The other part belonged nowhere else. It hurt, as he crashed back into the world. It was like smashing through a wall of flesh, of glass. It was like being born.

Frightened voices. Lochlan's face above his, there and then blurring out again. He reached blindly, felt a hand close around his fingers, recognized it as Rachel's seconds before an aftershock seized and shook him.

"Adam! Adam, what—"

"I know," he gasped, jerking upward. Somehow he was sitting, gripping the sides of his head. "I know where we have to go. I know."

Stares bored into him like drills. He managed a smile—through the pain there was exhilaration, the sense of once again finding his perfect place in the line they were bound to.

"I'll show you."

CHAPTER

TWENTY-EIGHT

Nkiruka watched them set the fire. She watched very closely. One watched everything closely, she supposed, when you knew it would be among the last things they would ever see.

Satya stood beside her, silently. There had been a lot of silence between them in the past day. There might have been attempted explanations, even arguing, but both seemed pointless. This seemed more and more like a decision that had been made a long time ago, that they were finally facing. Satya had always understood that truth.

It was why it had made her so angry.

"Soon," Satya whispered. Nkiruka nodded.

"Are you afraid?"

Nkiruka hesitated—then nodded again. "I don't know what happens after this."

"Shouldn't you be able to see that?" A flash of bitterness, like the lash of a tiny whip. Nkiruka closed her eyes and took it. There would be more pain later, greater pain: the pain she would have to bear for all her people. Each agony now was somehow precious.

"Maybe I'll be able to, when this is done."

Glowbugs were dancing in the branches. Not everyone was there, but a few were beginning to emerge from the shadows into the clearing. There was a fire scar in its center, a place of Naming in happier times. A powerful place. Another kind of center. On the black mound, a new fire was leaping and dancing, and as two young women tended it and coaxed it into a blaze, Adisa stood by, quietly.

In his hand he held a long, thin iron rod. Most of it was ornate, twists and spirals and leaves winding up its length. But the tip was simple, unadorned. In his other hand he held a syringe.

One would take her sight. The other would give new sight to her.

"You've barely been prepared." Now Satya sounded almost mournful. *Because she is already mourning me*, Nkiruka thought. *Every moment is a farewell.* "Usually there's more time."

"There is no time." Nkiruka turned to her, pulling her close. Satya stiffened but allowed it, and after a moment her body went loose, her head against Nkiruka's shoulder. Over her, Nkiruka saw Kae and Leila approaching through the trees, both of them dressed in white.

White, also a funereal color. It wasn't only for her. She knew that. It was for everything that was still to come.

"I wish you had chosen me," Satya whispered. "I'm sorry, Nkiru, I'm ... No. No, I'm not sorry. I wish *so much* that you had chosen me."

"I did." Nkiruka breathed the words into Satya's hair. She smelled of sandalwood and cinnamon. Nkiruka would still be able to smell that after this was over, and she breathed it in as if she could keep it in a corner of her lungs like a treasure. "I chose you. Just not in the way either of us wanted."

"I don't think I can do this."

"You can." Nkiruka pulled Satya's face gently away from herself, gazed down into her eyes, her thumbs tracing over Satya's cheeks. "We have to be strong now. It will hurt. But we have to be."

All the strength of all the Aalim in this place danced around her like the glowbugs. She was embraced and held by that strength, that power. The lights pressed into her skin. She tipped her head back and stared up at the stars, the other, older lights to which she would be eternally bound. A kind of marriage, one with all the secrets and the loves, the betrayals and the acrimony, the hidden violence and the sweetness that everyone could see, like any marriage. Long and painful and over too soon.

Love is so horrible, she thought, and she felt the stars agree.

At the time of her Naming, she had been gently forced to her knees. That did not happen now. Now she went alone, unaccompanied, splendid in her black robes gilded with silver stars—the night that went on forever wrapped around her. She could feel her people at her back, but all she could see was the fire and Adisa's face.

Somewhere, faintly, Satya was weeping.

This is death and this is birth, daughter. Ixchel in the fire, staring back at her with a shifting, beautiful face, young and old and back to young again. Ixchel the Aalim, Ixchel the death-dancer, Ixchel the Old Mother and the speaker for the stars. Ixchel the reader of the paths ahead and the weaver of orbits, Ixchel the spinner of stories, Ixchel the leader and Ixchel the lover and Ixchel the maiden and mother and crone, Ixchel the tired old woman, Ixchel going into the fire and the night and the light that burned the core from your bones.

All these things you must be.

No one spoke. No one ever spoke. Adisa stepped forward and plunged the iron into the flames. It began to glow, redder and redder, like a young star in the depths of a nebula. Then it was withdrawn and Adisa came to her and slipped the needle into her arm, flooding her with the nanobots that would remake her from the inside out. It didn't hurt. She looked up at him and his old eyes were shining and wet.

"Thank you," he whispered, and then the iron touched her and took her sight from her.

Of course she screamed. Of course she fell and writhed in the dirt as the fire knitted itself into her marrow. Of course she screamed again as the night split open around her. She was rising out of the flames, a firebird, a star.

All the dark and all the dancing.

Time folded in on itself. In the center of it—the true center toward which she had to go—there was a tiny green world, a woman, and a man, and she knew them because she had always known them, because this was where she had been going from the moment of her birth.

They were reaching for her. They could almost touch her. Then they were gone again, and she was alone.

She lay at last in silence, her face damp with tears. She felt herself breathing, and she stared up at the bright stars. Brighter than they ever were before. Bright and reaching for her, taking her as one of their own.

"You must tell them," she said as she began to push herself up on shaking hands, though her voice was strong as it had ever been. "You must tell them that we're going. Jakana and Suzaku. They don't have to come. They must choose.

"But you must tell them that Ashwina is going to Adam."

CHAPTER

TWENTY-NINE

The planet Peris was green and blue, and very small.

Lochlan had begun to learn, early in his life, to never discount what seemed ordinary or insignificant. Ixchel had beaten it into him—sometimes literally—and into everyone else who had been her student with him.

"You have to see, foolish boy. You think I can't see? You're not so foolish as that. Seeing isn't always seeing. Or rather, seeing can't be trusted. The universe is at least half what can't be seen with your birth eyes. Assume nothing. Withhold judgment. Open yourself."

He had tried, had made a genuine and honest effort. But it had always been something he struggled with. At first he had felt defensive about it, then resigned, then had worn his failure as a perverse badge of honor. It had been easier, especially young and angry, to judge at a glance. To be sure that he knew what he knew.

Then there had come Adam.

Still.

"Doesn't look like much," Aarons grunted.

Lochlan shot him an amused glance. "No, it really doesn't."

"That's good," Adam said. "If it doesn't look like much to us, it'll look like even less to them. I don't know how long we'll be able to stay here, but . . ."

"You're sure they'll take us in." Rachel appeared skeptical, as she had since Adam had shown them on the chart where they had to go. She hadn't said much, but Lochlan could practically see what she was thinking. It was ridiculous, it was stupid, there was no way Adam could know.

But Adam had healed her. Had showed her how to heal others. So perhaps she too had found it in herself to reserve judgment.

Besides, there was *something* about the place. Something somehow familiar. Lochlan turned his attention back to the planet, which rotated slowly beneath them as they orbited, its two green continents run through by low mountains, its single wide ocean. Peris, largely ignored by the Protectorate, was not exactly on the edge of their space but for the most part—given its sparse population and lack of any valuable natural resources—beneath their notice.

"Not *they*," Adam said quietly. "Her."

"A single woman." Rachel let out a laugh and shook her head. "This is insane."

Adam smiled at her. "She isn't only a woman. You'll see."

"Then what is she?"

"She used to be Bideshi." Adam nodded at Lochlan. "Powerful. Wise. She still is those things. An Aalim."

It came to Lochlan all at once, his recollection. It was old, from before his entire world had been torn apart at Caldor, when he and Kae had been children together, running and playing and getting into trouble . . .

Like stealing a Protectorate shuttle that a child, who would later go on to be one of the most gifted pilots of his generation and to lead an entire wing of escort fighters, had no business flying.

The memory lingered, not least because it was arguably his fault, no matter how intently he had denied it. He could see Kae now, back on Ashwina after two days of terror on the part of his parents, and—secretly—Lochlan himself. Kae being lectured by Adisa, his brow furrowed. Something had happened to him and he'd never told Lochlan everything, though he had talked about the woman, the house, the ship. Something had touched him. Changed him. It had been why he had been able to return safe, but that hadn't been that the only thing it had done.

All *she* had done.

He knew of only one banished Aalim who had made her home on a planet such as this one, whose line and orbit had touched theirs before.

"*Chere*," Lochlan murmured. Adam and Rachel turned to him, and he smiled. "Lakshmi. It's her, isn't it? That's who we're here to see."

Adam arched a brow. "Is that her name? She never told me." He didn't know, Lochlan realized. He knew a little, but only as much as he needed to in order to get them this far. "She's an Aalim, isn't she? But I don't understand why she's here and not on a homeship. I mean, I assumed she would tell us once we—"

"She's in exile," Lochlan said quietly. "She was an Aalim on a ship in another convoy. Very powerful. I never met her, but everyone knows what had happened."

"This is one of your . . . witches?" Rachel tripped over the word, as if she grasped more of its distasteful provenance—when it came from the Protectorate—than she had before. Lochlan shot her a look, but it wasn't as sharp as it would once have been. Maybe he was getting tolerant in his old age. Adam's bad influence.

"Our *Aalim*, yes. The mothers and fathers of our people. They guide us through the dark. They help us find the paths that we should walk. When we speak of them we do so with respect." *Says the man who routinely referred to Ixchel as "that mad old bat."* He caught Adam's eye and didn't quite smile.

"So what happened?" Adam frowned slightly, gaze intent, confusion mingling with curiosity. Lochlan briefly considered telling him in private—but what did it matter if these *raya* were privy to the more personal details of the Bideshi's lives? What could it hurt?

Hadn't they earned a small step through the door?

"No Aalim is allowed to favor any of their children, to hold them dearer than the others in their heart. Lakshmi did." He had always hated this rule. It had always seemed so unfair, so *wrong*. But it had also always been so, something so deeply rooted that it couldn't be argued with. No matter who it hurt.

Maybe we aren't so different from them, after all.

"You mean she took a lover," Aarons said. It wasn't a question.

"She had a lover before she took her place as Aalim for her people. But, well . . . their fare-thee-well wasn't as final as it was supposed to be. And they were discovered."

"And cast out," Adam said softly. "Her lover too?"

"No. She remained on board her homeship." Lochlan saw Rachel, Tamara, and Kara's eyes widen and felt a tickle of pleasure. *She.* "But she was never the same afterward. Losing someone like that . . ." His gaze shifted back to Adam. "You never completely get over it."

"She didn't follow Lakshmi?" Kara actually sounded upset, and Lochlan looked at her, surprised. She wasn't disgusted, not bewildered, but sad. "They didn't leave together? Why not?"

"They weren't allowed." Lochlan shrugged. This part . . . This was difficult to explain, not least because he wasn't sure that it would bear explaining. Not even to people who should understand it better than anyone. The power of what *was*. The difficulty in throwing it off. "They had . . . *transgressed*, I think the word was." His upper lip curled. "The shame for them was already great enough. If they could've fought back against the ship's council's decision, Lakshmi wouldn't have let it go down that way. From what I was told, she wanted to just . . . leave quietly. Live out her life somewhere well clear of everything that had happened." He nodded down at the little green sphere. "Guess this is where she ended up."

"All right," Rachel said after a moment or two of meditative silence. "Whatever else is going on here, we'll figure it out once we're on the ground. Tamara, you've got the coordinates for the landing site from Adam? Good. Execute the appropriate burn whenever you're ready and get us down there as soon as possible."

In the corridor, halfway to the mess hall, Adam caught Lochlan's arm and tugged him aside. Lochlan halted willingly enough—he was hungry, but not *that* hungry, especially when the only thing available were protein bars that tasted like salted sawdust.

"What's up?"

"How did you know?" Adam leaned forward. "How did you know it was her? How did you recognize the planet? You *did*, didn't you?" His eyes narrowed. "Have you been here before?"

Lochlan huffed a laugh. If this was all it was . . . Of course he wanted to know. "No, I haven't. But Kae has. Relax, I'm not keeping some deep, dark secret hidden away from you. It just didn't seem like something that bore going into in . . . mixed company."

Adam blinked. "Kae?"

"Yeah. He wasn't Kae, then. I mean, he *was*, but it was before—"

"Oh."

"Yes. He— Okay, look. What happened was that we were on Golen Station for supplies, and I dared him to nab a Protectorate shuttle, all right? And he did, and he got chased all the way to here."

Adam laughed, sounding shocked. Though only half. Maybe not even that much. "You *what*? Were you *insane*? No, wait." He held up a hand. "That's a really stupid question."

"Well, I didn't think he'd actually *do* it. I guess I got under his skin; I don't know. The guy *seems* so levelheaded, but he has some serious *fuguri* when he's roused. Anyway, he ran across Lakshmi, and she . . . I'm honestly not sure. Kae was never very clear about it. But she did something that got him home safe and whole, and that's all I cared about right then." Lochlan's mouth tightened with a ghost of old guilt. "*Khara*, I did feel bad about that. Could've gotten his damn fool self killed. Then again, *he* did it, not *me*."

Adam was smiling. "Exactly how hard did Ixchel whip your ass for that?"

"She didn't *whip* it," Lochlan said, a bit stiffly. "She *kicked* it. All the way up to her chambers, gave me an armload of books to augment the whole thing. Then back down for more and up again. About ten times. Kae only got sent to bed without dinner and scrub duty in the main kitchens for a week. Bastard. She always did like him better."

"I bet she did." Adam leaned up and pressed a kiss to the corner of Lochlan's mouth. "How could she not?"

"You're a bastard too." Lochlan hooked an arm around Adam's waist and pulled him closer, and then it was good that there wasn't anyone else in the corridor, and wouldn't be for a while.

The ship set down in a wide sienna field that stretched out at the bottom of a low, rolling hill. At the top of that hill was a house surrounded by reddish trees whose trunks and limbs twisted in a way that was at once gnarled and graceful. As Adam stepped down from the ramp onto the grass, he raised a hand to shield his eyes, glanced up at the trees, and thought of Ixchel's ancient hands.

The house itself was small, single-floored, and built of dull brown-red brick with a roof of wooden slats. Yet, there was something regal about it—and mysterious, though it was one of the most nondescript structures he had ever seen.

Lochlan drew up beside him. Some distance away, Rachel was talking to Aarons, their heads bent together, Rachel's focus intent on Aarons's face and her hand close to his. They had spent a lot of the last day in consultation, and Adam gathered that, while Rachel was content to be a kind of leader, she was also content to take advice from an older Protectorate citizen. Would that everyone in their band of refugees could be so flexible.

He glanced back at the house, a tickle of apprehension in his gut. He could see no one emerging to greet them. But he could feel someone there, all the same.

"Well, *chusile*?" Lochlan's mouth quirked, signaling amusement, but beneath his expression Adam could sense the same tension. Lochlan might be going into this knowing a little more, but he still knew almost nothing. "Are we going to seek an audience with Her Grace, or not?"

"Yeah," Adam murmured, and without waiting another second, he started up the hill.

There was a fresh breeze, and as they walked higher, it swept through his hair like cool fingers. Birds trilled somewhere, unseen. The sky overhead was mostly devoid of clouds, a blue so light it was nearly colorless, and if not for that lightness he would have been put in mind of the High Fields: their expansiveness and sense of an open world stretched out for the enjoying. But over those fields, there had always been the stars and the endless night they were set into.

Still, he could see why an exiled Aalim might make a home here.

But where were her Arched Halls?

Now he could see a garden set against the side of the house, a tree on one corner that bore small fruit in a variety of bluish hues, and a low line of purple flowers that ran along the house, their petals long and waving softly like delicate fingers. It was lovely in its way, and it didn't feel as though it would be out of place on Ashwina.

But there was a sense of loss here. It was gentle, but it was there.

Together, they crested the hill. Now it seemed higher than it had from below, and he saw the ship and the people gathered all around it, some in groups, some alone, standing and seated and lying on their backs in the grass, simply enjoying being on a world that wasn't inherently hostile. How long had it been since they'd walked in the grass? Enjoyed air that wasn't rank with filth and death?

Whatever else happened now, it was good that they were here.

He turned back to the house and Lochlan, and a Koticki was standing there in front of them, one foreleg raised and pincer open in greeting.

For a moment they regarded each other carefully. Then the Koticki nodded and lowered his leg. He was clearly advanced in years, his carapace a pale green, his back slightly bowed. But when he stepped forward, he moved well enough.

"So you're finally here," he clicked. "She said you would come. I am Skitss, and on her behalf I bid you welcome."

Adam hesitated, glancing at Lochlan, seeking direction. He had always been more comfortable talking to the insectoid creatures than any other Protectorate citizen he knew, but then his position had been solid, assured, and any kindness he extended was merely *noblesse oblige*. Now the dynamic had changed—he was a stranger and a guest, and he owed this Koticki a degree of deference. He lowered his head in something like a small bow.

"I'm . . . I'm not sure why I'm here. But I know I was called." He paused, looking past the Koticki to the door. "Can I see her?"

"Of course. Follow me." Skitss turned and headed for the house, and after Adam and Lochlan exchanged looks once more—and Lochlan shrugged—they followed.

The front room of the house composed most of the structure. On a small wood stove, a pot of something that smelled wonderful was simmering. Herbs were hung from the rafters, augmenting that smell with fresh, faintly spicy undertones. Shelves lined the walls, crammed with a clutter of dishes, books, pads, jars, and rolled paper. In that, it felt much like Ixchel's chambers.

Lakshmi had found as much of her homeship as she could. The rest, she had tried to bring with her.

"Here." Skitss gestured to a curtained door at the rear of the room. "She is resting. But she is expecting you. She'll be very pleased."

Adam started for the door. A few minutes ago, he would have hesitated, but now he was being drawn forward by the same tether that had drawn him to Peris in the first place. He couldn't go anywhere else. Or rather, he could, but then the entire tapestry would be unraveled and remade, and the chance to save anyone might be destroyed.

That couldn't happen. He lifted the simple, unpatterned curtain aside.

The bedroom was about half the size of the front room, the walls lined with more shelves, and the space dominated by a single bed on which lay the oldest woman Adam had ever seen. She was older than Ixchel, older than Adisa, thin and frail under her knit blanket with her white hair gathered in a braid to one side of the pillow and her eyes closed. Yet, despite her age and the deep lines etched into her brown face, he could feel her strength burning like a coal.

All at once she opened her scarred eyes, and they were milky and sightless and very, very keen. She turned her head, lifting herself on one elbow. It clearly took effort, but Adam hung back. She didn't need his help.

"Adam Yuga d'Bideshi." She smiled. "Lochlan Tomek Finnyfolu Jaabir d'Bideshi. It's so good to meet you at last." And she laughed in delight, sitting up fully and pushing the blanket aside.

"Old Mother," Lochlan said, with a reverence that Adam didn't think he'd ever heard before.

"Come, child. Let me look at you." She held out her hands, and Lochlan stepped forward, taking them in his. Seeing him, his bearing and the eager expression on his face, Adam understood something that made his chest ache.

Lochlan missed Ixchel. He missed her more than Adam had realized.

In fact, he had probably missed having an Aalim at all. They were the center of the homeships, Adam knew that much—the caretakers and guides, the people who made sense of an otherwise senseless universe. How long had he been away from his Aalim before? Away and not able to return? Try as he might, Adam couldn't feel the pain behind the questions. He hadn't been raised on a Bideshi homeship. He would never know what it was like.

There were ways in which he and Lochlan would never fully understand each other.

"It's been a long time since I set foot on your Ashwina," said Lakshmi. "Is she well?"

"Last I saw her, she was well." Lochlan ducked his head. "We . . . There was a battle. On the Plain. We lost—"

"You lost many. I know. I felt it." She sobered, turning to Adam, though she still held Lochlan's hands in her gnarled ones. "And you were at the center of it. You carry that with you, don't you? I can see it on you. The blood of the dead—you're soaked in it."

Adam sucked in a breath. He hadn't been able to resist coming here; now he suddenly wanted to run from that piercing sight beyond sight, to keep her from saying any more. He didn't have any words, not when the wound was reopening itself, raw and poisoned. But she answered for him.

"You chose to cover yourself in it, boy. You could have been washed clean a long time ago. All these months away from your arrogant people and you still carry their arrogance in your dance. Don't the *Kutub* say that holding to sin is the heart of pride? There's no sin here, but there's a vast gulf between repentance and guilt. One of them can heal you and the other will only keep you hurting."

She gently slid one hand free from Lochlan's and extended it to Adam. "Child, perfect one, let it go. It won't serve you in what's coming."

He almost didn't take her hand. There had been relief in finding his path, within and without; before then there had even been joy. Now there was overwhelming fear, because all at once he was sure that when he went to her and took her hand, there would truly be no going back. He would be locked into a trajectory, falling into a gravity well from which there would be no rising.

But Lochlan was there. Waiting for him.

He closed his eyes, took Lakshmi's hand, and the fear vanished. Warmth was flowing into him. Warmth and the breeze through the grass of the High Fields, the dancing light in the branches and twisted trunks of the Arched Halls.

When he opened his eyes again, Lakshmi was smiling, and she placed his hand in Lochlan's, releasing them both. "You feel it," she whispered, and she said nothing more. Adam held Lochlan's hand, and the sun came in through the open window and spread across their skin.

When Adam finally returned to the main room of the house, the light was lower, the sun dropping into afternoon. Lakshmi was hobbling ahead of them, leaning on a stick as old and gnarled as her hands. When Skitss stepped forward to help her, she waved him away with faint impatience.

"I'm not yet so infirm as that. Come, let's go out into the light. I want to feel it on my face. And I think there are some people waiting for me." She turned her head to the door and grinned. "Stealing from me, in fact."

Lochlan appeared surprised. "What—?" Adam followed his gaze toward the window and saw it: people from the ship were now milling around in the garden, some staring with hungry longing at the vegetables, a few bending to pick them. He could see the fruit tree from where he stood, and more people reaching up to gather the little blue things from the outstretched branches.

"Come," Lakshmi said again, and she didn't sound angry. "There won't be enough for them all, and they've been living on sawdust, eh, children? In need of fresh and growing things." She walked toward the door, wobbling slightly, but with every step she appeared to grow steadier and stronger. Bemused, Adam followed after, Lochlan at his side and Skitss behind, muttering to himself.

As they entered the garden, everyone glanced up, though Lakshmi was moving with no particular noise. Guilt flickered across many of their faces, and Rachel came forward, Aarons in tow. "Adam, I couldn't—" She halted, her expression uncertain. "Ma'am? I'm sorry, I couldn't stop them. They're hungry, and we—"

"Child, quiet yourself. Quiet your worries." Lakshmi stepped past her and into the garden, every eye was on her, but her focus seemed to be on the tree that stood at its edge. As she reached it, people shifted aside, silent.

They had never seen an Aalim. How could they understand what and who she was?

"What's she going to—?" Rachel started, but Aarons touched her hand.

"I don't know," Lochlan said. "Watch."

Lakshmi lowered her head in front of the tree as if in deference— or as if she was praying. What she said next was soft, and yet somehow Adam heard it, and he had only to see the assembled faces to know that they'd heard it too.

"I know, Ama. But I've been saving the power for so long. There can't be any harm in using a little, can there? Love, can't I?" She laid a hand on the tree's slender trunk, letting out a slow breath. "I can."

The air around the tree shimmered then, as if a heat mirage was settling over it. Rachel gasped, and Aarons murmured a curse that managed to sound more reverent than obscene. Adam found Lochlan's hand again and held on. Some time ago he'd accepted the existence of what might be termed miracles, though he still couldn't bring himself to believe in anything truly miraculous, truly guided by a supreme, unseen hand. Even so, this was something that was hard to deny. Not a god or some great, divine power but an old woman, reaching into the tightly woven strands of reality and tugging a few of them in just the right way.

Then it was over, and she almost fell back, Skitss rushing forward to support her. She laughed.

"Now there's enough. Everyone can eat, and eat their fill." She leaned heavily on Skitss, bowing her head again. "Divide the fish and the loaves among them. But they aren't fish, are they, Ama? No. They'll do, all the same."

Ama. Again, Adam gave Lochlan a questioning look, and Lochlan shook his head.

I don't know.

Lakshmi was returning to them, still supported by Skitss. Rachel opened her mouth and closed it, apparently at a loss.

"Let your people take what they want," Lakshmi said, laying a hand on her shoulder. "There will be plenty for everyone. They should feast while they can and recover their strength. There's work to be done." She turned to Adam. "As for you, boy: there's a village on the other side of this hill. In that village are people who are in need of you, waiting in the house farthest on the outskirts. I told them that you would be coming, but their time is running short, I think. Go now. Hurry."

Adam blinked. "Who?"

"No more questions. You'll see. What matters is that they need you." She made a shooing motion with one hand that was eerily reminiscent of Ixchel. "Off with you."

Lochlan started forward as well, but Lakshmi's hand shot out and curled around his wrist. He stared down at it as if he wasn't sure what he was seeing.

"Not you. You, young *voel*, stay with me. I have work for you to do, as well."

Lochlan looked from her to Adam, obviously discomfited. "What kind of work?"

Lakshmi grinned. "Work of a most important sort. I'll show you. Let your love go, he'll return to you in no time at all."

Adam glanced down the hill: the opposite side from where they had come. Yes, he could see it: a small collection of buildings made of the same red brick as Lakshmi's house, simple and unassuming. A dirt track led down into the little valley it was set in, and there was something about it that did indeed feel as though it were calling to him. Reaching into him, gentle but insistent, and tugging at his heart as every angle and shade seemed to lift itself and beckon.

"I'll be fine," he said to Lochlan, keeping his attention fixed on the track, the waiting valley and its lengthening shadows. "I promise. I'll be back."

It was strange, Adam thought as he headed down the path, how immediately he had trusted her. As with so many other things here, it had been a bit like Ixchel—he had met his first Bideshi Aalim with doubt, worry, deep uncertainty, but no mistrust or suspicion. He no longer had reasons to feel those things specifically, not of an Aalim, but this was a strange woman, an outcast, an entirely unknown quantity.

Except he did know her.

If only he knew where she was sending him.

The dirt track was surrounded by more open fields, but closer to the village the wild-growing grass and flowers became plowed and tended plots of land, stubby, thick-stalked grain and orchards with more of the fruit trees making up what crops he could see. Lights were beginning to come on in the village. The birdsong was louder, as if they were gathering somewhere unseen and sharing the gossip of the day—it struck him that he still hadn't caught sight of one of them.

Then he saw the little house and forgot the birds.

It was smaller even than Lakshmi's, almost a shack. Like all the others, it was red brick with a wood-slat roof, and through a white-curtained window, a faint light showed. It had no garden, but a copse of fruit trees stood nearby, unpruned, old, and twining around each other like mating snakes. A path off the main track led to the door of the place, and Adam stopped where it branched away.

His strange intuition had abandoned him. He had no idea what was waiting inside.

"They are in need of you."

Well, then.

Adam let out a heavy breath and started up the path.

It was a short way, only a hundred yards or so. Adam was no more than fifteen feet from the door when it opened with a jerk and a woman stumbled out. Her black hair was loose and wild, her brown skin sallow in the dim light, her body too thin. She gaped. She raised her hands and reached for him, and Adam stared at her, shocked to stillness.

He knew her.

"*You,*" Eva Reyes breathed, and tumbled into the dirt.

CHAPTER

THIRTY

Nkiruka pressed her hands together and the glowbugs came to her. She couldn't see them now, of course. Only she could, with a sight that had more in common with *feeling* than anything else. It was as if her senses had come together as one, and the picture that they gave her was so deep and so wide and so *complete* that she would never be able to process all of it.

She leaned forward from where she sat cross-legged, extending her hands, and the glowbugs landed on her fingers, pulsing like little dying stars. Over her head, the Arched Halls whispered with the voices of the dead and the voices of other things entirely.

She had come here after a time spent in seclusion and meditation, learning the new parts of herself and what they could show her. Part of her had been grieving, had been wailing with pain and loss, haunted by Satya's face, but the rest of her had been too focused on the world before her. She had wondered if that made her callous; then she had lost herself in the dance of distant stars and thought about it no more.

She wasn't alone. She was never alone. But someone specific was here, someone whose dance she recognized.

"Kae," she said, and didn't turn or rise.

He stepped from the shadows. "Old Mother."

She smiled. She could hear the half joke in the words, but also how serious they were. This was who she was and her age had little to do with her body. The universe was ancient. Now, so was she.

"You've heard from Jakana and Suzaku."

"Yes." Kae hesitated, then sighed and took a seat across from her. He held out a mug and she took it immediately, the warm, spicy scent of the tea drifting to her like a glowing mist.

"You're sweet, Kae. They said no, didn't they?"

"Of course you knew they would." He didn't sound angry; mostly he seemed resigned. Surely he had known too. "Adisa was furious, though naturally he was good at hiding it, at least until we broke the feed. I don't think anyone truly believed we would split the convoy over this. Their councils—"

"Were never easy with what happened on the Plain. I know." She sipped the tea, let it warm her hands. She could still sense the glowbugs circling, as if they were reluctant to leave her. "They're not wrong to feel the way they do. We were dealt a great hurt then, and something like that is hard to forgive." She lowered the mug and fixed Kae with her blind gaze. "But we have to, Kae. It has to be us. Someone has to take the first step, and we were the ones who did by taking Adam in. Now we have to take the next one, and we have to take it alone. I don't think it could ever have been any other way."

She lowered her head, closing her eyes, and sank a little way inward. "Another great Aalim taught us a prayer, once," she murmured. "You know it well. 'Forgive us our transgressions, as we forgive those who transgress against us.' It sounds so nonthreatening, doesn't it? But it's a warning. If we do not forgive, we won't be forgiven. And we have transgressed by abandoning them to their own mistakes, Kae. By setting ourselves against them rather than trying to fight the evil consuming them. Ixchel understood that. No one is innocent here."

"Who will forgive us?" Kae asked softly.

"You were taught that as well." She cocked her head. "You don't need a name. You don't even need to believe that it's one being only. You don't have to believe at all."

"I know. But I still wonder. Old Mother—Nkiru. *Are* we being guided by something? Or are we simply . . . fumbling our way forward in the dark?"

She set down her tea and gazed at him for a long moment. He was made of shifting forms of light and dark, a hundred billion little stars in their orbits. The stuff of stars, here for the briefest of moments in the body of a man, and when he went to the Halls, everything that he was would go to the stars again. Nothing was ever truly lost.

"Do you think there's any real difference?"

He let out a quiet laugh and shook his head. "You're already so much like Ixchel. It's . . . eerie."

"I know." She smiled again, but a second later the smile faded. "I'm— Kae, I'm not sure. I'm not sure what's happening, I'm not sure of anything. Do you know I'm still afraid? I should be so certain of the future, but I'm not. I don't know where this will end. All I know is that we have to keep moving forward."

Kae took her hand, squeezing. "I think Ixchel might have said the same thing."

"Yes. She would. She knew the limits of—of what we are. Of what I am." She tilted her head back, pulling in a long breath. It filled her, made her feel lighter. "We're going to slipstream." She held tighter to Kae's hand. "God, we're getting closer. I can feel it. Kae . . ."

He held on to her, her hand, and—when she tipped forward into his arms—all of her. She had to accept this as well. An Aalim couldn't stand alone. They had to draw strength from their people, accepting their own weakness. They had to be able to surrender to it. She felt Kae's strength flowing into her, the strangeness of him and everything that tied him to this place, where he had long ago discovered himself. And as the light swallowed Ashwina, it was enough.

It should have been Satya. But it was enough.

Isaac Sinder sat alone in his quarters and studied the pads arrayed in front of him. He was about to commit a blasphemy.

It felt like they'd been plunging aimlessly through slipstream for years, exiting at various points, scanning, looking desperately for any trace of the rogue ship. None had been found so far. There was no telling where it might have gone. Alkor had been coldly angry, then loudly frustrated, then cold and quiet again as they searched. He could feel her giving up, and she had every reason to. There was no way to find Adam Yuga, not now.

Except.

The calm certainty that had settled over him after the escape from the camp hadn't lifted. Nothing had changed. They were still being pulled toward something, a path laid out for them. For *him*.

All that remained was to find it.

It hadn't taken a great deal of research. Little was known in the way of the practical aspects of Bideshi witchcraft, but this much was in what records they had. The reading of stars. And it wasn't what he had thought—not only foolish astrology. It was something deeper, something that made both less and more sense to him. He could feel how it worked, though he couldn't have explained it to anyone else. Not that he would have tried.

They never would have understood. They didn't *feel* things the way he did.

His hands trembled as he spread them over the pads, and he clenched them, willing them to stillness. A wave of nausea twisted in his middle, and he willed that away as well. It might just be the drug he had snatched from the infirmary when the medic's back was turned, and injected into his own neck. It was an anesthetic, but taken in the right dose and in the right way, it had slightly hallucinogenic properties. He had known that the effects might be strange. But there was the power of the Bideshi, and once again he couldn't discount it. It was worth exploring. Every avenue was, now.

If this worked? What then?

Simple. Kill Adam, capture who he could, take what they knew and kill them too. Merely because they had useful knowledge didn't mean they had earned their right to exist. The Protectorate leaders' own arrogance might have blocked them from the possibility that some of the Bideshi's skills were genuinely effective, but that didn't mean the greater rejection of their nature was wrong.

It wasn't merely what you knew. It was how you used it.

Sinder closed his eyes.

Adam. He had been with him, had been less than a foot away from him. He had felt the man, had sensed his power and his . . . the spinning, melodic parts of him. The spaces in between and how full of *movement* they were. He might not have known at the time what the sensation was, but he knew now. No matter how distant the man was, that vibrating orbit was still there, singing across light years. Space was nothing here. All he had to do was listen and he would find it.

Adam. Where are you hiding?

There was so much. More than anything, he could feel his own body, his own vibration, the impossibly small lines that twisted and danced and composed him. He took a few moments to lose himself in that, fascinated.

But there was something wrong. Something *deep*.

He shook his head and wheeled away from it, outward again. He couldn't let himself be distracted. Because all at once, there the pattern was—faint but unquestionably there. He opened his eyes and studied the pads, the shifting images and the snaking sine waves.

Aletheia, faded and yellow but old and persistent. *Truth*. Allocer. Red and angry, its pulse enticing. *Revelation of the mysteries of the sky*.

A final one in the center. A blue giant, appearing almost crystalline in the image the pad showed, though its surface churned with endless storms.

Papaios. He knew it. A star around which circled only a few small planets, only one of them habitable by conventional, carbon-based sentients.

Peris.

"I see," he whispered, lowering his hands. "I see."

For some time he sat in silence, thinking. Alkor would never believe how he arrived at this knowledge, and in fact it would mean some undesirable consequences if she found out. But lying was easy. Something that Adam had said while imprisoned that he hadn't attached any significance to until now. Something with enough weight to persuade Alkor, and in any case, what else did they have to go on? Alkor was watching for anything. She was a shrewd woman, but she would be unlikely to ask too many questions at this point.

Slowly, he stood, walked over to his desk and hit the comm.

"Bridge. Let me talk to Captain Alkor. No, I can't wait. Get her now."

CHAPTER

THIRTY-ONE

A dam lunged forward without thinking, but he wasn't quick enough to catch Eva before she hit the ground. She was limp as she did, and as he reached her, part of him was sure she must be dead. But when he turned her over he felt that fine trembling that he knew so well by now.

Of course she was sick.

Her eyes were half-open, only the whites showing, and the trembling was getting worse. Heading toward convulsions? A wave of anger went through him—Lakshmi had known about Eva's state? Had let her languish down here? An Aalim possessed of the power she clearly was?

Or was this something that was beyond even her?

No more questions. He didn't have time. He closed his eyes, put one hand on her forehead and one on her chest, and dropped into her.

She was so much worse than Rachel had been, somehow worse than Naomi had been. It was instant blackness, instant cold. She was almost completely gone, maybe only minutes from death, though only months ago she had appeared whole and healthy. *So fast.* Blindly he pushed on, shoving his way past the choking tendrils of her sickness, searching for her roots.

But it was too much. The tendrils closed around him and dragged him down, too deep and too fast, and he twisted and tried to scream. There was no one else here to save him if he failed, no one to take his place and finish it. If he got lost inside her, he would never find his way out. He would die with her.

Eva! Eva, help me!

Lochlan should be with him. He should never have been allowed to come alone.

Eva, please.

But inside her own body, she wasn't alone. There was something, not a mind, not yet, but the possibility of one, the first hints of what it might become. That potential suddenly hit him, stunned him to the point where he forgot the choking blackness. He forgot everything but the tiny light that was reaching for him, almost extinguished in the dark.

And then Eva was there with him.

She was weaker than the light, barely there at all, but struggling to get to him through the depths that separated them, and he could feel the remains of the fierceness that had once been in her. He had only known her for the briefest of times, while they had been sorting through the aftermath of the battle on the Plain, but he had seen that Kyle had cared for her, and Kyle wouldn't feel that way about anyone without cause.

She was a fighter. Even now, at the last extremity, she was still fighting.

Help me, he gasped. *Help me. Help yourself. I'm not strong enough.* He never was; he never would be. On the Plain he had needed the Aalim. In the camp he had needed Rachel, and then he had needed her again. Now he needed Eva. He would *always* need someone.

It was all right to not be able to do this on his own.

He grabbed for her in one last, desperate lunge, and she reached him and held on. Instantly they flared in the dark, and at the same instant they hit the roots, a lurching nightmare of twisting and wrenching that was as terrifying as the blackness had been. But she was with him, fully with him, and if he was weaker, she was twice as strong.

Here. This is what to do. I'll show you.

But of course she already knew. She went into it, fearless, wrestling it free from herself, and though he went with her he could tell that she hardly needed him at all. Instead, he was once again captivated by that tiny, distant light, like her and yet nothing like her at all.

He knew what it was. He had known as soon as he felt it groping for him.

Then, before he had time to process what he sensed, it was over and he was being rocketed upward again, so hard and so fast that it was almost painful. Rising through the brightening world and out, falling back into the dirt as Eva raised herself with a huge, heaving breath.

He managed to meet her gaze in what was now true twilight, and she stared at him—her eyes clear, the color back in her cheeks. She was still far too thin, still trembling as she sat up—but she was *there* again.

And not only her.

"No," she whispered. "No, not me. Kyle, you have to help Kyle, he—"

Adam tried to turn over, tried to shove himself up, and dropped down again when his arms simply gave out. His legs didn't feel as though they were there. "I can't," he managed, his voice low and hoarse as if he had been screaming. "You . . . You know how, you have to—"

"What're you— No, I can't." She shook her head, pushing onto her hands and knees and starting to crawl toward him. The entire thing still had the unreal quality of a nightmare, and he held out his hands, trying to stop her. He was beginning to understand, now, how close he had come to his own death.

"Adam, please, you're the only one—"

"I'm *not*." The world was blurring away as tears welled and overflowed, hot on his cheeks. "You can. Don't argue with me, Eva, there's no *time*. *Go*."

She got slowly to her feet, still shaking her head, but with a last, bewildered look at him, she made her way into the house. Adam let his head fall back into the dirt and stared up at the sky.

The first stars were showing. He had seen those stars in a dream. He had stood beneath them, and he had known without a single doubt that he was exactly where he was supposed to be.

Was that still true?

If I make it back alive, Lock is going to fucking kill me.

From inside the house there was a cry, long and agonized. Then silence. The stars seemed to pulse and grow dimmer.

I've lost them, he thought. *I've lost all three of them.* Then he didn't think anything else for a while.

The edge of something pressed to his lips, wetness in it. Water. He hadn't even come fully out of the darkness that had enveloped him, hadn't even opened his eyes, before he was drinking like he hadn't had water in days, reaching up to grip the side of the cup as he gulped it down.

"Whoa, shit, Adam. You'll make yourself sick, cut it out." The cup was withdrawn, and he grabbed for it, making an embarrassingly childish whine. He managed to open his gritty eyes, blinking painfully in the light, and then something moved into his field of vision, blocking the worst of it.

A head. A face.

Eva.

He stared at her for a moment. Then he struggled to lift himself, every muscle in his body still weak and shaking. "Kyle. Is he...?"

"He's sleeping." She laid a hand on his chest and pushed him back down. She was also shaking a little, and her face was drawn and tired, but she was on her feet. And if she wasn't completely steady, she was steady enough. "I don't know what the fuck happened, I have no idea what you did, what I did . . . but he's alive. He's all right. I think."

Finally he could see past her and into the rest of the room—tiny, spare, illuminated by a single lantern and a fire in a stove at the far end, though it was close enough to the small pallet he was lying on to warm him. Against the wall and also close to the stove was a low bed barely large enough for two, and on it lay Kyle.

Or what used to be Kyle.

If Eva was thin, he was even thinner. He was wearing a thick beard that made him appear at least ten years older, and the gaunt lines of his face made him appear even older than that. And as Adam lifted his head and studied him, he could have sworn—though it might have been a trick of the dim light—that he saw gray at Kyle's temples.

He had been more than sick. He had been ravaged. Adam had seen terrible things in the camp: people wasted and tormented by their own failing cells and corrupted code. But he couldn't recall seeing someone who had been eaten through like this.

Maybe it was simply because he had known Kyle well before it had taken him. Had known what he was like.

"He got sick so fast," Eva said quietly, following Adam's gaze. "After I started to slide downhill, but . . . A lot more rapidly than me. Before I knew it, I was taking care of him."

Adam didn't look away from his old friend. He couldn't. That Kyle was most likely healed now didn't, for the moment, dull the horror. "How did you both get here? I mean— Why?"

"Like I said, we were sick. We were trying to find a way to help people, and then to get hold of you, but we lost touch with Kerry, and . . ." She sighed and tucked a lock of hair behind her ear. "We got desperate. We heard there was a Bideshi woman living here. That she had powers. We thought she could . . . But she couldn't."

"No," Adam said softly. "Of course she couldn't."

"But she said someone was coming who could. If we would hang on, if we'd help her . . . prepare."

Adam's brow lifted. "Prepare?"

Eva smiled. It was small, still a little weak, but there was a mischievous edge to it that was more like . . . More like *her* than anything else he had seen so far. "I'll show you."

Adam stared at the crates and pulled in a long, slow breath.

Getting up had been difficult, though not as difficult as he had feared, and with Eva's help he'd managed it, feeling more steady the longer he spent on his feet. Healing her had taken almost everything he had, but now it was coming back to him with remarkable swiftness. Eva must have been experiencing the same thing: she'd moved ahead of him with strong, easy purpose that spoke of her peacekeeper training, how skillfully she used the weapon that was her body.

And fortunately they didn't have to walk far. A door behind the stove led to a storage room at the back of the house. He blinked in the dimness, and Eva turned up the lantern in her hand, lifting it high.

The crates didn't fill the room. There were only seven of them in all, stacked neatly against the wall, plain and nondescript. Adam shot Eva a quizzical glance, but she only smiled again and stepped forward, setting down the lantern and bending to the nearest crate to pull off the top.

Guns.

Adam stared at them for a while. *Prepare.* Lakshmi was so much like Ixchel, and Ixchel had possessed a hatred and a great fear of war. She was a fighter, and she had gone to her death with her jambia in her hand, but she had never wanted that violence, had never sought it as an end.

And here was Lakshmi, who'd prepared arrival of hundreds of refugees with seven crates of guns in a shed.

"Pretty good, right?" Eva nodded, pride evident on her narrow face. "Took us a while to get them all together, and by the time we got the last one there was no way we were well enough to handle any more, but Lakshmi said it would be enough. Enough for what, anyway? I mean, clearly some shit's gonna go down . . ."

"I brought a lot of people with me," Adam said distantly. He stepped forward, lifted one of the smaller pistols and slid his hand around the grip. It was cold. "The Protectorate are looking for them. All of us."

Eva whistled. "You got yourself an army of fugitives?"

"I got myself a ship of refugees." He shook his head. "They're not soldiers, Eva. A few of them are peacekeepers, but the rest—"

"If the Protectorate is coming after you, you're either going to have to run or fight." Eva pointed at the crates. "And even if you run, you'll need time to do the running in. Or can you take off right now?"

"We don't have supplies and we're low on fuel," Adam murmured. He was staring at the crates again. "She knew. She sent me here for this."

Eva glanced at him and followed his gaze, her brows drawn together. "Who, Lakshmi? Yeah, she knows a lot. It's fucking creepy." She raked a hand through her hair. "How many are after you?"

Adam shot her a tight smile. "A recon fleet. At least three ships. Maybe more. It's not as bad as when they were after us before. It's still bad."

"How many people?"

"Two hundred? Maybe close to three? I don't know, we never counted." He laid the gun back in the crate and stepped away. "They were sick. They aren't anymore. But it's—"

"You healed them?"

"No. You saw me, Eva. There's no *way* I could heal fifty people without dying myself, let alone three hundred."

"Like me," she whispered, and nodded again. "Okay. Okay, yeah. So now they want to pull the rug over all of it. Great, 'cause that worked out *so* well for them last time."

"Part of it's that, yeah. Mostly I think they want me. I think *they* think I can tell them things. Make this all stop somehow." He was so tired. He hadn't fully appreciated how much. But somewhere, Lochlan was waiting for him. "I have to get back to Lakshmi's. Is there a groundcar? Some kind of transport—?"

Eva snorted a laugh. "About the best people have around here are carts and Terran cattle. A few solar-powered things. We're definitely not *cosmopolitan* out this way, my friend, and most people don't need to do much traveling anyway." She touched his arm. "You should go in the other room and rest. Tomorrow you can—"

"Lochlan is back there. He'll be . . ." It was difficult, all at once, to explain why it mattered so much, why he couldn't wait. But Eva was gazing at him with comprehension on her face.

"You were with him. I remember." She frowned as she glanced toward the door. "I don't like to leave Kyle. And he'd want to see you. But I can help you back up the hill. I feel . . . It's bizarre, but I feel pretty good. Better than I have in weeks."

"Yeah, funny how that works." Adam closed his eyes as weakness surged through him, making his knees shake. He might be feeling better too, but *better* was fairly relative. "If you're sure."

"Yeah, it's okay. Least I can do, really. And maybe I want to see these refugees of yours. C'mon." She slid an arm under his shoulders, and he leaned gratefully into her, letting her support him through the front room toward the door. She gave Kyle one last, lingering glance, then pushed open the door and helped Adam out into the night.

The way back up the hill was spent mostly in silence. It wasn't awkward silence, per se, but it was full of things that weren't being said, questions that weren't being asked. They boiled in Adam's mind, but he couldn't summon the energy to ask them, or even to know what they were. It would be enough to curl into Lochlan's arms and rest.

So it surprised even him when he spoke.

"Does Kyle know?"

He heard her let out a soft breath. "Know what?"

"That you're pregnant."

There was a very long silence. She didn't falter in her steps, but he could feel new tension gripping her, a tightness in her breathing, and all at once he understood.

"You didn't know, either. Did you?"

"No," she said, almost too quiet to hear. "You . . . You're sure?"

"Pretty sure. I felt it when I was . . . You know. Inside you. I don't know how else to say it."

"No, I know." She lifted her head, staring up the hill to the little lights of Lakshmi's house. The breeze that had felt gentle before was now chilly, almost biting. "We never talked about a baby," she said, still quiet. "I guess I assumed . . ."

"They never would have let you."

She snorted. "Are you kidding? Two people with a profile match like ours? Not in a billion years."

Adam smiled faintly. "Well, fuck them, I guess."

Eva laughed. "Yeah. Fuck 'em." She went silent for another moment. "He'll be terrified. Pitch a fit. Is it . . . okay?"

For a few seconds Adam wasn't sure what she was asking. Then he got it—the blackness, choking everything in her. And when the light had taken her . . .

It had taken all of her.

"I think so."

She let out breath. "Okay," she murmured. "Okay. That's good."

They went the rest of the way up without speaking, but the silence was easier, more comfortable. As they crested the hill, Lakshmi's door opened and out came Lochlan, hurrying, fists clenched—and halted.

"Line and fucking *orbit*," he hissed, rushing forward. "Adam, what in the names of all the stars did you—"

"You remember Eva." Adam gently shrugged away, letting himself fall against Lochlan's chest with relief that was almost overwhelming. Now everything was all right. Even if it wasn't. "She was sick."

"You—" Adam couldn't see Lochlan staring at Eva, but he could feel it, almost like a thrum in the air. "*Khara.*"

"Yeah," Eva said, amusedly. "Hello to you, too."

"There's a bed for you on the floor," Lochlan said, ignoring her. "For me too, I guess. Look, whatever, just . . . come in. You had to go and do that again, didn't you?"

"Yeah, I had to." Adam leaned his head on Lochlan's shoulder, his eyes closing. "Eva, thanks. I'll . . . I'll come by tomorrow and see Kyle. I promise."

"Or I'll bring him to you. He hasn't been out of the house in over a week." Still that dry amusement, but there was real warmth under it. "Sleep well, Adam. And thanks. Thanks for everything."

The inside of Lakshmi's house was quiet and warm. No one was in evidence—Adam guessed that Lakshmi herself was asleep, and Skitss was wherever Skitss bedded down. It had to be late, though how late, he had no idea. "How's everyone else?"

"Sleeping off a food coma. They ate Lakshmi's fruit until you could roll them down the hill." Lochlan stopped by a thin mat that had been laid on the floor and lowered Adam onto it. "I should stop worrying about you. You *obviously* don't give two shits about my feelings."

Adam laughed, lying back on the mat, which was a good deal softer than it looked. "I seriously don't know when you turned into my mother, but it's weird."

"You shouldn't have got me in *love* with you, then." Lochlan reached down to pull off Adam's boots, then pulled off his own. "Seriously, I was worried. She said you'd be back in no time. That was definitely time."

"I had work to do." Adam turned toward Lochlan as he lay down, settling one hand on the other man's hip. "What did Lakshmi have you doing that was so important?"

"Weeding," Lochlan said with clear distaste. "She really is exactly like Ixchel."

"Not completely." Adam closed his eyes and slid closer. "Don't ask. *I'm* about to go into a coma and I didn't even get any food. I'll tell you tomorrow."

He could feel Lochlan struggling not to say more. But to his credit, his more prudent side seemed to win, and he curled an arm around Adam's shoulders, pulling them chest to chest, so their legs tangled. Adam fell asleep with his head tucked under Lochlan's chin, and when he had dreams, they were—at last—peaceful.

CHAPTER

THIRTY-TWO

It appeared to be late morning when Lochlan opened his eyes. The sun was bright through the window, and an old woman was prodding him with a stick.

Ixchel?

"Aha. I knew you couldn't be dead yet. It's not in your dance. Your love has been awake for hours; you should join him." She stepped back with a smile, and Lochlan sat up, blinking at her. Now he remembered. Not Ixchel, but very like her.

Except not completely.

"Lakshmi." He scrubbed at his eyes. The mat next to him was, indeed, empty. Through the window came the faint sound of voices, Adam's among them. "What's going on?"

"Many things, boy. You should get on your feet or they'll run right by you." She nodded at the door, which stood open, admitting a warm morning breeze. "There's fruit and porridge under the trees outside. Not an endless amount of the latter, so I'd get to it before it's gone."

Still dazed, Lochlan rose and headed for the door. Some of the previous night was clear, but some wasn't, and it wasn't until he walked outside and saw Adam embracing a tall, dark-skinned man—who, though he was thin and weirdly old looking, was also profoundly familiar.

Then he remembered Eva—Eva, who was standing behind them, a hand over her mouth and tears glistening in her eyes. And he understood.

Adam stepped back, clapping the man—*Kyle*, his name was Kyle—on the shoulder, grinning widely. "I thought I wouldn't see you again," he said. "Seems like it was years. And here you—" He caught sight of Lochlan, waved him over. "Kyle, you remember Lochlan."

"I . . . Yeah, I guess I do." Kyle offered Lochlan a hand, which Lochlan grasped reflexively. Suddenly it felt as if things were moving too quickly, which wasn't a new feeling, but— "Good to see you again. Seems like we could have better circumstances, though. Adam's been telling me—"

"Kyle knows how we got here," Adam cut in. "And he knows that we're almost certainly being followed. Lock, we have to talk. All of us. Aarons and Rachel, too. Can we—" He gestured to a cluster of trees a little way away, at the center of which sat a much thicker grove, the trunks and branches woven around each other in a way that reminded Lochlan for all the world . . .

Here were her Arched Halls. The last piece of the homeship that she couldn't quite let go of.

At the edge of the trees, Aarons and Rachel were approaching— very close together. Aarons raised his arm in greeting.

"Right," Eva said, and started toward them. "Come on."

Finally together since the battle on the Plain, the full reunion— plus Rachel—was strange, though not awkward. Eva and Kyle appeared to know that Aarons was a friend, though they didn't seem easy around him. Rachel was clearly bemused, looking from one to the other as they headed further under the cover of the trees, but more than willing to go along.

Lochlan thought he knew how she felt.

"Okay," Adam said when they were gathered in a tight circle. "I'd say Lakshmi should be here, but I think she knows everything she needs to know. It's up to us now."

Aarons arched a brow. "You gonna tell us what *it* is?"

"The Protectorate are chasing us. They might've been chasing me at first, but now we're all involved." Adam grimaced. "I'm guessing I won't be popular if the rest of our fellow fugitives find out, but I can't help that now. They're coming. Eva told me last night that we have to run or fight, and I think she's right. Thing is . . . I don't think that's my call to make."

Lochlan glanced at Eva, then back at Adam. "How the hell would we *fight*?"

"We have weapons," Kyle said. "A lot of them. We've been stockpiling for a while now. They don't guarantee anything, but they're something. And Adam tells me that as far as he knows, none of the ships chasing you are equipped with orbit-to-surface artillery. That means they're stuck using fighters and ground troops, and if they're only recon ships, they won't have many of either."

"And they won't be expecting us to fight much," Aarons said, a smile pulling at his crooked mouth. "Isn't that so? Sure, we gave 'em a run for their money at the camp, but as far as they know, we're not *armed*, not more than a few of us. And they still don't know that everyone's healthy."

"Right." Eva nodded, a thin, tight smile tugging at her mouth, and watching her, Lochlan's gut twisted. "We have a shot, unless they show up with backup. But Lakshmi hasn't said—"

"Lakshmi knows?" Rachel's eyes widened, then she let out a laugh. "Shit, of course she does. Okay, so your witch feeds us prophecy, and that gives us an edge. What the hell, I'll take it." She fell silent for a moment, thinking. "But convincing the others that we should fight . . . Some of them will want to. A lot of them won't. They got free, and they fought for that, but now they're tired. They might prefer to run."

"So we don't stop them," Adam said quietly. "No one has to fight if they don't want to. But this . . ." He hesitated, then shook his head. "This isn't an ending. This is a beginning. I can't say how I know that, but I do. This is where everyone who's willing to stand up and fight for their people makes their choice. That's why we have the weapons. That's why we're here."

"What about after?" Lochlan's voice was low, hardly audible, but everyone turned to him. He felt sick. Because he remembered the Plain, the bodies, the screams and the pain, the countless dead, and Adam at the center of it, writhing in the depths of his agony.

All of that. And here they were again.

Adam met his gaze squarely, sadly. "I don't know."

"I can't." Abruptly, Lochlan spun, fists clenched so hard that his nails cut into his palms. "You do your talking. I'll be *weeding the garden*."

"Lock, *wait*." But he was already gone, striding away from the trees, head down and stomach roiling, a roaring in his ears that sounded like the wind on the Plain, lost and lonely and mourning for the dead.

Lochlan didn't weed the garden. He passed the house and kept walking, not toward the ship and the people taking the sun around it—so peaceful, so fucking *clueless*—but toward a little wood that lay at the bottom of the hill some distance beyond, the trees squat and thick in trunk and branch, their leaves a pale green tinged with purple. Here, the birdsong was louder, and he was grateful for it. It drowned out everything else.

He didn't enter the wood either, but instead walked along its edge, slowing, his hands loose at his sides. Here he was again, petulant Lochlan angry at not getting his way—except it wasn't that. It had *never* been about that. It had been about too much death far too young, and loss so deep it was as though a piece of his heart had been ripped from his chest. He had never wanted to feel like that again. He hadn't.

Until Adam.

And now Adam was going to war. That he hadn't outright said as much didn't matter. The implication was there. Clear.

He kicked hard at a tuft of grass, sending thin blades into the air—and that *was* a bit childish, but he couldn't bring himself to care. Kae would say that he was being stupid. Kae was probably right. But that didn't mean *he* wasn't right as well.

Hadn't there been enough death? Wouldn't it be better to run?

But *khara*, he hated running, too. He hated everything about it. Especially running once more, from something so big and bad that it assumed it would always win.

He kicked at the ground again, and this time a hidden twig broke with a *crack*. Instantly the trees to his right came alive with rustling and high-pitched calls, and from the branches erupted a huge flock of brightly colored things—things that, as they took to the clear sky, he realized were not birds in any form he knew but lizards with leathery wings, their heads long and narrow and beak-like and their bodies spattered with multiple hues of purple and blue and gold and red so vivid that there was no possible way it could be for camouflage.

They were beautiful, and he stared up at them, entranced, as they rose into the air and wheeled in a slow, graceful arc, settling back into the trees some distance away.

"They're called lenki birds," Adam said quietly from behind him. "Lakshmi told me."

Lochlan didn't turn. He gritted his teeth. "I gather she told you a lot."

"Yes, she did." Adam heaved a sigh. "There's things you need to understand, Lock. I think you know a lot of them already. You've seen the same things I have."

"Yes, I fucking well *have*." He whirled on Adam, his face burning. "You saw the Plain, right? What happened there? Now you want it to happen all over again? Seriously, are you stupid or really just that selfish?"

Adam looked stung. "This isn't like that."

"The *hell* it isn't."

"We're armed. There aren't as many Protectorate. We've got a decent chance—"

"You think my people weren't armed? You think every one of us wasn't trained in combat? We take an animal's life when we're children, an *innocent* life, just so we know what the cost is. You stupid fucking *raya*." The last word came out in a snarl, and part of him regretted it, but the rest of him was raging, completely absent thought, simply knowing that it was hurt and wanted to make the rest of the world hurt too. "You think this is what Ixchel wanted? More bloodshed? I hate your people, but I don't want to see more of them dead. I don't want to see *anyone* dead. It's always been like this, ever since the massacre on Caldor, and I *hate it*. I hate it *so much*, Adam."

Adam stared at him. Lochlan stared back. Behind them, the birds rustled and muttered at each other.

"I don't want to see that happen either," Adam said softly. "How could you think I did? How could you think that?"

"I don't. I don't . . . I don't *know*." Lochlan gripped his dreadlocks, pulled them behind his shoulder, and twisted half away. His eyes were prickling, and suddenly the idea of breaking down in front of Adam Yuga was the worst thing he could imagine.

Adam Yuga d'Bideshi.

Are you sure about that?

"Lock, they're *my people*." Adam took a step forward. "I don't think you understand. You never had to turn on yours. You never had yours turn on you. Do you have *any* idea how that feels? How helpless it makes you?" His voice was still low, aching, almost broken, and the world blurred before Lochlan's eyes. "Do you know what I was dreaming about? The nightmares? It was the Plain. Everyone was fucking *dead* because of me, and you—" His voice did crack then, and it was awful. "I couldn't save you. I lost you. I was losing you every *night*."

"*Chusile*," Lochlan whispered, something in him collapsing, and when he turned back, Adam was suddenly pressing against him, holding on so tight that the breath was almost squeezed from his lungs. Lochlan didn't care. He wrapped his arms around Adam, buried his face in blond hair, and made himself breathe.

My heart.

"There was never any other way this could have gone." Adam pulled back slightly, his face streaked with tears, and he reached up, rubbing away the wetness beneath Lochlan's eyes with his thumbs. "I understand that now. The second one of us reached for a weapon, we were both screwed. Completely fucking screwed. But you've seen it. You've seen what the leaders of my people do. They'll just *keep doing it*, setting the enhancements in place in each new generation, altering it, *poisoning* it, making people sick and killing anyone who gets in the way of their *empire*, until someone stops them. Saves them from themselves. You know another way to do it? *Tell me*. Lakshmi doesn't seem to think there is one, but she doesn't know everything."

Lochlan shook his head. He wanted to pull Adam even closer, burrow into him, hide inside him and forget everything else. "I still don't understand why it has to be us. Why it has to be *you*. Here. Now."

"Because these people have to know that they can do it. They have to learn that they can fight." Adam curled a hand around the back of Lochlan's neck and tipped their foreheads together. "Someone has to take the first step. Find me someone else and I'll cancel the whole thing. I'll do it right now."

Lochlan fell silent again. Then the silence transformed into his mouth on Adam's, fiercely pushing his lips apart, and he shoved Adam down into the grass, slid between his legs, and they both forgot the world for a short, precious time. Too short. Too precious.

"Promise me something."

Adam turned to face Lochlan more fully, and his touch was warm when he laid his hand against Lochlan's cheek. They were still tangled together, the grass itchy under Lochlan's side, the last of the sweat drying on their bare skin. Lochlan wasn't sure how long they had even been there, but it was getting on to midafternoon. Despite the time and his sudden realization that he was ravenously hungry, all he wanted to do was stay here until he couldn't anymore.

"Promise me," he said again, and Adam gave him a small, bemused smile.

"I can't promise you anything until you tell me what the hell I'm promising you."

Lochlan took a breath. He never would have believed that he would do this, but now he couldn't see himself doing anything else. It was his path.

Like everything else.

"If we get through this alive . . . *Chusile*. Marry me."

Adam blinked. Stared, his mismatched eyes widening.

"I know, I know it's . . ." Lochlan laughed, trying not to shift his gaze away. "Look, just tell me if you will. Don't leave me hanging in fucking midair like this."

"Why?"

This time the sound Lochlan made wasn't exactly a laugh. "That's not a yes or a no, perfect."

"No, I mean . . . Really. Why?"

That needed an answer. He hadn't expected the question, but it did. He searched frantically through the clutter that was himself, and it shouldn't be this hard to find words for what he was feeling, it *shouldn't* . . .

"Because I love you. Because I've never loved *anyone* like this. Because I . . . I want to be with you, you idiot; I want to make a life with you, I want to get old and disgusting with you, and I want . . . Adam, line and orbit, I *want you*, isn't that enough?"

Adam let out a soft breath and laid two fingers on Lochlan's lips, replacing them briefly with his mouth. "Yes. Okay? Yes, I will. Calm down, you'll rupture something."

"Oh." Had he expected a yes? What the hell *had* he expected?

Adam cocked his head. "What?"

"I guess I didn't think it would be this . . . easy."

"Oh, so I'm easy now. Thanks." Adam turned over onto his back, pulling Lochlan with him and nuzzling at his jaw.

"*That*, I think we've already well established." Lochlan slid on top of him, returning the nuzzle, the sun warm on his shoulders. It wasn't time to go back yet. He wasn't really all that hungry.

"Whatever." Adam sighed. "Just kiss me for a while."

Lochlan did. Then there was more than kissing, a lot more, and kissing in so many delightful places, sighs and laughter and soft cries, and by the time they pulled reluctantly apart, the sun was sinking and the shadows were lengthening, and they couldn't delay the future any longer.

But lines, it had been good. And it would be good again.

It would.

CHAPTER

✳

THIRTY-THREE

When night fell completely, they set a bonfire near the ship and gathered around it to roast the meat that someone had brought from the village. The village itself seemed wary of them, its people keeping a safe distance. Adam stood on the outskirts of the gathering and watched people mill around, talking, relaxing on the grass together. It was a warm night, in contrast to the cool one before, but while the mood was genial, Adam could sense an undercurrent of tension.

"I'm going to talk to them all after they've finished eating," Rachel said. She had approached without him noticing, but he didn't jump. Perhaps part of him had been expecting her. "Fill them in, offer them a choice."

"Good." Adam sighed. "I think . . . Tomorrow, something's going to happen."

"Lakshmi told you?"

"No. I don't know how I know. I just—"

"You just do. No, I get it." She laughed. "I mean, no, I really don't, but I do."

"Someone should get the children away," Adam said softly. Closer to the fire, Rachel's children were running and laughing, chasing two others about their age. "Maybe not only for tomorrow. Rachel, whatever comes after this . . . I don't think there will be a place for families."

"I know." She moved closer to him, her arms crossed over her chest. "I'll deal with that. I'm pretty sure that a few people won't fight. We can send them off with the kids. Get them as far away as possible." She paused. "We were always going to have to make sacrifices. I think a lot of us know that."

"The question is what we sacrifice," Adam murmured. "Yes. Okay, good."

Again, Rachel hesitated, and Adam could feel the shape of what she was preparing to say. "I'll take the lead in terms of talking. But I think you should speak too."

Adam squeezed his eyes shut. "I don't think that's a good idea."

"Are you kidding me?" Rachel snorted. "*None* of this is a good idea. There *are* no good ideas anymore. But I think you should. Even if they don't know exactly how you're involved . . . You're still at the center of it. You need to tell them who you are, what this is all really about."

Adam kept his eyes closed, as if he could simply block it all out. He wasn't a hero, and if he spoke to them, that wouldn't change. If anything, they might blame him, might hate him for what was going to happen next, despite the fact that they were free . . . And did *he* blame them for *that*? Would he have felt the same?

Maybe he wasn't giving them enough credit.

Either way.

"Okay. I'll do it." He opened his eyes, gazing at the gathering and then up at the stars. "The ones who don't fight should take the transport. They should go immediately, while they can. Stay at a distance and be ready to go to slipstream. If this goes to hell . . . There won't be a safe place on this whole planet."

Rachel nodded. "Yeah. We can set a return time. If they don't hear from us, they just keep on going."

Adam was quiet for a long moment. People would separate, loved ones from loved ones and friends from friends, and somewhere in that crowd was Lochlan, alone with his own thoughts. And yet not alone. Not alone ever again, or at least for the time they both had together.

Married. It defied belief.

"All right." He started forward, heading toward the fire without glancing back. "Let me know when you're ready."

"You know why we're here."

Rachel's voice was strong and clear, carrying over the heads of the crowd, and Adam was reminded a little of Naomi at the camp meeting. Rachel was younger, less certain, but that same solidness was in her, the sense of a backbone that could go to steel when it had to. When she spoke, people listened, and a realization stole over Adam. He wasn't merely looking at a leader for these people.

Rachel was a general.

"We're here because we ran," she continued. At her side, Aarons stood straight and firm, and again Adam noticed how close they were. "We ran because our own people were trying to kill us. They were trying to kill us because we had the *audacity* to think that we didn't deserve to die in a fucking cage."

There were nods and a murmur of agreement. A few people cheered, though the cheers weren't happy.

"They're not going to be content to just let us get away. We're too great a danger. They're going to be coming for us, and soon. So we have a choice to make." Rachel pointed at Kyle and Eva at the edges of the crowd. "These people have accumulated weapons. Enough for almost all of us. So we can do one of two things: We can run, or we can stop running. We can stand and fight."

Silence. Not even murmurs. Adam looked around at the refugees, but their faces were twisted and strange in the firelight, and difficult to read. Then he froze—there at the edge of the crowd was Lakshmi, leaning on her stick with an odd smile on her old face.

How long had she been waiting? How long had she known this was coming?

"Before we decide," Rachel went on, "I think you should hear from someone who's been at the center of this since the beginning. He didn't heal you, but he's the reason you were healed. Adam?"

Numbly, Adam stepped forward into the middle of the group. He was thinking of the meeting on the Plain, standing before the Aalim and begging for his life. Begging for his people.

It was still difficult to say if that had ended well.

He stopped beside Rachel and cleared his throat. Lochlan lingered on the outer edges; Adam caught glimpses of his brown face and the colored beads in his hair. His eyes. There was strength there, and Adam took it.

"My name is Adam," he said slowly, hesitating a second "I used to be sick, like you. And like the rest of you, I didn't do them a favor and lie down and die. I ran. I found people who would help me. I survived because of those people." The words were coming faster now, more easily. All he had to do—all he *could* do—was tell the truth.

"That was something the Protectorate couldn't forgive. Maybe you heard there was an *incident*? On a planet a long way from here, whose name most of you wouldn't know? That was because of me." *It was my fault.* "They were trying to *erase* me. They were trying to erase all of us . . . The Bideshi. I'm not one of them, but they saved me when they had no reason to do so. I think a lot of you know that they're involved in this, too. I think they will be until the end." Now there were murmurs again, and they sounded doubtful, but Adam steeled himself and pushed onward.

"I didn't mean to find you. But I did. You're why I came back. I don't want to see our people die, but that's where they're headed. As long as the people who want to kill you stay in power, there'll be more quarantines, more experiments, more torture. More death. You've seen that there's another way. I want to take that way to the rest of the Protectorate. But they won't let us. They're too locked into the way they've always done things, the way they've rejected everything the Bideshi are. Holding on to the things in which they were always taught to believe, no matter what they see. The only way we'll be able to make this work is by meeting force with force."

He sighed, his chest tightening. "I don't want to fight. I'd be happier not to have to. I've seen . . . so much death. I never want to see it again. But I don't think I have a choice anymore. We can fight, or we can die. Not just us. Everyone."

"Listen to him."

Everyone turned, startled. Lakshmi was stepping forward, supported by Skitss, lifting her stick as if in a kind of benediction. "Few know the cost of what he's saying better than he does. But you do. Haven't every one of you lost someone? There comes a time, children, when there are no good choices left. When all you can do is the best you can do." She lowered her head and appeared to say something under her breath, before she lifted her voice again. "It starts with us. With you. Here and now. You may choose one way, or the other, but no one can abstain from the choosing. No one can stand aside and watch it happen. Make your choices, and follow those paths to the end."

Once more there was silence, all eyes on the center of the circle. Rachel lifted her head and raised a hand.

"Everyone who's willing and able to fight, step forward. Everyone who isn't, take all the children and go to the ship. Don't hesitate. We've already stocked it with whatever supplies we could scrape together. It's not much, but it might be enough. Take off, head to the outer edges of the system, and wait to hear from us. If you've heard nothing two days from now, go to slipstream and get as far away from here as you can." She paused. "There's no shame in choosing that way. Not everyone's a fighter. And someone has to take care of the people who aren't."

There was a moment where no one moved. A log tumbled down in the fire, sending sparks up into the night sky like little gold and orange stars. Gradually, Adam realized that he was holding his breath, but only when he felt Lochlan's hand at the small of his back did he let it out.

Then, one by one, people began to divide themselves.

Adam had no idea how long it went on, that great separation: people stepping forward, people turning away. He knew only that it hurt, and he saw Rachel blinking back tears as Tamara took Becca and Dion by the hand and led them away. They were looking back over their shoulders, confused and clearly frightened, and Rachel pressed her hands to her mouth and closed her eyes.

This was good-bye. For some of them, maybe forever.

Then it was over. What they were left with was approximately a hundred people, mostly young and middle-aged, men and women alike. And there was something harder about them, something colder. A dark kind of understanding.

They knew what they had chosen.

"Okay," Rachel said softly, and lifted her voice again. "Tonight we'll hand out guns, make sure that everyone can use them. I think we're limited in terms of the strategy we can employ, and I'm not a peacekeeper, but I'll be talking to those of you who were. And I have someone who—" She gestured to Aarons. "He knows more than a lot of you, I think. You should listen to him. We'll work this out. I can't promise anything, but . . . we're in this together, and that has to count for something."

She paused and dropped her arms again. "All right. Let's get to work."

They exited slipstream smoothly, quietly, and Sinder lifted his head, gazing out the window of his cabin at the suddenly black space outside.

It was time. Or close to it, anyway.

He rose slowly, stretching his stiff legs; he had no idea how long he had been sitting there on the floor in silent meditation, but he felt rested. Refreshed. Ready to take on anything. He would keep that calm center in himself and it would rule him and replace his weakness with strength.

He went to the desk, and touched the comm a second after it chimed. "Yes?"

"We've come out of slipstream, sir. It's about three hours until we reach the planet itself. The captain would like to speak to you, if you'll meet her in her cabin."

"Straightaway, Lieutenant." Sinder began to straighten his suit, then stopped when he realized that merely straightening it wouldn't do the job. What was he thinking? He needed a shower and a change of clothes; he needed to present himself as he was. A sentinel, a knight—but in that capacity, merely a representative of something far greater.

Order would be restored, and he would exult in it. And all would be well.

Alkor met him at the door. Her expression was cold, stern, her bearing a little aloof. He wasn't bothered by it. She would see soon enough.

"Captain."

"Mr. Sinder." She stood aside and gestured for him to enter, which he did with a polite nod. She faced him as the door shut. "So here we are."

"Almost. They tell me that we're about three hours out, still."

"Yes. And then I guess we'll see if this *second sight* of yours really has something to it."

Sinder smiled. "You have a better proposition, Captain? I'm all ears."

"I just don't like the idea of my people being led on a snipe hunt."

"What are snipe, anyway?" Sinder moved toward her desk and lifted a small crystal trinket from its corner: a figure shaped like a graceful bird with its wings unfurling. It didn't completely match the rest of the decor and had the appearance of a gift; he wondered who had given it to her. "I know a lot about ancient Terra, but I don't know the origin of that phrase. Isn't it odd, Captain, how we use all of these things without any idea of where they come from? Their true purpose?"

Alkor arched a brow. "Well, clearly people used to hunt them. When was the last time you slept, Sinder?"

"You don't have a lot of faith in me," he said, turning back to her. "I know you said that you believed that I would find Yuga, but I wouldn't be surprised if you're doubting that now. I don't blame you. It's strange. I would doubt it myself if I wasn't so sure, and either way we'll soon know." He closed his hand around the crystal figure, feeling its coolness and weight. "Are your people prepared to make planetfall?"

"Yes. There shouldn't be any further problems." She shifted her shoulders and went to the cabinet on which sat the glasses and decanter. Again, whiskey as a kind of peace offering. *Good move.* "We'll take Yuga and the Bideshi—and Aarons—into custody if at all possible, but the officers at the quarantine told us to eliminate everyone else, and I think that's probably the best move. We don't have the facilities to hold that many people." Her mouth twisted as she poured. "I won't pretend to like it, though. They're civilians; some of them are children—"

"They're threats to the Protectorate. They're also dead anyway." He took a long drink, heaved a sigh as the heat of it settled in the center of his chest. "This is mercy, Captain. We can make it quick for them. What's their other option? Something slow and lingering and painful?"

"I suppose." Alkor examined her glass as if there might be an answer lurking in the whiskey's golden-brown depths.

"Regardless, be ready for resistance. These people broke out of a guarded Protectorate facility. And they almost certainly have Yuga. Don't underestimate them. Don't pull your punches."

"I don't intend to." Alkor looked up at him, her face set. "I want to be done with this, Sinder. I want this to be over. I want to go to my house on the beach and not think about it ever again. This whole business might be necessary, but it's *not* how I wanted to wrap up my career."

"I can well appreciate that, Captain. Nevertheless." He gave her a faint smile. "I know we didn't get off on the smoothest of terms, but I think we've developed a real working relationship. As I said, I'll make sure the right people hear about the job you've done."

"Thank you. But like *I* said, I don't want to think about this after it's all over." Alkor set her glass down on her desk and pinched the bridge of her nose. "I need an hour or so. I'll notify you when we're in orbit."

"Excellent." Sinder took a last swallow, then set his own glass down beside hers and turned toward the door. He was halfway across the room when Alkor cleared her throat.

"Sinder, can I have that back, please?"

He stopped and glanced down at his hand. The little figure was still nestled in his palm, now warm from the heat of his body. He returned to Alkor and held it out.

"My apologies. Thoughtless of me. It's very pretty," he added as she took it from him. "Where did you get it?"

"It belonged to my daughter." She set it back down on the desk, and kept her gaze on it. "I'll speak to you later, Sinder."

He nodded and turned away again. But that final image was strange. A great many things were strange now, were taking on the quality of a dream.

Sinder had always been dreaming. That much was clear. They were all living as the dreams of the universe, pulled along as inexorably as cars on a track.

He would play his part in that journey, to the last. He would fulfill it. He would see Yuga's blood on his hands, and he would know that he had done well.

CHAPTER

THIRTY-FOUR

N kiruka walked the halls of Ashwina.

Like everything else, she was relearning the ship, coming to understand it as it truly was. Humming with life, with chaos, with *movement*—these were things that she had always sensed, but now they were a blatant reality that crashed relentlessly in on her like waves on the shore. More than once she had to stop, head down, panting and gently turning aside the people who paused to ask if she needed help.

They weren't surprised, those few who had seen the last Aalim take her place. It always happened this way. Being born was an awkward business. It took time to find one's feet.

She followed the corridors and hallways and chambers down toward the center of the ship, toward the great hall that extended from the middle of Ashwina's bulk to her transparent top. As she exited the last corridor into one of the long galleries that circled around its side, she took a slightly trembling breath, something both more and less than a gasp. There was *so much* here. More than she could ever take in.

They were so close.

"Nkiru."

Some part of her had already known, had felt the approach of a familiar dance, graceful and lovely. A dance she had joined, once not so long ago. One she had expected to join to her own.

"Hello, Satya."

"You're looking well." The words weren't as cold as they might have been, but they were distant, as uncertain as Satya's body felt. She didn't know if she should approach, and Nkiruka wanted to reach for her, take her hands, call her "my love" and "dear child" and "*chusile, habibti*, my life."

SUNNY MORAINE

No. Not those last. Never again.

"I'm . . . becoming." It was the only word she could think of. She went to the railing that lined the gallery and laid her hands on it, feeling the space in front of her. A long way up, and a long way down. "It won't be long now."

"Yes. We're a few hours from the system. Adisa asked me to tell you." Satya paused, and it was heavy with her unhappiness. "I don't know why he did that. I don't know why I agreed."

"I do." She didn't quite smile. Adisa, too wise for his years. Ixchel had taught him well. "We share a home here, Satya. We can't be together the way we wanted. But we have to be together." She turned back, letting out a sigh. "We have to find a way to . . . move together. You know that as well as I do."

"We did move together." Satya sounded—*felt*—more helpless than anything else. At a loss. The past was chaining her to itself, dragging her down, and Nkiruka thought of Adisa and Ixchel and wondered if Adisa had faced the same thing: a life looking backward or a push forward into the terrifying, lonely unknown.

If so, she knew what he had chosen. What it cost him.

"Yes, we did." Despite her obvious pain, Satya was shimmering like a jewel, lit from within. Nkiruka had always known that she was beautiful, but now she saw her completely, all facets of her, and it made her heart ache almost more than she could bear. "Now the dance has changed. We change with it or we'll be destroyed."

"Do you know, I've spent hours lying in bed and thinking that being destroyed might be better?" Satya pushed past her, gazing over the edge of the railing. "The night you decided, I came out here and I looked down, and I swear to all the stars, Nkiru, I almost jumped."

Unsurprising. But Nkiruka's mouth went dry, her gut wrenching. "Why didn't you?"

"I'm not sure. Something stopped me." Now Satya seemed curious. "You always said I was too stubborn for my own good. Maybe I decided that you weren't worth it." She let out a breath. "No, that's not true. That's not why. I wish I could feel that way, but *chere*, I can't."

"It wasn't your time," Nkiruka said softly. Tiny stars danced through the air between them. "It wasn't in your dance or your orbit. Your path is taking you elsewhere."

316

Satya laughed softly. "Oh, fuck you."

Nkiruka bowed her head. She deserved that. She would have felt the same. Part of her *did* feel the same.

"I will always love you," she whispered. "If that's a sin, I'll be damned for it."

"Yes. We will." Satya faced her, hesitated for a moment, then reached out and took Nkiruka's hands in hers. A shock pierced Nkiruka through her fingers, lanced up her arms and into her throat and brain and heart, but she bit back her cry. She gathered the pain to herself and devoured its bitterness.

"I think this is good-bye," Satya murmured. "When we reach the planet . . . everything will change. Everything *is* changing."

"Everything is always changing." Nkiruka cupped Satya's face and leaned in. If they were seen, this might result in her exile, but she didn't care. One last moment together, one final sweet, terrible farewell. "Love, I'll carry your dance inside me. Always and forever, until the last star burns out and the night is empty and cold."

Satya drew in a breath that was more like a sob, and Nkiruka pulled it into herself when she erased the distance between their lips. She would keep it with everything else, like a secret treasure.

Now she had to close this love into her heart and turn her face to what lay ahead. To what she must do.

There was no time for mourning.

After Satya left, she stood in the gallery for a long time—and in fact, the time slipped away from her and became unimportant. Slipstream was violence done to space-time, a worm's tunnel burrowed through a forest of entropy. She was near the center of it, and so was the universe itself, and the center was pulling them in. It was the gravity well of a black hole, dragging everything into itself, and there was no escape.

When she felt Ashwina shivering her way out of slipstream, she bowed her head and whispered a prayer.

It had begun.

CHAPTER

※

THIRTY-FIVE

Things were moving quickly. By the time the transport was well away, Rachel and Aarons had commandeered a field comm unit from among its supplies, and were keeping its band open inside Lakshmi's house, posting someone near it at all times. The sun was still an hour or so from rising when the young man who'd been on watch found her sleeping beneath the trees and shook her, reporting that the transport had detected the recon fleet approaching. That they couldn't be more than an hour out.

She brought this information to Adam, who was sitting with Lochlan at Lakshmi's table; Lakshmi was seated in her rocker with her eyes closed. She seemed asleep. Adam knew she wasn't.

Gathered with the core group, he sat and listened as first Rachel spoke and then Aarons, the shape of the thing becoming clear, along with how badly the odds were stacked against them.

"There's three ships in all," Rachel said. The lantern sat in the center of the table, casting strange shadows over their faces, deepening their lines and hardening edges. "Which is a lot worse than one but a lot better than . . . Well, a lot better than anything more than three. Like we saw when we escaped the camp, they're not large, nor are they heavily armed, but they do have fighters and they do have peacekeepers, though Aarons tells me they can't land a huge number of people at any one time. Either way, they have enough firepower to knock our transport out of the sky. They're a threat. We shouldn't assume otherwise."

She produced a pad and set it on the table, tapping it to bring up a map of the surrounding terrain. "We managed to get the signal beacon out of the transport, though it was tricky. It has an external power supply, which won't last, but we think it'll broadcast long enough to get their attention."

"What we need more than anything else is cover," Aarons cut in. He pointed to the meadows around the little square that Adam assumed represented the house. "And we need to keep 'em as far away from the village as possible. Lakshmi told them this was coming a while ago. They're evacuating, spreading the word to others—the people here are good at removing themselves from harm's way. This place isn't far enough out of the way to completely escape Protectorate notice, but they'd just as soon make it look like there's no reason to come here. Apparently they have plans for this kind of thing. But let's minimize property damage all the same."

He smiled grimly. "So we put the beacon under the trees in this wood here." He pointed to the wood outside where Adam had found Lochlan the day before. "They'll head for it. The trees are thick, and they're easy to climb. We're stationing about a third of our people in there with rifles. They're mostly not snipers, but we do have two of those, and in any case, they'll have the element of surprise. If nothing else, they should scare the *shit* outta anyone who comes nosing around in there."

"Everyone else is taking cover in the other smaller wood behind the hill. There are some rock outcrops there that also give good cover." Eva sounded focused, almost excited. Like Rachel, she had a head for this. Rachel might be a general, but it would be good if she wasn't the only one. Of course, it would all depend on what Eva wanted. And the tiny life inside her—that might change things. But she probably wouldn't be content to sit by. "Once the peacekeepers are under the cover of the trees, those people move in and surround them. We're keeping some back to provide support if needed. We press, we take as many of them out as possible, and then we head back to the rocks and the trees before they can land more people and surround *us*." She let out a breath. "Rinse and repeat."

"Until they realize what we're doing," Kyle pointed out. "Which won't take long. They might be oblivious as hell to certain things, but they aren't stupid."

Aarons shrugged, though he was scowling even harder than usual. "*Thanks*. Yes, we're well aware. We can only work with what we have."

He paused, running a fingertip along the edge of the pad. "There's not going to be any *beating* them, you know that," he said. "Not this time. About the best we can do is push them back. Make them run for a while. But there's no winning in the picture here."

"*And* they won't be casually sweeping things under the rug this time." Adam sighed. So much of it always came back to this. "The Protectorate . . . They don't merely smooth over rough spots. They go after them with a fucking hammer. They'll mean to *end* us, and at least five people here have seen what that looks like."

"Then I see two more issues," Lochlan said. "We still have the fighters to contend with, and last I checked none of us had engines or wings strapped to our back or turret guns hiding somewhere in our heads, lovely though that would be."

Aarons snorted a laugh. "We don't? You're kidding. What's the other one?"

"Simply this: If they're coming after us with all hammers waving— and I agree they will—we can't stay here. Even if we do manage to chase them off temporarily, they'll come after us as soon as they can."

"Right," Rachel said, giving him a quizzical glance. "Which is why the transport will come back for us if it works."

"I don't mean that," Lochlan said patiently. "That's fine, good, I get it. But *after*." He was quiet a moment. "This is the start of something bigger, assuming we don't all get killed." If Rachel had seemed old, now Lochlan appeared ancient. And tired. Very tired. "You know I'm right."

"He is," Lakshmi murmured. She was rocking slowly, her hands in her lap, but her eyes were open and pale as a moon. "Ama," she said, even more softly. "*Habibti*, I know, I'm telling them. Hush, now." She turned her attention back to them, her mouth tightening. "For years I've seen this coming. Here, far from my Halls, far from my children, you think I can't still feel the dance? You think I can't still weave my fingers into the tapestry and pull just the right threads? You don't know what it is to see what I've seen, and know that no living being can change it."

She leaned forward then, gripping the arms of her chair tightly enough that her knobby knuckles went white. "For so long I had peace. Me and my Ama, waiting for the end, waiting to be together again. Then I dreamed waves of blood, and evil in the roots. I saw the Plain and a man, and then so many more people, like an oncoming tide. I would give anything to trade my place in this. But it's *here*." She stamped her foot on the floor, and they all jumped. "Here with you, at the threshold of this war. My role is to open the door. I will carry that to my death and beyond, that *stain* on my soul."

She went quiet again, and the silence of the others was heavy, stunned. Lakshmi had been peaceful, even happy, apparently pleased to finally see the people she had been waiting for and satisfied to play the part she seemed to believe had been set for her. Now all her muscles were tense; her face contorted with pain, and Adam wanted to go to her, though what he could do, he had no idea.

The question is what we sacrifice.

"Feel no guilt, children," she murmured. "Life is cruel. It can only ever be what it is, and the same is true of us all. Only know the nature of the door I'm opening before you. Know its nature, before you step through."

At first no one said anything. After a while, Adam realized that they were all gazing at him, all waiting for him to speak.

"We'll find a place to make a stand," he said slowly. "Look, I . . . I don't completely understand what's gotten us this far. I don't understand all of what's happening, and I sure as *hell* don't know what's going to happen next. What I do know is that there's something at work here that's greater than all of us."

He paused. Once he never would have imagined himself saying anything like this. But everything had changed.

"I don't know if you'd call it a god, or gods, or fate, or simply the way the pads fall. I don't know which of those I believe in anymore. But I do know I've gotten this far on faith. Not unquestioning faith, and I doubt everything all the time, but . . . None of it's been planned. I've just trusted that whatever's guiding this, it'll get me—get *us*—to where we need to be. I think that'll keep happening. So if we do live through this, I have faith that we'll find somewhere to stand."

They glanced at each other. Then Kyle laughed, shaking his head. "Friend, you are so fucking different."

Adam smiled, thinly. "Tell me about it."

"If only I'd known we were moving on the whims of a *mystic*," Rachel said, but she was smiling too. "Well, whatever. I don't know about the rest of you, but I don't care *why* we're doing what we're doing now, I only care that it works. We can get all metaphysical once we're on the other side and still breathing."

"Right. Let's get going." Eva pushed back from the table. Her face was drawn, her jaw tight, but her eyes were cool and focused. She wasn't looking at Kyle, had barely looked at him throughout the entire proceedings, and Adam wondered if she had told him yet. If she intended to.

Perhaps not until much later. Either way, it had to be her choice.

The meeting dispersed. Kyle and Eva had put themselves in charge of those using rocks for cover, while Aarons and Rachel were taking the other group into the trees. Adam watched them head toward the door, Lochlan still beside him.

"Which are you with?"

"The ones playing Klashorg in the trees." Lochlan took his hand. "You're going to stay here."

Adam turned to him, mouth twisting. It didn't feel exactly like a smile. "We're really going to do this again?"

"Not if you don't argue with me."

"You know the chances there." Adam raked a hand through his hair. He felt dangerously close to the sort of tantrum he remembered having occasionally as a child, screaming and kicking things and ultimately accomplishing nothing. "Lock, *seriously*, when are you going to treat me like a fucking *adult*?"

"When all has grown cold and stale and I no longer love you." He was standing placidly, his arms folded. "How many times do I have to tell you that you're not a soldier?"

"I can fire a damned gun."

"From a fighter turret. That's not the same as close-quarters combat, Adam, not one bit, and you know that. Look, you're right. Okay? You're right; I can't keep stopping you. I get that now. So when this is all over, we'll have lessons. I'll show you everything I know. In the meantime, you stay put. You help the ones left behind however you can. You stay *out* of the line of fire, or stars help me, I will kick your ass from here all the way to the Plain when I get back." He unfolded his arms and laid his hands on Adam's shoulders, his voice dropping into something thick and tight so suddenly it jarred Adam. "Do not—do *not*—make me terrified to lose you while I'm fighting for my goddamn life. Don't do that to me. Not again. Don't you dare."

Adam stared at him, mouth open. He'd had retorts, all manner of arguments, and they had died in an instant. What Lochlan was saying wasn't new, but the way he was saying it ... Choked. Desperate. Pleading.

"All right," he whispered.

"Yes," Lakshmi said, and they both spun, startled. Adam had forgotten that she was even there. She stood by the stove now, leaning on her stick and looking at Adam with an expression that he wasn't at all sure he liked. "You stay with me, child. We have work to do, you and I. I think you know what I mean."

All at once the dream—the *vision*—came rushing back to him, and he did. And he was terrified.

"On this ground, you may be an Aalim."

He eased himself from Lochlan's grasp and went to her, his head bowed. Everything in him was screaming *run*, get out while he could—but of course he couldn't. Not now.

"I don't know if I can."

"Yes, you do." Lakshmi tilted her head to one side, and Adam thought of a bird, the lenki birds, leathery and wrinkled but so lovely. "You know who and what you are, boy. Not for us, but for your own people. *If there arise among you a prophet, a dreamer of dreams ...*" She extended a hand. "We have to prepare."

Adam glanced back. Lochlan was standing only a few feet away from him, but the distance seemed vast and still expanding. Lochlan's face was a mask of confusion and unease, but try as he might, Adam could think of no way to comfort him.

Somehow, standing in the same little house, he was out of everyone else's reach.

"I'll come back," Lochlan said softly, then he went to the door and was gone.

I love you, Adam thought, perhaps called after him, but he was never sure. The door closed, and he was left alone with Lakshmi, with a wind rising inside himself. Out the window, the sky was lightening toward dawn.

CHAPTER

THIRTY-SIX

S inder gazed at the main screen, where Peris hung bright and green and soft blue in the dark. Not long ago, its blue sun had risen over its curving rim, and now that sun was behind them. He imagined the shape of their ship silhouetted against the star, bathed in radiance. Blessed by the heavens.

"You're prepared?"

Alkor nodded without a glance at Sinder. He had already known she would be. But it was good to ask her anyway. Good to make such things clear.

"Ma'am, we've picked up their signal. It's coming from the southern continent. It's . . . under some heavy tree cover. They must have thought that would hide them sufficiently."

"Excellent. What's the status of the other ships?"

"Stationed in lower orbit around the planet as you ordered. They're awaiting commands."

Alkor met Sinder's gaze directly, confidently. *You see. Now we can be done with it.* "No sense in waiting," she said. "Tell them to launch their landers. Launch our own too. Converge on that signal. Make sure they're armed, armored, ready to do whatever it takes to get Yuga and the other two into custody." She looked back at the officer. "Remember. Everyone else who was on that ship is expendable. More than that, none of them can be left alive."

Sinder inclined his head, satisfied. She was clearly still uneasy with the order, liked nothing about it, but first and foremost she was a soldier in the service of the Terran Protectorate, and she would do her duty.

More couldn't fairly be asked of anyone.

"I want minute-by-minute updates," she continued. "Stay in constant contact with the surface. The second they see anything, I want to know about it."

The view on the screen didn't change, but Sinder could practically feel the ship disgorging its small collection of personnel shuttles. No more than ten people aboard, but that would be more than enough.

Except that didn't entirely ring true, did it? There was something here beyond the obvious, something that he couldn't quite see. *Show me*. It wasn't a prayer to any deity, any conscious entity, but he sent it out into the universe and hoped that the universe would answer. *Show me what to do.*

"Captain, stay on high alert." She shot him a scowl, but he ignored her. "I have . . . a feeling. I'm not sure. Just stay sharp."

She gave a final nod to her officers, then turned to him, stepping close. "I've trusted you, Sinder. More than maybe I should have. More than I had reason to." There was a pause, and her jaw tightened. "You trust me, now. All right?"

She had lowered her voice and didn't sound angry, but there was a firmness in her tone that he didn't altogether like. He met her gaze evenly. Calmly. In these final moments, he wasn't going to lose himself. "All right," he murmured. There was something beautiful about her. Something weathered, like a stone shaped by years of wind and water. "I trust you."

The thing was, he did.

Lochlan shifted in his perch on the branch, and as the tree rustled, the shuttles screamed overhead, then pitched into a deeper hum. They were descending, setting down. Close.

This is it, Lochlan thought. If this was going to work, the peacekeepers couldn't be allowed a hint that anything was amiss. They would be ready for trouble. They might have taken the bait, but they weren't *stupid*.

A few more minutes. Nothing. Then, at the edge of the wood came bird cries, the flapping as a flock of them leaped into the air. The creak and rustle of the trees as people pushed their way in.

These are the cousins of the Arched Halls. It came to him as if from outside, sent by something other than himself. *This is your territory, not theirs. Your ground.*

Breathless, he waited. He had hated fighting to kill, feared it, been ready to stand against it with everything in him. Now he was focused only on doing it as quickly and as lethally as possible. He had been trained for taking lives, though not for taking joy in it. He could do it when he had to. He was ready. He would.

For Adam.

Now he saw white bodies moving in the dimness only ten feet or so below. Their rifles were raised, their footsteps deliberate, but they were still too confident, too convinced that they had already won.

And it was going to kill them.

There was no way of being sure how many of them there were, and it didn't matter. Someone was simply first, opening fire, and then everyone followed. Lochlan picked his shots, fired, picked more. Beneath him, the white bodies were falling among the trunks and roots and moss, birds were shrieking, shots were going wild. There were cries, yells, and under it all Lochlan's vision narrowed to a single sharp point as he aimed, fired, aimed, fired.

There was a pause in the chaos, though perhaps he imagined it. Then a shout went up from some distance deeper into the wood.

"Pull back! It's an ambush! Return fire and fall back; we can't see a fucking thing in here!"

He didn't see them retreating so much as he saw the white bleeding from the green and brown, retreating toward the meadow, and his middle clenched with fierce, awful joy. But as cheers rose, their shots rang out, and first there was one scream and then another, and the thump of bodies tumbling to the forest floor.

"They're in the fucking trees! Fire into the trees!"

Bullets whizzed past his ear and he ducked, dropping close to the branch. Here he had cover, but here he was also trapped, and it was only a matter of time until he would have to emerge. As had happened on the Plain, as happened every time he fought—even in training with Kae beside him—panic descended on him, covered by a detached calm. He had a choice, and neither option was good, so he had to take the less awful of the two. He swung down from the branch and dropped the short distance to the ground, gun still in his hand.

It was ridiculous, but he wished so much for his jambia. It was back on *Volya*.

"Everyone push forward!" Aarons, not far away. "Get them back into the meadow! Remember the plan!" All around Lochlan, more people were dropping down, starting after the retreating peacekeepers, ducking for cover behind the wide trunks. It was incredible, really—these were no more soldiers than Adam was, but they were moving well, responding to commands, apparently keeping their heads.

But they weren't Adam. He stepped over a prone body and knew that, though it hurt to see it, the hurt wouldn't last. He took a second to reflect on his own essential callousness.

Then he was shooting again, heading toward the morning light, watching more and more bodies fall, and fall, and fall.

Adam stood at the window. From here, he could see the wood and the rocky ridge opposite. He could see too much, and it was all he could do to keep still.

"Calm, child." Lakshmi spoke levelly from behind him, and he smelled the soothing aroma of her tea. "You can't do anything down there."

Adam gritted his teeth and didn't answer. In the green bowl of the meadow, where the grass was still dark and flattened from the transport, approximately twenty Protectorate shuttles sat like a clutch of white eggs. A swarm of peacekeepers had headed into the wood. Far overhead, he could hear more descending. Now, distant gunfire.

"You can't always keep your love safe," Lakshmi said, more softly. "Just as he can't always protect you."

"I know that." He turned, arms folded over his chest. Through the open window, the morning breeze held a chill. "But you know how hard it is. Don't you? You know that it's *impossible*." He stepped forward. Over the terror and the deep frustration, many things were finally becoming clear. "Ama. That's her, isn't it? The woman you were exiled for. You never saw her again."

"No, I did not." He had thought she might be angry, even offended; however, she simply regarded him patiently, her blind gaze sweeping over him. "But I saw her every night in my dreams. It was pain beyond imagining. Don't you think I wondered, every day after that, whether she had been worth it? Would it be a better love story if I said I was sure that she was? It wasn't an easy choice, perfect boy. In the end, my heart made it for me."

"You lost her anyway. You lost everything." Adam took a seat across from her. Suddenly, she didn't look so old. He could see a young woman in her, in love and in pain and very afraid. Aalim weren't special, that was the thing. More was asked of them than most. That was all. They still had to choose for themselves what to give.

What to sacrifice.

She inclined her head. "Yes. I did. Did that have to be? I don't know. What did your Ixchel teach you? That we know so much more? No. Perhaps sometimes we know more, but child, we are sure of so much less." More gunfire. Adam flinched. He wanted to see. He wasn't sure that he could bear to see. "Keep yourself at peace. Your time to act is coming soon."

"I should be with him." Adam stared down at the fine grain of the table, polished slick by many years of use. "Things keep . . . pulling us apart."

"You and he don't walk the same path."

He jerked his head up. "What do you mean?"

"You can't walk the same path, child. Every living thing walks alone. For a time yours might run side by side, and in that time you are companions. But in the end, all paths branch away, and then they end as well."

Adam took a breath, and then found himself unable to let it out. "What are you saying? Are you saying that he'll—"

Louder gunfire than before, and screams too. Unable to contain himself any longer, Adam shoved himself up from the table and rushed to the window, hands braced against its sill. Below him, the white mass of peacekeepers was retreating haphazardly out of the wood—

And was being boxed in.

They came from the wood itself, and they came from the ridge, a tide of people, advancing and shooting. Peacekeepers were ducking behind shuttles, returning fire, but they were falling. Not many of them, and there were still over a hundred firing, but they were stumbling, scattered and disorganized, overwhelmed by the men and women rushing at them.

It might work. It might. *It was.*

But in the mass of bodies, he was searching only for one, and didn't see it.

"Ma'am."

The ensign's voice made Sinder glance up, made him tense with disquiet—and with knowing. Here it finally was, the thing he hadn't been able to see, emerging into clarity.

Alkor lifted her face from her screen. "Report."

"It looks like our people have been . . . ambushed, ma'am. We're getting reports of casualties."

Alkor stared. The entire bridge crew stared. Sinder closed his eyes. *Yuga.*

Alkor rose slowly and stepped forward. "*How?*"

"They're all armed. We don't know how, but they're—"

"They're *supposed* to be *sick.* The officers at the quarantine told us they were *almost dead.* Maybe they made it out, but that was then. How are they killing trained peacekeepers? *How is that even possible?*"

Again, silence took the bridge. Everything in Isaac Sinder's body was slowly sinking toward the deck. He had heard Alkor angry, irritated, impatient, exasperated, shocked. But this was the first time that he had heard panic in her voice.

"I—" The ensign stared down at his console, at his hands, at the main screen, at anything but her. "I don't know, ma'am."

"So *find the fuck out.*" She whirled, her fists clenched. "Get me a clearer picture of what's happening down there. Get me whatever you have. And see if you can send a communique back to the quarantine. I want to know everything they know about this disease. *Everything.*"

No, you don't. Sinder clenched his own fists, fighting back the tremors that were suddenly surging through them. But he couldn't stop what was happening now. It was his fault that he hadn't foreseen it. He had sworn to not make Melissa Cosaire's mistake, to not underestimate the danger of the people he was dealing with.

And that was exactly what he had done.

"Send down the fighters," he said quietly.

Alkor shot him a frown. "What?"

"The fighters. Send them down." He met her gaze. "Boots on the ground aren't working. They have people, but they only have one ship, if that. Send the fighters and mow them down."

"You want to go to that extreme before we know anything more? We'll lose Yuga."

"Do you really care, Captain?" He cocked his head. "Do you think we have the *luxury* of caring about that right now?"

"How can we be sure they don't have air support? We didn't think more than a few of them had *guns*, either."

"Do you have a better idea?"

She let out a heavy sigh. "No. No, I don't. Lieutenant." She turned back to the woman, who swiveled away from her console.

"Ma'am."

"You heard him. Launch the fighters. Tell the other ships to launch theirs, too. I want everything moving in that area to *stop* moving, you understand?"

The lieutenant's brow furrowed. "What about our own people?"

"Tell them to pull back to a kilometer outside the landing zone and take whatever cover they can. Aside from that, they're on their own."

"Ma'am."

Alkor seemed to deflate then, bowing her head and letting her shoulders slump. She was losing people. She would lose others. In a mission that had, once, been about nothing more than sensor sweeps.

Sinder's heart broke for her, a little. Then he returned his gaze to the deceptively calm surface of Peris, and knew that, for now, he couldn't have a heart to break.

Nkiruka sat in the softly lit council chambers as organized chaos churned around her.

There was no panic, no worry. There was simply a lot of movement: people hurrying from one console to another, consulting with council members, carrying crucial messages to other parts of the ship. The center of all the movement was Adisa, overseeing and delivering instructions, but Nkiruka knew that, though she remained silent, the center of the ship and its people was herself, seated toward the rear of the curving room with her skirts gathered around her and her hands folded in her lap.

She needed no screen to see Peris. It was right in front of her, a tiny jewel in a black setting. Death sat on its surface like a dark flaw.

"The fighters will launch as soon as we're in orbit," one of the council was saying. "Ying and her staff have been alerted to receive casualties. We can see three Protectorate ships in low orbit, and we think it's unlikely there are more."

"How are they armed?"

"Not heavily. From what we know of this ship class, it's smaller, primarily for reconnaissance, and they have no orbit-to-surface guns or large missiles aboard. They do have fighters, and they're launching them now."

Ashwina was close, but Nkiruka could get closer. She tilted her head back, sending herself out through the lines and the orbits of everything that lay between Ashwina and the world they were rushing toward at nearly the speed of light. Because she *was* light, twining herself around the planet in the same bright dance.

And she could feel all of it. The wood and the grass, the rising sun, the warming rocks, the bloodstained moss, the terror, the gunshots, the screams, the stench of death. She felt it pierce her; her core twisted in sudden pain and grief. This was another part of the price she had paid and would pay for as long as she lived: no one's pain was closed off to her, and there was no agony that she wouldn't come close to and share. She felt all their hearts: how they would suffer, children who would never see them again, husbands and wives and lovers who would soak their pillows in tears, confusion at what was happening to them, the helplessness of feeling their lives slipping away. She shot through and among them like one of the bullets, hunting for what she needed. What Ashwina needed. What the people dying below her needed.

And then she found it, in the front room of a little house on a hill. Two faces, two dances, which she had joined with in a dream. At last.

Hello, Adam.

CHAPTER

THIRTY-SEVEN

It hit him so hard that for a moment Adam was sure that he had been shot.

He felt his whole body wrench backward, away from the window and toward Lakshmi. Her arms curled around him as his knees folded, and she bore him up. His body felt all of this, but it seemed to have nothing to do with him. It was merely a body. It didn't matter.

Not when *she* was finally standing before him, holding out her hands.

He took them. The flesh that had held him down might be sliding to the floor, but he was barely aware of it. He was at once above and over everything and deep in the roots, held and cradled by them, soaring higher than any understanding of *high*. It was like being Named, and it was like being healed on the Plain, and it was like neither of those things. Then, he had been alone with himself. Now, he was in the company of others: Lakshmi and the other Aalim and also *everyone*, their dance joining with his, their orbits intertwined.

Lakshmi took his other hand and the three of them formed a circle, and the universe took a breath around them.

Was this what the Aalim felt, each second of their lives? Even a fraction of this? This joy, this terror that ripped through the fabric of existence and nestled into his heart like coming home? Somewhere the fighting was continuing, and somewhere evil white bullets were hurtling downward and carrying death with them, but he could hold them in the palm of his hand.

He wasn't special. Anyone could do this. Anyone.

He was simply one of the first.

Guide them, Lakshmi said. *We must guide them. All together, we can. There—and there. Can you feel them? All the birds of Ashwina in flight.*

Yes, there they were. Wings upon wings of them, swarming from Ashwina's bulk not like birds but like angry bees from a hive. They descended on the hanging Protectorate ships, pelting them with fire, and others broke away and chased the smaller Protectorate fighters. Adam saw all this and was pleased, even as the pain of it lanced through him like a blade.

The people he had brought here wouldn't only see that they could fight. They would see who would fight with them.

Yes, come. The new Aalim drove all three of them upward, darting among the fighters. Where an aim was unsteady, they centered it. Where will faltered, they lent their strength. Where reflexes weren't fast enough, they curled their hands around the strands of time itself and slowed the spool. This, too, was a skill an Aalim possessed. And yet never before like this. This was new. This was a kind of birth, the blooming of something that had been closed too tightly for too long.

They lunged back down toward the surface of Peris, to where the fighters met in midair. Together the ships ducked and wheeled and tumbled, setting the air ablaze with the sheer force and number of their guns. Far below, a white wave was being driven back. All of it might be happening, or might only be possible, or might only be a dream. But carried and led by the others, Adam slipped into a dance that was pure instinct.

He had always known how to do this. Everyone did, even if they had forgotten. He had been waiting to do this since he had first emerged from the maelstrom at the moment of his birth.

Now, at last, he was free.

Lochlan was at the edge of the wood when he heard the fighters.

He froze, remaining under cover, staring up. He could hardly see them, little pale stars gleaming in the morning sun, deceptively pretty as they lunged toward the ground. How many were there? He had no idea. But in front of him, the peacekeepers were starting to push back against the wave of people that had them surrounded, starting to run for the other end of the valley, and now he understood why. He caught sight of Rachel and waved his arms.

"We have to get back into cover!"

"Fuck, I know!" She looked up, then around at the people nearest her. All of them were motionless, heads raised, some of them bleeding and some not, but every one fixated on the sky. "Have you seen Aarons?"

"A while ago. No idea where he went." He stared across the meadow, to where Kyle and Eva must be—if they were alive. Could they see? Would they know to run? There wasn't any fighting back against this.

There had never been any winning.

Adam.

Then the fighters bellowed above them, and the firing began.

If before had been chaos, what happened next was sheer madness. As one, everyone rushed back to the cover of the trees, away from the strafing fighters. Grass and dirt flew upward in explosions, people screamed and fell into the dirt, flailing as their bodies were torn apart. A few fell, tried to get up again, but were too late. Lochlan had a last glimpse of the people on the opposite side of the meadow, scrambling for the ridge—but he knew they wouldn't be fast enough.

Cursing, he almost tripped over someone, then righted himself and dragged them to their feet. He was mildly surprised to see that it was Aarons, bleeding freely from a graze on his upper arm but alive.

"This is turning into quite a party."

Lochlan only let out a thin laugh, hurrying on and trusting Aarons to follow. Overhead, more fighters were skimming low over the treetops, and he and Aarons were surrounded with falling branches and leaves as they began to tear the canopy apart.

"We'll hit the other side soon," Aarons grunted. "It's only more meadow after that."

"Yeah." Lochlan skidded to a halt. Suddenly it all seemed so *pointless*. There was nowhere to run. He had hoped, but he shouldn't have. Adam claimed a higher guidance, but here they were about to be slaughtered, and here he was, the superstitious Bideshi, and he simply didn't believe anymore.

Aarons stopped beside him, grabbed his arm. "The fuck're you *doing*? We move or we die!"

"We die anyway." Lochlan stared up at the white streaks across the sky. "I shouldn't have left him. We should have stayed together." He laughed. "I was actually going to marry him. You believe it? How *stupid* is that? I was going to marry him, and now look."

"You're outta your damn fool *mind*." Aarons yanked on his arm so hard that Lochlan was almost pulled off his feet. "I'll argue fatalism with you later. *Move*."

Lochlan whirled, gave him a shove. "You go. Fucking go if it's that important to you. I'm tired, all right? We're dying in the fucking dirt for no reason at all, and I can't—"

Pain lanced up and down his side in a bright spiderweb—the bruised side—and he faltered. Speechless, confused, he pressed a hand to the site of the pain and felt something warm and sticky.

Blood.

Aarons cried out and wheeled, and Lochlan staggered around after him. Nothing was making sense, now. The pain, the buzz of the fighters, and the peacekeeper standing in front of him, blast shield up and rifle still aimed.

"Don't—" he started, and Aarons shot the peacekeeper in the chest, in the head, and he fell backward, dropped his rifle, blood staining the dirt and the moss.

And lay still.

Lochlan stumbled to one knee, and then Aarons was at his side, trying to pull him up. "You stupid fucking Bideshi." Aarons spat the last word like an insult. "You're going to make me explain this to Yuga? You're going to do that to me, you selfish asshole?"

"I'm not," Lochlan murmured. The blood might be slowing. Maybe. He couldn't tell how deep the wound was, only that it *hurt*, and it was the bullet that should have pierced him back at the camp, finding him at last. *Adam*. Even if this ended, he needed to go to him. Hold him until it all came crashing down. It always should have been that way, on the Plain, here. "Aarons . . . help me, please—"

He stopped. Something cut through the roaring in his head, something new, both over and under the shriek of the fighters.

That *sound*.

It wasn't the fighters. He thought it was, at first, but it couldn't be. By now he knew the sound of the Protectorate ships, that awful screeching whine, but this was a deep roar; a noise that was bizarrely and deeply comforting.

Something familiar.

He stumbled up and back, gazing through the gaps in the canopy, ignoring whatever Aarons was saying. It couldn't be. It fucking *couldn't* be.

A small ship flew by, very low, so fast that it should have been a blur, but somehow its image was frozen before him, the beloved shape of it, the way it was at once clumsy and sleek, mismatched and harmonious, like the ship from which it came. The marking on its side, the twisting characters. The name.

"*Kae!*" He lifted his hands and screamed that name, the pain fading to unimportance. It was insane, *he* was insane, and he never wanted to be sane again. "Kae, you *glorious fucking bastard*!"

CHAPTER

THIRTY-EIGHT

"**M**a'am, we're under attack."

Alkor pushed herself up from the floor. She, like Sinder, had fallen when the ship rocked with three hard, fast impacts, and all around the bridge lights flared before they stabilized. "You don't say," she growled, and she didn't even sound surprised. "Who the fuck is it? Give me a damned visual."

"It's a large ship. It's— Oh. Oh no." The view on the main screen shifted, snapped into focus away from the planet, and Sinder sank backward, grateful that the seat was there to catch him.

The ship filled the screen. It was a mass of pieces, a patchwork of a thousand different smaller components, all welded together into a single massive hulk of a thing, rust-colored and somehow vaguely iridescent. It was immense, fantastically ugly, monstrous, an obscenity that flew in the face of every orderly aesthetic convention. It hurt to look at it.

It hurt to know what it meant.

"It's—"

"Bideshi," Alkor snapped. "I can tell. But homeships don't carry guns."

"They do carry fighters in large numbers," Sinder said quietly. "The defensive ones. Which, I imagine, this is."

"They're making another pass." The ship rocked again, though not as badly as before; Sinder gripped onto the sides of his chair and willed his nausea to subside. "The *Vanguard* and the *Superior* are both reporting damage. Some of it serious. If this goes on much longer . . ."

"Return fire. *Now*."

It was like a dance. He thought of that first time dancing in the High Fields with Lochlan, whirling and strangely joyful, pulling that joy from months of terror and pain. The terror of feeling the joy at all. Adam swept and spun between the fighters and the firing, which were like bursts of light and color that were somehow lovely, like new flowers on a white field.

Good, he heard, and he couldn't tell which of them it was. Perhaps it was both. He was grateful to them—teachers, helpers, placing him exactly where he was supposed to be. *It comes, all together in harmony. In the dance, child. In the—*

There was one in a fighter, one he knew. A soul he had touched. He stretched himself toward it without thinking—and just as he did, its side exploded in flame. This was like before, as well: crammed into the gun turret with Kae hurt below, and the helplessness and the rage that came with it.

Now Kae's fighter was spinning out of control, stabilizer charred and sheared away. He tumbled toward one of the white Protectorate ships, and as Adam penetrated the hull, pushing *in*, he could feel the man's fear. He could also feel time, its delicate threads. He could just see the tapestry of it, the way in which it was emergent in a chaotic quantum sea, parts of it coming into being and vanishing again, a beautiful riot of possibility. Everything happened everywhere. So things could change.

He felt the shattered body of the ship and flooded himself into those cracks. At the same time, he extended himself back, crying to the others. *Help. I can't do it alone. Help me.*

They came, and everything *moved*. Footage of a disaster in fast reverse. Tiny fires unburning themselves. Torn wiring knitting itself together. All bodies were bodies, all bodies were the same, and as Kae's ship healed itself and Kae's and the gunner's terror turned to confusion, Adam was flooded with joy at a new truth discovered.

Healing was healing. There was no limit to it.

Now, he whispered—to Kae, to the other two with him, to all the birds of Ashwina. *Now, together, we fight.*

He merely had to be there, be the link. Abruptly he sensed every single one of them, their lines and their orbits inextricably joined, as they always had been. They were separate parts of a whole, but they could move as one smooth organism, like Ashwina herself. Chaotic and beautiful and *alive*.

Kae's ship joined the dance and knocked the Protectorate fighter out of the sky with two hard blasts. The fighter twirled like a falling leaf and burst into a brief ball of flame and debris. Death. But he could grieve it later. He was accepting it, beginning to. If he could have escaped it, that would have been wonderful, but it would also have been a fairy tale.

Child, there is no life absent death. There is no birth absent violence.

As one, the fighters of Ashwina pushed forward, through the tiny shards of Protectorate firepower, and—ignoring them—hurled blast after blast at the great ships themselves.

And everything began to break.

"Captain, it's getting worse out there. It's . . . We're sending everything we have at them, but they're dodging around it like it's not even there. It's *impossible*."

Another officer spoke up, voice shaking. "We're getting a few of them, but there's a *lot*, and their flying is . . . It's like nothing I've ever seen before. Ma'am." She swiveled her seat around. "Please forgive me for speaking freely, but I don't think we can stay here much—"

Alkor held up her hands. The bridge fell silent.

"Sinder," she murmured, and turned to him.

He stared up at her, and he knew what she was going to say. He knew it, and his heart reared up at it, enraged. He was so close. *They* were so close. Adam Yuga was in reach, and all they had to do was last long enough to find him, catch him, *kill* him, end this whole wretched nightmare. He sent every remaining fragment of his will to her, to make her not say it. To not do this to him. Because if she did, there would be no gainsaying it. Not now.

And a smaller, more rational part of him knew that she was right. She had been ready for this to be over for a long time. She had been with him in it until the end, but that didn't mean just any end.

He wasn't going to be Melissa Cosaire. He wasn't going to pull the whole world screaming down with him. Not when this wasn't over. Not when there would be other chances; he could *feel* it. Slowly, painfully, he closed his eyes and nodded. If he had to fight his way back here with bare hands and a broken body, he would see that it wasn't the last. Given everything else, he was confident that it wouldn't be long until he found them again. Not long at all. He would be given everything he needed to end this properly.

Melissa Cosaire had given up. And he was not Melissa Cosaire. He knew when to pull back; he would know when to return.

"Go."

"Sir, they're pulling their fighters back." The young man who had been taking the lead in communications sounded excited, half-unbelieving, his voice strong but trembling at the edges. He would remember the Plain, how badly that had gone. He would understand how different this was. "We're getting reports from our people near the surface that the transports are lifting off as well."

Adisa sat back and let out a huge breath. Nkiruka was aware of this distantly as she slowly returned to herself. It was like waking up from a long sleep, except she was so tired. Almost too tired to move.

"Good," he said. "Give them a chance to get their people out. Don't pursue. I'm not interested in a massacre."

She smiled. Wise Adisa. He had never been much for vengeance. He wouldn't be now. She felt him glance in her direction, and knew that he saw her smile and took a degree of pleasure in it.

In some ways he was like a father to her, even if she had taken the mantle of Old Mother. In some ways.

"Recall the fighters?"

Adisa paused. "The ones still above the planet, yes. The ones closer to the surface . . . Order a contingent of volunteers to land and remain there until we can send proper landing parties. Tell Ying to gather some of her fellows and make herself ready for that. They'll have wounded. In the meantime, we need to ascertain their status."

"Kae's wing was taking the lead there. I'll tell him to pick a few of his people and set down."

"Good." Nkiruka lifted her head. Incredulity and exhilaration pulsed through her, not coming from her but as much hers as anyone's. "I think there's more than one person who will be most pleased to see him."

Things continued to wind down. They had lost fighters, and on the surface of the planet there were doubtless plenty of casualties, but this felt dizzyingly unlike the Battle of the Plain. People were congratulating each other, exchanging words of relief and even pride. No Bideshi fighter on the ship was in doubt of their skills, but the fact remained: they had taken on an armed Protectorate recon fleet and beaten them back. Won.

Except.

"Now it begins," Nkiruka said to Adisa when they managed to find a relatively undisturbed moment at the far end of the chamber. She sighed. "I wonder how many of them realize it."

"Some. Not all. But you did well." He laid his hands on her shoulders, and for a moment she thought he might be about to embrace her, but instead he only gave her a friendly squeeze and released her again.

He would want to maintain certain formalities. Even now. She would remind him too much of Ixchel.

"I did what I could." She felt Ashwina moving around her, felt the curve of the chamber under its golden, spherical sunlamps. "I did what I had to do." She paused. "I'll be going down with the landing parties. There's someone down there I have to see."

"You'll want to meet Adam, of course."

"Yes. But not only him." She folded her hands, and thought of that old hand in hers, the brief and complete peace she had known as she filled a space too long empty. "There's someone else. And I don't think she has much time left."

Adam didn't remember pushing his way out the door. He didn't remember running down the hill onto the meadow, didn't remember stumbling over the wounded and a few of the dead. He didn't remember the friendly roar of the ships and the quieter growl as they descended, and he didn't remember the cheering of exhausted people as they gathered, lifted their hands, waved their guns, wept.

Much later, he vaguely remembered Eva running into his arms—though she was limping—and Kyle doing the same, pulling him into a bear hug as if years had passed since they were last together. He remembered Aarons and Rachel supporting each other as they approached, Aarons opening his scarred mouth to say something, and Rachel framing his face with her hands, his scars as well as his unmarked skin, and kissing him, and this was not really so surprising.

Later he remembered some of these things. He didn't remember most of them. What he remembered, as he stumbled into the midst of them, was a tall man with tattooed brown skin and dreadlocks adorned with garish beads, blood staining his right side, staggering toward the dark-haired man who was just climbing down from the landed Bideshi fighter and embracing him so hard and so completely that they both almost fell.

He didn't have any qualms about breaking that embrace by joining it. He reached them both, stopped and stared, and then he didn't have to speak anymore, because somehow Kae was hugging him and Lochlan was kissing him, both at once, and untangling it all didn't matter.

It had come full circle. Full orbit. They were still flying.

It was enough.

APEX

They found Lakshmi on the floor of her house where Adam had left her in the last of his trance, Skitss bent over her. He looked up when they entered, and his features were so twisted with grief and betrayal that Adam almost turned around and walked outside again. He felt fragile. Like this last contact might be too much.

But he owed her this.

"She's alive," Skitss hissed. "No thanks to you." But from the floor there came a weak voice, and the fallen figure stirred.

"He did what he was meant to. As did I. Don't be angry with him, dear one." She lifted a hand. "Adam. Come to me."

He did, without hesitation, and dropped into a crouch beside her, reaching down to help her up—but she shook her head, nudging his hands away. Behind him, he heard Kyle and Eva murmuring, Eva letting out a quiet sob. He felt Lochlan's silence, and he felt Kae beside him.

Felt so clearly it was almost sight.

"Boy, you know now what you can do. It's yours for a reason, as it belongs to everyone. Use it. Give it to the others." She stroked her gnarled fingers through his hair, but he could tell that she wasn't really perceiving him anymore—or that, rather, her perception was fading in and out between what was around her . . . and somewhere entirely other.

"Ama? Yes, love, I'm coming to you. Give me a moment. Just one."

Adam covered her hand with his. He wasn't going to say that Ama wasn't there. For all he knew, she was.

"I still need . . ." She smiled, and she seemed to be seeing through him. "Aha. Here she is."

Adam glanced back toward the doorway—and froze. There, standing on the threshold, was a small woman with skin such a dark brown that it was almost black, her hair hanging down her back in a complex series of braids. She was young, certainly no older than him and perhaps even a few years his junior, but her eyes were the ancient white eyes of an Aalim.

And still raw, healing. She was new. *Newborn.*

"You're—" he murmured, and she nodded.

"You've seen me. You'll see more of me." She went to them and bent, and the instant her hand touched Adam's he felt a jolt as though she were electrified, and gasped. It was like it was with Rachel . . . But stronger. Deeper. Lochlan stepped swiftly forward, but Adam held up his other hand, shaking his head.

"It's all right." He paused. "You're . . . Nkiruka." He knew the name as if he had always known it, and she nodded.

"You're the prophet."

"What? No, I'm—"

"Yes, you are." She sighed. "Don't argue. He is, isn't he, Old Mother?"

"Yes." Lakshmi laughed softly. "*Old Mother.* But that, young *voel,* no one has called me that in . . . I don't even know how long. And you." That strange sight-without-sight was directed past them again, and Kae started. "Child, here you are, all grown and as you should be. Come and let me look at you."

Kae did so, glancing at Lochlan—who laid a hand on his arm, a touch that said more than even an embrace would. Kae nodded and turned to them again, kneeling opposite Adam. His face was relaxed, his eyes both distant and seeming sharply focused on something only he could see.

"It's been a long time, Old Mother."

"Yes, boy, it has. *Boy.* Yes, that was it. I couldn't quite see it at the time, but that was it. It's so good to see you whole."

"We can help you." Tears were shining in Kae's eyes. "We can get you back to Ashwina—or just down to the valley. We have healers, Ying is the most—"

"Others are more in need of your healer's skill than I am, child. My time is finally over. I am going to my Ama, who has been waiting for me for years upon years." She let out a shuddering sigh and closed her eyes. "Carry me to my Halls. My Arched Halls, in the grove. Lay me inside, and tonight at dusk you will give it—and me—to the fire. Give me a little light to speed me on my way home."

Kae only nodded, clasping her other hand in his. Adam watched. That second sight had not left him, the sense that everything around him was possessed of an additional dimension that he could almost see. Kae's pain was like a light in itself, radiating from him, but it was a complicated pain, and loss was only part of it. Something more had happened here than merely a foolish child helped by the skill of an Aalim in exile. Something much, much deeper.

Perhaps someday Kae would tell him. Perhaps not.

"All right," Nkiruka said, her voice quiet. "She'll be sleeping soon. Let's move her as gently as we can."

It was late afternoon; sunset wasn't going to be long in coming. The sun itself was warm on their backs as Kae, Nkiruka, Eva, and Adam carried Lakshmi from her house, Lochlan walking with them, Skitss following along behind and weeping in the way that Koticki wept, a soft hiss like the sighing of the wind in dry grass. Before them, leading the little procession, Kyle, looking somber and confused. She had meant a great deal to him and Eva as well, Adam knew. She had sheltered them when no one else would, given them comfort, hope, direction. Given them what she could. They would still have those things, now. But what was coming next would be hard.

Everything that was coming would be hard.

The grove seemed larger in the afternoon sun, with the shadows beginning to lengthen. Overhead, more Bideshi landing craft were descending, and in the valley Adam thought he could see Ying, organizing people to carry the injured toward the canvas shelter she had already erected for them to receive treatment—Protectorate and Bideshi alike. He would have to go to her, when this was done. She would want to see him, to embrace him. There were many more reunions still to be had, some happy and some less so. But now he turned his attention back to the trees gathering around him, how they wound themselves into an enclosed space ahead, barely higher than Lakshmi herself but enough like the Halls that she would have felt at home. Into this they carried her, and laid her down on soft moss and soil.

"Ama," was all she whispered. "Ama, I am here."

They left her. It was a slow leave-taking, bit by bit, but in the end only Adam and Lochlan remained seated in the grass beyond the edge of the grove, gazing out over the valley and watching the sun sink lower behind the hills. Beyond them, outside the enclosure, Skitss was sitting silent vigil, his head bowed. His and Lakshmi's full history—probably complicated, certainly long—was something else he might never know.

"We made it," he murmured. He paused and ducked his head. "Well. Most of us."

"Somehow." Lochlan took his hand and slid even closer, so that their shoulders and hips were pressed together and his arm was around Adam's back, wincing only a little at the pressure on his much abused and bandaged side. Adam leaned gratefully into him. He could sleep. He could sleep for about ten thousand years. And at the end of it . . .

A kiss to wake him.

"There's still one more thing to do."

Lochlan laughed. "There's a *fuck of a lot* to do, *mitr*, or did you nap all the way through our little adventure there?"

"You know what I was doing."

"Yes," Lochlan said, quieter now. "Yes, I do."

They were silent for a moment. Then Adam butted his head against Lochlan's shoulder. "Well?"

"Well, what?"

"What do you think about it?" He wasn't exasperated, but he was pressing. He felt the need to press. Nkiruka was below, helping Ying with whatever could be done, and Kae, Kyle, and Eva were doing the same. He wasn't sure where Rachel and Aarons had gone, but he suspected that they shouldn't be disturbed, and in any case, despite his bond with Rachel, he didn't think she would really understand. He was alone, except for Lochlan, and what had happened was gnawing at him and wouldn't leave him be.

"I think . . ." Lochlan laughed again. "I think you might be about the strangest man I've ever met, *mitr raya*."

Adam rolled his eyes. It was good to know that, despite the weariness and the grief and the relief, he was still *capable* of being exasperated by Lochlan. "Thank you. Thanks, that's very helpful."

"I mean it. I think you're strange. I think that this is pretty much normal for you. For us. Everything about you has always been strange, Adam. For all you insist that you're not special . . ."

"But I'm not." Adam pulled back enough to look into Lochlan's eyes. "That's the whole point of this. Or one of them. What I did . . . *anyone* can do it. Anyone's capable. Bideshi, Protectorate . . . We've all got that—that connection, that *tether*. That line. All we have to do is find it."

"They said you were a prophet."

"I'm only one of the first." Adam shook his head, a small, tired smile pulling at his mouth. "Don't you know what a prophet is? It's only someone who reminds people of the obvious."

"Oh," Lochlan said, and didn't argue anymore. They sat together, Adam sinking into Lochlan's heat and solidity, letting himself briefly forget about everything else. Everything that had happened and that had yet to come. Down in the valley, people were setting light to little campfires, hanging lanterns.

"So what's there left to do?"

Adam raised his head slightly. "Mm?"

"You said there was something left to do." Lochlan gave Adam a shake. "C'mon, *chusile*, don't fall asleep and leave me in suspense."

"Oh, right." Adam nodded to himself. It wasn't as though there was a decision to be made. It had been made already. "We have to get married."

The fire burned on the hill. At sunset, Kyle and Eva had returned with Kae and Nkiruka, and together with Skitss they put burning clumps of dry grass against the old, twisted wood and fanned it. The wood itself was also dry, though parts of it were living, and it caught quickly. They stood in silence, watching the smoke billow up toward the starry sky.

"I will return to the village," Skitss said presently. "A woman there has agreed to take me in. An apothecary. I know something of herbs from what Lakshmi taught me, so even an old Koticki might be of use."

"The village," Adam said, remembering it with a start. "Are they all right? Was anyone down there hurt?"

"No one was there." Kyle nodded toward the flames. "The evacuation Lakshmi advised went off without a hitch. They're returning home now. If trouble comes back here, they'll know how to hide themselves again."

Adam let out a breath. Their luck—their amazing, unbelievable luck—had held. It had held where the luck of so many others had failed. Down in the valley, volunteers were digging graves. Not so many, but enough. Ying's makeshift clinic had almost more patients than they were equipped to handle. But here they were, and but for minor hurts, they were whole and well.

It had the feeling of a good beginning.

Or a high place from which to fall.

"Leila is coming down with the next transport," Kae said softly. "She'll be here in about half an hour. She'll want to see you, Adam. Lock."

Lochlan had been standing with his head lowered, quiet, but now he looked up, almost grinning, though there was something a bit forced about it. "The love of my life? Here? Kae, it can't be so, I can't be *so blessed* that—"

Kae shook his head in wonder. "You can't even shut it off at a funeral."

"This isn't just a funeral." Adam stared into the fire and found a smile, let it come. "She wouldn't want it to be only that."

"No, she wouldn't." Nkiruka turned to them, pulling her scarves closer around her shoulders. The night was cool, though not yet really cold. "We see life braided with death, never to be separated. There's much life here tonight amidst the death. They can't be without each other. We mark the passing of both; celebrate each in its time." She laid a hand on Lochlan's arm, on Adam's, and it felt like a blessing. Somehow her face was both joyful and grave, even sad. Knowing and profoundly experienced.

"Don't hesitate to seize that life. All that you can. Don't hesitate for a moment."

There were witnesses, though there were no lights but the stars and the distant fires. Light felt unnecessary when there was already so much of it everywhere. They were some distance from both the little encampment in the valley and Lakshmi's funeral pyre, nowhere particularly special. Adam knew that in the daylight he might not even be able to find this place again. But it wasn't the ground that mattered. Everything was its own center, and they would carry theirs with them.

Adam could feel their friends, but they had no more real impact on him than the wind in his hair. He gazed at Lochlan, standing there with the starlight silvering his skin, and sensed two lines and two paths twining around each other, forming a knot. Time might undo it. But a lot of time would be needed.

There were no rings and there was no ritual, not even any words that meant much. There were his hands in Lochlan's, his smile, their lips and the way they fit so perfectly, and the few words that they both held like treasures but didn't need to say.

I'm yours. I promise. My dance, all my lines and my orbits. My heart.

He didn't know what was coming next or where they were going. All he knew was who he would share the path with. Whatever happened, this moment would always exist, clear and perfect, woven into the fabric of the light, and the dance, and the night that went on forever.

# GLOSSARY

Aalim .... Bideshi scholar, teacher of laws and traditions, one possessing great wisdom
Chere .... Stars, used as an exclamation
Fuguri ... Balls, testicles, guts
Habibi ... Beloved, as said to a male person
Habibti .. Beloved, as said to a female person
Khara .... Shit
Kutub .... The ancient holy books of the Bideshi
Lovina ... Strong, rich Bideshi liquor
Mitr ...... Friend
Raya ..... Landowner, with intensely negative connotations of being the possessed rather than the possessor
Shala ..... Hallucinogenic drug derived from the roots of the Bideshi's ancient trees
Voel ...... Bird, with racier connotations in slang; a cocky person

Dear Reader,

Thank you for reading Sunny Moraine's *Fall and Rising*!

We know your time is precious and you have many, many entertainment options, so it means a lot that you've chosen to spend your time reading. We really hope you enjoyed it.

We'd be honored if you'd consider posting a review—good or bad—on sites like **Amazon, Barnes & Noble, Kobo, Goodreads, Twitter, Facebook, Tumblr,** and your blog or website. We'd also be honored if you told your friends and family about this book. Word of mouth is a book's lifeblood!

For more information on upcoming releases, author interviews, blog tours, contests, giveaways, and more, please sign up for our weekly, spam-free newsletter and visit us around the web:

Newsletter: tinyurl.com/RiptideSignup
Twitter: twitter.com/RiptideBooks
Facebook: facebook.com/RiptidePublishing
Goodreads: tinyurl.com/RiptideOnGoodreads
Tumblr: riptidepublishing.tumblr.com

Thank you so much for Reading the Rainbow!

RiptidePublishing.com

ACKNOWLEDGMENTS

As always, thanks go first and foremost to Rob for remaining married to me through the literal years of trying to make this book—and the one that follows—happen. He's an amazing man. Or he has a very high pain tolerance. Or both.

Thanks also to the rest of my family, especially Mom and Uncle Richard for the cheerleading and for not being quiet about how much they loved the first book. To Emma also, whose music recommendations continue to give me life.

As usual, more thanks are due to the entire crew at Darrow, for continuing to give me a writing outlet that makes this kind of writing easier and less stressful. Special thanks to Ashley and Leah for, well, everything. Including forbearance when I'm unmanageable.

Yet more thanks go to Elise Tobler for much-needed advice and counsel; to Izzy, Andrea, and Jason for making me feel like this really was worth doing; to Marco Palmieri for general encouragement; and to literally everyone who has ever hung out with me at a con and given me reason to believe I could actually do this job.

To everyone at Cyborgology, for everything.

To everyone at Riptide, especially Sarah, for being willing to look at this and then being willing to give it a home when it desperately needed one, and Caz, for working on it with me and really making it something I'm proud of.

And finally to Megh. She is why this exists. These characters, this world . . . It would not be here at all without her.

ALSO BY
SUNNY MORAINE

Labyrinthian
Lineage (coming soon)

Root Code
Line and Orbit
Sword and Star (coming soon)

Casting the Bones
Crowflight
Ravenfall
Rookwar

ABOUT THE AUTHOR

Sunny Moraine's short fiction has appeared in *Clarkesworld*, *Strange Horizons*, *Nightmare*, *Lightspeed*, *Long Hidden: Speculative Fiction from the Margins of History*, and multiple Year's Best anthologies, among other places. They are also responsible for the novels *Line and Orbit* (cowritten with Lisa Soem), *Labyrinthian*, and the Casting the Bones trilogy, as well as *A Brief History of the Future: collected essays*. In addition to time spent authoring, Sunny is a doctoral candidate in sociology and a sometime college instructor; that last may or may not have been a good move on the part of their department. They unfortunately live just outside Washington, DC, in a creepy house with two cats and a very long-suffering husband.